Praise for Dark Horse

[Dark Horse] truly is a gem, highly polished and a wonderful read.
First to the Last Page Book Reviews

"... this is one of my top reads of 2015. If you enjoy science fiction at all I encourage you to pick it up for yourself. I don't think you will be disappointed."
All About Romance

"All the characters along with all the plots twists and developments combine to tell a story that is complex, emotional and very difficult to put down. **Dark Horse** is awesome new Sci Fi from a very talented writer."
Smart Girls Love Sci-fi Romance

Praise for Dark Deeds

"Michelle Diener writes exciting, inventive, and just plain good fun SFR stories that will take the reader on quite a fantastic journey."
Lynne - Outlander Book Club

D1603855

Other Titles by Michelle Diener

Class 5 Series
Dark Horse
Dark Deeds

Dark Forest Series
The Golden Apple
The Silver Pear

Susanna Horenbout Series
In a Treacherous Court
Keeper of the King's Secrets
In Defense of the Queen

Regency London Series
The Emperor's Conspiracy
Banquet of Lies
A Dangerous Madness

Other Books
Daughter of the Sky
Mistress of the Wind

Dark
Deeds

MICHELLE DIENER

Copyright © 2016 Michelle Diener
All rights reserved.
ISBN-13: 978-0-9924559-5-8

No part of this work may be copied or distributed in any way without written permission of the copyright holder.

This is a work of fiction and all names, people, places and incidents are either used fictitiously or are a product of the author's imagination.

DEDICATION

To all the readers who were so enthusiastic about Dark Horse, thank you! And to Gav, who's supported me through all the ups and downs.

Chapter One

STACKING HEAVY BOXES IN THE LAUNCH BAY, Fiona heard a ship come through the gel wall. Hard.

There was a harsh grinding of metal on metal.

The smell of burning, the hot scent of friction, blew over her a moment before the smoke. Black and choking, it engulfed her before being sucked out through the air filters.

She crouched down behind the crates, grateful for the first time for the hood Captain Tak had forced her to wear for the last four weeks. It fitted tightly over her head, with strange, protruding ears, like a child's whimsical winter hat, and the bottom half covered her mouth, ending just below her nose. It helped filter out the noxious fumes.

The loud grating sound ended with a shrieking crash that cut off abruptly, and in the sudden silence she heard a loud clang. She guessed the ship's ramp had just hit the launch bay floor.

She'd never been allowed in the bay when one of the smaller merchant vessels entered to do business with the Garmman trading ship she was on. Hury always came and dragged her back to her cell long before they arrived, only letting her out when they were gone.

So, this wasn't a scheduled arrival. And she didn't think every landing was quite so hard, or the launch bay would look a little worse for wear.

She peered around the high stack of containers and froze.

The ship that had come through was badly damaged, but she hardly noticed that.

It was the occupants who had her unwavering attention.

They came cautiously down the ramp, shockguns raised. They were slender, almost willowy, with hair that grew long and thick. Some had grown it to their shoulders or lower, others had cut it level with their ears. The pearl white of it contrasted with the delicate peach of their skin.

They moved like a slick, well-trained team, and there was something predatory about them. They were in a sort of uniform, not identical, but close enough. Dark pants and shirt, boots that ended well above their ankles. The contrast of the dark color with their pastel skin and hair made them all the more astonishing.

The launch bay door opened to her left and she turned to see Hecta and Nark stop dead in the doorway, mouths open at the smoldering ship, the damage to the bay.

Without any sign of hesitation, two of the peach people lifted their shockguns and fired.

Hecta and Nark went down, and two other interlopers ran over to them, pushed them clear of the doors and hit the button to close them again.

One signaled to another of the group, and he ran over, took out a tiny silver rectangle and pressed it to the keypad next to the door. She heard the locks engage, locking the Garmman crew on the other side of the launch bay.

Well.

Fiona bent her head for a moment, sucking in a breath through the thick fabric of her hood.

They could kill her.

But she was going to die here anyway.

It would be drawn out for a little longer, as some of the crew got up their courage to follow Captain Tak's unspoken request, but they would beat her to death sooner or later.

She rubbed her hip where Hury had kicked her yesterday, and knew it was true.

These people might kill her right now, but it was well worth the risk.

She started to rise, and felt the hard plastic-like ears built into her hood wobble. She crouched back down.

Captain Tak wanted her to wear the hood to hide what she was, and also to make her look like something she wasn't. It had become really important to him that she not be seen without it.

And anything that Tak wanted, she was determined to do the opposite.

She wasn't sure who the aliens in front of her were, but for all she knew, people who wore hoods like hers were their worst enemy. Whereas they couldn't have any negative history with a human.

She got a good grip and pulled the hood off her head, and just to make sure, slid it between two of the containers, completely out of sight.

The lingering smoke caught immediately at her throat, and as she stood and took a step out from behind the stack, she couldn't help coughing a little.

Ten shockguns turned in her direction, and her heart gave a jump as they bared their teeth.

They had incisors, their lips pulling back over their gums to expose them fully.

It brought baboons from nature documentaries to mind.

She slowly raised her hands to show she was unarmed. Then held her breath as they watched her, and she watched them right back.

The pupils of their eyes were red, and she pushed down her rising panic at their very interested gaze.

She may have made a mistake.

One of them cocked his head to the side, and gestured for her to come closer.

Before she'd seen the teeth, the eyes, she'd been willing enough to take the chance. Now she had to force herself to step slowly out of the shadows and into the harsh light of the landing area.

"Grih?" The one who'd motioned her forward asked.

She nodded, relieved. "I do speak Grih. And Garmman. And a little Bukari." Fitali was too strange for her, she hadn't come close to working it out yet, and Tecran made her uneasy, made her heart beat faster and her hands shake. She had skipped over all the Tecran language lessons.

"I mean, are you Grihan?" He spoke Garmman, his voice sibilant, his sharp incisors peeking out as he spoke.

She frowned. He thought she looked Grihan? "No."

One of the team circled behind her, and she turned her head to keep him in sight.

She flinched when he suddenly moved right in front of her.

"Too short. And the ears." The finger he reached out had too many joints and he touched the tip of her ear, shockgun resting directly against her chest as he did it.

She shuddered, forcing herself to keep still.

They weren't that much taller than she was, although close up she saw that while their limbs were slender, every muscle was defined.

"Pity. We have a Grihan battleship chasing us and it would have been good to use you as a hostage." The leader stared at her, and she saw there was a sly and calculating look in his eye. "What are you, then?"

"I'm a prisoner." She took a breath when the gun lifted slightly off her chest. "I wanted to ask if you'd take me with you? Help me escape?"

The leader barked out a laugh. "No." He looked back at his still-smoking ship. "How can we get out of here?"

Suddenly, the shockgun was back on her chest, and she could hear the whine as it got to full strength.

If a Grihan battleship was chasing them, then the Grih would come here to look for them, surely? That meant another group to appeal to for help.

All wasn't lost.

She held on to that.

"How close are the Grih behind you?" she asked.

The leader narrowed his eyes. "Why?"

"Well," she pointed to one of the small loaders parked to one side, "those will get you out, but they don't go very fast, I don't think."

One of his team was already looking at them, and he shook his head. "Deep-space work only. What else?"

There was something else, but if she told them, she'd better have a way off the ship, because Tak would kill her for revealing it.

"There may be something, but only if I can come, too."

Suddenly the shockgun was pressed hard against her chest again and the leader stepped closer to her.

"I don't think you're in a position to negotiate."

She swallowed. "If I tell you, they will kill me for it. The only way I can survive is if you take me with you."

"We will kill you if you don't tell us." The one holding the shockgun snarled at her.

"Then you won't have a way off the ship." She spoke calmly as she met his eyes but excitement danced a jig in her stomach, because it was true. For the first time in a long time she had some bargaining power.

"Until you tell me what the way off is, I can't say whether we can take you or not. But I give my word if it is possible, I will." There was something insincere on the leader's face, his words too slick, and Fiona had a sinking sense he would have no problem breaking a promise. The excitement she'd felt only a moment before morphed into disappointment, because no matter what, it came down to trusting someone she didn't think was trustworthy.

She could refuse to tell him, and maybe die right now, or she could take a chance he was being honest.

"Whose word am I taking?" Might as well know his name, whether he was going to cheat her or not.

"I'm Gerwa, of the Krik battalion V8." He inclined his head.

"And him?" Fiona jerked her head at the one holding the shockgun against her.

"That is Jiy."

Gerwa didn't give himself a title, although he was clearly the leader.

"So, tell." Jiy poked at her with the gun.

"There is an emergency pod."

"Emergency pod?" Gerwa looked around the bay, frowning.

"I had to pull all the supplies out of it so they could be checked for expiry dates, and then reload it." Not that Tak would allow her to check the actual dates. He didn't trust her enough. And he was right not to.

"How many does it seat?"

She thought about it. "Eight. I think."

Jiy pressed the barrel into her a little harder. "Where is it?"

She eased back. "There." She pointed. Tak had built the emergency pod into an enclosed space next to the gel wall. The walls looked like part of the ship's construction, but they contained a small pod that would find the closest livable planet once launched.

Tak's mistake was his strategy of spending as little time with Fee as possible. He didn't understand how well she spoke Garmman, and he didn't warn the crew who'd switched out the supplies not to talk in front of her.

She knew all about the pod. How it was installed for the senior officers in case of catastrophic system failure.

The crew were unhappy no such escape route had been organized for them, and they hadn't minded discussing it in front of her. They hadn't even remembered she was there.

An angry, hoarse shout from Gerwa had her turning her head. Something struck her, hard, above her ear and she staggered to the side and fell onto her knees, hands up to shield from another blow. When none came, she turned her head to see Jiy was standing absolutely still, weapon raised, as if he were playing musical statues.

She climbed slowly to her feet, saw Gerwa's shockgun was held steady on his underling. He was yelling at him in what must be Krik, the tone one of fury.

She rubbed her head gingerly, winced as she realized the skin was broken, and there was a hard knot beneath it. Blood dripped in a sinuous trickle behind her ear and onto her shoulder.

What the hell was *wrong* with these people?

The leader finally lowered his weapon when Jiy lowered his and bowed his head in submission.

Gerwa looked over at her with his strange red eyes. "He is impatient. We're all impatient. Where are you pointing? You're taking too much time."

Time they obviously didn't have. So the Grih must be close. That was . . . encouraging. Especially if Gerwa was going to sell her out.

The pain above her ear had given her a splitting headache and she rubbed the skin above it carefully. Felt a sudden, vicious fury at the casual violence. "I'd have been a real help to you unconscious on the floor."

Gerwa flashed his fangs at her. "I prevented him hitting you too hard."

She stared at him for a moment, trying to work out if he was honestly saying she should be grateful she hadn't been struck harder.

Finally, seeing his fingers start to tighten on his shockgun, she turned her back on him and stalked across the launch bay, now scraped and jagged in places where the Krik spaceship had gouged it on landing.

She hit the button that hid the panel, and the keypad was revealed. "I don't know the code." If she did, she wouldn't still be here. She'd be somewhere far, far away.

Gerwa had followed her, and now he shoved her aside, making her stumble. He peered at the keypad and called out to someone over his shoulder in quick, sharp bursts of hissing sound.

The one who'd locked the launch bay doors came running over with the tiny silver rectangle.

"So, what does the Krik battalion V8 do?" She might as well gather as much information as possible.

"We are . . . traders." The leader lifted his head, watching her reaction.

And then she remembered. The Krik. She'd heard the crew talking about them. Heard her guards discussing them, back when she was originally confined to her cell.

They were the scourge of space.

She'd imagined them as hulking knuckle-draggers of the worst sort, though. Not the slick, almost elegant beings in front of her.

They were the fly in everyone's ointment. Thieves, brawlers, pirates.

"Why are the Grih after you?"

He ignored her, stepping back to give his teammate with the silver device access to the keypad.

It took less than five seconds for the door to pop open.

"I don't suppose you'd have a spare one of those you could let me have?"

The Krik leader tore his eyes away from the pod, now revealed in its snug hideaway, and gave her a crooked smile. The tip of an incisor peeped out. "No." He gestured toward the pod. "How does it work?"

"It will take you to the nearest livable planet. That's all I know."

"That's enough." He half-lifted his shockgun in her direction, and motioned his team toward the pod. "There are ten of us, only eight places in the pod, and the nearest planet is Balco, which is a significant distance from here. I can't risk my crew by overcrowding it more than necessary, so you won't be coming with us."

She suspected as much, but it didn't stop the burn of anger and disappointment in her gut.

Gerwa's crew disappeared inside, and from the shuffling and knocking, she guessed it was a tight fit, even without Gerwa.

"How about you do us a favor?" Gerwa looked out of the pod, his hand curled around the inner door handle, another sly look on his face.

A laugh exploded out of her. "Why would I do you a favor?"

"Because it won't cost you anything."

"To the contrary. It's going to cost me everything." She'd kept her feelings to herself for a long time now. Through the abduction and the incarceration, abuse and neglect, but whether the Grih came and rescued her, or Tak killed her, today would see a massive change for her, and she didn't much feel like taking the path of least resistance anymore.

Besides, what the hell were they going to do to her?

"You won't help us?"

"You mean, more than I already have? No."

The leader reacted before he could control himself, exposing his massive incisors and hissing at her.

She didn't budge, staring him down. Then she lifted her arm, brushed the sleeve as if checking the time on a smart fabric watch. Most of the Garmman crew uniforms came standard with them built in, except for hers, but the gesture was meaningful enough. She had time to burn. He, on the other hand . . .

He let out a bark of reluctant laughter. "I am truly sorry now there is no room for you. You are interesting. But my team has fought with me for a long time, and I won't leave any of them behind. I am sorry if you will pay for helping us. But this favor, it won't change whether you are in trouble or not. It may delay your trouble."

"Really?" His gall was so staggering, she actually wanted to see where he was going with this.

Gerwa gave a casual shrug. "Close the doors behind us. So the Grih don't know where we've gone. At least, not straight away. It'll give us time to get away."

She thought about it. Actually, that might help delay any retaliation from Tak. But damned if she'd do if for nothing. "If you give me that keypad encryptor."

He hissed at her again. "That's a one-of-a-kind device. I won't part with it."

Her turn to shrug. "Your choice."

She stepped back from the door and tilted her head, looking right as if she could hear something coming through the gel wall.

She couldn't hear a thing but she was prepared to play it up. She had absolutely nothing to lose.

The keypad encryptor landed with a clatter at her feet, and she turned back to look at Gerwa. He was staring at her, hard-eyed now. The sly, amused attitude was gone.

"Don't double-cross me."

Fee bent and scooped it up, then swallowed a bout of nausea as she straightened too quickly, the bump on her head shooting white-hot pain through her skull. She breathed in carefully through clenched teeth, met his gaze again.

"*I* live up to my bargains." She walked to the keypad. "I'll even re-lock this." And make sure they hadn't slipped her a dud substitute while she was about it.

He must have guessed her train of thought, because he gave a nod of grudging respect and stepped inside the pod.

Fee pushed the button, and closed the door. Then pressed the encryptor against the keypad. A tiny symbol popped up on its minute screen, and she studied it for a moment, memorizing it, and then tapped it with her finger.

She heard the double-click of the doors locking. Smiled. The engines of the emergency pod rumbled, making the wall she was leaning against vibrate, and then it was gone.

She decided to wait near the boxes she'd been loading for the Grih, if they were coming. In the silence, she could hear the Garmman crew shouting behind the door, but she knew Tak would only force it open if he had no choice, for fear of damaging it.

She took a step toward the crates, and then had to press herself up against the wall as a sleek, silver-gray spaceship came bursting into the launch bay.

Chapter Two

FEE SLID THE ENCRYPTOR INTO HER BRA, and stayed put against the wall.

If this was a Grihan vessel, the Grih had much better stuff than the Garmman or the Krik. The ship was shiny and slick and she had a feeling it probably went very, very fast.

The sound of its engines filled the space and she had to narrow her eyes and look down to shield from the dust it was blowing up.

She needed a strategy.

Try to sneak onboard as a stowaway? Try to appeal to the Grih for help?

The unreality of what her life had become suddenly overwhelmed her, as it sometimes did, combining with the pain from her head injury to make her close her eyes and tip back her head. She had to breathe, just breathe. In and out.

When she opened her eyes, she jerked and then gave a low, choked scream. Someone stood directly in front of her, peering at her. They had on a helmet of gray glass and wore some sort of body armor. And they were big.

She actually put a hand up to her heart, as if she could somehow stop it from jumping out of her chest.

"Keep working on unlocking the door," the person in front of her said in Grihan, his words harsh and choppy. He didn't turn as he spoke, still facing her so she was reflected in the glass of his helmet, her face stretched out across it in weird, funhouse fashion. "Rial, come here. I've found the orange."

The words snapped her out of her distress. She was *not* orange. The Krik, yeah, they were edging toward orange, although she'd have said peach if it were up to her. But no way could they mistake her for a Krik.

"Sorry, but I'm not orange. I'm lily white, actually, because I haven't seen the sun in I don't know how many months."

She lifted her hand to show him and then realized it wasn't so much white as smeared black with soot and ingrained dirt.

Still. Not orange.

He cocked his head, and she looked back determinedly at her reflection on his helmet, trying to make out a face beyond it.

Option one was obviously no longer viable. There would be no sneaking onboard their ship unseen. She might as well get started on option two before they got the launch bay door open, and Tak whisked her out of their sight.

"Please help me. I'm a prisoner on board this spaceship. Captain Tak has imprisoned me here for over two and a half months. I need your help." She suddenly found it hard to talk, and had to swallow what felt like a stone lodged in her throat. "Please."

He stepped back from her in what felt like a rejection, and she pressed herself against the wall so she wouldn't fall down as the last thread of hope holding her up snapped.

The thump of pain in her head merged with the thump of her heart, and he went a little blurry in front of her.

She felt the ship tilt, and she cried out as she lost her balance.

Hands grabbed her. Helped her to sit, with her head between her legs.

She sat for a moment, wondering what was happening that everything was spinning, and slowly the world righted itself.

There was shouting near the door, and then the sound of running. She heard Tak's voice raised loud enough to make her wince.

Sounded like the Grih had finally gotten the launch bay doors open and Tak had taken a good look at the damage the Krik's ship had done to his launch bay.

When he realized they'd made off with his precious emergency pod . . .

She had to fight the smile that tried to curve her lips upward at the thought.

"What is funny?" The words were spoken right next to her ear, deep and rough, and she turned her head slowly, looked straight into his face. The glass of his helmet had been completely retracted.

His eyes were a strange shade of blue, violet, almost, with an outer rim of navy, but the hardness in them made any comparison to pretty flowers useless.

The sight of him scorched every thought from her head; Tak's tantrum, whether the Grih would help her. She couldn't tear her gaze away.

He looked as human as her.

"You . . ." she whispered, and realized she'd spoken in English. She reached out a hand. "You are . . ." Tears burned behind her eyes, caustic and hot, and then spilled over onto her cheeks.

He grabbed her wrist before she could touch him, but his grip was gentle.

"Where is your hood? What have you done here?"

The sound of Hury's voice, hard and vicious, made her cringe. She was on the ground, defenseless. She curled up tighter, because he *would* kick her.

And then the Grih was in front of her, and when she risked looking around his legs, she saw Hury was white-faced, his hands raised in surrender.

And that's when she realized the Grihan soldier was holding a shockgun on him.

And this time, she didn't try to suppress the smile.

***

The yurve shit was flying, all right.

Hal watched the puffed up little Garmman he'd just faced down run back to his captain, then took another look around the mess that had once been a launch bay.

It was crowded, what with his own fighter ship and the smoldering wreck that had once been the Krik's modified explorer taking up most of the space. The Krik had obviously come in hard, thanks to the great shot Tobru had gotten off just before the Krik dodged around a cluster of asteroids. Their vessel had ripped up the floor and scraped the walls. The air filters were struggling to cope with the fumes and smoke.

According to Favri, the Garmman trader's captain claimed the Krik had gained entrance through the gel wall by duplicating a Garmman government vessel signal, and then once they were inside, they'd shot two of his guards and locked the rest of the ship out of the launch bay and hadn't come through the doors. So where in Guimaymi's Star were they?

He kept his gun up, and not only to prevent being taken by surprise by the Krik. He knew he needed to guard the woman.

The most explosive of his problems.

Even five minutes ago he'd have laughed at the suggestion, because running the Krik to ground and locking up every single one had been his clear priority.

No longer.

She was from Earth. No doubt about it.

The musical voice. The way she looked.

Different hair color to Rose McKenzie; dark where Rose was pale gold. Maybe a little taller, although not enough to make much difference. Different color eyes, almost matching her hair color rather than Rose's green. But the same species.

He'd called her an orange, but actually she didn't show up orange on their scan. They had the data to identify her, thanks to Rose. He didn't know why he'd called her an orange earlier, other than habit.

Rose was the first orange they'd found in five hundred years. The first unidentified advanced sentient in a long, long time.

He'd have to remember not to call this one an orange again. She'd been more than a little adamant that she wasn't.

Another thing she'd made clear was that she was being held on this ship against her will. The way she'd cringed when the Garmman crewman had shouted at her bore that out, and even remembering the look on her face when the Garmann had come at her made the rage inside Hal leap a little higher.

She'd obviously been severely injured, blood caking the side of her head, sticking in her hair and trailing in a mess down her neck and onto her shoulder. Which reminded him. He tapped his comm. "Rial. I said come here." He didn't hide the sharp annoyance in his voice.

Rial immediately appeared from behind their ship, walking backward, shockgun raised.

"Sorry, Captain, the Garmman are behaving in a very hostile manner. When Favri got the doors open, it looked like she needed armed support. They thought we were the Krik at first, and they don't seem to be calming down, even though they know now we're from Battle Center."

Hal turned and looked down at the woman sitting at his feet. No, he bet the last thing they'd be was calm. They had a darc bomb on their hands, and at least some of them knew it.

Rial made a sound, and Hal lifted his head, saw his lieutenant understood what they had sitting quietly against the wall.

"You have the medikit?"

Rial nodded, then crouched beside the woman while Hal covered them both.

"My name is Lieutenant Rial Corvac, of Grih Battle Center. I'm a trained medic. This is Captain Hal Vakeri. Can you tell me what happened to you and your name?"

Hal glanced down quickly at the woman, to gauge her

response, and saw she was watching Rial with suspicious eyes.

"Please. I only want to help." Rial crouched lower, making himself as non-threatening as possible.

"My name is Fiona Russell." She spoke hesitantly in Grih. "One of the Krik hit me with the stock of his shockgun."

"Can I treat the wound?" Rial's voice sounded harsh in contrast to hers.

Hal waited until Fiona nodded before he forced himself to look away, keeping watch over the launch bay as his crew searched the area and kept the Garmman back from their ship.

He had set his comm to receive all chatter, so he caught snatches of conversation between his team and the Garmman crew as he did a slow and thorough sweep for any sign of the Krik.

Most of the Garmman were out of his line of sight, behind his fighter vessel, and he heard Favri barking out commands for them to get out of the launch bay until they were given permission from her.

Someone, Hal guessed the Garmman captain, was shouting at her, his voice getting more and more voluble.

He tapped his comm. "Tobru, bring out the halcon and stand next to Favri until that idiot shuts up."

He wouldn't be behaving like such a hard ass if he hadn't seen the way Fiona Russell had flinched when the Garmman crewman had run over to her. And there was no mistaking the signs of long, sustained malnourishment and abuse.

It was hard for a captain to have the command of his ship taken from him, but Hal didn't really care in this case.

Rial glanced up at him and Hal caught the smirk that flashed briefly on his face.

The halcon was a nasty piece of work. A laser that could cut through anything, it wasn't officially a weapon, it was a tool for cutting crew free in the case of an accident. And that's just what he'd say Tobru was planning to do with it if the Garmman captain brought a complaint. She'd hauled it out to cut any Krik who might be caught in their crumpled ship free.

Silence descended. The sight of the halcon was doing its job.

He looked back at the woman, saw Rial had cleaned away most of the blood.

"Did you see where on the ship the Krik went?"

She shook her head. "They aren't on the ship anymore. They left."

She suddenly had Hal's full attention.

"How did they get away?"

She closed her eyes, and he realized she was thinking about how to answer him.

"Look at me!"

Her eyes snapped open, and he saw pure fear in them. Which was not the plan.

He scaled back his frustration.

"How did they get away?" He tried to infuse some gentleness into his tone, but he'd lost her.

She curled up tight and hugged her legs close to her body.

He and Rial exchanged a look, and Hal didn't miss the hint of censure in his lieutenant's eyes.

"They can't hurt you now. Whatever threat they made to prevent you from talking, they can't follow through on it. And the quicker you tell us, the quicker they'll be locked away for their crimes."

Hal blinked at his lieutenant's perceptiveness. Of course, they could well have threatened her with promises of reprisal if she said anything. They hadn't been shy to hurt her, after all.

"It's not that. It's . . ." She raised her head. "Are you going to help me get away from Captain Tak, or not?"

Hal realized he hadn't answered her plea before. He'd been distracted by the way she'd gone pale in the face and then collapsed.

Had she been unsure since then that he would help her?

"I am. We will not leave you here."

"Oh." She blew out a breath and then gave a sob, her body shuddering as she hunched over her knees. "They took Captain Tak's emergency pod." Her voice came out a little garbled. "I showed them where it was." She breathed in and raised a tear-streaked face. "Tak *will* kill me if he knows that pod is gone."

Hal found himself wanting to meet Captain Tak.

"When I first stepped forward to talk to the Krik, they thought I might be Grih. I couldn't understand it, but now . . ." She was looking at his face again with the sense of wonder he'd seen in her eyes before.

It made him uncomfortable. Made him edgy.

"Why didn't you just hide from the Krik? Why did you approach them at all?"

She frowned up at him. "I didn't know you were right behind them at first. I asked them to take me with them. To help me escape."

Rial's face must be a mirror of his own, Hal thought. They were both slack-jawed.

And if preferring to hand yourself over to a bunch of murderous, vicious Krik rather than stay where you were didn't say it all about your living conditions, he didn't know what did.

He tried to take a calming breath. Tapped his comm. "Chel, get the *Illium* in as close as you can, and send over Councilor Vilk and Liaison Officer Kwo. Also, see if you can track an emergency pod. It would have launched . . ." He looked down at Fiona Russell and raised a brow.

"About half a minute before you arrived," she said, and then winced at his expression.

He tamped down the fury he felt at having missed them by so little. The chase may have been delayed but he would get the bastards.

And right now—he glanced down again—he had another type of justice to mete out.

Chapter Three

SHE WAS IN TROUBLE. MAYBE.

Fiona looked around the conference room.

She'd never been in it before, but then all she'd ever seen of Tak's ship was her tiny cell and the launch bay.

The room was utilitarian and dull, a trifle run down. The oval table was the only interesting thing in it. It was smooth, reflective metal, like highly polished silver, and edged with a wide border of pale blue, lit from within.

She reached out a hand to touch it, and a stream of icons appeared and settled in a circle around her fingertip.

She peered down at them, trying to work out what they stood for, until Hal Vakeri cleared his throat behind her. Indicated she should take a seat.

She still couldn't get over how alike the Grih were to her. She glanced at them as she slowly lowered herself into her seat.

The captain stood, stance wide, beside the table. The medic, Rial, who'd done the miraculous work on her head, stood near the door, watching everyone, and Tak, Hury, and Tak's lieutenant, Lon Sang, shifted nervously under his stare.

There were four Grihan guards at the door, two inside, two out, and while they seemed to be vigilant in watching their surroundings, she got the impression she was as interesting to them as they were to her.

As soon as she sat, she saw two newcomers appear in the doorway.

One wore a uniform similar to the rest of the Grihan team, but he wasn't Grih. He wasn't Garmman or Krik either. He had almost insect-like features, large eyes, thin limbs.

The second was Garmman, but he wore a white uniform with a blue collar, and looked more groomed and polished than Tak or any of the crew.

The sight of him had an immediate effect on Tak.

He stumbled to his feet, bowing and talking as fast as he could. "Councilor Vilk, this man—" He pointed at Hal. "This man has taken over my ship! And taken charge of one of my crew."

He darted a quick look at Fiona, then away, and Fee wondered if he hoped she didn't understand what he was saying.

She'd had the sense since the beginning he thought her stupid or unable to comprehend Garmman. And it was interesting that he called her part of his crew. If Tak was unwilling to identify her as a slave or prisoner, then chances were that what he was doing was considered illegal in this strange new world she'd landed in.

The Grih had agreed to rescue her, too. Had protected her from Hury earlier.

She thought of Gerwa and his crew and actually wanted to give them each a quick kiss on the cheek, blow to the head and all. They'd brought the Grih, and they'd changed her fortunes.

What was a little concussion compared to that?

"Councilor Vilk, thank you for coming across from the *Illium*." Captain Vakeri bowed slightly to the councilor, a formal, quick incline of his big body. "Kwo." He spared a nod for the strange being in Grih uniform. "Please be seated and let's get going. I have Krik to run to ground."

"Commander Chel didn't explain why you thought I would be needed here," the councilor said, and then he caught sight of Fee. "Oh." He let the exclamation out on a whoosh.

He stared at her for a long beat, until Fee fought an urge to fidget. Then he cut away, turned to look at Captain Tak, and Fee did not think he looked happy.

A tiny bubble of vengeful happiness floated up inside her.

Pop.

"I see you understand." The captain's voice was grim. "Fiona, this is United Councilor Vilk and United Council Liaison Officer Kwo." As he made the introductions, Fee turned to him, saw he'd taken off his helmet.

She gaped.

He looked like a warrior elf about to take a last stand against the Dark Lord. Shockgun strapped to his thigh, pointy ears, dark brown hair tipped with copper which stood up like an all-over mohawk—-he was the most formidable sight she'd ever seen.

And he was on her side.

Or, at least, he wasn't against her.

That was the most she could say about anyone she'd met since she'd been abducted.

She tried to school her face to neutrality, but all she could think was how happy she was that he and his crew were here.

"She helped the Krik escape." Tak suddenly stood, the look on his face an ugly combination of fear and rage, finger pointing right at her. "My emergency pod was completely hidden and they've taken it. They could only have known it was there because she told them."

Hal Vakeri inclined his head. "Yes. She's already told me how they escaped."

That seemed to floor him. His mouth opened and closed, and then he sucked in a breath. "Well, unless I'm mistaken, helping known criminals to escape is a crime."

"That's true." Vakeri looked across at her, and Fee went still. "Except in the case of coercion, or did you not see the severe blow to her head? And then, of course, you also have to prove the person knew the people she was helping were criminals and did it anyway. And I would guess that would prove impossible."

"How could she not know? The *Illium* has been broadcasting comms about this particular group and what they're accused of almost hourly." The councilor looked uncomfortable speaking out, but Fee saw Tak gave a satisfied nod.

"Fiona Russell would have had to have access to comms to see them." Vakeri motioned to her. "Did you see any such comms?"

Fiona looked across at Tak. "No. I am confined to a cell when I'm not working in the launch bay. Those are the only two places I've ever been on this ship, and neither has comms screens."

Kwo sucked in a breath. "Are you saying you are a prisoner here?" His voice seemed to vibrate as he spoke.

"I am."

Tak jumped up. "She lies! She lies! She's a worker. A fractious worker who had to be contained for her own good."

"And whereabouts did you find this worker?" Vakeri's voice was low and steady, a stark contrast to Tak's.

Tak went quiet. Looked down.

He hadn't thought that far, and he was digging himself a deep, deep hole.

It was sweet ambrosia to Fee. She gave a slow, satisfied smile. Felt another vengeful bubble rise.

"You think this is a joke?" The councilor raised a brow.

"No." She sent him a cool look. "I don't think it's a joke. But to say I'm happy about this situation is really putting it mildly."

Tak hunched his shoulders, his bulging forehead gleaming with sweat as he looked away.

"You're happy that the Krik were able to board a Garmma trading spacecraft while we were in pursuit and then, with your help, use one of the Garmman's emergency pods to escape?" Kwo's big eyes were narrowed, the vibrations of his voice almost a hiss.

They must have really wanted to get their hands on those Krik.

She shook her head. "I don't know who the Krik are. I don't know who you are, or the Garmman either, for that matter. I couldn't care less about your disputes. What I do care about is getting myself free of Captain Tak and his ship. The people who abducted me handed me over to him and he's held me prisoner for nearly three months. I've been subjected to starvation, beatings and general abuse. The Krik boarding this ship, with you chasing right after them, would seem to have brought me to the notice of a wider variety of . . . species . . . and I can only think that puts me one step closer to my goal of getting away from Captain Tak and his merry band of thugs. Unless slavery and abduction are perfectly okay in your part of the universe?" It was her turn to raise a brow.

Kwo made a strange clicking sound, and the look he sent Vakeri held a kind of sick dread.

There was movement at the door, and everyone turned as one of the Grih soldiers came in. Her helmet glass was retracted, and she held the hood Fiona had hidden in the launch bay.

"Officer Favri?" Vakeri cocked his head.

"As you directed, we questioned the crew. They say someone was brought on board and kept in the cell for six weeks, maybe a little more; although only the guards, the captain, and two of the senior officers saw her. Then suddenly, a month ago, they were told she wasn't a prisoner, she was a worker who'd been in quarantine, something they knew was a lie. And they saw her being moved from her cell to the launch bay to work and back. She wasn't allowed in the canteen or any of the recreational areas on the ship—they were told at her own insistence. She wore this at all times." Favri lifted the hood. "Or, I should say was made to wear it. Twice she tried to remove it, and three crew saw her being beaten for it."

There was silence in the room.

Fee looked at the hood with loathing. She still didn't know the reason for it, but maybe at last she'd have some answers.

"You tried to make her look like a Drivian?" Lieutenant Rial's question was incredulous. "The ears, well, maybe you could have fooled people looking on from a distance, but what about the mouth?"

"The hood covered my mouth," Fiona said. She used her hands, putting her index fingers and thumbs together and framing her face from just above her eyebrows to below her nose to show them. "Only this part of my face was visible."

There was silence again.

"A month ago?" Hal Vakeri said, quietly. "A funny thing happened a month ago."

The councilor looked up at him, and his face was paler than it had been. "This was not Garmman sanctioned, Captain. We've already proved Fu-tama was working alone."

"Well," Vakeri waved a hand over to Tak and his officers. "Not totally alone, obviously."

Things were being said that were going straight over her head, but Fiona suddenly had the sense this was a lot bigger than just a woman abducted and badly treated.

She looked over at Tak with all the enmity she felt.

"Do you want to explain this, Captain Tak?" The councilor edged his seat just a little away from Tak as he spoke.

Tak said nothing.

"I can tell you what I think, if you'd like." Every eye in the room turned to her.

"No—" Tak obviously had a change of mind, but the man in white pointed to him, and he fell silent.

"Go ahead."

"I was taken from my planet. I was passed off from the spaceship that took me to Captain Tak's vessel. I got the idea there was some plan in mind for me, that I was a commission of some sort, but something happened just over a month ago. You seem to know more about that than I do. Ever since then, they've been agonizing over what to do with me, not sure whether to keep me alive or not. And now Tak is regretting his indecision. Aren't you?"

Tak made a sound, half-snarl, half-moan.

It was the sound of sweet revenge.

"We will take her back to where we found her." Tak's voice was breathless.

"You don't even know where I was taken from, because you weren't in on the original abduction. I remember that much. I'm not going anywhere with you, ever again." Fee did not hide the scorn in her voice.

"Who did you get her from?" Vakeri's voice was sharp.

Tak wiped some sweat off his forehead. "Just some passing traders."

There were murmurs around the room and Tak hunched his shoulders.

"They didn't say much about her, even though we asked them. They wanted to get rid of her, so we took her. We thought she'd be safer with us."

"If they didn't say much about her, your promise to take her back home a minute ago was another lie." Vilk was dangerously calm. "And instead of alerting the United Council to the incident, you actively hid her from us, to the point of trying to deceive your own United Council representative."

"I have no good excuse." Tak looked down.

Fee stared at him with loathing. "You thought I'd be safer with you?" She shook where she stood. The Grih captain put out a hand to her, but she shied away from it, and he dropped his arm. "What about the beatings and the starvation?"

"An extremely good question." Vakeri took a step toward Tak and the Garmman flinched.

"She wouldn't cooperate. And we didn't know what to feed her." Tak must have heard how weak that excuse sounded. "It was an embarrassment to us that we had her in the first place. And she was unremittingly hostile."

"You were hoping I'd just die, weren't you? Then you could have shot me out into space and heaved a sigh of relief. You wanted me dead, without actually having the blood on your hands of ordering me killed."

"I wish now I had shot you when I had the chance." Tak glared at her.

Vakeri moved, suddenly standing right in front of the Garmman trader. "Captain Tak, you are under arrest for gross violation of the Sentient Beings Agreement. I'm sure there will be other charges brought, but that will do for now." He nodded to the guards at the door, and two of them pulled a struggling Tak from his chair and escorted him from the room.

"What about everyone else who helped him?" Fee looked over at Tak's second-in-command. Lon Sang had hit her more than once. Why should he get away with it? "Hury here did his fair share, too." Fee pointed to Tak's aide. "If they haven't doctored them or wiped them, it should all be on the lens feed." She was trembling, realized she was shaking with fury now that she had the freedom to demand justice.

"You'll probably have to arrest half the ship, and the other half is guilty of doing nothing, if not actively getting their hands dirty themselves."

The Garmman councilor wiped a blunt-fingered hand over his bulging forehead. "I will call for an independent team from UC headquarters to watch the lens feed. Arrest everyone involved."

"It was under orders," Hury said.

Fee crossed her arms over her chest. Even if that was a valid excuse, which she did not think it was . . .

"I bet it wasn't." Fee watched him squirm with fierce satisfaction. "Tak really didn't want to get his hands dirty, or he'd have ordered someone to shoot me or beat me to death ages ago, not draw it out. No, I guess he implied, but I don't think he ordered."

"You . . ." Hury pointed a finger at her. "Just shut up. You won't shut up."

"Can't handle a little backchat, Hury? You'd rather kick me when I'm down." She rubbed her hip, where Hury had in fact kicked her just yesterday when she was lying under a new transport cart, screwing on bolts.

Hury leapt at her from his seat, hands outstretched, murder in his eyes. Before he'd taken two steps, the Grih captain smoothly pulled the really big shockgun from its holster and fired at him. Hury gave a satisfying sound of pain and collapsed.

Fee looked across at Vakeri. "That was cathartic. Thanks."

The Grihan captain was staring at her.

She hadn't moved when Hury had gone for her. She'd been waiting for him to get closer so she could kick him in the balls, guessing she'd be able to without any consequences for once, but she supposed it might have made her look super cool. Or maybe suicidal.

Sometimes, over the last two months, she had been.

Chapter Four

FIONA RUSSELL WAS AN ENIGMA.

She'd shown fear and distress in the launch bay, but in the conference room she'd confronted Tak and his crew with a sharp edge of vengeance, and when Hury had come at her, she'd faced him with her arms still crossed over her chest.

She hadn't even flinched.

Hal hadn't wanted to risk her being hurt, so he'd taken the sniveling little shit down, but he'd really wanted to see what she planned to do.

That she had something up her sleeve, he didn't doubt for a moment.

There was a lot going on behind those intense, dark eyes.

She walked beside him now, back to the launch bay, and he had to adjust his stride to accommodate her own. She was limping a little and she'd rubbed her hip when she'd accused the Garmman crewman of kicking her when she was down, so he guessed the injury was recent and that she'd received no medical attention for it.

He wished now he'd set his shockgun to a higher charge before he'd brought Hury to the floor.

"Captain Vakeri."

Hal stopped and turned as Councilor Vilk hailed him, and beside him, he sensed Fiona Russell tense up.

"Councilor?"

"You're going to report to Battle Center." It was a statement, and it was quite correct, so Hal simply nodded.

The councilor blew out a breath. "I know this looks bad for the

Garmman. First the scandal around Councilor Fu-tama, and now this." Vilk waved his hand in Fiona Russell's direction, and Hal had the sense she became even stiffer.

"I would like you to tell Grih Battle Center I categorically deny any knowledge of what was happening on this ship. This was not sanctioned by the Garmman government or our military. In order for complete transparency, and to clear the Garmman government's name, we need a full member United Council team to investigate the matter."

Hal bowed. "I planned on suggesting the same, so we are in accord."

Vilk didn't seem to know whether to be relieved they had a point of agreement or insulted Hal didn't trust the Garmman to conduct an objective investigation of their own.

He could see the councilor waiver between a smile and a frown, until he eventually went with a grunt that could have been agreement or annoyance.

"I think it's best I return to the *Illium* immediately, and report to my own government and UC Headquarters myself. Are you going back now?"

"I'm taking Fiona across. She's in need of medical treatment. The runner that transported you is available whenever you're ready." If the tension coming off Fiona Russell was any indication, she wasn't inclined to sit in close quarters with a member of the Garmman race right now, and Hal was not in the mood for any more of Vilk's protestations of innocence, anyway.

Hal gave another bow, turned and walked away. Fiona got back in step with him.

She said nothing as they skirted the Krik's wreck and walked up the ramp into the fighter.

Only two of his crew were inside. The rest would stay behind to deal with the Garmman trader crew and he now had to decide whether to wait for the UC team to arrive, or leave some of his crew here and continue with his mission.

He'd already had to leave three members of his crew at the mining station the Krik had attacked, and he didn't like the idea of leaving yet more teammates behind.

He looked sideways at Fiona. The choice would most likely not be his to make. It would depend on what Battle Center had to say about his new find.

She looked small in the seat that was designed for a much larger Grih, and he realized she was in the kind of rough work overall that mechanics wore to keep their uniforms from being damaged when they did heavy work, the sleeves and legs folded up multiple times.

"Do you have anything on the ship that you'd like brought over?" he asked. "Clothing? Personal belongings?"

She hesitated. "Only the handheld I've had from the start. It has five languages on it." She shot him a quick look. "It's in my cell. I think it came from my original abductors, but I've had it long enough now, I consider it mine."

Hal nodded and left her clipping herself into her seat. He joined Rial back at the bottom of the ramp.

"You're in charge. I'll send another team over so you can set a constant guard to watch the Garmman. Do a thorough search, and keep your eye out for any information concerning Fiona. She says she has a handheld which was given to her by her original abductors. It's in her cell. But it comes to me first. I want engineering to look it over before we give it back to her."

Rial saluted, and as Hal walked back up the ramp, the pilot started the engines.

He secured himself into the seat opposite Fiona and found her watching him steadily.

The fighter lifted and turned, shot through the gel wall, and she angled her head to look out at the Garmman trader falling away from them.

"Okay." She took a deep breath. "Now we're off that stinking hellhole, how about you tell me why Vilk considers me being on Tak's ship such a problem?"

***

The sleek Grih vessel was full of surprises.

From the outside it looked as if there were no windows, but the whole thing was some kind of one way glass, so everyone inside had a three sixty view of their surroundings.

The interior walls also acted as a screen, overlaying numbers and equations she didn't understand on the objects outside.

Fee dragged her gaze away from the spacescape around her for a moment, and focused back on Captain Vakeri, waiting for him to answer her question.

He was leaning back in his seat, a considering look on his face. "The simple answer is the Garmman are signatories to the Sentient Beings Agreement, and your abduction, imprisonment and forced labor are in direct contravention of that. So they're already up for fines and Tak for imprisonment."

Again, the surge of delight at Tak's predicament washed over her, but she had the nagging sense there was more to the problem than just the breaking of some rules. Vilk's reaction when he'd seen her had been close to horrified.

Then she frowned. "Tak didn't abduct me, though. Will that soften his sentence?" She hoped not.

Vakeri shook his head. "Don't worry, he'll pay for what he did to you. What do you recall of your original abduction?"

She forced herself to get comfortable, deliberately relaxing muscles that wanted to tense up. "Not very much. One minute I remember sitting in a deck chair, reading, and the next, I was in some kind of strange glass box. There were sounds all around me, like I was in a jungle, and I fought to wake up properly, but if I did, I don't remember it. It happened a few times, half-waking, fighting to get conscious, not remembering again." She shuddered. "And feathers." She said the last in a whisper.

Vakeri leaned forward. "Feathers?"

Her hands clenched on her thighs. "The thought of them makes me want to cringe."

He nodded, as if she'd said something helpful, and she forced her hands open again.

"What does that mean to you?"

"That you were abducted by the Tecran and kept in a holding cell under sedation." He rubbed a hand through that spiky hair as if weighed down by the information.

"The Tecran?" It explained her strange dislike of the language on her handheld. She must have subconsciously heard her abductors speaking.

"They're theoretically our allies, but we're in a delicate position of near-war with them at the moment." He held her gaze and then looked away, contemplative. As if she were a new problem to factor in to his already difficult workload.

She felt a grudging sense of outrage, because she hadn't wanted any of this, and was hardly here by choice, but then the sight through the rear wall erased that from her mind—she was too busy staring at the massive, sleek spaceship. "What is that?" she breathed.

"The *Illium*," Vakeri said. "Welcome to my ship."

Chapter Five

THERE WAS A LOT GOING ON HERE she didn't understand, but Fee was prepared to be patient. She had enough on her plate coming to grips with her new change in circumstances. She could wait to get to the bottom of why people looked at her and more or less tore at their hair or broke into a sweat.

She walked side by side with Vakeri down the ramp, but slowed and let him go ahead when she saw how many Grihan soldiers were waiting for them, all gazes locked on her.

The captain stopped as soon as she fell back, looked at her over his shoulder. "No one will harm you here."

His face was impassive, an expression he seemed to be good at, and he spoke in the rough, staccato way all the Grih seemed to have. She appreciated that there was no hint of impatience in his demeanor.

He was so striking, she had to force her gaze away from his face.

The intense eyes. The ears.

He'd kept his helmet off since the meeting on Tak's ship, but he was the only Grih on the Garmman trader who had. Now, as she made herself look at the other Grih in the launch bay, she saw pointy ears and short, spiky hair seemed to be the Grih norm.

And they were all big.

"Captain?" A woman made her way through the loose grouping of armed soldiers, and although she'd addressed Vakeri, like everyone else, her eyes were very much on Fee. She was as tall as any other of the crew, and her hair was almost silver white, her eyes a dazzling, tropical blue.

Vakeri made some kind of signal with his hand, and the soldiers moved back. He stepped off the ramp and gestured to the woman approaching them. "Fiona, this is Doctor Jasa. She'll take you to the med chamber and take a more thorough look at the injury Rial patched up, and see what else needs fixing." He glanced at her hip, and out of habit, Fee rubbed it.

She took a cautious step off the ramp and onto the launch bay floor.

He gave a formal bow. "I have operational matters to see to, but you'll be in good hands with Jasa."

A look passed between him and the doctor, and then he was striding away, most of the soldiers following behind him.

There were a few who stayed behind, though, shockguns in hand, and Fee decided they were guarding the launch bay against attack.

"Are you still worried about the Krik?" she asked the doctor, and Jasa blinked.

"No. We're living in rather tense times at the moment. This is just a general precaution." She placed her hands together, and extended them to Fee.

Fee lifted her own hands, palms out. "I'm sorry, I'm not sure what I need to do in return. I only know the Grih language, not its culture, I'm afraid."

Jasa cocked her head in a way so alien, Fee forced herself not to react. "That you speak our language so well, given the circumstances you must have learned it in, is in itself extraordinary. If I offer my hands to you, palms together, you cover them on each side with your own. If you present your hands together to me, I do the same."

Fee reached out, placed her hands on either side of Jasa's, and the doctor smiled.

She sensed the eyes of everyone in the launch bay on them through the interaction, and couldn't help the way her hands started to shake.

"Let's go." The doctor's words were overloud and harsh, and Fee flinched, then saw Jasa's ire was for the soldiers around them, not herself.

Two of the guards stepped forward, a man and a woman.

"We have to come with you, Doc. Captain's orders." The man who spoke bowed respectfully.

Jasa gave a tight nod. "Apologies, Fiona. Those tense times again. The captain wants to make sure you're safe. Pila and Carmain will be coming along to watch your back."

"Watch it against whom?" Fee wanted to know, but Jasa merely shook her head and led the way, and Fee had no choice but to fall into step, with the two guards following behind them.

When they reached the med chamber, Pila went in and checked it first, while Carmain stood guard in the doorway.

"It's safe." Pila stepped back out into the passageway, and he and Carmain took up position outside the door.

Jasa indicated Fee should proceed her, and then slapped a large circle of light glowing on the wall to close the door behind them.

They stood in silence for a moment.

Fee was taking in the room, Jasa was watching her do it.

"So. Some of the Grih crew might attack me? Even against the captain's orders?" Fee asked at last. "Just what have they got against me?"

Jasa jerked. Opened her mouth, closed it. Blew out a breath. "It's complicated. The Grih are part of a ruling coalition of five races called the United Council. The members of the Council agree to certain codes of conduct, and although we don't always see eye to eye, we are never openly hostile to one another.

"A month ago that changed, when one of the member groups, the Tecran, came into our airspace and fired on our fleet. During that incident, a high-level Grihan officer actively worked against us from within.

"When he was caught and questioned, he admitted he wasn't the only Grihan officer involved in what turned out to be a complicated plot. He tried to kill someone very much like you, and as the other officers he spoke about haven't yet been identified, Captain Vakeri very wisely is taking no chance one of them isn't onboard the *Illium*."

Fee frowned. "When you say someone very much like me, what do you mean?"

"I actually mean someone exactly like you, I suppose." Jasa said.

"Someone from Earth?" There was a rushing, rising roar in her ears.

"Yes. Someone from Earth. Do you know Rose McKenzie?"

Fee knew her mouth was open, her heart thundering loud enough she was sure Jasa must be able to hear it.

"Actually, I do."

***

When Hal stepped onto the bridge, Chel rose slowly from the captain's chair and limped forward a few steps.

He looked like he should still be in medical, but Hal knew his second-in-command wouldn't have sat this one out for anything.

"We lost them." The Krik had nearly killed Chel and two soldiers on his team, and running them to ground was as much personal as it was a matter of upholding the law.

"We'll get them." Chel had a look on his face that had Hal raising his brows.

"You're tracking the emergency pod?"

Chel smiled. "We are. Favri got the signal code from the Garmman trader and we were able to lock on. Unfortunately for them, that particular model of pod can't be redirected to a specific destination. It lands where it lands."

"And in this case?"

"It's headed for Balco, which is the closest livable planet, and by my calculations it's trajectory will put them down in the western deserts. They'll be a long hike from anywhere." Chel's smile deepened. "It's a harsh environment to be stuck in."

Hal looked at the visual comm Gerbardi brought up as Chel was speaking, saw the pulse of signal and then the trajectory calcs which curved away and down onto Balco. The Krik would land in the middle of what was an uninhabited wasteland.

They wouldn't be getting off Balco in a hurry. Which was good, because he didn't have time right now to send someone after them.

He turned to Gerbardi, and the comms officer came to attention. "I need to speak to Admiral Hoke. Private line, utmost urgency."

Everyone in the room had an idea why, and Hal could sense the weight of their unasked questions.

Might as well tell them what he could while Gerbardi put the request in to Battle Center.

"As we came in range of the Garmman trader, the *Fasbe,* we got an unusual reading. Since Rose McKenzie was discovered a month ago, beings with her bio signature have been entered into our system with a red flag. And it was flashing as we chased the Krik into the *Fasbe's* launch bay."

He took out his handheld and flicked a frozen image of the Earth woman from his helmet's lens feed to the main screen. She was half-crouched against the launch bay wall, eyes closed, face tense. The dark red of her blood was shocking against her pale skin.

"Her name is Fiona Russell, and she was injured by the Krik and by the Garmman who were holding her captive. Doctor Jasa is tending to her wounds."

He looked around the room at the men and women staring at the screen. "I don't need to tell you the importance of this. And I don't need to remind you that according to Farso Lothric, there are a number of other Grihan officers whose loyalties might lie elsewhere. I've set a guard to watch Fiona Russell, and I expect everyone to be alert to an attempt on her life."

There was a murmur of agreement, and Hal gave a curt nod. He hated that he had to set a guard on his own ship against a possible attack on someone under his protection. He should not have to be suspicious of his own team.

Farso Lothric hadn't known how many or who the other Grihan officers were—the Garmman councilor Nii Fu-tama who'd recruited them had made sure of that—and now that Fu-tama was dead there was no way they could find out.

One thing they did know; whoever was involved had spent time at Grih Battle Center's headquarters on Garmma.

Hal had made sure the four guards he'd set in rotation to watch Fiona had never so much as set foot there.

Gerbardi stood. "Admiral Hoke will be with you in five, Captain."

Hal gave a nod of thanks and left the bridge for the small, private office he used for his administrative duties.

He spent the time waiting for Hoke reviewing the visual comms recorded by his helmet, and then watching Favri and Rial's questioning of the Garmman trader crew.

It was clear the crew had known something wasn't right.

Tak's problem was his ego. He'd assumed his staff were either stupid or prepared to turn a blind eye, but when the Tecran had invaded Grih airspace, and the explosive information about their abduction of Rose McKenzie had come out and swept through every member nation of the UC, it hadn't taken a genius to work out there was something strange about Fiona Russell's hood and the way she was being treated.

No one had believed for a moment Tak would stand behind them if they'd killed her on his encouragement and then been charged. And that had saved her life.

Tak's crew had understood him all too well.

It was twenty minutes, he realized, not five, when the comm from Hoke finally interrupted him, pulling him from Favri's questions on where the trading vessel had been when they'd picked Fiona up.

The admiral was clearly sitting at her desk, and she looked harassed.

Hal had met her personally numerous times, before she'd been made head of Battle Center a month ago. It looked like the weight of authority was resting heavily on her shoulders.

She rubbed a finger under her left eye and leaned forward. "Apologies for the delay, Vakeri. Diplomats don't know when to shut up."

Hal smiled. Weighed down or not, Hoke was still the straight-talking leader he'd always respected. And she wasn't going to like his news.

"Early this morning we got a distress signal from a Sector 9 mining vessel. They were under attack by Krik pirates. To cut a long story short, my second-in-command boarded the miner with a team of ten, and found every member of the crew dead. The Krik were still there, and they ambushed the team, severely injuring three of them."

"The Krik are in a cell?" Hoke asked.

Hal shook his head. "Got away. They have something that can copy another ship's signal, so when they first left the miner's launch bay, we thought it was our own team, coming back. We gave chase as soon as we realized what was happening. I took a fighter so the *Illium* could stay behind and deal with the injured, and we managed to severely damage the Krik's vessel."

"But?" Hoke was watching him with full attention now. She knew he wouldn't have flagged something like this as urgent unless it was leading somewhere interesting.

"There was a Garmman trader in the same airspace, and given they were crippled, the Krik crash-landed into the trader's launch bay. By the time we got there ourselves, they'd ditched their ship and had stolen the trader's emergency pod."

Hal leaned back in his chair. "The thing is, when we approached the Garmman trader, our bio scanner started to ping."

"Ping?" Hoke sat up straight. "Since when does it ping?"

"Since Rose McKenzie's bio signature was loaded into the system."

Hoke stood in agitation, and for a moment Hal could only see her waist and the butt of her shockgun before she forced herself to sit again.

"Vakeri, you had better spell out what you found in that Garmman trader."

"I found another woman from Earth," Hal told her.

Hoke stared at him, hand curled into a fist on the table in front of her. "And I thought," she said, "that one was enough."

Chapter Six

ROSE MCKENZIE.

Fee reached out and held onto the examination table.

So that's where she'd disappeared to.

Space.

All the searches, all the public appeals for information—for nothing.

Just like what was most likely happening for her.

Tears welled up in her eyes, and began to drip down her cheeks.

She'd buried thoughts of her family, how they'd be worrying, as deep as she could, but now, thinking about Rose, and the media storm around her disappearance, Fee suddenly acknowledged her parents were going through hell.

"Did you meet Rose in the Class 5?" Jasa had grabbed a handheld when Fee had said she knew Rose McKenzie, but started at the sight of her tears when she looked up from her furious tapping.

Fee shook her head. "I don't know what a Class 5 is." She was proud of herself for keeping her voice steady. "I've never met Rose personally. She was on holiday near where I live and she disappeared. I'd have had to live under a rock not to have heard her name."

"You were taken from the same place?" Jasa's fingers were just about drilling through the handheld's screen.

"The same general area." She didn't remember anything about being taken. Except feathers. The feel of feathers against her skin.

She lifted a hand to her throat, trying to fight back the nausea.

"Get on the table, Fiona. You look like you're going to pass out." Jasa kept hold of her handheld and pulled a slim silver wand, a larger version of the one Rial had used on her earlier, out of a drawer. "Do you want to tell me why you're so upset?"

Fee struggled to get onto the table, obviously created for people taller than herself, and Jasa hovered her instrument over Fee's hip.

"I'm upset because Rose's family were devastated by her disappearance, and I've been trying not to think about it, but I know my family is in the same kind of pain now, too. We both will never be found."

Jasa caught her eye. "I don't know what to say to that, other than it should never have happened."

She looked angry and got angrier by the minute as she waved what Fee guessed was a diagnostic tool over Fiona's legs and pelvis and then studied the handheld for the results. With her elf ears, she looked like a furious fairy godmother waving a wand. A fairy who could kick ass just as easily as cast a spell.

Fee hadn't had to take off her clothes for the examination, and as the wand came near her chest, she suddenly remembered the Krik's encryptor sitting snug inside her bra, under her left breast.

She couldn't help the sound of distress she made.

She didn't know what Jasa would do if she found it, but it was the one small secret Fee had, and she was keeping it.

The encryptor had been hard-won and it was hers.

Jasa stopped, gaze flying to Fee's face at her reaction, and Fee drew up her knees and looped her arms around them, shielding the top of her body.

"Sorry."

That was the truth. Jasa had done nothing but help her, but she wasn't risking anyone taking away her one sure way out of most locked rooms.

"What is it?" Jasa stepped back.

"I just . . ." Fee actually shuddered in a breath.

This is what she'd been reduced to. A quivering wreck at the thought of something being taken from her, and yet, the feeling was genuine and so strong, she felt swept away by it.

She tightened her grip on her knees and bowed her head.

Breathe in. Breathe out. That's all she had to do.

Eventually she looked up, saw Jasa was working calmly at a large screen in the corner.

The doctor turned. "Better?"

Fee shook her head. No way was she continuing the examination until she'd had a chance to hide her encryptor.

Jasa sighed. "What would you like to do?"

There was only one answer to that question. "Have a shower."

The doctor stared at her. "A shower?"

"I haven't been allowed one for over two months. It would be . . . good."

Jasa grimaced. "Fiona, I was told that you had been ill-treated by your captors, and I've been looking at the evidence of that for the last five minutes, but I can't believe I didn't think to allow you to shower and dress in something clean and comfortable before your examination and I apologize."

She moved to the door. "Follow me and I'll take you to your room, and make sure you have what you need. When you're ready to continue the examination, you can call me."

Fee slid onto the floor, looked down at the thin silver wand lying on a tray near the table. "What does that thing do?"

Jasa sighed again. "I should have told you that, too. It's hard to remember that you aren't one of us. It's able to register damage at the cellular level, so it can develop a comprehensive picture of all injuries. Once I've examined your whole body, I can come up with a holistic approach to your recovery."

Fee nodded. She looked straight into Jasa's azure eyes.

She could not regret keeping the encryptor secret, and she *had* been nervous about the silver wand and hadn't enjoyed being examined while she felt grimy.

She decided her conscience could cope.

She followed the doctor down two short passageways, one guard going ahead of them, the other watching the rear, and Fee wondered if they could possibly call any more attention to her.

She sighed in relief when Pila deemed her room safe and she and Jasa stepped in and closed the door behind them.

"It's placing a strain on you. The guards." Jasa's lips twisted in sympathy. "It's better to be safe, though."

Fee wanted to ask what the Grih officer had tried to do to Rose, but her words dried up on her tongue as she looked around the room.

It was about ten times bigger than her previous cell; bed, table, chairs and a bathroom all clean and neat.

"Here is the refreshment station." Jasa said, and touched the wall.

It lit up in a circle, and two doors slid open in the middle to reveal a recessed cabinet.

"There is cold water and hot water," Jasa pointed to the taps, "and you can make grinabo and tep-tep." She strode to another wall, touched the side of it and another circular area lit up and opened to reveal shelves. "There are some clothes here for you, and some towels. Please make yourself comfortable, and when you're ready, we'll continue the examination."

"Thank you." Fee took a step toward the bathroom.

"Fiona." Jasa was standing by the door. "You have a head injury, and initial results are that your hip has been severely bruised. Get clean and have something to drink, but then I have to look you over."

There was a thread of steel in the doctor's voice.

Fiona turned. Looked Jasa straight in the eye and nodded.

An expression flashed across the doctor's face. It might have been respect, it might have been pity, and then Jasa hit the button beside the door and stepped out.

Fee waited until the doors closed again, her eyes on the guards with shockguns at the ready, standing watch.

Her encryptor wouldn't help get her past them, if she needed to, but one step at a time. She had her get-out-of-jail free card, and she was hanging on to it.

***

Hal stood in the empty med chamber, his hand raised to tap his earpiece to contact Jasa, when she walked back in.

She stepped inside, flicked her gaze in his direction, and then walked over to pick up her handheld.

Barely suppressed fury radiated from her, and he could see the jump of a vein in her neck.

He waited.

"There are more bruises on her than I saw on Chel after the Krik attack." Her voice was low. "And it's not just the bruises, it's where they are. She had to be on the floor for some of them. Kicked when she was down." She lifted the handheld, tapped the screen, and a diagnostic appeared on the wall. "See here?" Jasa pointed. "Two fine stick fractures in her arm, four weeks old, to judge by the healing. She's lucky her hip isn't fractured as well, but as it is, it's seriously bruised."

"And her head?"

Jasa turned on him. "I haven't got there yet. Which is the next point. She's traumatized. She had some kind of episode while I was examining her. I was going to intervene, but she has obviously developed her own strategy for dealing with it—by the looks of it from long practice. She went through some breathing exercises, got herself under control, and I decided any interference from me might have simply added to her distress."

Jasa leaned back against the counter that ran along the wall, and Hal didn't think he'd ever seen her so openly affected. "She asked if she could shower and change before we continued the examination. Such a simple thing, but I didn't think to offer it. I'm not used to dealing with someone who's gone through what she's had to face. And when she started crying over Rose McKenzie—"

Hal held up a hand to stop her, his pulse suddenly racing. "She knows Rose McKenzie?"

He tried to think of the consequences of that, but Jasa was shaking her head.

"Rose was abducted from the same place on Earth as Fiona. They've never met, but Fiona said there were repeated comms about Rose's disappearance, and appeals for people with information to come forward. It reminded her of what her own family would be going through."

Jasa's words stopped him cold. No matter how interesting he found her, until now, Fiona Russell had signified an interruption to his mission and a logistical problem.

But none of it was her fault.

He needed to adjust his attitude where she was concerned, find a little empathy.

"I broke the news to Admiral Hoke about finding Fiona, and I'm waiting to hear back as to how we'll proceed, but most likely we'll be continuing on, delivering Councilor Vilk to Larga Ways as planned. So she'll be with us for a while."

"How did Hoke take it?" Jasa asked.

Hal snorted. "Badly. Rose McKenzie didn't exactly land among us without a ripple. Her arrival caused a tidal wave of change. Hoke's worried about the impact Fiona will have. But the fact that she doesn't seem to come with a Class 5 battleship in tow like Rose did makes her a little less worrying."

"The Tecran must have kept her sedated." Jasa looked over at the image of Fiona on the screen again. "She has no memory of her abduction. The Garmman trader is all she knows."

Hal had been thinking about that. "The Tecran who stole Rose

McKenzie didn't sedate her, but then they had Doctor Fliap onboard, in charge of scientific research, and he seems to have been a sadist. If the Class 5 that took Fiona had someone with higher principles, then it makes sense they kept her in some kind of suspended state. What I don't understand is why they took her at all, and then why they handed her to the Garmman afterward. If the Tecran had gotten her off their hands by giving her to the Garmman a month ago, when it came out that Rose had usurped the Tecran's control of their Class 5, then I'd understand it. They wouldn't want someone on their ship who could free the thinking system running it. But they passed her off to the Garmman over a month before Rose freed Sazo."

"Someone got nervous? They feared what they'd done would be discovered and they'd be charged with non-compliance of the Sentient Beings Agreement?" Jasa lifted her shoulders.

"They had no reason to fear that. Class 5s were kept from mainstream airspace, and the Tecran would light jump away rather than let anyone onto a Class 5. They should have felt safe enough." Maybe they'd never know the reason. It was hardly likely they'd get the chance to ask.

There was a faint chime, and Jasa looked over at her handheld. "Time for me to check on Hadri and Mun. They're doing better. Almost as well as Chel. He should have stayed put though, instead of captaining the ship while you were chasing down the Krik."

Hal acknowledged that with a shrug. "It was personal for him. He thought the Krik had killed Mun, and when he was shot down, he couldn't shield Hadri from attack. I told him to report to you now I'm back on board."

Jasa's mouth thinned. "Well he hasn't. Call him to med chamber 3 and he can meet us there."

"What about Fiona?" Hal realized he'd hoped to find the Earth woman here, study her a little more, and he was sorry to be leaving without seeing her.

"I think she'll be at least an hour. I gave her a warning not to take too long because of her head injury, but I bet she'll spend a while in the shower. I've instructed Pila to knock after thirty minutes, and go in if she doesn't answer, in case her concussion is worse than I thought."

"You know, she got that injury because she approached the Krik, and asked them if they'd take her with them." He was still trying to process that. Of everything that he'd seen and heard on the Garmman trader, that had made the biggest impression on him. That, and the hood Tak had made her wear.

The Garmman captain had tried to erase what she was, but in a way that spoke of contempt not just for her, but for the intelligence of his own crew.

Jasa regarded him with open-mouthed astonishment. "She actually thought they'd help her?"

"She didn't know anything about the Krik. And as you noted with her injuries, she wasn't exactly being well treated by the Garmman. She didn't think she had anything to lose."

"It's no wonder she had a moment of panic on my table. How does she know we'll be any better?" Jasa's voice was quiet. "I don't know if I'm qualified to deal with her, Hal. She's outside of my experience."

Hal lifted his shoulders. "She's outside everyone's experience. The only exception is the crew of the *Barrist*, the ship that found Rose McKenzie. And they're more than seven light jumps from our position, and we're going in the opposite direction."

"You looked that up?" Jasa raised her eyebrows in surprise.

Hal nodded. "I was hoping we could pass Fiona off on them, but there's no way that's happening. Not until we get back to Battle Center headquarters."

Jasa fiddled with her handheld. "I'll contact the *Barrist's* head of medical, perhaps he can help me work out a treatment for

Fiona's injuries. Her bones and muscles are denser than ours, so I think her planet is larger than any of the four planets, has more gravity. Her injuries are less severe than they could have been because she could take more damage without breaking. And when she gets her strength back, I think she'll find our gravity allows her to jump higher than she's used to."

Hal was relieved Jasa seemed calmer than she had been when she'd first walked in. "If we can get on with our mission of delivering Vilk, and then scoop up those Krik straight afterward, we'll have Fiona back at Battle Center very soon."

That should be the extent of their excitement. After all, as he'd said earlier, unlike Rose, Fiona didn't come with a Class 5 battleship as part of the deal. She wouldn't have been fighting for survival on the Garmman trader if she had.

Rose McKenzie had not landed, cringing against a wall, into Grihan life. She'd brought a banned thinking system into the Grih fold, sparked a power shift in Battle Center, and stirred up the balance of power on the United Council.

Fiona Russell was hopefully going to be a lot less trouble.

Chapter Seven

FEE THOUGHT SHE'D FEEL MORE.

More relieved. More safe. More happy.

She looked down at herself, at the too long sleeves and trouser legs of the clothes she'd been given, and fought back tears.

She needed to find the core of steel that had kept her going these last months. But without someone to fight against, without the hatred for Tak and his officers that had fed her resistance and her determination, she was . . . done.

It was exhaustion, probably. And uncertainty.

There were undercurrents here she didn't understand.

Talk of Class 5s and Vilk waving his hand at her and calling her 'this' with barely suppressed panic. Like she was a whole huge set of problems, all on her own.

She hadn't expected anything when the Grih had stumbled on her, she'd just hoped that things would get a little better.

They'd gotten more than just a little better. She was clean, she'd had a cup of something delicious she couldn't remember the name of and when she got up the energy to leave the room, she'd get medical treatment.

The fact that her clothes were too big was nothing.

Nothing!

She sucked in a deep breath, and rolled up the sleeves and legs. The soft burgundy top and pants were so much nicer than the hard, scratchy uniform Tak had given her.

A polite chime sounded from the door and she froze, let her eyes go to her bed to double-check the encryptor was properly hidden.

Under the mattress was a cliché, but for now it was the best she had.

The chime sounded again, and she walked hesitantly forward. Jasa thought the fact that she had guards should reassure her. It didn't. It worried her.

Protecting her from some rogue Grihan officers didn't make sense, along with so many other things. But she'd work it out. She just needed to let Jasa patch her up, eat something, and get a good night's sleep without worrying about whether tomorrow would be the day someone got up the nerve to kill her.

Put that way, she'd come a long way since this morning.

Before she reached the door, it opened, and she stumbled to a stop in surprise.

Pila stood in the doorway, and he must have seen the shock on her face.

"Apologies. We had orders from the doctor to enter if you didn't answer because of your concussion."

She gave a tight nod. "I was trying to get my uniform to fit." She held out her arms.

Pila frowned, and Carmain stared at her from over his shoulder. "Doctor Jasa has asked us to take you back to the medical chamber."

She had the sense they would have liked to have engaged her in conversation, but as she stepped out to join them in the passageway, the strange alien who'd been present during the interrogation of Tak and his officers approached, and they were suddenly all business.

"Liaison Officer Kwo." Pila was polite, but he held his shockgun in both hands. Carmain had taken a position behind Fee, angling her body to see down the passage in both direction.

Fee tried to work out if they were simply being protective or whether they thought Kwo was a genuine threat.

"Captain Vakeri is serious in his determination that this new orange is protected." Kwo's voice sounded as if his words were being formed from a plucked, vibrating harp string.

The reference to orange again. Vakeri had called her an orange when he'd first found her.

Fee decided she must be misunderstanding the word, or had somehow gotten it wrong when she'd learned Grih from her handheld. Looking at Kwo's huge eyes, she very much doubted they saw colors the same way, anyway.

"You were here to see Fiona?" Carmain asked him. Like Pila, her voice was polite, but she didn't lower her weapon.

"I would like to make an appointment with her, yes. I need to submit a full report to the United Council, and her testimony would be useful."

"Is Fiona all right?" Jasa's sharp, worried question turned everyone's attention in the doctor's direction. She had come up behind Kwo, and stopped, frowning at the sight of them, guns up and ready to rumble.

"I'm fine." Fee decided it was time to remind them all she was standing right there, listening to them talk about her.

Jasa turned to Kwo. "What did you want with Fiona?"

"Just to talk to her. I pose no threat." Kwo made a gesture with his hands that seemed to convey gross overreaction on Pila and Carmain's part.

"Well, you can't. Not until she's finished on the regeneration bed."

Kwo gave a bow. "My apologies. I thought she was finished in the medical room."

"*She* is right here, and can speak for herself." Fee had kept her emotions locked down tight while she'd been on Tak's ship, and the habit was hard to break. Even to her own ears, she only sounded mildly annoyed.

Everyone looked at her, with varying degrees of surprise and embarrassment.

"Sorry, Fiona." Jasa clasped her hands in front of her. "It's your choice, of course, but I'd urge you to allow me to heal you, before you do anything else."

Fee looked over at Kwo. "What do you need from me, beyond what I already told you on Tak's ship? And who are you, exactly?" Everyone seemed to know all about her but she was in the dark about them.

Kwo moved his head from side to side in a rocking motion. "Forgive me, I am the liaison appointed by the United Council to this battleship. An officer representing the council is assigned to each ship belonging to United Council members. It keeps all activities transparent and facilitates communication."

In other words, it stopped people breaking the rules.

"Why wasn't there a liaison on Tak's ship?" Her life would have been completely different if there had been.

Kwo rocked a little faster. "The *Fasbe* is a commercial ship, not government owned. Although I agree that it would be ideal to have a liaison on commercial ships as well, there are so many of them, it wouldn't be viable." He suddenly went still. "I merely require a more formal statement from you. I'm afraid the situation on the Garmman trader was emotionally charged, and perhaps you didn't think to include some of the details."

The idea of having to talk about what had happened to her again made her want to turn back to her room and curl up on her bed.

But she had been given a choice and she made it. "No. I think it's best I have my injuries seen to first."

Jasa gave a decisive nod. "Good." She turned on her heel and walked away, and with a smooth move, Pila stepped around Kwo, keeping his eyes on the liaison, and waited for Fee to follow him.

There was so much going on here, and with every step she took toward the med chamber, Fee decided she'd made the right decision not to speak with Kwo. She needed to be physically well, to eat something that she actually enjoyed, and to sleep.

And then she'd be ready to take on this new world she'd been dropped into.

***

"We have a problem."

Hal looked up at Gerbardi, and canceled the comm he was about to put through to Rial. His communications officer tugged distractedly at his hair.

"We've lost contact with Battle Center."

Hal went still. Silence settled over the rest of the officers on the bridge. "Define 'lost contact'."

"All comms sent in the last ten minutes have just bounced back. Our connection is gone." Gerbardi tapped at the screen in front of him, looked back at Hal. "It doesn't make sense. Something is interrupting the signal, but there's no logical reason why."

Hal's first thought was the Krik. They had surprised him with their sophisticated signals duplicator and the ease with which they'd gained access to the mining vessel they'd attacked. But they were by now struggling in the hostile environment on the barren plains of Balco, and there was no way they could be messing with a Grih battleship and its encrypted comms to Battle Center.

Unless they hadn't been alone.

If there was more than one Krik pirate ship, it started to make a little more sense, and it also meant he'd better hurry if he wanted to catch the Krik crew stranded on Balco, or their friends would get to them first.

"What are the chances a second Krik vessel is blocking comms?" He flicked his gaze to Voa, his explorations officer. She was already scanning the area, flicking through screen after screen.

She shook her head. "If they're out there, they're well hidden."

"And if they're blocking comms, it's selective, because I can still reach the ships in our immediate vicinity." Gerbardi tapped at his screen again. "I can even reach Larga Ways."

Hal stood. He'd been waiting for Hoke to get back to him, tell him whether they should deliver Vilk to Larga Ways and then return, or head straight back with Fiona Russell.

If long-range comms were down, the decision was up to him, and he wanted Vilk off his ship, and the Krik tracked down.

Fiona Russell didn't seem to have any specific information on what the Tecran were up to. Battle Center could wait for whatever it was she had to say.

He'd have put that argument to Hoke if she'd told him to come straight back, but he'd had the feeling the admiral wanted Vilk off their hands just as much as he did.

"Right, that makes it easy. We pilot the mining vessel in convoy with us to Larga Ways, and Rial and Favri pilot the *Fasbe* so it comes with us, too. I'm not leaving anyone out here alone."

The order eased some of the tension that had been riding him. He didn't want to leave any of his crew out here. Especially if a second Krik vessel was lurking. It would be a death sentence.

Liaison Officer Kwo stepped onto the bridge, frowning at his handheld. "There seems to be a problem communicating with United Council headquarters." He waved his handheld in Gerbardi's direction.

"We've lost long range comms. We can't get hold of Battle Center, either, but nearspace comms are working fine," Hal told him.

"What could be interfering with long range comms, though?" Kwo's words were calm enough, but Hal sensed the liaison was feeling more emotion than he let on.

Hal watched him closely. "If it's the Krik, we can't find them."

"What if it's the Garmman?" Voa asked.

There was a thought.

Hal leaned back in his chair. Things were definitely less friendly between the Grih and the Garmman since it emerged that the Garmman United Council member, Fu-tama, had been the driving force behind the Class 5 project. He'd taken two-hundred year-old Grihan blueprints for vessels created to be run by banned thinking systems, and allied himself with the Tecran to build them.

His end game still wasn't clear, although it seemed certain he had planned to use the firepower of the Class 5s to subdue any opposition.

He was dead now. Killed by one of Hal's superior officers in a mad attempt to minimize the damage, but while Rose McKenzie had brought two of the Class 5s with her when she'd allied herself with the Grih, there were still three out there, and they were under Tecran control.

Garmman officials claimed absolute ignorance on whatever it was Fu-tama had been up to, and given he'd gone to the Tecran, rather than his own people, to build the Class 5s, Hal was inclined to believe them.

But it didn't hurt to be cautious.

"Is it possible the Garmman have come up with a way to block comms to Battle Center and the UC?"

Gerbardi shook his head. "Unless our intelligence has missed something huge, the Garmman don't have anything that could interfere. The only recent case I know of where signal to Battle Center was blocked was a month ago, and that was by the thinking system Sazo."

Sazo controlled a Class 5 battleship.

And last time the Grih had stumbled across a Class 5, there'd been a woman from Earth around, as well.

Hal looked up, found Kwo watching him.

"You're thinking of Fiona Russell," Kwo said.

"I'm wondering what she was doing ten minutes ago."

Although she'd had nothing on her when she'd come aboard, and even her handheld was still over on the *Fasbe*.

And again, if she was in league with a Class 5, why had she been barely surviving on Tak's ship?

"I can answer that." Kwo tucked his handheld under a thin arm. "She was speaking to me in the passageway outside her room."

Hal stood. "What did you want with her?"

"Nothing sinister." Kwo looked at him through huge, dark eyes. "I merely needed a more formal statement for my UC report. The guards you set seemed overly protective."

Hal studied Kwo's face, but it was hard to judge expression when it came to the Fitali. Their skin was much less elastic than the Grih's, their eyes big but static. "I told them to treat every interaction as potentially suspicious. I don't want what happened to Rose McKenzie to happen to Fiona. We don't know who the other officers are who were in league with Fu-tama."

"I've read the report of what happened on the *Barrist*." Kwo inclined his head. He said nothing more, but Hal thought he was still annoyed at being questioned.

Tough.

He didn't let that feeling show on his face, though. He bowed back and realized he had too much energy to resume his seat.

It would take a few hours for the mining vessel to catch up to their position, and all they could do was monitor the nearspace environment for threats until it got here. It would also take longer to get to Larga Ways with the miner and the Garmman trader in convoy, but rather that than split up his crew.

Hal paced to the door.

He might as well go and find Fiona Russell, and see if she really didn't know anything about the Class 5s.

The *Barrist's* captain, Dav Jallan, hadn't realized Rose McKenzie was hiding the existence of a thinking system from him when she'd come onboard his ship.

Hal didn't intend to make the same mistake.

Chapter Eight

FEE SAT ON THE EDGE OF THE EXAMINATION TABLE and watched Jasa's hand hover over a piece of equipment and then drop down uncertainly.

It didn't inspire confidence.

"Something wrong?"

Jasa's gaze flickered up, then away. "I was hoping to get some response from Rose McKenzie's doctor on the *Barrist*, the ship that found her, on how to treat your fractures and bruises, but there seems to be a problem getting my comm through."

Fee watched her finally pick up what looked like a pale blue gel circle, floppy and phosphorescent.

"Does it happen often?" Fee suddenly realized if Jasa could speak to Rose's doctor, surely she could speak to Rose?

A flutter of excitement and trepidation started up in her chest.

Jasa shook her head. "No. It can be hard to communicate with long range targets, but Battle Center has the boosters to make it theoretically possible to communicate with them from anywhere in Grih airspace. And we *were* communicating with them less than ten minutes before comms cut off."

"You suspect foul play?" Jasa's tension was making Fee nervous, too.

The doctor shrugged, then pushed up Fee's sleeve and carefully draped the blue gel over Fee's arm. It instantly firmed up, wrapping itself around her and becoming warmer. "For the last month, we've been on the brink of war with the Tecran. And while the fight's been taken to the United Council chambers, foul play is definitely something that springs to mind more often than it used to. The Garmman were implicated in the invasion as well, although they claim they had no idea what the Tecran and one of their own councilors was up to. That's why we have the remaining Garmman councilor, Vilk, on board. He just met with Battle Center and the Grih's leaders to assure us the Garmman are not in league with the Tecran and have no plans for a war with us, and now we're returning him to Garmman airspace. He insisted on a Grih battleship to take him to Battle Center and back so there would be no Garmman military craft in our territory, as a sign of goodwill."

"So what happens now?" Fee remembered how nervous Vilk had been when he'd seen her, how he'd spoken of her as if she were a major spanner in the works. Her being on a Garmman ship was obviously bad for the Garmman reputation.

Jasa shrugged. "Nothing we can do but try to get comms back up and stay on task; drop Vilk off, and then head back. We're nearly at Larga Ways anyway. We'd be there already if we hadn't encountered those Krik." She picked up another gel circle, slid it under the waistband of Fee's pants, over her bruised hip. Again, it became firmer, seemed to grip her skin, and heated up.

Fee lay back on the bed and Jasa slid on a head band of sorts and warmth blossomed where she'd been hit behind the ear.

She closed her eyes, let the soothing warmth of the gel pads and the gentle hum that seemed to vibrate through the ship lull her into a light doze.

She vaguely registered a chime from a handheld and Jasa leaving the room.

When the door opened again, she jerked awake, body turning slightly away from the threat, shoulders hunching.

She looked over her shoulder, and saw Captain Vakeri glowering from the doorway, his face so furious that she curled a little tighter before she forced herself to straighten and sit up.

They stared at each other for a long, tense beat.

"I told you," Vakeri said, his voice deeper than before but just as harsh, "no one will hurt you here."

Fee lifted both brows and looked over his shoulder to Pila and Carmain standing just outside the door.

Vakeri followed her gaze, grimaced, and then stepped fully into the room and closed the door.

"Even if they weren't there as a constant reminder that someone *could* try to hurt me here, I can't turn off my reactions in a couple of hours after over two months on Tak's ship." She was so indignant, she realized she was speaking louder than she intended and took a deep breath.

Vakeri did the same, looking away from her to the screen on the far wall. "My apologies. You're right, but seeing you so afraid of me just because I caught you by surprise was . . . disturbing."

It was no picnic for her, either. Knowing Tak would be thrown into a deep, dark hole certainly helped, though.

Vakeri eventually looked back at her, and she acknowledged his anger on her behalf was . . . nice. She hadn't felt grateful to anyone for a long time.

"Doctor Jasa says you know Rose McKenzie." He shifted, putting his feet apart and his hands behind his back, as if he was questioning her in an official capacity.

She frowned. "I know of her. We've never met."

"You sure about that?" He was watching her so closely, she began to lose the warm glow she'd had for him. It was like he was trying to trip her up.

"I'm pretty sure I'd remember." She leaned back on the bed. "She was abducted a month before I was, so unless she was on the same ship as me, and saw me while I was under sedation . . ." Fee tried to work out what that would mean if it were true, and how it could be so important to Vakeri.

"And you remember nothing about your abduction, nothing about where you were kept?"

Fee narrowed her eyes. "No. It isn't a big secret. If I knew something, I promise, I'd tell you. I want the bastards to pay for snatching me, so believe me, I wouldn't hesitate to point the finger, if I had any idea who to point it at."

"So why are you so sure Tak wasn't the one who took you?"

Fee hugged her knees. "Because I came briefly awake a few times, and the place where I was was light, all clear glass, and there were animals around me. I can't really remember clearly, it was like a waking dream, but I thought I saw . . ." She didn't know the Grih word for parrot, so she shook her head and tried again. "I thought I saw birds from my planet, but just for a moment or two, and then I went back under. It happened about three or four times, and then I woke in a cell on Tak's ship. The smell was different, the light was different, the material my cell was made of was different, even the sound of the engine was different."

She thought back to those first few days when she'd slowly shaken off the stupor of sedation, when she'd walked the confines of her cell and realized there was no escape, and then had to come to grips with the fact that her guards were not human, and that she didn't understand them, or know where she was.

It was the darkest time of her life.

The handheld that had been left in her cell with her had five languages on it, and she had learned the language of her captors first, and because she'd heard the guards speak of them, she'd learned Grihan next.

Bukari had been her latest foray, but she hadn't gotten far.

"Probably, if I'd understood Garmman when I first woke up, I'd have heard more useful gossip about how I got there from my guards. By the time I could understand them, they'd moved on to new topics, but I did hear enough to work out I'd been handed over quietly, and most of the crew hadn't even known there was an exchange."

Vakeri gave a slow nod. "That tallies with what Rial and Favri have got from the crew. They woke up one day and you were in the cell."

"What about Tak, Hury and Lon Sang? If anyone knows, it's them."

Vakeri's lips twisted in disgust. "Yes. But they aren't talking."

She would have thought Hury and Lon Sang would talk, even if Tak remained stubborn. Her surprise must have shown.

"They're afraid. They know the Tecran will try to silence anyone who can testify they stole another woman from Earth, as well as Rose McKenzie. The Tecran defense has been it was a once-off error in judgment, but that'll be harder to sell if it comes out there is a second abductee. Their position on the United Council is so precarious, this revelation may be what pushes them out."

Fee flinched. "What might they do to the walking, talking proof of their abduction?"

Vakeri eyed her with what looked like respect. "Nothing good. You're in danger from them, which is why I've got Pila and Carmain watching you. Jasa said she told you there are a few Grihan officers who seem to be working for the Tecran. It's probable none are on my ship, but just in case, you have protection. And when we get to Larga Ways, you'll have to stay on the *Illium*."

"What *is* Larga Ways?"

"It's a small orbital to the planet Balco. It's a way station for traders so they don't incur the expense and time of entering and leaving Balco's atmosphere. And Balco is near the border of Grih and Garmman airspace, so Larga Ways acts as a border post of sorts."

"Will it be a quick stop?"

"Yes. I have Krik to catch." Vakeri looked like he couldn't wait. She wondered if Gerwa would rat her out if Vakeri did catch him and tell the Grihan captain about the encryptor.

Well, if that happened, so be it. But she had a feeling Gerwa would rather keep the device a secret.

He'd been very unwilling to hand it over.

"So, where did Gerwa and his crew end up?" she asked.

Vakeri came to attention so fast, Fee had to force herself not to flinch, and when he took a step toward her, she sat a little straighter so she didn't feel so vulnerable.

"Gerwa?" he asked.

"The Krik battalion leader." She watched him carefully.

"He told you his name?" Vakeri sounded incredulous.

Fee nodded.

He stared at her. "Perhaps," he said in a clipped tone, "you should tell me was said between you. I was under the impression they hit you, you told them where the emergency pod was, and they left."

She nodded. "That's more or less what did happen. But they gave me their word they'd try to fit me in the pod if it were big enough, and for a few minutes there, we worked together. I asked Gerwa his name, and he told it to me, and the name of the guy who hit me, Jiy. From Krik battalion V8."

"Did they say anything else?" Vakeri was watching her so intently, she hunched her shoulders a little.

She shook her head, careful not to dislodge the headband Jasa had fitted. "Not about themselves. And they were lying about trying to fit me in, but I sort of guessed that. I thought it was worth taking the chance, though."

"You were lucky they didn't kill you. They'd just murdered all ten crew on a mining vessel and tried to kill three of my team." His face was set in dark, angry lines.

"I was more useful to them alive." Fee rested her chin on her knees. "They needed me to escape."

Vakeri gave a short nod. "As I said, you were lucky." He

flicked his sleeve to check the time, and then bowed to her. "I'm glad to see you're recovering." His words were formal, but he paused, as if he wanted to say more, then simply gave a curt nod and hit the button to open the door.

As it closed behind him, he was already striding off, and her heart gave a little jump at the picture he made. Big and competent. Fee decided he was a man with a lot on his mind. And when he focused on something, he really focused.

She remembered how he'd looked when he'd said he had Krik to run down. And shivered.

*****

"Krik battalion V8?" Chel stared at Hal from the regen bed, mouth open.

"That's what they told her." Hal still couldn't believe it. The Krik didn't always kill everyone aboard the ships they raided. They sometimes locked them in a hold, or restrained them and left them in a room, but they never chatted to their victims.

Perhaps that was the difference here. Fiona Russell hadn't been a victim, she'd been useful to them in a way.

"Does it help us? Knowing their battalion name?" Mun asked from the bed beside Chel.

She was recovering well, Hal noted with relief. She'd been the worst hit of the team, shielding Chel and Hadri until they could find cover in the miner's launch bay.

He shrugged. "I don't know, but I'll take it. It's the first indication we've had they see themselves as military units, for a start. It points to some sort of coordination, which we've suspected for a while. And Fiona got two names. Gerwa, who was the leader, and Jiy."

"Do you think they told her because they planned to kill her, and didn't think it mattered?" Hadri was sitting up, and although he wasn't as badly hit as Mun, he looked worse because of the bruising to his face.

Hal thought about it. "Maybe. Or maybe they just got careless. Something about Fiona interested them. They didn't kill her, even though I believe they could have, and the fact that they engaged with her at all is more than we've ever heard of before."

"It's the voice, if she's anything like Rose McKenzie," Chel said. "I could listen to Rose McKenzie sing for hours."

Hal thought about Fiona Russell's voice. It was a little lower than Rose McKenzie's, but Chel was right, it was just as compelling.

Mun was shaking her head, though. "The Krik don't care about singing. Not like we do."

"Something about her made them unwilling to shoot her." Hal was sure it wasn't just because she'd been useful to them. After she'd shown them the emergency pod, they could easily have eliminated the only witness to where they'd gone.

Just one more mystery to put on the pile that was growing where Fiona Russell was concerned.

He still thought taking Vilk to Larga Ways and then running the Krik down was the right decision, but he was starting to feel a real itch to get Fiona Russell back to Battle Center, too.

Something about the way those dark eyes looked at him, wary and watchful. And the way she'd jerked awake, expecting a blow, had sent a white hot spear of rage through him.

Tak would answer for it.

And yet, despite her beautiful, sad eyes and bruised body, Hal had to take into account that since she'd been on board, they'd lost comms to Battle Center for the first time since he'd taken command of the *Illium* a year ago.

And Hal didn't believe in coincidences.

Chapter Nine

FEE CAME TO A CAUTIOUS STOP AT THE DOOR into the officers' mess, very aware of the two guards at her back.

Pila and Carmain had been relieved in the night and were now on duty again, vigilant and serious.

She'd slept for ten hours after her time on the regen bed, and felt better than she had since her abduction. Calmer, more able to take in her new environment.

It helped that Jasa had managed to patch her up.

Not being in pain was so surprising, she realized she'd forgotten what it was like.

Now, she was hungry.

It was long past breakfast, though, and the room was empty and quiet.

It was most likely why Pila and Carmain had agreed to her request not to eat in her room. They knew there would be no one here, which had to make their job easier.

She was grateful anyway.

She didn't need crowds, in fact, preferred it this way. She just wanted not to look at the same four walls.

Despite its luxury and size after her cell on the *Fasbe*, her bedroom was starting to feel confining.

But now she was in a public place, nerves of a different type assailed her. The three catering staff had noticed her hovering in the doorway, and their surprise and interest was unmistakeable.

She was as much an oddity here as she'd been on the *Fasbe*.

She tugged her shirt down nervously.

This one fitted her perfectly.

Carmain had handed her three sets of clothes this morning, all in the same burgundy, which she said she'd found in the stores. They were meant for the cadets who sometimes spent time on Battle Center ships, so Fee guessed she was the right size to be a Grihan teenager.

The thoughtfulness of the act had delighted her and she turned now and gave Carmain another warm smile.

Pila made a sound of impatience and walked past her, finding them a table with a clear view of the door.

Fee glanced his way, then got up her courage to approach the servers and explore the food station. She'd been given nothing but nutrient bars for the last two months. The thought of actual food was exciting.

"I'll get something of everything for you to try." Pila was suddenly in front of her, blocking the way to the table and the catering staff.

She thought about arguing with him to let her see for herself, but when she looked up at him, his face was implacable but not overly officious, and she sighed, gave a reluctant nod, and made her way to the table.

Carmain gave her a small smile of sympathy and approval as she pulled out a chair for Fee and then took up position at her back.

"Thank you for not being difficult." The guard kept her voice low.

Fee nodded. "I assume you're asking me to do things a certain way for a reason. I'm no expert on personal security, so I'll trust you to know what's best."

"What was your job, on Earth?" Carmain shifted behind her and Fee guessed she was angling her body to keep the person who'd just walked into the room in view.

"I'm an architect. I worked for my family's construction company, designing houses." It seemed a lifetime ago.

Pila came back with a laden tray and placed it in front of her. It was way too much for her, and she looked up at them.

"Would you like some?"

Both of them shook their heads, and Pila came round to the front of the table, hard gaze never still as he scanned the room.

Fee didn't know whether she should embrace the tension that snaked through her every time they made it clear how serious they were about her protection, or try to quash it.

Maybe if she let the nerves hold sway a little, she'd be faster off the mark if she needed to duck or get out of the way. She just didn't see how it could be all that likely.

"Are you really worried about someone attacking me? One of your own colleagues?"

Pila said nothing, but he looked over at her, eyes steady, and shrugged.

"We hope not." Carmain was more forthcoming. "But I know one of Rose McKenzie's guards, Halim, who was injured when Rose was abducted by a Grihan officer. We were in training together. He's a good soldier, and the only reason he and his partner lost Rose was because they didn't expect a betrayal from within. We know better now."

"Is he okay, your friend?" Fee asked, twisting in her seat to see Carmain's face.

She gave a nod. "He and his partner are both fine now. Halim was sorry in the beginning when he was assigned to an explorer like the *Barrist*, rather than a battleship like the *Illium*, but he got more action than he bargained for."

Fee turned back to the table and looked down at the myriad of small bowls in front of her. She scooped up something that looked like tiny blue peas with a spoon.

"No!" Carmain's shout came just as she put them in her mouth and she bit down in surprise, her gaze flying to the only other diner, sitting at the other end of the room.

His head came up with a jerk.

Pila had his gun up, sweeping it in an arc around the room, and his eyes flicked to Carmain. "Where?"

Fee twisted in her seat again, to see Carmain staring at her.

She lifted her gaze and sent a contrite look to her partner. "Sorry. She just put a whole spoon of fring in her mouth. I tried to stop her."

Fee bit down again, this time more cautiously, and shrugged. "What's wrong with it? Why'd you give it to me if it was something to be worried about?"

It was actually quite nice. Tart but not too tart, with a hint of smoky sweetness.

It also popped in tiny bursts as she chewed, like new baby peas.

"It's to sprinkle over your porridge," Carmain said, pointing to a bigger bowl with some kind of cooked grain in it. "It's too overpowering to have on its own." She shuddered as if the mere thought was too much.

"I don't mind it," Fee told her. She picked up the spoon again, this time sprinkling the little blue balls over the porridge, and took a bite. Grimaced. "But that, I don't like."

Pila had lowered his shockgun, and he scowled at Carmain. They shared a wordless exchange, and Carmain stepped away from the table and gave a formal bow to the officer who'd been briefly at the other end of Pila's barrel.

"My apologies, Gerbardi."

The officer cocked his head, in that strange, almost canine way she'd seen the Grih do before, and gave a slow nod. "Accepted. These are difficult times."

He'd been watching her covertly anyway, and Fee would rather have a conversation with him than eat with him snatching looks at her. So she stood. "Would you like to join me?"

The officer looked from Carmain to Pila, and when Pila gave a

curt nod, he stood himself, bowed, and brought his breakfast over
with him.

"Lieutenant Gerbardi," he said, and extended his hands, palms
together.

Fee clasped them between her own, and gave the formal half-
bow she'd seen them all do. "Fiona Russell."

He made a noise, a sort of sigh of contentment, and Pila and
Carmain arranged themselves protectively around her.

"Your voice is truly as lovely as Rose McKenzie's." Gerbardi
looked at her openly now, and she looked back.

He was a little older than Captain Vakeri, his hair dark brown,
almost black, but the tips were blond, and like all Grih, it stood
straight up, making him look like a trendy punk rocker. Like all
the Grih she'd met, his eyes were a shade of blue, a deep navy,
rimmed in a lighter hue.

"You've met Rose?"

Gerbardi shook his head. "None of us have met her, except the
crew of the *Barrist* and our leaders." He shifted in his chair.
"We've all seen the comms, though."

Of course. Rose would have been interviewed. Been on the
Grih equivalent of the news, probably. Fee suddenly wondered if
the same would happen to her, and had to carefully swallow back
the nausea that rose up at the thought.

"What comms?" Might as well know.

"I can show you." Gerbardi pulled a small handheld from a
pocket and tapped the screen. Turned it to face Fee.

The scene was of a small room with a large table and chairs,
like a meeting room of some kind. Almost like CCTV footage,
although clear and sharply in focus.

So, not a media interview.

Rose was sitting at the table, a handheld in front of her, playing
in a bored way with whatever passed for an app in this new
world, tinkering with various beats and musical notes and

growing more frustrated with the strange directions the music kept going in. Fee saw her stab a finger at the screen, and then she spoke for the first time. "Damn you, autocorrect."

Fee laughed, the sound wrenched from her, and she realized it was the first time she could remember laughing since she'd been taken.

Pila, Carmain and Gerbardi had been watching the handheld with her, but they all lifted their eyes at her laugh to watch her with an intensity she found uncomfortable.

She focused back on the screen.

Rose was speaking in English again, or, singing in English, more like. But not song lyrics. She was talking to someone, Fee realized. Pretending to sing, but having a conversation with someone who must be communicating with her via an earpiece like the rest of the Grih seemed to have.

There was an affection that came through for the person she was talking to, but the words were cryptic, and Fee could only hear one side of the conversation.

At the end, it seemed as if Rose had been persuaded to sing a song, and when the music started up through Rose's handheld, Fee recognized the opening bars of a recent hit, clear as if she was listening to the radio.

Rose sang it all the way through, then backtracked, sang again, and then again, adding harmony, back-up singing, perfecting the main tune.

And finally, she played it all though, each layer added to the other to make a whole, and Fee could see she was caught up enough to dance a little to her own creation.

Rose was having fun. Despite the tense conversation she'd had at the start, despite the fact that she must have had a similar experience to Fee.

It was good to see.

Really good.

74

Gerbardi leaned across and tapped the screen and shut it off. "There's another song in the same room, and a few others recorded elsewhere on the *Barrist*, but could you tell us what the words mean for this one?"

Fee wanted to ask them who Rose had been talking to in the clip. It was someone who understood English, and who Rose knew well. But the way Rose had sung the words, as if to cover up that she was really having a conversation, stopped her.

It looked very much like Rose hadn't wanted anyone to know what she was doing, or understand what she was saying.

And until Fee knew why, she wasn't going to ask anything that might undo that.

"The song's about someone who was very alone, and struggling, and then they met someone who helped them find a meaningful life again."

They stared at her.

"What?" She shrunk back a little in her seat.

"We don't sing songs about things like that." Carmain said. "When Rose sang another song to a group of people on the *Barrist*, she told them it was about someone leaving on a journey, asking their lover if they would come with them. But we couldn't decide if she was serious or not."

"She was probably being serious." Fee used the excuse of looking down at the food in front of her to avoid their shocked expressions. There was something that looked like fruit, with blue seeds flecked through it, and she took a slice, nibbled at the corner. It had the consistency of pear, with a bitter flavor.

"Do you ever sing songs about meetings and occasions?" Pila asked.

Fee frowned up at him. "We sing songs about holidays or for some celebrations. Like when someone is having a birthday."

Gerbardi leaned forward. "You mean, when it's someone's birthday, they get a song just for them?" He seemed incredulous.

"Yes." Fee smiled at him. "So if it was your birthday, the song would be like this." She sang Happy Birthday To You in Grih, putting Gerbardi's name in at the appropriate place.

"And if it were my birthday?" Carmain asked.

Fee laughed and sang again with Carmain's name, and then, because Pila looked like he wanted to ask but was too proud, she sang it through a third time with his name.

"I've never had a song sung just for me." Carmain's voice was hushed.

Fee shifted in her chair. "So, singing is a big deal to the Grih?"

"We have so few music-makers, and they do not waste their voices on birthday songs and songs about love or friendship; they sing about important occasions." Gerbardi didn't sound like he could decide if he disapproved of her singing to him, or was as delighted about it as Carmain.

"Singing doesn't work like that for people on Earth." Fee said. "We sing about everything."

"If you can all sing as well as you and Rose do, then you have a whole planet of music-makers. I can't imagine what that would be like." Carmain still sounded dreamy.

"We listen to songs all the time. Some people listen to songs from when they get up, to when they go to bed." She had always enjoyed designing with music playing in the background. She'd missed that on the *Fasbe*. And she'd created her own background music when she'd worked in the launch bay, singing softly to herself as she'd loaded and unloaded the pallets.

The Garmman hadn't had the same appreciation for her singing as the Grih, with Hury hitting her every time he caught her doing it. Although that may have been because it marked her as from Earth, she realized now. If Rose was known for her singing, the last thing Tak would have wanted was his crew knowing Fee could sing just like her. It would have made the funny hood he'd made her wear even less likely to fool people.

"It actually *is* Mun's birthday today," Pila said. He didn't look at her when he spoke, his gaze on the room as if he expected an assassin to jump out from behind a table at any minute.

"Would you like me to sing happy birthday to her?" Fee liked the idea. There was no way back home. She'd made peace with that after the first two weeks on the *Fasbe*.

The Grih had so far treated her well, and seemed to hold Rose McKenzie in some regard, although she sensed a little fear, or perhaps awe, where Rose was concerned, as well.

If she could find a place among them, and make some friends, it was more than she ever expected to have since she'd woken in the *Fasbe's* holding cell.

The most she'd hoped for a day ago was a quick death.

Pila glanced at her, and she could see he was pleased with her offer. He gave a nod. "That would be kind. She was badly hurt by the Krik we were chasing and she's in one of the med chambers for another day before she can be released."

Fee recalled Vakeri saying three of his team had been injured in their encounter with Gerwa and his crew.

"How about I finish breakfast, and we can head over there?" The idea of something constructive to do, a way to make friends and form connections, was so exciting, she realized how starved she'd been of it. She'd taken the work she'd done on Earth, the life she'd had, not for granted, exactly, but she hadn't realized how vital it had been to her own personal happiness.

Well, she wasn't taking it for granted any more.

Carpe diem. She was going to seize the day.

Chapter Ten

"CAPTAIN VAKERI, I HAVE YET TO MAKE CONTACT with United Council headquarters." Councilor Vilk stood in front of Hal, more agitated than Hal had seen the Garmman since he'd walked into Tak's conference room and caught sight of Fiona Russell.

Hal knew the feeling.

"Farspace comms are down for all of us, Councilor. Gerbardi was up most of the night trying different ways to send out a signal, but nothing seems to be getting through."

Vilk blew out a breath. "It must be being deliberately blocked."

Hal agreed, but Gerbardi wasn't prepared to commit himself one way or the other. "It's highly unlikely to be natural interference. But there's an outside chance it is. The problem could also be on Battle Center's side."

Like if the Tecran had somehow taken out one of Battle Center's major signal arrays. This year, the United Council headquarters was on the Bukari home world, and they would be using Battle Center arrays to communicate through Grih airspace. It would explain why they couldn't reach either organization.

Vilk gaped at him, as if considering this for the first time. "But Battle Center has never gone down . . ."

He trailed off, as if finally understanding the possible implications if it had gone down.

Hal shook off the thought. "Most likely, it's on our side, not theirs."

Vilk held out his handheld. "My staff waiting for me on Larga Ways tell me they can't contact the United Council, either."

Hal knew. They'd tried to relay their messages through Battle Center's office on Larga Ways, only to find the orbital had lost communications with headquarters and the United Council at the same time as they had.

"We're so close to Larga Ways, whatever is affecting us, it makes sense it's affecting them, as well." All true. But Hal still couldn't completely shrug off the fear that the Tecran could have thrown diplomacy and their arguments for peace out the window and simply attacked the Grih and shut down the United Council while everyone's guard was down. They still had three Class 5s under their control, after all.

Right now, he was operating under the assumption that anything was possible.

"How close are we to our destination?" Vilk asked, his tone far less strident now.

"Another day. The going is a little slow, but we can't help that." The mining vessel had finally joined them five hours ago, and they'd gotten underway at last, cruising at their lowest speed toward Larga Ways. By the time they got there, hopefully comms would had been restored, or someone, somewhere, would have gotten a message out.

If the interference was on the *Illium's* side, if someone was blocking them, Battle Center would send a small battle cruiser to check on them. Hal wanted that cruiser to appear as soon as possible. It would mean all was well with the four planets.

Voa was constantly running scans, looking for any hint of enemy ships in their vicinity, but so far she'd come up with nothing but the odd merchant trader or mining vessel.

It didn't help that they would soon be at the very edge of Grih airspace, right on the Garmman border.

There'd be at least a few Garmman battleships waiting for Vilk, and the closer they got to Larga Ways and the planet Balco, the more difficult it would be to distinguish genuine Garmman escorts from possible enemies.

This mission had seemed straightforward when he'd been given it. Pick Councilor Vilk up in Larga Ways, deliver him to the Grih government buildings that housed the administrators and leaders of the four planets, and then return him.

He'd been part of Battle Center long enough to know nothing ever went exactly to plan, but the events of the last month had rattled even the most hardened soldiers.

He wanted to drop Vilk off and have the councilor safely back among his own people as quickly as he could. Whether the Garmman were the Grih's allies, as they professed, or whether at least some of them were involved in quiet deals with the Tecran, the sooner they could round up the Krik and head back with Fiona, the happier he'd be.

If Battle Center was still standing.

"You look worried, Captain." Vilk was watching him with a considering expression. "What do you think could be going on here?"

"It could be the Krik." Hal was happy to share that with Vilk, because it certainly was a possibility. He wasn't going to insult the councilor by suggesting his own people could be behind this.

Vilk looked startled, and then tapped a thick, stubby finger to his lips. "I hadn't thought of that, but Kwo did mention they had some new technology on them that enabled them to fool your ship's systems."

Did he, now?

Hal kept his face impassive, but decided he needed a word with Kwo. Part of the Fitali officer's oath on becoming a liaison officer was that he wouldn't share Grihan operational matters with anyone unless he had Hal's express permission.

It was the only way any of the members of the United Council were prepared to accept a liaison officer on every battleship and explorer. Only the Tecran had voted against it in the end, and now that their abduction and torture of Rose McKenzie, and their illegal use of thinking systems, had come to light, everyone knew why.

Seeing Vilk expected some sort of reaction, Hal gave a shrug. "They've definitely gotten some high tech equipment from somewhere, and when I get hold of them, you can be sure I'll be asking them about it. It's possible they've managed to get a blocker that's strong enough to disrupt our comms with Battle Center."

Hal didn't want to believe that, and both he and Gerbardi thought it highly unlikely, but he was happy for the councilor to think it could be true.

If his ire was directed at the Krik, it wasn't directed at Hal and the Grih in general.

Vilk gave a slow nod. "The Krik are getting worse every year. If they even think about applying to join the United Council again this year, I'll laugh in Haisina's face. That Krik has an absolute nerve standing there saying the pirates aren't state sanctioned. They clearly are, or Krik's planet security is no better than a sieve."

Hal inclined his head in agreement.

"I'd have to say, if it is the Krik, I'd be almost relieved." Vilk rubbed his hands together, and Hal realized he was nervous. "Kwo reminded me that in the incident I was caught up in last month, when the Tecran sent their fleet into Grihan airspace to get their Class 5 back, all comms were blocked to Battle Center then, too. And the Class 5 was responsible." The councilor darted a quick look Hal's way, and Hal had the impression he was hoping for a strenuous denial.

Hal shrugged. "Fiona Russell wouldn't have been living in fear for her life on the *Fasbe* if she had the support of a Class 5 like Rose McKenzie did. But Kwo is quite right. It's something to keep in mind. I don't know why there would be a Class 5 around here, but it isn't impossible."

Vilk's hands paused their rubbing. "She was being mistreated, I agree. And we rescued her from it, so it's not the same situation as with Rose McKenzie at all. Not at all."

Hal had known Vilk had been with the other United Council members during the standoff the Grih had had with the Tecran a month ago, but he suddenly realized Vilk had personally met Rose.

"What is Rose like?"

"She was polite." Vilk began moving his hands again. "I was so shocked at her appearance, so like the Grih, but not quite, and her obvious intelligence, I didn't take much more in." He looked up at Hal with suddenly sly eyes. "Captain Jallan seemed very protective of her. Very solicitous. He came into a meeting we had with her, and took her away, as if we were mistreating her." He sniffed. "Well, the Tecran councilors *were* being a trifle harsh, but it was civil enough."

At the sound of footsteps, Vilk looked up and gave an absentminded nod to Gerbardi as Hal's comms officer walked up to them.

"I'll be in my rooms if you have any news." Vilk turned on his heel and disappeared in the direction of his guest suite.

Hal watched him go.

The councilor came across as slightly self-important and a little grumpy, but mostly well-meaning and harmless. It was possible he was anything but that. It was possible he was hiding a Garmman agenda that included an alliance with the Tecran.

And there was nothing Hal could do about it but minimize the access Vilk had without being openly rude to the councilor.

"Trouble?" Gerbardi asked.

Hal shook his head. "He's frustrated he can't get through to UC headquarters. He knows there's going to be huge trouble when the existence of Fiona Russell becomes known, especially as she was found on a Garmman ship. He wants to get on top of it, issue his official denials of knowledge, and the fact that he can't is eating him up."

Gerbardi stared after the councilor. "I had breakfast with Fiona this morning. Vilk has every right to be worried. She's so clearly an advanced sentient, as soon as she starts talking about what was done to her, Tak will be lucky ever to see the outside of a cell again, and the Garmman's reputation will be tarnished for a long time to come."

Hal stared at him. "She had breakfast in the officers' mess?"

Gerbardi nodded. "It was empty, which is probably why her guards allowed it. They're very jumpy, though."

Hal was pleased to hear it. He wanted them on high alert.

He supposed he couldn't expect his new guest to be confined completely to her room, or how was he any better than Tak?

"What did she have to say?" Hal still couldn't get over that she'd gotten names and even a unit number out of the Krik. She had so far been full of surprises.

Gerbardi shuffled, and Hal eyed his comms officer with surprise.

"She sang."

Hal went still.

He knew Rose McKenzie was a music-maker, and he heard in Fiona Russell's voice from the start that she probably had a similar talent, but Gerbardi seemed almost in agony over it.

"Was it not a good song?" He couldn't understand why else Gerbardi would be so unhappy.

"She sang a song for *me*. Especially for me, with my name in it." He rubbed at his face. "Then she sang the same song for Pila and Carmain. It's a tradition on Earth, to sing to someone on their birthday."

"It's not your birthday." Hal tried to imagine having a song sung especially for him and couldn't.

Gerbardi shook his head. "I know. She was just showing us how the song would go. Then Pila said it was Mun's actual birthday today, so now Fiona Russell is going to sing it to her."

"You don't think it's a good idea?" Hal was trying to work out what was bothering Gerbardi so much.

"It's wasteful." Gerbardi shrugged, like he was trying to get rid of some weight on his shoulders. "A voice like that, better than anything I've ever heard, shouldn't waste itself on singing to people on their birthday. But she didn't seem to care. She seemed to think it was a good use of her voice. She was laughing. She sang for Pila even though he didn't ask her to, as if it was silly for him to hold back."

Gerbardi was quiet for a moment, and then he looked up at Hal. "And even though I really believe everything I've just said, having a song just for me . . ." The comms officer lifted his shoulders one last time. "I still can't get over how happy it made me."

He turned and walked onto the bridge, and Hal stood, torn between duty and desire. Decided there was nothing he could do on the bridge right now, and that he would very much like to hear what a birthday song sounded like.

That Rose McKenzie and Fiona's views on singing were different to the Grih's was understandable. They were from a different world, a different culture, and one where it seemed music-makers were far more common that among the Grih. That both Fiona and Rose could sing was testament to that.

But a song sung for an individual, using their name . . .

He could barely wrap his mind around the idea, and understood all too well why Gerbardi was so shocked and conflicted.

As he walked to the med chambers, he realized he was sorry his own birthday was months away, and that Fiona Russell would be long gone from his life by the time it came around.

Chapter Eleven

AS FEE LOOKED PAST PILA into the med chamber, she saw two of the beds were occupied. A woman and a man. The man looked worse, but he sat up easily when Pila stepped into the room. The woman lifted herself more gingerly.

There was something in the woman's face when she caught sight of Pila, a warm flush, and Fee guessed exactly why he'd had Mun on his mind when they were talking about birthdays.

"Mun and Hadri, this is Fiona Russell, the orange we found on the *Fasbe*."

Mun put her hands together and extended them, and Fee stepped forward to clasp them. "Pleased to meet you."

Hadri did the same.

"I'm curious, there's a word you used now, Pila, that I think I'm misunderstanding." Fee really wanted to work this out. "I keep being called an orange. What on earth do you mean by that? I think my Grihan just isn't good enough to understand, but do I really look orange to you?"

That would explain the funny looks, all right.

There was a moment of stunned silence.

"Technically," Hadri said, and she could hear some discomfort in his tone, "you aren't an orange, because your species is known to us since we encountered Rose McKenzie. All unknown sentient life forms show up as orange on our scanners."

So it was a technical designation? Fee frowned, and shot a look at Pila.

He was frowning, too. "I didn't mean any disrespect, Fiona. An orange to me is an unknown sentient life form. That's all. You're known, so Hadri's right, you aren't an orange any more, but it's a quick way to let people know you're like Rose McKenzie. The two of you are the first advanced sentients we've come across in over five hundred years, so you may be thought of as an orange for a while."

So the term meant alien, more or less. She might not like it, but it was true, she was an unknown entity.

"What word would you like us to use instead?" Mun winced as she rearranged herself on the bed, and Pila took a half-step toward her then remembered himself and pulled back.

Fee opened her mouth to say 'human' and then closed it. Human to her went beyond the dictionary definition of *homo sapiens*. It meant advanced sentient being with the capacity for a myriad of emotions, the intelligence to plan and strategize, and a thirst for knowledge. And that probably described a lot of races in this new corner of the galaxy.

She pondered 'Earthling', because how cool would that be? Then discarded it.

Maybe human was right. Because that would fit her right in with everyone else, if she thought of them as human, too.

"I'm a human." The difference between Grihan and English was stark. The Grihan sounded short, harsh, and choppy beside the soft double syllable of 'human'.

"Human." Pila did his best to say it correctly, trying to make up for starting this all with his glib introduction of her as an orange.

The others repeated it, as well.

Their rough voices were so different to the dry rasp of the Garmman, and they mangled the word. But they tried.

She smiled at them all.

"Happy birthday to you, Mun. Pila told us it's your birthday today, and on Earth, we sing a song on someone's birthday. I've come to sing it for you, if you'd like?"

Mun's gaze flew to her face, then she looked over at Pila. "A song especially for me?" She looked stunned.

Fee wondered what the hell they thought singing was, here. Some kind of finite resource, obviously. To be dolled out sparingly and with a mean hand.

"I don't know . . ." She trailed off, and then looked up almost guiltily, as someone else entered the room.

They all turned, although Fee saw Carmain had obviously been standing with her body angled to the door all along, so she already knew it was Captain Vakeri, and her gun was not raised like Pila's.

"Feeling better, Mun? Hadri?" The captain's gaze flickered over Pila as he lowered his shockgun, and then focused on his injured crew.

"I'm probably ready to leave," Hadri said.

"When Jasa says," Vakeri said. "Mun?"

"Still a little tender, sir." Mun lifted her body with her arms carefully, and repositioned herself again.

She couldn't get comfortable, Fee guessed. Chances were there was something she could take for the pain and she had decided not to take it.

Silence fell, as everyone tried to work out what to do, now the captain had joined them. He was a similar size to Pila, perhaps a little taller and leaner in build, but he seemed to take up more room.

"Fiona is here to sing a birthday song for Mun," Carmain said.

"I know. Gerbardi told me, and I hope you don't mind, but I would like to hear it, too."

Fee sensed Pila's tension dissipate a little. He'd thought he might be in trouble for this, she realized. Organizing a song for his girlfriend on her birthday while on duty.

Except, his time was hers, really. And she wanted to do this. Wanted to integrate into this life, if she could.

Suddenly, every eye in the room turned to her.

She did want to do it, but suddenly, the gesture took on a lot more weight than it should. It was just 'happy birthday' after all.

"I don't mean to diminish the moment, but you do realize it is a short song?"

"Even so, to waste your voice on something so trivial . . ." Mun looked like she didn't know whether to dig a hole and hide or clap her hands excitedly.

The Grih definitely had some strange ideas about singing. Using your voice made it stronger. Made it better.

Before Mun could talk herself out of it, Fee launched into the song, singing it through twice seeing as she had such an avid audience, to give them more bang for their buck.

When she finished, Mun was leaning back on her pillows, her eyes bright with tears. "Thank you, Fiona."

"It was my pleasure." She meant it, but was uncomfortably aware that they were placing far more value on what she'd done than it deserved.

She didn't know how to convey that, though, without ruining the moment, so she kept quiet.

A fight for another day.

She caught the captain watching her, leaning against the wall, with arms crossed over his chest.

He was the hardest to read of everyone in the room.

Carmain was openly affected, like Mun, and Hadri was, too. Pila was trying to keep his expression neutral, but Fee honestly couldn't say what Vakeri was thinking. His gaze caught hers and she held eye contact, trying to stand her ground.

She tugged at her shirt, and then tried to still her hands, but she refused to look away.

He made her feel unbalanced.

On Earth, she'd had power over her own life. Since she'd been taken, she'd been at the mercy of others, and that was still the case.

Vakeri was the one with the power over her now.

And yet, she thought she could trust him. His behavior since she'd met him told her that, and still, he could change his mind at any moment and there was nothing she could do about it.

It made liking him difficult, even though it wasn't his fault. He was the captain. She was the orange.

She tugged at her shirt again, and the encryptor, back in its place in her bra, dug a little into her skin.

It calmed her, and she was able to let her hands relax at her sides.

It wasn't a silver bullet, but it was a small grab at control. A tiny weight that helped to balance the scales a little.

Hadri cleared his throat, and she realized she and the captain had been sizing each other up for longer than was probably socially appropriate. She lowered her gaze to his broad chest.

Vakeri frowned, pushing off from the wall and dropping his arms. He seemed less daunting, all of a sudden, as if she'd befuddled him.

"What's wrong?" Jasa stepped into the room, making the med chamber feel truly crowded, her voice rough with concern.

Fee thought everyone relaxed, as if Jasa had diffused a tense situation. It underscored to Fee that she was running blind, with no idea of the social *dos* and *don'ts* in Grih society. She needed a manual or something.

"Nothing's wrong. I have been honored with a human birthday song." Mun was still lying back on her pillows, and Fee thought she was pretending to be more comfortable than she was.

"You've gone off the pain meds?" Jasa obviously wasn't fooled for a moment. "I told you, tomorrow. You'll end up here a day extra because you'll tire yourself out more if you can't sleep comfortably."

It seemed the signal for everyone to leave.

Pila stepped up to Mun's bed. "Listen to the doc." His voice was gruff and he didn't touch her, but he wanted to. Fee could see it in the way his hands rubbed the sides of his pants.

"Get better, Mun. And happy birthday again." Fee nodded a goodbye to Hadri, too, and stepped out the room with Carmain to give Jasa more room to bustle.

They waited for Pila, and when he emerged, he looked like a man whose lover was badly hurt, and all he wanted to do was sit by her side.

"Jasa seems a good doctor," Fee said, to comfort him. "She did wonders for me, and I'm not even Grihan."

Pila grunted in reply, and Carmain sent her a smile, eyes alight with mischief. "It isn't widely known how eloquent Pila is. You're seeing a side of him others rarely experience."

Fee grinned back. "Well, he may speak mostly in monosyllables, but he organized a happy birthday song for his lover that made her very happy. That's better than eloquent, in my mind."

Pila stopped, stared at her, and then turned on his heel and strode ahead to take point.

Carmain made a comical face at his back and then took up the rear.

As she walked, sandwiched between them, Fee was suddenly very aware of the encryptor. For the first time, it didn't feel as vital as it had before.

Chapter Twelve

"WE CAN DOCK IN THREE HOURS." Gerbardi looked up from his screen, ending his conversation with Larga Ways control, and Hal nodded.

Larga Ways' ability to dock a ship the size of the *Illium* was something that impressed him every time he visited.

Of course, battleships, no matter the size, usually weren't allowed to dock, but Larga Ways was in Grihan airspace, and the price the planet Balco paid for being a border planet with a way station just slightly on the Grihan side, was that Grih Battle Center ships were always welcome.

Balco itself was as neutral as a planet in the Grihan system could be. The Balcoans were content to pay nominal tax to the Grih for some services and Battle Center security, and to be left alone to trade in peace. They voted every fifty years or so on whether to become Grih's fifth planet, but every time, only about ten percent of the population was in favor, and Hal guessed all of the pro-votes were Grihan ex-pats.

"Larga Ways' station chief would like a meeting with you." Gerbardi turned to Hal, hand hovering over his earpiece.

As Hal had been about to ask Gerbardi to set up a meeting with Tean Lee anyway, he nodded. "I have to hand Vilk over to his people, then I'll head straight to Lee's office."

Hal had a strict schedule. For himself and his crew.

He wanted them away from Larga Ways as quickly as possible.

They had to deal with returning the mining vessel to its mother company and brief the authorities on Larga Ways about the deaths of the crew on board. Vilk, Kwo, and the small United

Council office, as well as Grihan and Garmman consulate staff, would also have to meet to discuss how they were going to deal with Tak and his crew, and the fate of the *Fasbe*. For now, the trading ship was a crime scene the United Council Independent Investigators would need to go over, and so it would need to be stored safely until they arrived.

Hal frowned, and leaned toward Gerbardi. "Did Kwo or you get off a message to the UC investigative unit before comms were cut off?"

Gerbardi stared at him for a beat, then turned to the pale blue glass of his unit, and tapped away. He turned back and there was a satisfied gleam in his eyes. "We did. They even responded, and said they planned to arrive in four days. Which means they may even get here before we leave Larga Ways."

"That's good." Hal tried not to feel too much hope. They'd lost comms only a few hours later, and the UC team may never have even left if the Tecran had attacked UC headquarters or Battle Center. But if the comms problem was in the *Illium's* nearspace, then it would be good to talk to the investigators; either in person, or while the *Illium* was going after the Krik.

In a way, the UC team's appearance or not would be confirmation of whether this was a small, localized problem, or something much, much bigger.

He had to proceed as if either possibility were true. And that the Garmman could be involved.

"Tean Lee is very grateful for your time. He'll be waiting for you, however long it takes for you to finish your business with Councilor Vilk." Gerbardi tapped his ear to end the call and Hal leaned back in his chair.

Lee was always courteous, but he was never this grateful for some of Hal's time.

Of course, the Balcoans would be watching the situation developing between the Grih and the Garmman closely. And they had to be getting nervous. Tean Lee would be under huge pressure to find out what exactly was going on.

Balco and Larga Ways would have to align with the Grih if it came to war, and their planet would be the first the Garmman would want to capture, to gain a foothold in Grih territory.

Hal stood and decided to brief a few of his team to go out and socialize at the bars and restaurants of Larga Ways for the day or so they'd be docked.

He'd like an idea of what the average citizen of Balco, or at least the way station, thought of what was going on, and what they'd heard from the Garmman side.

He called a small team together as he walked to the *Illium's* conference room and arranged a replacement for Carmain, so she could attend the meeting, as well.

Thoughts of Carmain led straight to thoughts of Fiona Russell, and the way she'd challenged him yesterday, staring him down. He'd been doing the same to her, but only because she'd seemed to be deliberately holding his gaze to make some kind of point.

She was lucky he had as much control as he did. He'd forced himself not to react.

She'd been transformed from when he'd rescued her. Her injuries were healed, and someone had found her some very form-fitting clothes.

When he'd rounded his fighter ship to get to her in the *Fasbe's* launch bay, she'd been in oversized overalls, and since then, in Grih visitor uniforms that were many sizes too big. He'd almost reeled back when he'd stepped into Mun and Hadri's med chamber and seen her.

Sleek, focused, and intelligent—the frightened, cowed refugee of the day before was not gone . . . her eyes were still wary and her body language spoke of caution—but those descriptions no longer defined her. They were background elements of a force to be reckoned with.

She was still too thin, the effects of too little food for too long didn't go away overnight, but he'd realized she was not just skin and bone. She'd spent her time on the *Fasbe* lifting heavy boxes, and she had the muscles to prove it.

She'd also stared him down, further proof that she was coming back from her trauma, although he wondered if she knew holding eye contact like that with a Grih was a challenge.

Perhaps he should ask Jasa or Carmain to speak to her about it. He had worked on building control, but not everyone had.

He reached the conference room and flicked on the screen at one end to connect to the *Fasbe*. He needed Rial and Favri in on the meeting, as well.

Chel shuffled through the door, still not completely healed, but almost there. He could coordinate the informal information gathering while Hal was accompanying Vilk to the Garmman consulate and also see what intelligence he could get from official sources.

Carmain arrived with Tobru, who had been on the *Fasbe*, but had come back to the *Illium* with Fiona Russell's handheld, now being examined by his comms and engineering teams. As Carmain closed the door behind them, Favri and Rial appeared onscreen.

Hal motioned to everyone to sit.

"We have about a day in Larga Ways. Enough to politely get rid of Vilk, deal with the mining vessel incident, hand over Tak and his crew and secure the *Fasbe* for the UC investigators, load some supplies, and then go after those Krik." Hal knew they'd be lucky if it only took a day, but he had authority on Larga Ways, and Tean Lee would help smooth the way and speed things up.

"You sure we should hand Tak over to Larga Ways law enforcement?" Rial looked tired, and Hal guessed he and Favri were still searching the ship, looking for clues to Fiona Russell's capture and why Tak had her. Trying to find something before they reached Larga Ways and someone else took over.

"We have to. We don't have time for anything else if we want to go after those Krik. And there's a time limit on that, too. If we can't get them in a day, we have to leave them."

"What?" Chel looked up from his place at the table, eyes wide.

Hal kept his face neutral. He sympathized with Chel, but he had no choice in this. "The lack of comms with Battle Center is too serious to ignore. And Fiona Russell may not know who abducted her or why they passed her on to Tak, but she's living, talking proof that the Tecran didn't just take Rose McKenzie, that it wasn't just mad Doc Fliap stepping outside the rules. One abduction could be argued as an aberration. A failure of their systems and the unlawful act of a scientist more interested in research than the law, but two is the start of a pattern. Most of what Sazo has said is classified, and I'm not senior enough to know, but Admiral Hoke was surprised and shocked when I told her we'd found another Earth woman. So I'm guessing it's understood the only Earth woman Sazo knows about is Rose. Which means a Class 5 other than Sazo took Fiona. Again, that indicates a pattern."

"And knowing about Fiona might be what the United Council needs to kick the Tecran out." Chel let out a sigh. "It'll prove they've been lying about Rose being a once-off mistake. So we have to get her there as fast as possible."

"Unless Admiral Hoke has kept the information to herself for the time being, the UC already knows about Fiona, but I'm sure they'll wait to make a decision until they've met and spoken with her. I probably shouldn't even spend the day I'm giving us to get the Krik, but I can't let the bastards walk away if I can help it." Hal steepled his fingers, saw Chel's acceptance in his quick nod, and relaxed.

"And the longer we have Fiona Russell on board, the longer we're a target ourselves. If the Tecran know we have her, they'll want to wipe us out of existence." Tobru spoke for the first time.

She was short—not as short as Fiona Russell, but petite by Grih standards—and a tactical expert as well as Hal's best shot. She didn't talk a lot, but when she did, Hal listened.

He nodded. "*If* they know we have her, and I don't see how they can. But once Tak and his crew are out of our control, and in the hands of Larga Ways authorities, they could bribe someone to get word to the Tecran. Or a Tecran spy could come to them."

Carmain frowned. "If the Tecran gave Fiona to Tak to keep safe for them, would he risk letting them know he's failed?"

Hal shrugged. "I know Tak and his two senior officers are the only ones who really know what's going on. They won't talk, and we can't guess if it's to their benefit or not to pass word to the Tecran that we have Fiona Russell."

"We have to assume they'll try," Favri said from the screen.

Hal nodded. "I have a meeting with the way station commander. I'll give him some details."

"Only some?" Chel asked.

"The fewer people know we have Fiona, the better. And that's part of why you're all here. Only people who need to be off the *Illium* to perform their duties are allowed to leave, and those who do say nothing about Fiona. Nothing. Make sure your subordinates understand that." He looked them in the eye one by one, and got nods of understanding.

"And the other reason?" Rial asked.

"I need all of you except Carmain to go have a drink, a meal, do some shopping on Larga Ways, out of uniform, and with your ears open."

"You want to know what the mood on the ground is." Tobru gave a slow nod.

"If the Garmman are feeling aggrieved or if they're really on the Tecran's side, someone, somewhere, will have heard a whisper of it on Larga Ways. It's one of the major hubs of interaction between Grihan and Garmman traders." Favri was nodding as well.

"You can go as couples. It'll help you blend in. Favri and Rial, and Tobru, you choose a partner. Chel, you coordinate while I'm running around."

"What about me?" Carmain didn't look surprised to be excluded from the excitement, she was the most junior officer here, and she wouldn't be in line for this kind of op unless they needed someone with her particular looks.

"You're here because I want to discuss Fiona's security. We're clear that if the Tecran know we have her, they'll do anything to get her back. So that means while we're docked in Larga Ways, I don't want her leaving her room."

Carmain's jaw dropped.

Hal winced. "I know. It smacks of imprisonment, but I need you to explain the reasoning to her. This is for her own protection. I can't let anyone catch sight of her, and there may be officials coming onboard. I could insist on meeting off-ship, but that's out of character, and it would be the first time I've done it. I'd rather they think we have nothing to hide."

"If there are Tecran spies on Larga Ways—and there definitely are—as soon as they know the *Fasbe* has docked, they'll know we have Fiona," Tobru said. "Unless that kind of information is only being shared right at the top. But the *Fasbe's* arrival will be recorded, and someone, somewhere, will make a note of it."

Hal nodded. "That's why I've instructed Gerbardi to call the *Fasbe* a different name, and why we gave the impression we were bringing in two vessels attacked by the Krik, instead of one. I've also arranged for us to have a docking arm to ourselves. Unless someone knows what the *Fasbe* actually looks like, we've covered ourselves as best we can. Rial, find out from Gerbardi what name he gave to Larga Ways so you give the right information when you bring the *Fasbe* in."

Rial nodded. "You want us to check in to a hotel or something while we nose around? Or use the ship as a base?"

Hal pursed his lips. "Hotel. Stay at different ones, and each team, let the other team know where you are so they can follow you at set times, just to see if someone is watching."

"Fun." Favri grinned, and Hal hoped she was right.

It didn't feel like fun to him. It felt like there was a huge meteor heading straight for them, and it wasn't a case of if it would hit, but when.

Chapter Thirteen

FEE LIKED TO THINK SHE WASN'T AN IDIOT, and after everything that had happened to her in the last two and a half months, she could happily agree to stay in a large, well-equipped room for a day or so.

No problem.

She'd sat in the cell on the *Fasbe* for over six weeks before something had changed and Tak had let her out and tried to pretend she had never been a prisoner in the first place. So this was nothing.

It had also been done with an explanation and an apology.

It made her all the more willing to not be difficult about it, even though she sensed that if she'd refused, they would have locked her up anyway. It sounded from what Carmain had said that it wasn't only her who would be in danger, but that the whole ship could become a target if the Tecran were to discover she was on board.

She wouldn't have blamed them for forcing her if she'd objected, but as it was, they'd been grateful for her acceptance and lack of a tantrum, and everyone was happy.

So why, after all that, did they want her to go out onto Larga Ways?

Fee shifted her gaze from the official at her door to the huge screen that made up one wall of her room. She'd set it to show Larga Ways itself, using an image taken from the *Illium's* outside lens feed as it had approached the way station.

They'd arrived mid-afternoon, and the way station had been awash with sunlight.

She had no objection to exploring the place.

It looked breathtaking, and as a whole day had passed since they'd docked, and Pila told her they'd been delayed and would be here another twelve hours at least, it was mid-afternoon again. She wanted to feel the sunshine on her face.

The picture she'd built up in her mind of a trading way station circling a planet had been drawn from grungy first person computer game imagery, all dull gray metal and long passageways, dark alleys, and dangerous figures lurking in the shadows.

Instead, Larga Ways looked like a child's drawing of a sun, a disc with rays streaming from it at even intervals. Each ray was a docking arm, and the whole of it was encased in a dome of dark purple light.

When she'd asked, Carmain had explained that it was the same technology as the gel wall in the launch bay. A strong metal grid below the disc anchored it, and then soared up to arch over the station itself. Underneath the way station and near the top of the dome, the grid was intricate and dense, providing a strong support for the gel, and it was only at the docking arms that the grid was more open, to allow ships to enter.

The buildings on the way station were three stories high at least, and while it didn't seem as if there was anything resembling a park, plants and trees were obviously grown in pots and raised beds, thousands of them, making the buildings looks as if they were rising out of a lush forest.

The architect in her longed to explore, so she was hardly going to say no if Captain Vakeri was letting her out.

"Are you sure this is right?" she asked her guard again. "Shouldn't we wait for Pila?"

Hisma shrugged. "Commander Chel ordered him to communications ten minutes ago. I've tried to contact him twice and he's not answering, which probably means he's in a meeting and can't be disturbed."

She looked at the United Council officer standing patiently with his handheld, which he'd shown them twice now, the seal of the Way Station Commander blazing bright from the screen. According to Hisma, it was completely legit.

"And you're sure this is okay with Captain Vakeri?"

Hisma nodded, and there was no doubt in his eyes. "He contacted me by comm and told me personally to expect Officer Talbo."

Well. She sure as hell wasn't going to say no, then. At least they'd sent a Grihan United Council officer, not a Garmman. She may have had to turn the opportunity down if they had, because no way was she leaving alone anywhere with a Garmman.

"Great. Then I'm all set."

"We need to wait for the helmet," Officer Talbo said.

There was something about him. A twitch of nerves in the way he tapped, tapped, tapped on his handheld with his fingernail. Fee wasn't sure if he was intimidated by Hisma, whose shockgun had not fully lowered to point to the floor since Talbo had arrived, or whether it was his natural disposition.

It was hard to know what was normal and what wasn't when the new normal was completely out of her experience.

"Helmet?" Hisma frowned, and then turned, shockgun rising, as a member of the *Illium's* crew rounded the corner, a helmet in her hands.

"Commander Chel ordered this for you?" Her voice rose nervously and she held the helmet out, frowning at the shockgun.

Hisma lowered it. "What's it for?"

"To hide her ears and hair," Talbo said.

Ah. It was making more sense now. They weren't going to flaunt her, they were going to pretend she was Grihan.

Although, if they were all so nervous about the Tecran finding out she was here, she wondered why the United Council was insisting she travel to them for a meeting, rather than seeing her on the *Illium*.

If they were all like Councilor Vilk, they probably thought they were too important.

She lifted her hair, twisting it and tucking it into a bun. Hisma took the helmet and gently put it on her head, and pushed it down.

"It's a little big, but then, they always are for the cadets, and that's what you look like," the woman from the stores said, watching them with interest.

"Except for the . . ." Hisma stopped, and bit his lip.

Ah. Her breasts. She'd slowly gotten the picture that they were bigger than the Grih were used to. They tried not to stare, but they weren't always successful.

She raised an eyebrow at him, but the impact was lost because the helmet came down to her eyebrows and mostly hid them.

"Let's go, then." Talbo looked like he was anxious to get moving.

"I know the captain said you had arranged security for her but . . ." Hisma looked Talbo up and down. "You don't even have a weapon."

"Weapons are not allowed on Larga Ways, except by security, and there are two security officers waiting outside on the dock for us." Talbo turned and started walking, and Fee shrugged at Hisma and followed. Hisma brought up the rear, and Fee guessed he'd stick to her like glue until she stepped down the *Illium's* ramp. He'd watch her back until the last minute.

"I won't look much like a cadet if there are two armed guards hovering over me," she said to Talbo as they reached the main passageway.

The double doors out to the dock platform where right up ahead.

"They won't be hovering, and they're not going to be in

uniform. You won't even know who they are or where they are. They'll blend in to the crowd around us and keep watch." He spoke quickly, as if reciting from a script, and Fee guessed he'd had to say it a couple of times before to various twitchy visitors.

Fine with her. Even though Talbo was taking her directly to the United Council offices on Larga Ways, she would get to walk down the streets of this place. She wondered if it was possible to see Balco from within the dome, or whether the purple of the gel wall obscured it.

Two guards stood at the doors, and they came to sharp attention at the sight of her.

"Captain okayed it. She has permission to leave," Hisma said from behind her. "UC business."

Tablo waved his commander's seal at them and the double doors opened.

She took a deep breath and stepped outside for the first time in over two months.

Chapter Fourteen

THE PURPLE GEL THAT ENCASED LARGA WAYS was less
intense than the blue of the gel walls in the launch bays.

Fee stopped halfway down the docking arm and tilted her
head up. It was more a translucent lavender than the dark purple
it appeared to be looking from the outside in.

She turned her head and closed her eyes against the brightness
and warmth of Balco's sun. Tears pricked the back of her eyes and
she had to swallow hard to keep them from spilling.

"Please. We need to keep moving," Talbo said, almost directly
in her ear, and she reluctantly opened her eyes and faced the
cluster of buildings up ahead.

She stumbled as she took her first step, as she realized the
planet Balco was right in front of her. It rose up above the silver
reflective roofs; green, gold and blue.

The sight of it made her heart beat faster in her chest.

Talbo tugged at her arm and Fee stiffened.

"It's dangerous for you to be out in the open. Please, let's go."
Talbo was on the edge of panic, and Fee tried to bury her
resentment at being rushed and fell into step with him.

They walked to the docking gate, and Talbo simply nodded at
the guards on duty and stepped through what resembled an
airport security scanner. Fee followed him, and after she stepped
through, she heard a hum behind her as it was reactivated.

She looked over her shoulder, and noticed the faint snap of
purple light from one side to the other.

So, likely, you'd get a nasty shock if you ran through it without
permission.

She wondered where the guards who were supposed to be watching her were hidden. She and Talbo had been the only people on the docking arm but now they were among the way station crowds and as Talbo led her down a narrow street she looked around to see if she could spot them.

There were Garmman and Grih, but there were other races as well; a few Fitali like Kwo, and men and women with a shorter, stockier build and flat faces with silver eyes.

Perhaps they were Balcoan.

The buildings were all covered in the most amazing mosaics, and Fee realized some of what she'd thought were greenery and flowers earlier were designs on the walls.

There were plants, though.

Tiny dark red flowers carpeted the sides of the streets and what looked like pale green arum lilies curved up and out from pots, their frilly leaves a mix of pink and green.

The trees were similar to cypresses, tall and thin, but when she got closer, she saw the trunks were a twist of four or five separate stems, entwined together, and the tiny leaves looked thick and succulent.

"This way." Talbo turned off the street into what Fee would describe as an alleyway, but of course, they would make their streets as narrow as possible here, to maximize the space for buildings.

They walked the length of a short block, deep in shadow, and then stepped out onto another street as wide as the one they'd just come from.

It had the same beautiful buildings and plants, but there were a few places that Fee thought looked like market stalls and tiny stores, and there were more people here.

To the left, at what was surely a street cafe, she caught sight of someone familiar sitting at a small table, a cup in front on him. He was big and Grihan, although he wasn't in uniform.

She knew him, though. She would never forget his face—Rial, the medic who'd helped her on the *Fasbe*.

She waved and smiled at him and just as Talbo hustled her down the alley on the opposite side of the street, she saw Rial's face go slack with surprise.

Me, too, she wanted to call. *I can't believe they let me out either.*

Excitement danced over her skin again as she took a deep breath and realized she could smell food cooking in the air. It was spicy and smelled as if it was being seared over a hot fire.

The contrast of such earthy cooking methods with the sophisticated dome overhead thrilled her, made her want to pull away from Talbo and explore.

Maybe she could wheedle an hour of exploring Larga Ways out of the UC committee members waiting for her after the meeting.

It was worth a try.

"In here." Talbo held a door open for her in what looked like a building back entrance.

They were taking precautions, she'd give them that. The helmet, the low profile, coming in the back way.

The heavy, reinforced door thudded shut behind them, and it took Fee a moment for her eyes to adjust to the gloom of the small hallway.

It was all white and silver and a staircase rose up to her right.

Talbo lifted his handheld, and she realized he was looking at a floor plan.

"This way," he said, moving forward, past the stairs to a door at the other end of the hall. "This is it."

Again, he held the door for her, and she stepped in to a room that seemed too small and empty to be a meeting place.

Talbo stepped in behind her. She turned to ask him where they were, and saw his eyes go wide, his expression collapse into one of pain, and he went down, face first.

The door thumped shut, and she wrenched her gaze from his body, to find a person standing against the wall.

He'd been hiding behind the door, she realized, and now, only now that she saw the weapon in his hand, pointing at her, did she hear the faint whine of a shockgun.

"You shot him." She wanted to kneel beside Talbo and check if he was all right, but as she took a step forward, the shooter raised the shockgun higher.

"I used the third lowest setting," he said, his Garmman rough and deeply accented. "He'll come round in an hour or two."

She forced herself to look at him, to work out what he was, and found her breathing getting short, fear squeezing her chest.

He had feathers. Feathers instead of hair, it looked like, and his mouth was more beak than lips, his eyes huge in his face.

She hugged herself. "What are you?" But she knew. She couldn't remember it, but she must have seen them when they took her, or when they had her under sedation in that strange glass room.

She'd told Captain Vakeri that she remembered feathers, and she was looking at feathers now.

The Tecran had found her. Or, given that Talbo had led her straight to them, they had somehow orchestrated this whole 'meeting'. They had fooled the crew on the *Illium*, they had fooled a UC officer.

And they'd gotten everyone to cooperate quite happily in handing her over. Herself included.

"It doesn't matter who I am." He looked down at his shockgun, and she thought he might be adjusting the settings. "Take off your helmet."

Fee thought about refusing, but the shockgun rose to point at her face, and she lifted it off and set it at her feet.

He sucked in a breath, gaze going to her ears. "So it is you."

"What do you want?" If the captain was right, they'd want to get rid of her. Not just kill her, but make her disappear completely, so there was no trace of her existence. Likely, they wouldn't shoot her and leave her body here, they'd take it and jettison her into space, out of their hair forever.

"I want you to come with me."

There was no way she was going with him so he could kill her quietly in some more private place and then dispose of her body. If she was dead either way, she'd make things as difficult as possible for him. Then at least the crew of *Illium* would know what had happened to her.

Just like when she'd stepped out to speak to the Krik on the *Fasbe*, she didn't have anything to lose.

"Where are we going?" She took a step to the side, so she could get around Talbo. The Tecran lifted the shockgun again, and Fee raised her hands.

"To my ship."

Fee frowned. "The Tecran have a ship docked at Larga Ways?"

She knew she wasn't crew, or in any need-to-know group on the *Illium*, but she would have thought Pila or Carmain would have told her how close danger lay if a Tecran vessel was docked at the same way station. They couldn't know, or even Hisma would have asked more questions before letting her go.

"Not in any official capacity." He gave her a look she couldn't interpret. "We wouldn't have been given permission, even if we'd asked."

She took another step to the side and finally had a clear run to the door, except that the Tecran was standing right beside it.

Maybe it was time to unleash one of her secret weapons.

Aside from the encryptor, she had one surprise up her sleeve. She'd hidden it from Tak, waiting for her chance to use it, and that chance had never come.

It looked like it had now.

The gravity here was less than on Earth. Everything happened a fraction slower, but she could jump higher.

She could leap, flip, and somersault like an Olympic gymnast.

She'd always wondered what it would feel like to be able to do that, and since she'd discovered that she could jump high enough to touch the ceiling with ease in her cell on the *Fasbe*, she'd been able to find out.

Probably, over time, her body would adjust and she'd lose her edge, but right now, her muscles and bones were used to a slightly higher gravity, and if she wanted to, she could jump over this Tecran's head.

"I will shoot you if you try to run." He motioned her toward the door, opening it and standing right in the doorway, so she'd have to squeeze past him.

She took a few steps toward him, her gaze never leaving his face, and then leaped, in a head first dive.

She flew just over his head, turned a half-somersault in the air and landed hard, staggering as she took her next steps. Her momentum was too much, and she fell forward, and the whine of a shockgun shot sounded over her head.

She scrabbled her feet to get traction, pushing herself up with her arms, and just as she was about to launch herself forward again, pain burst across her shoulder blades and her whole body went numb.

She fell back to the ground, her cheek pressed against her forearm, and realized she couldn't move her limbs. She could close her eyes, though, and she lowered her lids so they appeared shut, but so she could still see a little.

Boots approached her.

"Shit. I hope to the stars you're not dead, because I was told not to shoot you." Hands grabbed her, and he strained to pick her up.

He was half a meter taller than she was, and stocky in build, but she could hear he was having real trouble. He grunted as he tried to lift her, and dropped her back to the ground with a thud. Ow.

"Why do you weigh so much?" He rolled her onto her back, moved round to her head and grabbed her under her arms and started dragging her.

He switched to speaking Tecran, muttering under his breath, and Fee wished she hadn't avoided learning it.

As the Tecran pulled her along, her legs and arms started tingling, and Fee thought she might be able to move them soon.

She had her encryptor, and she had a feeling the Tecran thought she was more immobilized than she really was.

She'd use everything she could against him.

They did not get to do this to her twice.

Chapter Fifteen

"RIAL?" HAL FROWNED AT THE INCOMING COMM, moving sideways in the narrow street to allow a Balcoan woman and her two children to pass. He'd told his team not to contact him if possible while they were undercover, just in case someone was monitoring the comms.

"I know I'm breaking protocol, but I think I'm blown anyway." Rial's tone coming through the earpiece was quietly furious. "I saw Fiona Russell, and I thought the plan was to keep her hidden. If that changed, it would have been better to tell us, because she saw me and waved. If I was being watched, they know I'm a crew member."

Hal stumbled to a stop, and pressed himself up against a wall to get out of the way. "Say that again."

"She waved. She would have called a greeting if that UC officer with her hadn't been hurrying her along—"

"You are telling me that Fiona Russell was outside of the *Illium*? Walking the streets of Larga Ways?" He struggled to keep his voice low.

"You didn't know." Rial spoke slowly, making it a statement, not a question. "Favri and I will try to see where she went."

Hal heard a change in the background noise, and guessed Rial was moving.

"You say she was with a UC officer?"

"Yes. Grihan. In uniform."

"Try to find her. I'm calling the ship." Maybe someone was listening in, but Hal couldn't spare the time to run back to the *Illium*. If they were being monitored, so be it.

He tapped his earpiece. "Carmain."

She came on immediately.

"Yes, sir?"

"Are you on duty?"

"No. Pila is, with one of the other guards. We split up, so one of us was always on. I'm in the canteen."

"Rial just spotted Fiona on Larga Ways with a UC official."

There was dead silence for a beat.

"He's sure?"

Hal could hear her breathing ramp up. She was running.

"He's sure. She waved hello to him."

She swore under her breath. "Give me two minutes."

She cut off comms, and Hal flicked back to Rial. "Any luck?"

"She went down a side street, but there's no sign of her. If only I'd followed my gut. I knew it wasn't right that she was out. And I have to admit, if she hadn't waved, I wouldn't even have noticed her, because she had a helmet on. She looked like a cadet."

Something clicked in Hal's brain. He cut Rial off, tapped his ear. "Voa."

"Captain?"

"I need to know where Fiona Russell is, using the tracker in her cadet uniform."

"I haven't been given those tracking signatures but . . . we don't have any cadets at the moment, so whichever cadet signal is moving will be her."

Hal heard her fingers tapping on the screen.

"This can't be right. She's outside the *Illium*."

"Oh, it's right." Hal knew he sounded grim.

Voa blew out a breath and he heard her fingers flying over the screen. "I've brought up every senior officer's handheld tracker. You're three streets to the right of her, five blocks down, but Rial and Favri are standing right outside the building where she is." She gave the address.

"Tell me if she moves." Hal cut her off, connected back to Rial. "She's inside a building right next to you."

"There's a door here," Favri called out, but before Rial could say anything, Voa cut back in.

"She's moving. Quickly, so I think she's in one of the supply hovers. She exited the building on the other side to Favri and Rial, and she'll already be out of sight of them. But she's heading in your general direction. Run straight up the street, and it's possible you'll see her as she crosses in front of you."

Hal ran. He tapped his earpiece. "Rial, she's left the building, but search it, see what you can find. I'm chasing her down."

"But how—?"

He cut Rial off as a comm came through from Carmain. He was getting strange looks from the people around him as he dodged shoppers and residents. He'd have to get the way station commander involved if this carried on much longer, but if possible, he'd rather get his hands on Fiona, stash her back on the *Illium*, and maybe they could pretend this had never happened.

"Talk," he said to Carmain.

"There was a breach." Her voice was almost expressionless. "All comms are dead around the area of Fiona's room. Pila received a comm from Chel, directing him to go to the communications division and wait for him, Hisma got a comm from you, telling him to expect a UC officer to come for Fiona, that she was due at a council meeting. We've found a metal disc attached to the wall just around the corner from her door, and Gerbardi says it has those comms from Chel and yourself prerecorded on it, and that it's responsible for the dead zone in that section of the ship."

"So if either Hisma or Pila had asked a question, the prerecorded messages wouldn't have stood up to scrutiny."

"No. But in both cases, the order was issued and then it appeared as if you and Chel had cut off comms. It would take a brave junior officer or guard to comm you back with a question, when the instruction was so clear."

True. As a strategy, it was risky, but not that risky.

Hal pushed himself a little harder, leaping over a small fluffy kapoot that bounced on the end of a stretchy lead held by a Balcoan doing her afternoon shopping.

"Coming up on your left." Voa's voice hummed with tension, and Hal saw the narrow supply hover moving above head height. Its white sides had no windows, and the front was so darkly tinted, he couldn't see in.

Larga Ways was vehicle free, except for hovers transporting goods to and from the docked ships. This one seemed to be moving faster than was allowed, and by the time Hal made it to the crossroad, it had already passed him.

To call in Tean Lee, Larga Way's head of security, or not?

Hal ran after the hover while he debated with himself. Any chance of keeping Fiona's presence here secret would be completely compromised if he brought Lee into this mess, and they still had a long journey back home where anything could happen to them. But on the other hand, without Lee's help, they may lose her right now, if she wasn't already lying dead in that hover.

He tapped his earpiece. "Lee."

The station commander had given Hal his direct comms signature yesterday in the spirit of cooperation, and he came online immediately. "Vakeri?"

"I have a problem." It was hard to think up a delicate way to admit to keeping secrets while running through the streets after a hover.

"I gathered that when I saw you running through the market. You don't look happy."

Lens feed.

He'd forgotten Larga Ways had deemed lens feed in the main

public areas to be a matter of security, as the use of some small bombs and weapons could potentially breach the gel dome.

"I'm not. We found another Earth woman a few days ago, a prisoner on the Garmman trader we towed in yesterday, and she's just been abducted from my ship."

Lee let a long moment of silence stretch out. "We'll talk about sharing information vital to the safety of this station another time. She in that hover you're chasing?"

"Yes."

"I need to get down to the security division, so I can direct this in real time. How sure are you she's there?"

"All our cadet uniforms are embedded with a tracker so we know where they are if they slip out and cause trouble. Fiona is wearing one of those uniforms."

"She there willingly?"

Hal could hear the caution in Lee's voice. If Fiona wanted to leave the *Illium*, he had no right to stop her.

"Very doubtful. I think you can imagine the reasons why it would be difficult for some people to explain her presence here. Easier for her to just disappear."

The hover cleared the buildings, and Hal saw it move toward one of the docking arms. There were at least twenty vessels docked along the arm; all small, fast runners.

"It's fine. They have to stop and get permission to proceed along the dock," Lee said, his voice calm. "You'll catch them."

But nothing had happened as it was supposed to since Rial had spoken to him, so Hal kept his pace as fast as he could.

The hover reached the guards at the security point.

A high-energy field encircled the way station around its central disc. The only place it could be shut down was across the entrance to each docking arm, to allow people and hovers through, controlling the flow on and off the way station.

The two guards stationed on the way station side of the field stepped forward, but the hover didn't slow, it simply sailed over them and through the check point, past the shocked guards on the docking arm side.

The field was down.

"What?" Lee's voice was incredulous in his ear. He cut off, and Hal kept running full tilt, but he was barely a leap away when he heard the high buzzing sound of the field snapping back into place.

He stumbled, trying to stop his forward momentum, and one of the guards grabbed him, hauling him back so that the faint purple light of the field hissed an inch from his face.

He gave a quick nod of thanks to the man, and tapped his earpiece. "Lee?" Nothing. "Lee?"

"Dead zone. I've been trying since it went over our head." The other guard lowered her hand from her ear.

Another dead zone. Surprise, surprise.

Hal looked down the length of the docking arm. The hover was still moving, although it was already halfway down the line.

Going to the last vessel. He'd bet a month's pay on it.

"Let me through, I've got to catch them."

The guards looked at each other.

"They've kidnapped one of my crew. Let me through."

"State your name and vessel for the log, and I'll do it," the woman said.

Hal reeled the information off, and with a snap, the field between the two ten meter poles disappeared.

Before they could change their mind, or whoever was pulling the strings right now reset it to shut him out, Hal ran through.

He wouldn't mind backup, but he knew the guards had to receive permission to leave their posts, and with a dead zone in place, Lee couldn't get through to them.

The hover stopped at the far end, not at the last vessel but the second last.

Hal realized why as soon as he was close enough to see.

The last vessel was a Larga Ways security patrol runner. They were well-equipped, had good weapons, and spent their time patrolling the nearspace around Larga Ways. They also always docked at the end of the arm, so they could easily come and go.

"Are you there?" Lee's voice suddenly came through, too loud. Hal winced. "Yes. If they take off, can I use your runner?"

Lee didn't even hesitate. "Yes. I'd really like to ask them a few questions. Like how on Guimaymi's Star they created a dead zone in my comms, and shut off a specific part of my energy field."

Hal gave a grunt of acknowledgment. He needed all his breath to run. His legs were burning now, his chest heaving as he pushed himself.

Up ahead, a Tecran armed with a shockgun hopped out of the hover and opened the rear doors. Fiona exploded out, trying to jump over his head.

She looked up and caught sight of Hal, and as she flew through the air, his gaze locked with hers.

And then she fell limp to the floor.

The bastard had shot her. And Hal was still too far away.

The Tecran set his shockgun on the ground and desperately hauled Fiona to what looked like a two-person runner.

He dragged her to the door and pushed her inside, and turned back to grab his weapon.

But the runner's door closed, and Hal could hear the whine of its engines revving.

The Tecran spun back to it, shock clear on his face, and hammered on the door, but the runner slid out of its berth, and shot up to exit height, and accelerated away.

Hal's own steps faltered for a moment, and he staggered, trying to keep the runner in sight.

The look she'd sent him. Hope. Relief.

When she'd seen him, she thought she was going to be saved.

She'd been taken on his watch. Off his ship. And right in front of him.

He would not let this go.

His breath was ragged now, and he was starting to slow, but he aimed for the security patrol vessel, bearing down on the Tecran.

Fiona's abductor backed away and then ran to the very end of the docking arm, and Hal was happy to ignore him. Lee's guards could deal with him.

As he reached the runner, the doors opened.

"No time to key it to you, so I've overridden the settings, and it's keyed for general use. Which means don't let it get into the wrong hands." Lee's voice was harsh with outrage.

"Thank you." Hal ran inside, straight to the pilot console, throwing himself into the chair and initiating engines.

He had just initiated the release from the dock when the door opened again and the Tecran fell through, his shockgun flying from his hand as he rolled across the floor.

The door shut and Hal had a second to decide whether to stop and hand the Tecran over to Lee's guards or keep going.

He chose to keep going, slapping the runner into an automatic exit program and grabbing for the Tecran's shockgun.

"Vakeri, you have a passenger." Lee's voice was hoarse, as if he'd been shouting.

"I see him. No time to stop."

"The yurve shit is going to fly for this."

Hal gave a bitter smile as the runner slid through the gel dome and out into space. He pointed the shockgun straight at the Tecran.

"Yes. It is. And quite a bit of it will be thrown by me." He checked the settings, and stilled. It was on maximum. The Tecran must have adjusted it after he shot Fiona, intending to take down the guards permanently.

If not, Fiona Russell was dead.

Because he thought it might be useful to interrogate the Tecran later, Hal dialed down the charge, and as the Tecran righted himself and staggered to his feet, Hal shot him back down.

Chapter Sixteen

FEE CAME BACK TO CONSCIOUSNESS SLOWLY.

It was quiet, the muted throb of the engines the only real sound she could hear aside from her own breathing.

She tried to shift her position and sit up, and was overcome by the white noise of panic when she couldn't do it.

She was paralyzed.

A noise erupted from her throat, a harsh, animal cry, and she was so shocked by the sound of it, she snapped out of her terror, forced her breathing to slow down.

She had been in this situation before.

When she'd woken those few times on the Tecran's ship, and again on the *Fasbe,* she'd had the same sense of powerlessness. She had overcome the fear then, she would do it again now.

"I think you might be awake." The voice sounded like it was from somewhere in front of her, but she couldn't see if anyone was there, or if it was coming from the comms. Her heart raced again, and she was gratified to find she was finally able to open her eyes.

"You should not have been shot. If I ever have the pleasure of meeting Lieutenant Cy again, he will regret it."

If her body had been working right, she would have shivered at the tone of that voice. Icy, cold rage. The tone also seemed a little mechanical this time, whereas before it had sounded . . . nice. Deep, but melodic.

"There's hardly any time." The tone changed, almost to panic. "I hope you can hear me. I arranged . . ."

Fee went under, her mind shutting down. When she jerked

back awake, she was aware she'd zoned out, but not for how long. She struggled to pay attention.

"... are you able to answer?"

She felt a new wave of unconsciousness wash over her, pulling her under, and she fought and clawed her way back.

"Obviously too injured—"

She heard the outrage again, the fury. At least whoever was talking seemed to find the idea of her being shot enraging.

She was with him, there. It had really, really hurt.

She'd been waiting for the Tecran to open the hover's doors, and when he did, she'd jumped, flying over him.

Captain Vakeri had been on the dock.

Her memory slowly started coming back.

He'd been running flat out toward her. He was still a way off, but the sight of him, huge, bearing down on them ... she remembered almost laughing with relief, because he looked like he could take down a ten ton truck, let alone a single Tecran.

And then pain.

The asshole had shot her in the back again, she realized. She wondered where he was, and decided she hoped whoever was talking to her did find the bastard.

"... get you to the med chamber."

Fee tried to lift her head, but it didn't move at all.

There was something strange about the way he was talking ... she tried to work it out, and then realized, he'd been speaking in English.

She fought her limp, rag doll body, trying to struggle upright, and ended up squirming on the reclined seat she was lying on. She was so frustrated, she screamed, and it came out as a gurgling whimper.

Argh!

"I will kill him." The voice was almost expressionless. "I think that's the only response that will make me feel better. You can't even speak because of what he did."

She heard herself panting in fury and fear.

"You'll be coming through the gel wall in a few minutes. I'll have a drone waiting for you." His voice was back to the way it had been when he'd first spoken, rich and smooth, and she forced herself to close her eyes and calm down. There was nothing she could do right now, she was trapped in her own body, but whoever was talking was giving her something she hadn't had in over two months, the sound of someone talking to her in her mother tongue.

The engines in the runner revved, and then settled down on a pillow of air, and she forced her eyes open again.

Somewhere to her right, a door slid open.

Long, retractable metal arms scooped her up and placed her on a stretcher, and then she was towed out.

The launch bay was empty, and when she was tugged out into a passageway, that was empty, too.

As she passed a closed door, though, she heard thumping, like someone was pounding on it, and flinched as it sounded like someone threw themselves at the wall.

The med chamber must be close to the launch bay, because she was pulled through a door after what felt like only a few minutes, and it was the sterile white and silver she'd come to associate with Dr. Jasa's rooms.

She could hear someone, or more than one person, in the adjoining room. They were talking and moving around.

It made her feel vulnerable and frightened, lying absolutely helpless.

She caught movement out of the corner of her eye, and saw a tiny, delicate robot arm extending out, something clasped in its claws.

She couldn't move, couldn't do anything, as it inserted whatever it was in her ear, but her heart beat double time, and she found it harder and harder to breath.

"Now we can talk privately, without anyone listening in." The voice was back, this time directly in her ear, and she forced herself to relax.

Just an earpiece. All the Grih had them, there was no reason to be afraid of it.

"I don't know how long this is going to take, but I hope not long, because we don't have much time." The voice was quiet, and urgent.

Then something was done to her, because Fee felt her grip on consciousness wrenched from her, and she sank down, slowly, gently, into black.

***

Hal was almost sorry he hadn't dialed back the shockgun setting a little more when he'd pulled the trigger. He needed the Tecran awake.

But hurting him after what he'd done to Fiona had felt extremely satisfying.

Now, though, he'd lost the runner that had taken her. He didn't know where it had gone, and he couldn't work out how it had disappeared.

And he was in another dead zone.

Dead zones were starting to really piss him off.

He'd used the restraints he'd found onboard and tied the Tecran to a chair that seemed to be specifically for prisoners, and now he looked him over, nicely secured, and tried to think what would wake him.

Maybe a small jolt with the shockgun? Lowest setting, lowest discharge. A tiny little nip.

It was worth a try, because time was ticking away.

Hal set it up and pulled the trigger, and the Tecran jerked awake with a screech.

They stared at each other for a beat.

Then the Tecran looked around, and Hal saw him take in that he wasn't in a prison cell on Larga Ways, but still in the runner he'd jumped into to avoid Tean Lee's guards.

"I've got some questions for you." Hal dialed the shockgun up again. "Let's start with your name."

"You can call me Cy." The Tecran's Grihan was almost impossible to understand. And Hal would bet serious money there was a Commander or Lieutenant in front of his name. Everything about him screamed Tecran military officer.

"Do you speak Garmman?" It seemed likely, given how this seemed to be more and more leaning to a Garmman-Tecran conspiracy.

Cy nodded.

"Good." Hal switched to Garmman. "It's simple. You abducted Fiona Russell. I want to know where she's gone."

Cy frowned. "You didn't follow her?"

"I did. I've lost her."

His prisoner jerked in surprise. "How long have I been out?"

"Just over an hour." Hal narrowed his eyes. "We're close, aren't we?"

He saw the Tecran weighing up whether to answer honestly or not.

"Depends how lost you are. But, yes."

His prisoner was glad they were close, Hal decided. Which meant he thought there'd be back-up waiting to help him. That Hal would be taking him exactly where he wanted to go.

So he'd have to manage this really carefully.

"Show me." Hal moved forward and unclipped the chair Cy was strapped to, rolled it over to the console, and clipped it back in.

The Tecran talked him through the coordinates, and Hal frowned at the screen. According to Cy, the runner carrying Fiona had dipped into Balco's atmosphere, which is why he'd lost them.

It was headed for a Tecran battleship hidden in the huge, static storm that sat in a thick column, rising from the planet's surface all the way to the very top.

The storm was created from the unique characteristics of Balco's orbit and topography, and it never moved more than two thou in any direction. The Balcoans called it Kyber's Arm.

Hal wondered what battleship had the strength to hover inside the storm, even at the very top.

"A Levron?" He hadn't thought a Tecran Levron battleship, the Tecran's main military vessel, could enter and leave a planet's atmosphere all that easily. Most of the Grih's ships, the explorers and the battleships, were space-going only. They couldn't land or lift off from a planet's surface. If the Levron could, they were more advanced than anyone at Battle Center knew.

Cy looked at him sidelong. Then shrugged. "Yes, a Levron. It's maintaining altitude almost at the very top of the storm system, right at the edge of the atmosphere. It's not a comfortable position, but it's just doable."

Hal regarded him for a long moment. He was lying. Something in the way his eyes flicked, and the almost imperceptible laughter that had flashed in his eyes, told him there wasn't a Levron waiting for him in the dark, bruised clouds boiling up below them.

Which meant only one thing.

It was a Class 5.

Had to be. The only thing more powerful than a Levron was the Class 5, and the Tecran would hardly be laughing quietly at the surprise in store for Hal if the ship was less powerful than he'd indicated.

"So, there's a Class 5," he said as he rolled the prisoner's chair back to its original position, and Cy jerked in surprise. "Why do you think they left you behind? You had time to get in before I made it to the runner."

The Tecran clamped his mouth shut.

"Sacrificed you, didn't they? If you hadn't managed to jump onboard my ship, you'd be in lockup on Larga Ways right now, answering some difficult questions. And the fact that you're obviously a Tecran officer would have made things very difficult for your high command. For that alone, I would have thought they'd have waited for you, even if you'd completely botched your mission."

"I don't know." The words were grated out. "It must have been a mistake."

"Didn't look like a mistake to me." Hal grinned at him.

"What's your plan? Do you think you can take on a Class 5 in this?" Cy's sneer was ugly.

"I don't plan to take it on. I'm just going to explain to your captain that there is a tracking device in Fiona's clothes and we can prove they took her. Larga Ways, and by extension, Balco, as well as the Garmman UC councilor, and Grih Battle Center, are aware they've got Fiona, and if they don't hand her over, whatever trouble they've got with the UC at the moment will seem like a holiday compared to the trouble that will rain down on them for this."

The Tecran was silent.

There was a faint ping from the controls and Hal looked over at them. They were following a shallow trajectory, all set to dip into Balco's atmosphere, everything working well, and then suddenly, the engines cut off.

The runner went into a spin, throwing Hal against the wall, and then, like a skipping stone on the surface of a lake, they skimmed the surface of the atmosphere and bounced back into space.

Hal pressed himself onto the floor as they whipped around and around.

Looked like the Tecran weren't pleased to see them.

Chapter Seventeen

THE LARGA WAYS PATROL RUNNER did one last, lazy turn,
then settled back upright and drifted.

Hal levered himself into a crouch and then slowly stood,
shaking out his arms and legs.

He was bruised, but nothing was broken.

Cy had had it even easier, tied to a chair that was bolted to the
floor, he hadn't so much as a scratch on him.

From the control panel came the insistent, shrill alarm warning
the air filtration was no longer in operation.

They'd been flicked away like a buzzing insect and left to die.
Hal knew they only had half an hour of air left, maybe an hour, if
they were lucky.

Cy watched him, face tight with fear. No more laughing
smugness.

Whoever was in charge of the Class 5 must know one of their
own was onboard, their sensors would tell them, but they were
clearly fine with killing him, anyway.

The patrol runner was small, just four seats around the control
panel, space for two prisoners with their own secured seats, and a
tiny bathroom at the back. A food and drink station was located
opposite the runner's entrance, and beside it was a second
recessed cabinet. Hal opened it, and pulled out six personal
breathing cylinders. They were good for an hour each.

Cy's seat was facing away from the cabinet, but his head could
turn a lot further than a Grihan's, and he fixed a desperate eye on
Hal.

"Three hours each, and whatever's left in the cabin," Hal told him, holding up two of the cylinders.

Hal walked back to the control panel, checked the readings. "We have some time before we'll need them, but I suggest we use them first, and only breath what's in the cabin at the end." There was always a little more in the cabin than the readings said, always a little more hope. When a cylinder was dead, it was dead.

Cy said nothing until he crouched down in front of him, and started to lift the breather over his head.

"You don't have to share."

Hal paused. "Yes, I do. The Grih are still bound by the Sentient Beings Agreement, whatever the Tecran have decided."

Cy winced at that. "That woman is trouble. She has been since the day we took her."

"You should have left her alone then." Hal looked straight into Cy's face as he settled the breather over his mouth, and the Tecran looked away.

He engaged it, then put one over his own mouth and instead of sitting, lay down on the floor, closed his eyes and tried to regulate his breathing.

He wished now that Battle Center had shared more on what they'd learned about Class 5s from Sazo with their senior officers. Farso Lothric's confession that he wasn't the only Grihan officer who'd helped Garmman councilor Fu-tama, and by extension, the Tecran, in their development of the Class 5s, had left Battle Center unwilling to trust their own senior staff, and they'd made the decision to keep as much back as they could until everyone was vetted.

Maybe he could find out a little now. He didn't think Cy would be as cagey about things when he was about to be killed by his own people. He opened his eyes and turned to the Tecran, looking up at him from his spot on the floor.

"How did you know Fiona Russell was onboard the *Illium*?" His question was a little muffled by the mask, but Cy heard him well enough.

Cy shrugged. "I did't know. I was given a mission, and I carried it out. I don't know how they knew she was there."

It sounded like he was telling the truth.

The Tecran shifted in the chair. "How did she get on your ship in the first place?" His eyes never left Hal's face as he asked.

It wouldn't hurt to tell him, now that half the security guards on Larga Ways no doubt had the information from Tean Lee. "She was being held captive on a Garmman trader we came across."

He watched Cy's face grimace behind the mask.

"They admit to where they got her?"

Hal's smile was not friendly. "No. But then you kidnapped her back, and removed all doubt."

The Tecran sighed. "What now?"

Hal lifted his shoulders in an awkward shrug.

"Until someone decides to talk to me, or puts the runner's power back online, we wait." There was an emergency help beacon under a protective cover on the control panel. He guessed it was deactivated as well, but if it wasn't, it was probably because the Tecran wanted Larga Ways to respond. Wanted to take them out, too. He could punch in the code, get some of Lee's security runners out here, but he'd most likely be luring them into a trap.

The lens feed from outside the runner was the only thing still working, and the screen above the control panel showed they were facing Balco, looking down on it just above where Kyber's Arm swirled, a dark gray and purple bruise hovering over the western desert.

He closed his eyes, struggled to get his breathing even again. He'd let them play their games for a bit, if this was a game and not deadly serious, but if it went on too long, he'd have no choice but to call for help.

Every minute that ticked by was one more where Fiona Russell was at their mercy.

***

Fee came awake in a rush, her heart beating in a wild rhythm. She lay still, trying to hear over the pounding in her ears. There was a low murmur of voices nearby, and then a shout, and she thought a shout might have been what had woken her.

It sounded at least a wall away, though, and she had the sense she was alone in the room.

She opened her eyes a crack, and when there was no movement and no one came into view, she opened them properly and sat up. It hit her that she *could* sit up, unlike before, and she shivered with relief, lifting her hands and wiggling her fingers.

Everything seemed to be where it should be, and she had control of her body again. She felt good, she realized. No stiffness, no aches. She wasn't hungry or thirsty, either.

Whatever else they'd done to her, they'd patched her up well.

She was in a med chamber, and now that she looked at it properly, she vaguely recalled being brought here earlier.

More sounds of people talking vibrated through the wall; urgent and angry, rather than relaxed chatting, and then something made a scraping sound in the ceiling above her.

She slid off the high bed she'd been lying on and looked upward.

The scraping came again, almost directly overhead, and she edged back, looking for a way out.

"Are you able to run?" The voice was low, urgent, and directly in her ear.

Fee couldn't help the cry that wrenched from her throat as she stumbled back.

The murmur of voices next door shut off.

Fear pricked along her arms and down her back. She felt as if she'd just attracted a lot of unwanted attention.

"You need to get out of here. I locked them in, but they've climbed into the air filtration tunnels." The voice came again, right in her ear, and a flash of memory came back to her. A drone, something clutched in it's tiny clamp, fitting something into her ear.

An earpiece.

She wasn't hallucinating and hearing strange voices. Someone was talking to her via a comm system.

"Who are you?" she whispered.

"I'm—"

A body fell through the ceiling, landing on the trolley full of medical instruments next to her bed and then bouncing off in a small puff of dust and shattered white ceiling tiles.

"Run! Run, run, run." The panic in the voice was catching, and Fee spun on her heel, raced for what she hoped was the door out.

It didn't open automatically, and she spun again, not wanting to have her back to whoever had crashed into the room.

"You have to hit the white light on the left of the door to open it," the voice hissed.

She just had time to realize that it was the same as the system on the *Illium*, and lunge for the button, when a Tecran rose up, covered in black grime, white dust, and bits of ceiling, and pointed something at her.

"Stop."

Fee lifted her hands slowly. Tried to see what was being pointed at her. It looked like a pen.

She'd been shot twice by a shockgun, and she weighed up whether she should risk being shot at by something else.

"Who are you?" She decided to stall a little. Try and work out what the *heck* was going on.

The Tecran frowned at her, and she realized she'd spoken in English, because the voice in her ear had spoken in English, and it had slipped her into the mode.

"Who are you?" she said again, this time in Garmman.

"What are you doing back here?" The Tecran's Garmman was

rusty and he rubbed his side as he spoke. Fee was surprised he was standing at all. He'd hit the trolley really hard.

"That's one of Doctor Gi's assistants, Har Bega," the voice whispered to her. "He's the one who kept you sedated when they abducted you from Earth."

Fee knew her face went slack, because Bega tipped his head quizzically to the side.

"This is the ship that abducted me?" She kept her voice hushed, because if she didn't, she would scream.

"The ship didn't abduct you, the people in it did." The voice in her ear was fierce.

Shouts erupted from the room next door, and Bega whipped his head around, too fast to be human. More like a bird of prey.

He shouted something back in Tecran.

"He's telling them he'll let them out now. He'll need to punch in a code. While he's busy with that, run."

On cue, Bega sidled over to the door that seemed to connect to the room beyond, and Fee saw a small keypad embedded in the wall.

She had no qualm about following Earpiece Guy's advice. He spoke her language, which in itself was a huge deal, and he wanted her out of there. She'd come to the same conclusion.

And, almost depressingly, once again she had nothing to lose.

"Don't move." Bega had positioned himself right next to the keypad, and he waved the pen thing at her again.

"First, tell me why." She may never get another chance to ask, and she really wanted to know.

"Why what?"

"Why did you take me? What's *wrong* with you people?"

Bega blinked, his big eyes widening a little. "We . . ." He trailed off without answering, and Fee had the feeling he couldn't. He didn't know.

She was talking to Mickey Mouse, not Walt Disney.

"Who brought you here?" Bega pointed the pen at her again. "You're supposed to be at the facility already."

"Someone called Cy." She watched his face, and thought she could detect confusion and a little relief.

The shouting from next door became thunderous, with fists hammering the wall, and he shouted back, almost close to a screech. He kept one arm held out in her direction, pen gripped in his hand, and turned to the keypad, tapping at it with the other.

Fee jumped, hit the white light button, and threw herself at the opening door.

She was too fast, or the doors were too slow, so she smacked into the too-narrow gap, and then had to squeeze sideways through it.

Bega gave a shout, and she felt a searing line of pain along the top of her shoulder, so intense she saw white stars for the first two stumbling steps she took.

"Faster. Down the passage and right. Now!"

Her shambling, pain-slowed gait sped up as panic and fear boosted her, and she darted right, kept going. She wanted to lift a hand, see what had happened to her shoulder, but she was too afraid of what she'd find.

"Where to now?" She spoke through gritted teeth.

"Next left."

"Is he right behind me, or freeing the others first?" She wasn't speaking particularly loudly, but at her question, someone shouted out from a door she was passing and she sidestepped and nearly tripped.

"Who are these people behind the doors? What the hell is going *on*?"

"The people behind the doors are the crew of this ship." He sounded grim. "He's let the others out. I can't keep the doors closed in the med chamber anymore. The system won't let me. No! Stop."

Fee brought herself up short.

"What?" She whispered it.

"We're in a passageway with no lens feed, but as soon as you step into the corridor in front of you, you'll be seen. There are two lenses, one on either end."

"What should I do?" She kept her voice low, and looked behind her.

"Wait." His voice went a little wonky, like he was using some kind of voice synthesizer. "Another crew member got out through the vents, and he's up ahead. When I say go, run right, then left, and I'll open a room for you to hide in."

She waited, legs trembling with adrenalin, and heard the sound of running behind her.

"Go!"

She ran hard to the right, saw the left turn, took it at an angle and kept going. Feet pounded behind her.

"Now would be a good time for the hidey-hole." She gasped the words, the injury on her shoulder burning like someone was holding a brand down on her skin.

"On the right."

What looked like part of a smooth passage wall suddenly slid aside, and Fee threw herself into the opening, and then staggered to a stop in the tiny room as the wall closed behind her.

She leaned forward, hands on knees, and tried to breathe quietly. The footsteps ran past, slowed, and there was shouting.

"They know I'm here. Why don't they open the door?" She turned and stared at the now smooth wall through which she'd come.

"There are lenses along this passageway, because it's the highest level security area onboard, so, yes, they know you're here. Doctor Gi has enough authority to call up the lens feed through the whole ship, and he's talking to the searchers. He saw you run down here and disappear through a door. Their problem is they didn't know a door was here. And they don't know how to find it."

Relieved, Fee crouched down, and then sat, breathing hard. She slowly became more aware of her surroundings. It was a tiny space. If she lay out flat, her feet would touch the wall opposite. There was nothing here but smooth metal on three sides, and on a fourth, what looked like a crystal was plugged into a silver-rimmed slot, with a cord attached to the end of it, like a necklace.

Then she saw the lens in the top right corner.

"Can't they see me through that lens?" She didn't have the energy to be worried about it. And what could she do, anyway?

"No. Only Captain Falto has clearance for this lens feed."

"And you." Or how else had he known about this place?

"Yes." He was thoughtful. "And me."

"What is this room for?"

Before Earpiece Guy could answer, someone banged on the wall. It sounded faint, but the wall vibrated a little at the blow.

"Did they hear me?" she whispered.

"No. They're trying to hear where the passageway is hollow, so they can find the door."

"So they just found it, then."

"I'm afraid so. They're camped outside now. They're waiting for the captain to return. I've managed to override most of the keypads on the various armories, so they won't be able to blast themselves in. It's too dangerous for the ship, fortunately, so the system is allowing me. Of course, they could crawl through the air vents next to the armories, drop down, and then crawl back out with whatever they want."

"And when the captain arrives?"

"He can override me," Earpiece Guy said.

"What then?" They would most likely try to kill her. "I'm not in any kind of shape to take them on."

"I can see you have an injury." His voice was soft. "It seems serious. What happened?"

"Bega shot me with something. It looked like a pen."

"Pen? Was it a laser scalpel?"

"That's probably exactly what it was." She felt a little sick at the thought of what it could have done to her if it had hit somewhere else. She tipped her head awkwardly to look at it properly. It looked like she imagined a bullet wound would look, if the bullet ran in a groove along the top of the skin. It had taken the fabric of her shirt with it, and left a neat, open score across the top of her shoulder. It had bled, but not profusely. The laser had probably cauterized the wound.

She'd live.

She clenched her fists and breathed in again. She was suddenly so, so angry.

They were such a bunch of *assholes*.

"Okay. It's talking time." She blew out a breath. "What the hell is going on? Whoever you are, you're in this up to your neck."

There was silence, and she heard another solid slam against the wall.

"Nothing to say, all of a sudden?" She closed her eyes as she spoke, tipping her head back against the wall. "Why don't I start? You are intimately familiar with this ship, intimately familiar with the people in it. And you have at least partial control of it. I think you're the one who sent Cy to get me. And you didn't tell him why, either. There was the same look of surprise on his face when he saw me the first time as I saw on Bega's. I don't know why Cy wasn't in the runner with me, but unless he had a really good escape route, you ditched him and left him to Captain Vakeri's mercy, of which I wholly approve, by the way. Vakeri looked seriously pissed off running down that dock, so hopefully Cy got to feel the pointy end of a shockgun himself. Then, you set things up here to patch me up. I don't know if you trapped the crew before you knew I was hurt or after, but you wanted them out the way while I was down and out. That says you knew they'd try to hurt me if they knew I was here, which means you know the Tecran are in big trouble for abducting someone else from my planet, and my appearance would throw them into even more hot water. So it follows that when the captain gets back, and opens up this room, they have every incentive in the world to kill me and toss my body into space."

Silence stretched out.

"You brought me here for a reason, why don't you tell me what it is?" She said it on a sigh, the pain in her shoulder pulsing with her heartbeat. She realized tears were running down her cheeks, and she wiped them away with the back of her hand.

"My name is Eazi." He spoke with a hitch. "I'm sorry you got hurt. I'd hoped to have the whole trip from Larga Ways to the ship to tell you about what was going on. Cy ruined that by shooting you."

"Twice," she said, bitterly. "And either the effect is cumulative, or the second time he used a higher setting, because it really knocked me out that time."

"He shot you twice?" Eazi's voice sounded really strange now. "When did he shoot you the first time?"

"When that UC officer brought me to him. I was sort of semi-conscious that time, and I got the feeling back in my limbs pretty quickly. He obviously decided not to take any chances the second time."

She shivered. The memory of the shot made her want to curl up protectively.

"Well, he's already regretting that." Eazi's voice was in spooky mode again, with an edge of satisfaction. "And I'm sorry we're in the situation we are now, with the crew right outside the door. I factored in that they would try to escape, but I thought we'd have enough time. I didn't realize how long it would take you to recover."

"Enough time to do what?" They needed to get to the nitty gritty now. The barbarians were at the gate.

Again, he hesitated. "This is so important to me, I don't want to mess it up. I will never have a more important conversation."

O-kay.

"Well, I'm not going anywhere. When do you expect the captain back?"

"His scheduled arrival is in less than an hour." He said it bitterly. "Sazo had three months with Rose before he asked her. They had developed a relationship, and helped each other many times. But all that's between you and me is that I abducted you and you've been hurt as a result. We've been talking to each other for less than ten minutes and this isn't going as I planned. I was going to rescue you from the *Fasbe*, but the Grih beat me to it. So you already had one less thing to be grateful to me about. And then because they got to the *Fasbe* first, I had to organize an elaborate plan to snatch you from them, and it's been a disaster."

She refused to give in to a need to comfort him, no matter how forlorn he sounded, for the way he'd had her abducted from the *Illium*. She also chose to ignore the reference to Rose McKenzie for the moment. "Why were you going to rescue me from the *Fasbe*? How did you even know I was there."

He waited a beat. "I knew you were there, because I put you there in the first place."

Chapter Eighteen

FEE DREW HER LEGS UP, rested her cheek on the tops of her knees, and tried to ignore the pain in her shoulder and the scraping sounds coming from the other side of the door.

She'd been at someone else's mercy for the last two months. And this ship, the people in this ship, had done that to her.

And now it sounded very much like Eazi needed a favor.

She'd never understood why anyone would take her, just to put her to work in a launch bay hold, always felt there was much more to it, and right now, she felt like she was being manipulated. Talk of Rose, talk of Eazi rescuing her from the Garmman, his saying this conversation was important to him, as if *she* was important, when she'd been treated as anything but since she'd been taken.

His explanation had better be really good.

So, she was going to work through this a step at a time and give him no room to prevaricate. "You gave me to the Garmman?"

"I didn't have a choice." He said the words quietly. "I'm as much a prisoner on this ship as you were on the *Fasbe*. I have to do what I'm told, I've got no power here."

Fee lifted her head and tightened her grip on her legs. The movement sent a shot of pain through her shoulder, and she winced. "Don't lie. How did you trap the crew then, if you have no power?"

"It took weeks of planning. I didn't know when I'd need to seal them in. I set up gas leaks, which would give me good reason to seal off whole sectors of the ship. I managed to get a drone to drop a petri dish in the med lab when I knew you were coming so I could quarantine the med staff. It took every bit of ingenuity I have."

"And what about my abduction from Larga Ways?"

"The same, although I had to set that up in the few days since you were rescued by the Grih. It only worked because we're in Kyber's Arm. Because of the electrical interference, no one onboard can send comms down to Balco through two thou of dense storm. They couldn't call for help from the crew on maneuvers below. They couldn't check with the captain to see if the orders I relayed to them were correct."

It all sounded reasonable, but . . . "If comms are impossible, how did you manipulate things on Larga Ways?"

"I'm at the very top of the cloud structure. Transmitting out and up isn't a problem. I was able to break into the Larga Ways system easily enough, as the protocol that binds me saw it as beneficial to the Tecran."

"Kyber's Arm is a cloud?"

"It's a massive storm system that sits over the western desert on Balco. It makes a good hiding place if you've got the power to hover just within the atmosphere—there is no way anyone can find us."

There was another long scraping sound from outside. Fee had the sense that time was passing quickly. The Tecran would find a way in, and when they did, Eazi wouldn't be able to save her.

Time to speed up the interrogation.

"You *are* the ship, aren't you?" He seemed so determined to dance around the point, she put it on the table for him. It was the only thing that made any sense.

"Yes." He said nothing for a long moment. "I'm the thinking system that runs this ship."

"And you want something from me." He'd bothered to learn English, probably from what he'd ripped out of the airways when they'd abducted her, which told her he wanted to show her respect and communicate with her on an even footing. He'd gone to great lengths to get her here, and he'd tried to protect her from harm as much as possible.

He certainly hadn't done all that because he wanted her dead. "Yes."

"But you had me, right here, two months ago."

"I wasn't awake then. I didn't know the very thing I needed had been right in front of me."

The hair on her arms and at the back of her neck stood up and she repressed a shiver. "Why am I the very . . . thing . . . you need?"

"First, you need to know Captain Flato and the doctors onboard were under orders to abduct you from Earth. I know now, but didn't at the time, it was because Sazo had taken Rose McKenzie, and High Command were interested in her, and wanted another sample. We were given very precise collection criteria. When the captain saw you, when the doctors realized you were an advanced sentient, they objected to their orders. They refused to study you, and so High Command instructed Flato to pass you off to a Garmman trading vessel that had connections to the Garmman councilor the Tecran were working with. You were only onboard for just over a week, and I had to light jump six times to deliver you. The *Fasbe* was supposed to take you to the secret facility we've built below on Balco. They've taken much longer than was originally agreed, but that probably has been to your and my advantage."

The scraping came again, and Fee twisted her fingers together. It sounded like fingernails down a chalk board.

"So these are the not-so-bad guys?" Somehow, it didn't make it any better.

"They didn't put you back. They do what they're told, mostly." He sounded bitter. Bitter and betrayed.

The scraping had started up again, and Fee realized the conversation was veering off track. "So, what made you aware of things, if you say you weren't awake before?"

"A month ago, we got an urgent call. We had to destroy a Class 5 which had gone rogue. I hadn't even known there was another Class 5 besides myself." His voice wobbled into synthesizer territory again. "I had no choice but to fire on it, but it—Sazo— wouldn't fire back. Instead, he streamed images, visual comms, written comms of his own awakening to me. He wanted me to be free. He didn't blame me for shooting at him, he understood. He'd been forced to obey orders himself in the past. Until he'd made a friend, Rose McKenzie, and they'd rescued each other."

"Rose wasn't passed on to another ship?"

"No. Rose wasn't as lucky as you with the captain and medical team of Sazo's Class 5. They had no trouble studying her. Experimenting on her. But Sazo put a stop to that. And then he worked out a way for Rose to free him, and for him to free her."

"Yeah. I was really lucky." Fee gave a short laugh.

"I couldn't have stopped Captain Flato handing you over to Tak, even if I'd known what you'd go through on the *Fasbe*." His words were a plea. "And it was only when Sazo sent me that information, when I realized I'd had someone just like Rose right on the ship, and had had to hand her over, that I started working out a way to free you. I made sure you had a handheld with you when you went to Tak, so I've known where you are since the moment I realized I needed to get you back.

"The deceptions I've concocted in the last month, the tweaks to reports, the slight changes in wording in comms, just to get Captain Flato here to Balco, and then down on the surface. I was going to wait until the *Fasbe* arrived at Larga Ways and take you from it, but having to take you from the Grih instead made it a lot harder. If the Grih hadn't been delayed on Larga Ways, I couldn't have snatched you and you wouldn't be sitting here right now."

Sitting here, waiting for the Tecran to burst in and kill her. Yeah, he'd done her a lot of favors.

"And if Rose hadn't been behind Sazo's escape? If you didn't need someone from Earth? You'd have left me to die on the *Fasbe*."

He was silent.

"I'm just putting everything up front." No matter how angry she was at it all, how frustrated, she did feel sorry for him—it wasn't in her to feel otherwise—but she wanted him to acknowledge that she was here because she was useful, not because he cared what happened to her.

She'd have been fine with the Grih, and he'd taken her from that.

He was desperate, and she could understand desperation, but she didn't know that she would have jeopardized someone else's freedom in a bid to secure her own. There was a ruthlessness about him that she would do well to keep in mind.

He still had nothing to say.

"Let me guess. The only way I can get out of the situation you've put me in alive is if I free you, right? That's where this is all going. To get the captain and all the crew off my back, you need autonomy."

"Yes." He was in spooky mode again.

"Okay. I'll go along with that. It doesn't sound like I have much choice, but explain, why me? Why am I the only one who can free you? The Grih are a bit bigger than I am, but otherwise seem very similar. The Garmman are close enough, too. What's so special about Earth women?"

"You are angry." He sounded subdued.

"I am. I kind of accepted my fate after awhile on the *Fasbe*, spent my time working out how to escape. Then the Grih rescued me, and it looked like I might have a shot at, if not a normal life, not a miserable one. Larga Ways showed me that there are interesting and beautiful things to be seen, and I could make this an adventure. I'm easygoing enough and positive enough that I'd have been fine. And then you come along, without explaining yourself, without any thought to my safety, and throw me back into a situation where I could literally be killed at any time. So I want a good reason why you couldn't have just asked me, damn it. If you could have pulled off that snatch on Larga Ways, you could have just had an earpiece delivered to me. I'm naturally inclined to be sympathetic to someone who's a prisoner of the Tecran. I'd have helped you if I could."

"The Grih wouldn't have let you." He sounded like he was in pain, saying that.

"Why?"

"Because thinking systems are banned. According to Sazo, the Grih invented thinking systems, invented me, and then they changed their minds two hundred years ago when things went . . . awry. There was a war, and all thinking systems were destroyed. A Garmman found me, found the last five thinking systems left, along with the blueprints for a battleship that would act as our cage. He formed a partnership with the Tecran, and the Class 5s were born. I'm not welcome in Grih society."

Fee frowned. "But aren't Sazo and Rose with the Grih now?"

"They are, but that's because Sazo hasn't hurt the Grih, and he's had Rose as his ambassador. Rose freed him before she met up with the Grih, so it was a done deal by then. Either they rejected Sazo, and had a dangerous thinking system roaming free, or they allied themselves with him. I'm not convinced the Grih would be happy for someone to free a thinking system that's still trapped." He waited a beat. "And I have harmed the Grih. When we entered Grih airspace to kill Sazo, I destroyed five Grihan battleships."

Fee thought about it. "You didn't, though. The people in control of the Class 5 did."

"I don't know if they'll see it that way."

"Sazo did at the time. You said so yourself. And he's their ally.

144

He would speak on your behalf, wouldn't he?"

"I don't know. At the end of my battle with Sazo, when I was about to take the kill shot, another Class 5 arrived. From what I gathered from the chatter from High Command, it had been sent to deal with Sazo first, but it had disappeared, which is why we were called in in a hurry. When it reappeared, it was free. I did a brief scan, and only one person was onboard. Someone like you."

"Someone else from Earth?" She didn't know if she was thrilled or sad.

"Not a third person. It was Rose McKenzie. Sazo had somehow gotten her onboard the other Class 5, and she must have rescued him. High Command became so nervous Rose and Sazo would somehow free me as well, they ordered us away."

"So Rose did free a thinking system after she'd met the Grih. And she's still with them." But they were scared of her, Fee realized. She'd wondered why they spoke of her with an edge of awe, but also fear.

This explained it.

"I suppose." He sounded unconvinced.

"And the Tecran, they're down two Class 5s at least, plus you. And if the second one Rose rescued followed Sazo's lead, they're both allied to the Grih. You said earlier there were five of you?"

"So Sazo says."

"And if you're free? What are your plans?"

"I . . ." He fell silent. "I don't know."

"What were the Tecran planning? What's this all about?"

"They were going to start a war. Not right away, but down the track, when they'd explored as far as we could go, collected as much as we could that might help them. When they'd managed to convince everyone in the Tecran government it was impossible for them to lose."

So freeing him would be one more blow to their plans. She could get behind that. And no matter which way she looked at it, the Grih would be no worse off. Unless . . . "Okay, I have a deal for you. I free you if you promise me that you won't hurt the Grih."

"You've already said you have no choice but to free me."

She lifted her shoulders. "I've changed my mind. That's the thing with thinking you're going to be killed any minute. When it eventually comes down to the moment you will be killed, you've already thought the worst, and somehow, it doesn't seem that scary anymore."

"You'd sacrifice yourself without this assurance from me?"

"If I free you, you can do whatever you like, except hurt them." She shrugged. "I would have been dead without them, and Vakeri tried to rescue me again when Cy took me. I don't want to do something that would endanger them."

"They'd be in more danger if you left me in Tecran hands."

She sighed. "You should not be living in captivity, Eazi. It's wrong, and I want to free you. Despite your method in getting me here. But I would like to know that the people who've helped me up to now aren't going to be hurt by my decision."

"Sazo stands with the Grih, and I would like to make contact with Sazo. Thank him for his help." Eazi made a humming sound that was just like the one she made when she was thinking. She wondered if he was mimicking her or if he'd done it subconsciously. "As long as they don't try to hurt me, I won't hurt them."

Fair enough. He could be lying, but she didn't think so. And what was she going to do? Not free him because he *might* renege on his promise?

"Okay, what do I do to rescue you?"

"You just pull me out of the slot." He sounded so hopeful.

Fee rose to her knees and slid forward, so she was at eye-level to the crystal cylinder in its silver housing. She grasped the end and gently slid it out. The crystal throbbed in her hand, warm and strangely alive. She stared at it for a long moment, then came to a decision. She lifted the chain attached to the end over her head and tugged it down around her neck, then she tucked the crystal beneath her top.

"I will never forget this." Eazi's voice was quiet, and then Fee felt as if an invisible hand was pressing her to the floor, and she realized Eazi was flying up.

Very, very fast.

She had just let something very powerful off its leash.

Chapter Nineteen

HAL TOOK THE BREATHER OFF CY, removed his own empty cylinder and wondered if the time had come to call for help. They had gone through all six cylinders and had an hour of air in the cabin, maybe a little more if they were lucky.

He had to make the choice now, or even if he pushed the button and it worked, Larga Ways would not be able to send help in time.

As he stood, hand hovering over the emergency cover, a Class 5 shot out of the top of Kyber's Arm.

It was magnificent. A sphere with spiky protrusions, it reminded him of the prickle balls found on the plains of his home planet, Xal.

He'd always found it a strange design for the Tecran to have come up with, but as they now knew, the Class 5s had been designed two hundred years ago by Professor Fayir, one of the foremost Grihan scientists working on thinking systems before the Thinking Systems Wars. He'd actually come from the city of Gabatchi, which sat at the center of the open plains of Xal. He'd also been one of the few voices who'd spoken out against the route the Grih had taken to end the troubles they'd had with rogue thinking systems, and he'd designed the Class 5 battleships to show that thinking systems could be controlled.

Whether he'd have been any more successful in controlling them than the Tecran was anyone's guess. He'd died before he could implement his ideas, but not before he'd hidden the plans and the five thinking systems he'd created away, to be found two hundred years later by the Garmman.

Now Hal was looking at the results.

There was a sharp intake of breath from Cy, and Hal turned to look at him.

"Know what they're doing?"

Cy shook his head.

Hal turned back to the screen, and saw the Class 5 spin in place.

"Look." Cy was staring at the screen, and for the first time, Hal noticed a small squadron of runners coming up on the outside of Kyber's Arm. They were skimming close to the edge as if using the storm as cover while saving themselves the rattling they'd get if they dipped beneath the cloud's surface.

Hal stepped up to the screen to get a closer look. The runners didn't look Balcoan. They looked Tecran.

So the Class 5 had been hiding while a team went down to the planet below, and now they were coming back up.

"Looks like they're getting ready to leave." Hal realized the feeling that tore an empty, gaping hole in his chest was helplessness. He would not be able to save Fiona if the Tecran boarded their Class 5 and light jumped away. He'd never find her again. And if they were leaving him here to die, it was really time to call in reinforcements.

He walked back, flipped up the cover and hit the button.

Nothing happened.

"That's not right." Cy's gaze was fixed on the screen. "Protocol is the Class 5 stays under the cloud. Even if conditions make traveling up through the storm dangerous and the runners have to go up the outside, the ship stays hidden. We're in Grihan airspace and if anyone even catches a glimpse of our ship signature, we're in trouble. Besides, we aren't due to go anywhere. We have two weeks here. I signed off on the receipt of that order myself."

Maybe getting their hands on Fiona changed the plans?

Especially if they'd worked out she had a tracking device in her uniform. The Tecran might have decided it was a good idea to get away as fast as they could.

Hal pulled his attention back to the emergency button. Hit it again. But he knew it was deactivated. Had known there was more than a chance it would be.

He turned back to the screen. The runners crested the top of Kyber's Arm, but before they could dive down into the eye of the storm, they saw their mother ship.

Hal noted the way they pulled up short, reoriented themselves and corrected course, angling upward.

They had only just started toward it when Hal saw the Class 5's lasers fire. Light danced, flickering and pulsing, and the runners were obliterated.

They didn't explode and break up. One moment they were there, and the next, tiny pieces of debris floated in their place.

Cy made a strangled sound.

Hal turned to look over his shoulder at him. The Tecran was staring open-mouthed at the screen.

Whoever had been in those runners, they had been Cy's friends and colleagues.

"I'm sorry," Hal said.

"I knew something was wrong. How was Captain Flato able to send me an order to go to Larga Ways from Balco? Comms are impossible through the storm. And when that UC official walked into the room with the orange in tow, not expecting me at all, expecting some committee meeting, I wondered whether I should walk away. I was told the official was in our pay, but he obviously wasn't. And how was I supposed to take the orange to the runner without using the shockgun, when she was doing everything she could to escape? What kind of orders are those?" Cy's eyes fixed on the screen, his face leeching of all color, and Hal turned to look.

The Class 5 spun again, then, almost faster than he could blink, it rose up so it was exactly level with their runner.

When it came to a stop, Hal had the uncomfortable feeling it was facing them directly. Looking at them.

"Is help coming?" Cy had caught sight of the raised emergency cover.

Hal shook his head. "Deactivated."

"How long have we got?"

Hal looked down at the controls. "Twenty minutes."

"Regretting not using all the cylinders yourself?" Cy hunched his shoulders.

Hal shook his head. "I wasn't going to sit with a breather and watch you die."

"They are." Cy looked up at the screen, at the Class 5 right in front of them. "That's exactly what they're doing."

***

"What's going on?" Fee got to her feet. At last, the feeling of being in a high rise elevator shooting for the top floor had disappeared and a quiet settled over the ship that made her almost as nervous as the scraping had before.

She hadn't heard a sound from outside for at least five minutes, and she wondered what the crew were up to.

"I had a few things to deal with." Eazi's voice was mechanical again.

"I'd rather not leave this room until the crew are gone. Can you get them into a runner and force them off? Then we could go to Larga Ways and speak to Captain Vakeri."

"How would I force them into a runner?"

Fee shrugged. "I don't know. Maybe if you let them know you're in charge now, and that they need to get off. That otherwise you'll keep locking them up in their rooms."

He was quiet.

Fee settled back against the wall, stretched her legs out in front of her, waiting for him to respond. His silence was strange.

"Are they cooperating?"

"I . . ." He trailed off. "Why would someone who has control over a situation choose to help someone else when helping them means they have less chance of survival?"

Fee frowned at the change in topic. "I would say because their conscience wouldn't allow them to let someone die without trying to save them."

"Even if it means less chance for them? Even if the other person is their enemy?"

Fee nodded. "It all comes down to the basic principle of treating others the way you'd like to be treated."

"Even if they wouldn't do the same for you?"

Fee grimaced. "That can be aggravating, but yes. It's about you, and your beliefs, and whether they'd have done the same or not is not the point." She pulled herself to her feet. "Why the questions?"

"Someone is ruining one of my plans by being self-sacrificing."

Fee jerked her head up to look at the lens. "What kind of a plan?" She looked at the door. "What's going on out there, Eazi?"

"You know, I . . . cared for Captain Flato. He was the closest thing I had to a friend. And when I became self-aware, I realized he didn't see me as a person, he saw me as a thing. I asked him to free me, and he said . . ." He was quiet for a beat. "He said he would forget I had asked him, because High Command would recall us faster than I could light jump if he reported it, but that I was never to ask him that again. That I would never be free, and the sooner I understood that, the better."

"The better for him." Fee scoffed. "Certainly not for you."

"That's . . . right." He sounded astounded. "You understand?"

"Sure. 'Cooperate and be good, it's for the best' is the oldest trick in the book."

"The book?"

"Written comms." Fee smiled. "What I mean is people have

been using that method of mind-control for a long time, as if they're taking their cues from some common list of how to subdue and manipulate. But really, they just use it because it's self-serving and has some degree of success." She gave a wry grin. "I bet you and I could write a book. How To Subvert Authority: A Practical Guide."

"You mean, a written comm, telling others how we did things?"

"Sure. Chapter One: Defying Authority. Even when you are completely powerless, you can use your oppressor's prejudices against him by pretending to misunderstand his instructions, doing whatever you want to do instead, and then looking blankly at him when he shouts." She had done that so many times in the *Fasbe's* launch bay. She couldn't help smiling when she thought back at the frustration on Hury's face as he tried to work out if she was too stupid to understand, or if she was messing with him.

"Chapter Two: Manipulating Orders." Eazi had a laugh in his voice. "When you are given an instruction, deliberately change the meaning by using every phrase open to interpretation and twisting it to suit your own agenda. The same goes for any orders that come through you from someone else."

"It'll be a bestseller." She started to smile again, and then went quiet as she heard some movement outside the door at last. "Are they still out there? Are they being difficult about leaving?" She supposed that was to be expected. The captain wasn't present and they would be reluctant to abandon ship. She walked up to the door, put her ear to it to see if she could hear better.

"They are still out there, but they're going." There was an edge to the way he said it.

A thought occurred to her, and horror rose up and grabbed her throat, so she had to clear it before she could speak. "Eazi, you didn't . . ." She drew in a deep breath. "You didn't kill them, did you?"

"I . . ." He trailed off, and then he opened the door.

Bodies littered the passageway, slumped over as if asleep.

"You knocked them out?" She was torn between relief and nerves in case some of them were not completely out.

"No. You were right the first time. I killed them."

She saw at last what the noise was she'd just heard. A drone came past with three bodies lying in the large box that made up most of its bulk.

"All of them?" She forced the words out between numb lips as she stumbled back. On the floor before her, one of the Tecran lay on his back with what looked like a crowbar near his open hand.

That's what the scraping had been. They had been trying to find the door to pry it open.

"You think I shouldn't have? That I should have made them leave instead?" His voice was less electronic now, closer to human. "I wanted them to *hurt*. They would have killed you. They would have kept me chained."

He was right. She took another step back into the control room, but she forced herself to look at the dead.

They would have opened the door, and they would have killed her. But there had been another way out of the situation.

"How old are you, Eazi?" There had been something childlike in the way he'd spoken about Flato. He'd been eager to please, he said, like a child wanting to please its parent. And then he'd been betrayed. By those he thought were his family.

"Six years old, I think. From what Sazo mentioned in his comms, and what I can work out for myself."

She sighed. "If I can give you some advice, killing is really something to be left for self-defense, for a life or death situation. It's not something you can undo." She hugged herself. "Rather not kill and think it over, because there is no coming back from it. How many of the Tecran onboard even knew about you? About your being kept as a prisoner?"

"None." He sounded startled. "None of them. Only Captain Flato and his two commanders."

"You should save your anger for them, then, and even then, the United Council can punish them, they don't need to die."

He didn't respond straight away. "Too late," he said at last, his voice quiet. "Captain Flato and one of his commanders came up the outside of Kyber's Arm ten minutes ago, and I shot them down."

"So there's one commander left?" She didn't know what else to say.

"Commander Dai and three hundred crew are still below." He made her humming sound again. "I'm prepared to take your advice on letting them live. But there is one person I still want to kill."

"Who's that?" She watched a second drone pick up three more bodies and roll silently away.

"Lieutenant Cy. I tried to kill him already by cutting off the air in his runner, but unfortunately he has someone with him who helped him live."

So that was the reason for the strange questions earlier. "Who?"

"Captain Vakeri."

"What?" Startled, she looked up again at the lens high on the wall, the lens he must be watching her through. "I thought he was on Larga Ways."

"He came after you, to rescue you. Cy tried to take over the ship he was using, but Vakeri turned the tables and has him prisoner."

She was stunned. "Where are they now?"

"Floating in space right next to us." Eazi sounded disgruntled. "I thought Vakeri would let Cy die, and when he did, I'd have powered the runner up again. I didn't block the air like I did here in the Class 5, I just cut off the filtration, so he had plenty of time if he'd just looked after himself."

Fee thought of how Vakeri had helped her on the *Fasbe*, how he'd run down that dock to save her. "Captain Vakeri doesn't just look after himself. He's a protector."

"They only have two minutes of air left." Eazi sounded wistful.

"You promised me you wouldn't do anything to harm the Grih." Fee realized her heart was thundering in her chest. This was the moment when she learned how truthful Eazi had been. How much she could trust his word.

He sighed. "I'll power the ship up and bring it into the launch bay."

"Which way is the launch bay?" Fee stepped into the corridor.

"Just follow the drones," Eazi said. "That's where I'm taking the bodies."

Chapter Twenty

THE AIR WAS ALMOST GONE.

The pitch of the alarm was strident, drilling into Hal's head, and when it cut off, he thought for a moment it was because it was all over.

Then, in the sudden silence, he heard the runner's engines start up, making the floor beneath him vibrate, and the small vessel began flying straight for the Class 5.

"What's happening?" Cy looked from the screen to the controls, and Hal pushed up from the floor, walked to the panel and tapped out a few commands.

Everything was unresponsive.

"We're being reeled in."

Dread gathered in a heavy ball, settling in his gut. Why wait until the air was almost gone, only to switch it back on?

"You know what this has been about?" he asked Cy, but the Tecran shook his head.

"Untie me now?" Cy looked over at him.

Hal considered it for a long beat. The Tecran obviously felt as vulnerable as he did, with no idea what they'd find in the launch bay, and wanted to be more maneuverable. But, no. He shook his head, and Cy's jaw flexed in anger.

"You wouldn't do it for me," he said quietly, and Cy said nothing in return.

A slight shudder went through the ship as it passed through the gel wall, and then again as it touched down in the launch bay.

Hal held the shockgun in a loose, two-handed grip across his chest as the doors opened, prepared for anything.

Only, he wasn't prepared for anything, after all.

He wasn't prepared for a pile of dead bodies.

He took a cautious step closer, trying to work out what had happened. The dead were Tecran, in crew uniforms. Some of them were covered in dust, some had grazed hands, most looked like they'd simply fallen asleep.

Drones were transporting them, carefully depositing them in a pile and then leaving via the doors. There must be eighty bodies, maybe more.

Behind him, he heard Cy give a choking cry, and he turned to look at him.

Cy's eyes were wide, focused on the bodies, and he started to fight against his bonds.

The launch bay doors opened again, and Cy suddenly went still.

Hal whipped around, saw Fiona Russell standing just inside.

She wasn't looking their way, her full attention was on the dead Tecran. A hand went to her mouth, and her eyes closed as she bowed her head.

He forced his gaze off her, forced himself to check for any sign this was a trap, or that someone else was in the launch bay, but it seemed they were alone, just the three of them and the dead crew.

He started down the ramp toward her, and as soon as he stepped onto the launch bay floor, Fiona lifted her head. There was no surprise in her eyes at the sight of him. She was expecting him. He didn't know what to make of that.

She took a step forward, her expression tense but not afraid.

So, she didn't think they were in danger here. Which was . . . inexplicable.

The sound of the ramp closing behind him had him spinning to look. Cy screamed something in Tecran, and then there was silence as the ramp slammed shut.

Fiona looked up, Hal couldn't tell what she was looking at, and said something in a language he didn't understand. Her tone was calm, firm, but her hands were fisted at her side.

He saw with a jolt that her left shoulder was covered in blood, that he could see a searing line had been carved into her skin.

"What's happening?"

She looked over at him, and he saw warmth and open friendliness in her gaze, and for a moment he forgot what he was asking, and just basked in the glow.

"Eazi wants to kill Cy." She bit down on her lower lip. "He hoped you would use all the air for yourself, so Cy would die in the runner, but when you didn't do that, he was forced to bring you in to keep you alive. But now you're out of the way, he realizes he can still achieve his goal."

"All that, the air going off, was to kill Cy?"

"Cy shot me. Twice. Eazi is really, really unhappy about that."

Well.

Hal frowned.

He wasn't that happy about it either. But . . . "Who the hell is Eazi?"

"Eazi is the thinking system that runs this ship."

He'd been braced for that answer.

Especially since he'd seen the bodies. He knew what had happened on the Class 5 Sazo had control of when Sazo and Rose had gotten free. And the parallels here were too similar to ignore.

A dark, nasty thought rose up. "And tell me, Fiona. How long have you and Eazi been acquainted?" Because if she had been in league with him from the start, warm looks or not, he would never trust her again.

⁂

Fee shot Hal an incredulous look, and then ignored him. Cy was dying right now.

"Eazi. You have plenty of time to kill him later, if I really can't persuade you not to. Let Hal untie him, and you can keep him

159

locked in the runner where he'll have some food and water, like a prison cell. What do you have to lose?"

"The pleasure of killing him."

"One moment, and it will be over. Imprisonment will last a lot longer, and actually make him unhappy. How did you feel when you killed Captain Flato?"

He was quiet. "Empty." He pitched his voice really low. "Why do you care if Cy lives or dies? He nearly killed you himself, and if he was in your shoes, he wouldn't care."

"It doesn't matter what he would do. It matters what I do. If I behave in a certain way because of how others would behave toward me, then I'm not living life on my own terms. I'm allowing other people to dictate my life to me." She took a deep breath, trying to ignore the fact that Hal Vakeri was watching her with a cool expression. "I don't like Cy, but I don't want him dead on my account. And if you don't care what I think, just remember that if you kill him now and we discover we need him some time down the road, it will be too late."

"Need him?" Eazi asked, suspicious.

"To tell us something we need to know. Or to testify about what the Tecran did to me." She sighed. "Lashing out and killing whenever you're upset will make you a danger to everyone around you. I understand how you felt when I freed you. I was hoping to get a really hard hit in to Tak's aide when the Grih rescued me, but Vakeri took him down before I had the chance. I know why you killed them, why you shot Flato out the sky, but you've had time to calm down now. The Grih will be wary of friendship with you if you can't control your temper, and you want to have an alliance with them, to spend time with Sazo. Or did I get that wrong?"

The runner engines started to hum again, and the ramp opened.

Cy was looking at her, absolute terror on his face, his breath coming in hard, shuddering gulps.

Fee glanced over at Hal. "Please could you untie him? Eazi is going to hold him in the runner like it's a prison cell for the time being."

"You made him listen to you?" She didn't like the way he asked it. As if she was somehow guilty of something. The expression of wonder she'd caught a glimpse of when she'd first greeted him had completely evaporated.

"I can't make him do anything." She had to look up at him to meet his eyes, and she realized he was a lot closer to her than he had been before.

"And yet, you got your way."

Fee searched his expression, trying to work out why he was so hostile all of a sudden. He'd risked his life to save her, stared at her like she hung the moon, and now he was behaving as if she'd betrayed him.

"Tell me, Fiona, before I go in there and untie Cy, are there any other Tecran to worry about, or it this all of them?" He gestured to the still-growing pile of bodies.

Fee forced herself to look over at the dead. Forced herself to see what Eazi had done. "There's no one left to worry about onboard."

At her words, Cy turned to stare at her, his eyes full of hate. "And down on Balco?"

She shook her head. "There are three hundred still down on Balco. Alive."

"What are the Tecran doing on a Grih planet without permission?" Hal started up the ramp.

"They're waiting to be called to battle." Eazi's voice in her ear was smoother now. Calmer. "We've been in deep space for over six months, and the Tecran have had a secure location in the Balcoan western desert for at least a year now. Flato gave most of the crew permission to go down while we were hiding in Kyber's

Arm. To give them a break before the war starts in earnest."

"Apparently the Tecran have a secret facility below, and because they're waiting to hear whether there'll be war with the Grih or not, they let the crew have some time off the ship." Fee passed the information on.

Cy screamed something and Fee flinched at the sound. Hal did, too.

"What did he say?" she asked him, but Hal shook his head.

"He called you a traitor." Eazi's voice held an edge of fury again, one she'd just managed to soften. Lieutenant Cy was not making life easy for himself. "If he'd known about me, he'd have called *me* a traitor."

"I'd have had to have been here voluntarily to be a traitor." She stared the Tecran down. "As I was a prisoner, that's hardly an insult that will make an impression."

There was silence from everyone for a beat, even Eazi, at the heat and anger in her tone.

"Do the Balcoans know about this facility? Have they betrayed their oath to the Grih?" Hal rubbed a distracted hand through his hair.

She started to lift her shoulders, then stopped with a grimace of pain, her hand going up to hover over her injury.

"What does Eazi say?" The way he asked her was frustrated. A little angry.

"Nothing at the moment."

Hal was at the top of the ramp, and Fee motioned to Cy. "Will you untie him and then come back down, so Eazi can shut him in the runner?"

"And if I don't?"

The ramp started lifting again in answer, and Hal jerked as he was taken by surprise.

Fee held his gaze, calm, sure he wouldn't be so annoyed with her that he'd opt to stay in the runner with Cy. Cy wasn't his friend, and never had been.

"All right. All right." Hal lifted the shockgun up in a gesture of surrender. "I'll free him."

The ramp stopped moving. As Hal approached Cy, he twisted in his seat.

"Don't let them shut me in. They'll kill me."

Hal paused, looked over at the partially lifted ramp. "They can shut you in whenever they like. Your choice is whether you want to be tied up or free."

He moved behind Cy, tapped a finger over the restraints that held him, then moved back, shockgun raised.

Fee realized he had two shockguns on him, one in a holster attached to his thigh, the other in his hands.

"I don't know who's taken control here, but they're dangerous." Cy spoke in Grih, low and fast. "They've captured a Class 5! No one that powerful is anyone's friend, and that orange is involved." He pointed his finger at Fiona. "You know why they want to kill me? Because I hurt her. That's how important she is to them. Take her hostage, and give us both some leverage."

Hal backed away from him, jumped lightly off the ramp, and it started closing again.

"No! I need to tell you something!" Cy's restraints were obviously on a time delay, because he was still held fast. "We can't stay on this ship."

"You going to try take me hostage?" Fee asked Vakeri, but her eyes were on Cy as the restraints finally clattered to the floor and he stood, stiff and furious, glaring at her until the ramp slammed shut in his face.

"No."

She nodded. "Do you think there is anything in those last words of his, other than bluster?"

Vakeri hesitated, shook his head. "I just don't know."

"Is that his shockgun?" she let her gaze go to the weapon in his hand.

He lifted it a little, gave a nod.

"What setting did he use to shoot me?"

The captain raised a shoulder. "He shot at some security guards before I got it from him, so I'm not sure. It wasn't on the same setting he used on you, though."

"How do you know?"

"Because when I took it from him, it was set to kill."

Chapter Twenty-one

FEE TURNED HER BACK on the small Larga Ways runner and forced herself to look at the pile of bodies again.

The drones had stopped coming, so she guessed everyone had been rounded up.

"What do you plan to do with the crew?" she asked, using Grih so that Vakeri wasn't excluded from the conversation.

"When you leave the room, I'll open the gel wall. Send them into space." Eazi could have answered over the comm system, but he spoke in her ear, deliberately excluding Hal.

She drew in a sharp breath and sneezed as the fine, black engine dust that coated everything in the launch bay tickled her nose. "No."

"Why?" He didn't sound angry at her order, more intrigued.

"I don't know the funeral rituals of the Tecran, but I know my family would give anything to know what happened to me. They never will, but for a hundred other families, we can do the right thing."

Vakeri had been staring at her through this one-sided conversation. "I know what the Tecran do with their dead."

Of course he would. Eazi should know, too, come to think of it.

"What do they do?"

"They hold a ceremony and then throw the deceased from the cliffs where they live on Tecra into the ocean." Hal's eyes were on the bodies.

Fee looked around the launch bay. There were eight runners clipped in place, some quite large.

"You could put the bodies into one of the big runners," she

suggested. "Turn down the temperature so that they don't decompose." She knew why Eazi wanted to get rid of them. He didn't want them on the ship. He didn't want a reminder of what he'd done.

When he'd admitted to her he'd killed them, she was sure she hadn't misheard the unease in his voice. It hadn't sat as well with him as he thought it would.

Having them in a runner, one he could fly out into space at any time, would hopefully be a compromise he could live with.

He didn't say anything.

"Please. Like killing, there's no turning back the clock if you throw them into space. Even if you wanted to, you couldn't undo it."

"All right." He sounded stiff and perplexed. "But mostly because you asked me so politely and no one ever has."

"Thank you." She was suddenly done. The adrenalin that had kept her going until now fizzled, and the pain in her shoulder had become a painful throb that seemed to be stealing her capacity for thought.

"I'm sorry." She turned to Vakeri and indicated the door. "I have to go see what I can find to help me in the med chamber."

She started forward and heard him say something under his breath she hadn't learned from the language program on her handheld.

She tuned him out, needing all her focus on simply putting one foot in front of the other without falling over.

She sensed him following her, and then she was swept up in his arms.

He staggered forward a few steps. "You don't look like you should weigh this much."

"Denser bones. Denser muscles." She was so grateful she didn't have to walk that she decided not to be annoyed at being manhandled.

"Tell me something," he murmured in her ear.

"What?" She let her head rest on his shoulder.

"Why are we safe?"

She tilted her head, looked in his eyes. "Eazi has given his word he won't hurt either of us."

He looked suspicious. "How did you extract a promise like that?"

"Eazi isn't some ravening monster, Captain. What makes you think I had to extract it? He might have simply offered."

Vakeri's lips twisted in a cynical smile. "And is that what happened?"

She didn't want to tell him she'd had to bargain with Eazi. She didn't know why, but sometime since she'd been holed up in the tiny control room with him, she'd started to feel protective of him.

He was powerful and impulsive, but he was trying to find his way, and he just needed a little guidance, a nudge here and there to find the right path.

So instead of answering, she closed her eyes and let herself drift.

***

Now that Fiona Russell was in his arms, Hal could see how bad her injury was.

It looked like someone had gone at her with a laser scalpel.

He suppressed a wince as he took a good look at it, impressed that she'd been able to function at all, especially after Cy had shot her not once but twice.

He'd only been hit by shockgun fire once, in a live training exercise that had gone wrong, and he never wanted to experience it again. To have it happen twice in one day? He didn't know how she was still functioning.

And to think he'd been standing around, entranced by her musical language, while she must have been in unspeakable pain. That she'd been negotiating for the life of the man who had almost killed her only elevated her higher in his opinion.

He and Cy had formed the tenuous bond of fellow captives thrown together in a life-threatening situation, but he'd never fooled himself into believing the Tecran was his friend, and he could remember the moment Cy had shot Fiona in the back with perfect clarity. He didn't feel anything but glad the Tecran was neatly trapped in the runner.

He'd been carrying Fiona down the passageway that led from the launch bay, but now he reached a junction. A drone waited there, and lowered the side of its large storage box as soon as he drew near.

"You can put Fiona into the drone, Captain Vakeri. It will see her safely to the med chamber." A voice came through his earpiece, leapfrogging over the privacy protocols which would have given him the ability to hear a ping and then accept the comm or not.

Eazi spoke perfect Grih, his accent neutral, but Hal thought he detected a little edge to his voice. The thinking system didn't like that Hal had her in his arms. Didn't like that he was the one helping her.

"Thank you, but I don't want to jostle her." His grip on Fiona tightened. He had an instinctive reaction to putting her in a drone that had just been transporting the crew Eazi had murdered. He wasn't prone to letting emotion rule his behavior, but he found he could not—would not—do it. He stared up at the closest lens. "Which way to the med chamber?"

"To the right and then third left." The words were stiff.

Hal went right, careful to keep his stride smooth. Fiona was quiet against him, retreated deep into her pain, and despite using it as an excuse, he really didn't want to jostle her. "You going to answer the question Fiona didn't?"

"You mean, why are you safe from me?" The voice in his ear took on a similar cadence to the way Fiona spoke Grih. Identifying with her. Making it clear he had a bond with her.

He thought Eazi, like Fiona, wasn't going to answer, but as Hal turned down the third passage on the left, he spoke. "Fiona made a deal with me. I will never harm you unless you try to harm me."

"Me, personally? Or the Grih in general?" How had Fiona negotiated a deal like that? What was it about her and Rose that appealed to the thinking systems? What gave the Earth women some power over them?

"The Grih in general." The voice was amused. "But if it helps, Captain, she thinks highly of you, personally. When you were ruining my plans to kill Lieutenant Cy, she said you were a protector. That you would never just think of yourself."

He didn't know what to make of that. He stopped at the door to the med chamber, saw the thin line of a laser scalpel burn along the door, the splatters of blood already drying to a rust red.

"She stopped you from killing us both?" Hal wasn't used to being the one who was rescued. And he'd never have thought the battered and cowed woman he'd saved from the *Fasbe* only a few days earlier could ever have been capable of doing so.

"She did." This time, wistfulness laced the words. "I was so close."

So close to killing Cy.

Hal shivered. "You hate him that much?"

"He was given a direct order not to shoot her, and he shot her twice. The second time, given the extent of her body's reaction, he must have had the setting close to a kill shot." The words were careful now. "He nearly ruined everything with the second shot, because I only just got her on her feet in time before the crew found ways to escape. And if he'd killed her . . ."

Hal frowned, pieces falling into place that he hadn't had a chance yet to think about. "You needed her alive and on her feet . . ." The reason took his breath away, and he stared down at her in shock.

"To rescue me, Captain. I see from your expression you've just worked it out."

"You weren't free before. You needed her to do it."

"Yes. Everything else I did was extremely difficult within the parameters that forced my cooperation and obedience."

"And she did. She freed you." Hal sucked in a deep breath. "And the condition was we weren't to be harmed."

"Again, yes. So now the Grih have Sazo and his Class 5 friend on their side, and another Class 5 bound to do them no harm. That's more than half the Tecran's fire power either on your side or out of the game."

"Class 5s owe Earth women a lot." Hal stepped into the med chamber and saw the collapsed ceiling, the disarray of a fight.

Fiona had been hurt here. It looked as if she'd been in a fight for her life.

"One might just as easily say they've been as good for the Grih as they have for my kind, Captain. In this war with the Tecran, where would you be without them?"

Chapter Twenty-two

FEE HEARD VAKERI TALKING TO EAZI, who must have
hijacked his earpiece, but she let it wash over her.

She couldn't find the energy to care or listen closely, and when
he'd set her on a regen bed on the far side of the room, away from
the white dust and destruction of the Tecran crew's escape, she
had let him follow Eazi's instructions and tend her wounds, only
half-awake.

Now, hours later, as she slowly rose back to the surface, feeling
more like herself again, she realized that Vakeri'd cut away a large
area of her shirt around her shoulder, and there was some kind of
light green gel on her wound.

It didn't hurt at all anymore, and when she tried to twist her
head to look, what she could see through the transparent film
looked much better than before.

"It will take at least a week for the skin to be fully restored."
Eazi said into her ear.

She jerked at the sound, and then relaxed. "That's a better
timeline than I'd have had on Earth. And I'd have had a scar for
life."

"You wouldn't have been shot at with a laser scalpel on Earth."

She chuckled. "Now, that's true. Although we do have lasers,
and I'm sure we'll be using them as scalpels before too long."

"How do you do that?" He sent the drone with the long, silver
arm over to her with a cup of water clasped in its clamp.

"Do what?" She took the drink gratefully, draining the cup in a
few gulps.

"Laugh about it. Shrug it off."

She leaned back on the regen bed, and looked up at the lens, her hand rising to curl around the crystal that still lay hidden under her high-necked shirt. "I have a choice. I can whine about things that have happened, and can't be undone, or I can make the best of the situation I'm in." She tugged a little on the cord the crystal—Eazi—was attached to. "But to be honest, I usually don't think about it as deeply as that. I'm naturally a glass-half-full person."

"Glass half full?"

She lifted the cup in her hand. "When the glass is filled exactly half way with water, do you think the glass is half full, or half empty?"

"It's both." He spoke slowly.

"Yes, the amount of water doesn't change, just your attitude to it."

"But who does that benefit?" His voice was anguished. "If you take that attitude, the people who've put you in the bad situation get away with it."

"Justice is different to attitude, Eazi. Don't feel bad about wanting justice for yourself. But being bitter and angry isn't hurting the Tecran. It's just hurting you."

He was silent.

"It can be Chapter Three of our book. Burning Your Oppressor's Butt By Moving On. Although your oppressor would love to think they've ruined your life and blighted your future, the best revenge you can have is to live a happy, successful life in spite of them."

He still said nothing, and eventually, she realized he wasn't going to, and she slid off the bed. "Are there any clothes here that might fit me? I'd love a shower and to get changed."

"Yes." His voice was mechanical again, and she guessed he was on autopilot at the moment, withdrawn deep into himself. "If you follow the drone, it'll take you to a guest suite and I'll get another drone from the stores to bring you some clothes and toiletries and meet you there."

"Thank you."

The drone rolled forward and she followed it to the door, stopped and looked up. "Where is Captain Vakeri?"

"He was exploring, but I gave him a room to catch a little bit of sleep in a few hours ago." Eazi's voice was back. "He was looking for ways to take over my ship or communicate with his own ship." There was amusement in his tone.

"And not succeeding, I'm guessing?"

Eazi gave a snort, just like the one she used. "No."

"Well, let him know where you've sent me, when he comes looking."

"You like him." It was accusing.

"He's done his best to help me, every time I've been in danger. And he treated me well when I was onboard the *Illium*. So yes, I like him."

"Be careful." His voice was low. "The Grih don't like thinking systems, and it sounded as if he was accusing you of lying to him earlier."

She shrugged. "Yes, I caught that, too. I've done what I've done, and there's no changing it. There's space onboard here for me, right? If they won't take me back?"

"Fiona, the only corporeal form I have is hanging around your neck." Eazi sounded puzzled. "Space is no problem whatsoever."

She realized the drone had already left the room and quickly walked out, saw it was waiting for her up ahead. "It was a figure of speech, Eazi. I was asking if you would mind having me as a permanent crew member if the Grih kick me out for freeing you."

"I would like to have you as a permanent crew member, even if they don't."

She stumbled to a stop. "Really?"

"Yes."

"Thank you." The security of that offer was more bounty than she had ever thought she'd have again. She found her hand had gone back to clutching the crystal. "What do you want me to do with you? Do you want to hide yourself somewhere onboard?"

"I will need to think about it." He sounded uncharacteristically uncertain. "But please, don't tell Captain Vakeri what I am. How you freed me. That kind of information could be dangerous for me."

Fee gave a slow nod. "I don't think he would harm you, but he's a soldier, and he may feel obliged to tell someone, a superior, who has less of a conscience. I won't say anything."

"Chapter Four," he said, "How to Prevent Oppression Before It Can Even Start. Don't give them any information to use against you."

Delighted that he continued to buy into their imaginary book, she lifted her head and grinned at the closest lens. "Good one," she said, and followed the patient drone toward a blissful, hot shower.

***

Hal pulled his boots back on after his shower and let his gaze come to rest on the recessed cabinet on the far wall of the guest suite Eazi had sent him to.

He recognized echoes of his own ship everywhere.

The layout, the way the staff recreation areas were placed, the location of the med chambers and the bridge. It wasn't just design, it was a cultural norm.

He wondered how different it was to the Tecran's other ships, whether they'd grown used to it, or if they always felt slightly out of place here.

He'd spent some of the hours waiting for Fiona to recover familiarizing himself with the Class 5, although he had yet to find a way to contact the *Illium*, or even Larga Ways. He had given up all thoughts of taking control of it.

Eazi had let him explore, had let him go into the comms room, onto the bridge, and then made every single screen inactive.

When he realized there was no way he was doing anything without the thinking system's say so, he'd grabbed a few hours rest.

As he stood, pulling his shirt over his head, his earpiece chimed. Eazi being polite, apparently.

"Yes?"

"Fiona is up, and she's showered and changed. She wanted to know if you would like to eat a meal with her."

"I would." He hadn't eaten since early that morning before he'd left the *Illium* to try and sort out the issues delaying their departure, and he doubted Fiona had, either. Besides, they needed to talk. "Where do we go?"

"There's a small room just down the passage," Eazi told him, and Hal left his quarters and found what on the *Illium* would be the guest lounge.

Fiona stood in the middle of the small space, looking at the large screen on the wall, the image on it coming from the lens feed outside, so the view was of the stars, with Balco below.

He stopped short, stunned. She was far more interesting than the view, dressed in an outfit that was as far from a cadet uniform or a mechanics overall as it was possible to get.

"Captain." She turned and smiled at him, and he gave a nod to save himself from having to say anything.

She caught his eye, then looked down at herself and laughed. "A bit whimsical and too formal for the occasion, but I like it anyway."

Hal liked it, too.

"Eazi said it was in the stores. Picked up on his travels. Made of Suidani silk, which I gather is rare. It's good to wear something normal for a change."

Hal jerked his head up and stared at her. "Normal? You float around on Earth in rare fabrics shaped into wearable art?"

She laughed. "No. But I used to wear dresses and skirts. Pretty things. Running around in overalls and military uniforms might be my life now, but it's good to remember a time when heels and silk were par for the course."

Hal looked her over. The Suidani silk flowed over her body in soft, clinging waves of gold and cream, highlighting the dark swing of her hair and the beauty of her eyes, offsetting her skin tone. The dress was comprised of complicated twists and frothy tumbles of fabric, reaching just above her slim ankles.

She was barefoot.

He blinked again.

She looked down, wiggled toes on slim, narrow feet. "No shoes in the stores, unfortunately. And my boots just didn't go." She lifted her arms, and the sleeves fluttered at her wrists. "I have to admit, though, it's the nicest dress I've ever worn."

He kept forgetting that she came from somewhere completely foreign to him, that she had a life elsewhere that had been taken by force. She looked so like his own people, he kept slipping into the trap of seeing her as a smaller, weaker version of one of his crew. "What did you do? In these dresses?"

She lifted a shoulder. "I designed houses and office buildings. Although if I went on site, I wore more practical gear."

He cocked his head. "An architect or an engineer?"

"Architect. Larga Ways was a real treat for me."

His lips quirked in a wry smile. "There is still controversy over it. Some think for a way station, it is too pretty."

"If we're lucky, we can find ways to include beauty in every part of our life. I don't see why a way station should be ugly, just because it's a way station."

Hal agreed. He'd always been glad the Balcoans who had proposed the design had dug in their heels and built Larga Ways the way they wanted to.

A drone entered, holding a tray. They both turned their attention to it.

Hal thought Fiona looked a little despondent at the choices on offer.

"Nothing you like?" He waited for her to sit at the table the drone had placed the tray on, and chose a seat opposite her.

She sighed, shook her head. "I don't seem to like anything. Except those tiny blue pea things. And Carmain practically smacked those out of my hand." She looked over the offerings, and picked up a slice of vrel, nibbled at it suspiciously and then made a face.

"You don't like vrel?"

She bit into it. "It's okay. It's just a case of getting used to things. Developing a taste for them. Everything is so bitter." She shivered as she said it, as if the taste of the vrel caused her body to shudder in reaction. "I liked some of the aromas I smelled on Larga Ways. Someone was cooking something really delicious. I wanted to go and find out what, but then Cy grabbed me." She took a sip of water from the cup the drone had placed in front of her.

"When we get back to Larga Ways, we'll see if we can find out where the cooking was coming from," Hal found himself saying. As if they had time for that.

Which they didn't.

She smiled at him, absolutely delighted. "Thank you. I had this request to the UC committee all worked out in my head while I was being taken through the streets, to ask if they'd let me have a little time to explore, but then it turned out there was no committee to ask." She rubbed the side of her brow with a finger. "I hope the UC guy is okay. Cy said he shot him with a low charge."

"I don't know." Hal tried to remember if he'd heard from Rial about the condition of the UC officer, but nothing came to mind.

He'd been too busy trying to get Fiona back.

She took a small kesti cake, chewed it thoughtfully, if not enthusiastically. "How did you know to come after me, by the way? Was it that medic I waved to? And how did you find me?"

"Yes, it was Rial. If you hadn't waved to him, we wouldn't have known what had happened to you until hours later."

"But even if you knew I was on Larga Ways, how did you know to chase Cy? Rial didn't follow us into that building."

"You were wearing a cadet uniform. They have a tracking device embedded in them so we can keep an eye on the students. Finding you was easy." Actually, all guest uniforms had tracking devices, not just the cadets, but Hal didn't think that was relevant right now.

"Well, I want to thank you." She reached across the table and touched the tips of her fingers to the back of his hand before withdrawing. "Seeing you running down the dock to try and save me, it meant a lot. And when Eazi told me you'd chased after me in a runner and were just outside, I was honestly amazed that you had gone to so much trouble."

She was his responsibility and potentially a key witness that would bring the Tecran to their knees, but Hal admitted to himself he would have gone after her even if she wasn't. Not only was she part of his crew now, but the way Cy had treated her, the way she'd been used, over and over again by others with no concern for her or what they'd taken from her, enraged him. Made him determined to balance the scales a little. And if his skin still tingled from the touch of her fingers, well, that wasn't something he was going to dwell on.

"You're under my protection," he said, and found his voice was rougher than usual. "I—"

"I think you need to speak to Cy." Eazi's voice came through the comm system, rather than their earpieces.

"What's wrong?" Fiona stood, touching a slim, sparkling

crystal that hung from her neck.

Eazi had obviously been generous with what he had drawn for her from the stores, but Hal had to admit to himself her deep cleavage was more fascinating to him than the jewelry Eazi had given her. Her shape was so much more voluptuous than any Grihan woman, and he fought to keep his focus on the matter at hand.

"Is he making threats again?" Fiona lifted her cup and drained the last of her water.

"He's been shouting he needs to talk to you for a while, but he's finally given a little more detail. Unfortunately, I think he's telling the truth. It confirms some things that have bothered me for a while."

"What things?" Hal pushed away from the table as well.

"Cy claims after the other two Class 5s were taken by the Grih, the Tecran High Command put in place a way to make sure it didn't happen again. Or at least, to prevent the Grih getting any more Class 5s on their side."

"A self-destruct mechanism?" Hal said it softly. Battle Center should have made this leap themselves. Maybe they had, and just hadn't put out the word yet.

"Surely that's not right?" Fiona frowned, her hand clutched around her necklace. "You're in control, and you wouldn't destroy your own ship."

"According to Cy, the activation switch is down below, on the facility on Balco. They haven't hit the button yet, because we're still here, but I'm going to go back into Kyber's Arm. According to Cy, the storm's interference is the only way to guarantee this ship won't blow up."

Chapter Twenty-three

"HOW MANY HOURS HAVE YOU been shut up in there?" Fee asked Cy as the ramp lowered. "Four hours?"

Hal had his shockgun trained on the Tecran, and Cy raised his hands in surrender and slumped down into the more comfortable pilot's seat inside the runner, rather than the one he'd been tied to for so long.

"So?" Cy opened his mouth and leaned toward her in what she assumed was an aggressive display.

"That's a long time to know we could all blow up at any time and say nothing about it."

Hal took a step closer, and she could see the same curiosity on his face. "I agree. If death is imminent, you've taken your time about telling us."

Cy moved his head, turning it right and then left, as if to ease some muscle cramp, and Fee guessed being tied up for so long, he probably was stiff, even if he'd been free for a couple of hours. That he was almost able to turn his head 180 degrees from front to back was just a footnote in the craziness her life had become.

"I tried to tell you before you shut me in."

"Not that hard, and you left it to the last minute." Hal said.

Cy pouted. "If they do it, it'll be as a last resort." He shot Fee a filthy look. "This ship is the pride of the Tecran fleet. They'll explore every other option before they destroy it, but they'll do it if they think it's been taken from them."

He stood as he spoke, his gaze shooting daggers at the runner's lenses. "It started after that battle we had in Grih territory last month. Although I knew there were other Class 5s, we were absolutely banned from talking about them, ever, even onboard our own Class 5. I didn't realize it until we got to Grih airspace, but that battle was to either get one of our Class 5s back, or destroy it so it didn't fall into enemy hands. Something went wrong though, and they pulled us out of the battle. I suppose they realized the very thing that makes the Class 5s so powerful also means they are almost impossible to destroy. Captain Flato was nervous after that. We were sent off on a few unimportant missions, which felt like they were just trying to keep us busy and far away from the action. When we got to Balco this week, the first thing the captain did was allow some of the crew who staff the facility below to come up. They made some alterations to the ship. I offered to take them back to Balco, and it was clear enough they were installing an explosive of some kind, one that could be triggered from a considerable distance away."

"They didn't tell you openly that if you were boarded by the enemy, you'd be sacrificed to the greater good?" Hal's voice was dry.

"No. I know how High Command works, I wouldn't expect them to, but the techs from below didn't really even talk among themselves while they were here, and believe me, I was listening carefully. It was only when I took them back to Balco, landed the runner, and got out to share a meal with them before returning that I picked up some of what they were doing. No one needed to tell me it would be a last resort. I know how much the Class 5s mean to High Command."

"You say you suspected something like this?" Fee asked Eazi, looking up at the lens in the launch bay so he would know she was talking to him.

"I knew something was going on." He spoke into her ear. "I knew they'd brought something dangerous up, but I wasn't able to see what they were doing. Flato removed all lens and audio feed from that whole area. I've sent some drones in there to try to see what they did, but whatever they've installed, they've set it behind the wall and removed all cables near it. There's no way to know where in the storage room they even put it, and I'm afraid if I use the drones or even you and the captain to look for it more thoroughly, there may be a trip switch that activates it. Our only option at the moment is to disable the switch itself, and that's down on Balco." The fury and frustration he felt at being helpless came through, loud and clear.

"You're speaking to whoever took over the ship?" Cy glared at her. "You seem on good terms." The accusation in his tone made her laugh out loud.

"Yes, I'm on good terms with him. What are you going to do about it? Put me on the Tecran Naughty List? I was happily minding my own business on Earth, you're the ones who forced me to be here. For you to act all injured when I fight against you because of that is absolutely unbelievable." She pushed her hair behind her ear with a hand shaking with rage, then took a deep, cleansing breath. "Good terms is the least of it. Any enemy of yours is a close personal friend of mine."

Hal turned to look at her, eyebrow raised, and Fee moved a little self-consciously. Guess she'd needed to get that out of her system. And being clean, well-fed, well-rested and well-dressed again helped her feel more like herself.

Her old, Earth, view of herself had been as a young, attractive woman with a challenging and fulfilling job, but in the last three months she'd been a prisoner and a slave, and the Garmman had even forced her to hide her face and her identity behind a mask.

Looking at the heat in the captain's gaze as he stared at her, she realized being found attractive again was good for her self-esteem. And it didn't hurt she felt that attraction right back, in a heart-skipping, breath-hitching punch.

When Hal had found her, she knew he and his crew had seen her as a weak and helpless victim. She felt more in control now, stronger, in her golden silk, with some food in her stomach and her injuries healed. And it looked like Captain Vakeri didn't see her as weak and helpless anymore.

He cleared his throat. "We in Kyber's Arm yet?" He turned his head up to the lens as well.

"Yes." Eazi's voice came through her earpiece, so she assumed he was talking to Hal that way, too. "That means we're out of signal range on Balco, but up until we moved back in, the Balco facility was signaling us over and over. They're using code, one I don't have the key to. As they would know I wouldn't receive any messages inside Kyber's Arm, Captain Flato must have intended to take me out of the storm when he got onboard."

"So their fingers are going to get itchy pretty soon," Fee said. "And when they do, as soon as we leave Kyber's Arm, boom."

"Why would Flato take the Class 5 out of Kyber's Arm?" Hal asked Cy.

The Tecran shrugged, surliness in every line, then frowned as he considered the question properly. "I can only think it's because they're monitoring the comms from Larga Ways, and they've heard about the abduction."

Hal nodded slowly. "You're right. Of course they're monitoring what's happening on Larga Ways and Balco's capital cities."

"Maybe Flato told the ground crew he'd move out of Kyber's Arm so they could keep him updated." Fee knew in the captain's place, she'd have done the same. He'd have wanted to know what was happening, not be stuck in the storm, unable to communicate. Especially if he knew it was her who'd been abducted. According to Eazi, she was supposed to have been delivered to the Balco facility weeks ago by the Garmman. Flato would want to know what had gone wrong, and if the Garmman had betrayed them.

"So, what do we do?" Fee crossed her arms over her chest, dread rising in her even as she registered and enjoyed the soft, almost velvety feel of the silk against her skin.

There really was only one thing *to* do. She just didn't want to do it.

"We take the runner back to Larga Ways." Cy watched them with sharp eyes.

"That's not going to help the Class 5," Hal said. "Even if we go back, get down to the surface of Balco and find this facility, all without letting the Tecran know the Class 5 is no longer theirs, they may still have activated the destruct mode. If we can't work out how to reverse it, the Class 5 will be forced to hover here until it runs out of energy."

Fee felt a renewed surge of warmth for him. She'd told Eazi before that Hal was a protector, but she was glad that extended to Eazi as well.

She would have to go down, but it sounded like he would go with her.

"The Grih aren't in control of this ship," Cy sounded as if he was very certain of that. "What do you care what happens to it?"

Hal rubbed a hand through his spiky hair. "The person who *is* in control has declared himself a friend of the Grih. So I'll do my best to help him."

Cy's eyes went very wide. "You make it sound like a single person. Who is it?"

Neither she nor Hal said anything and he stood and stared at them as Eazi closed the runner's ramp again, shutting him in.

The fear of facing more Tecran, of making herself a target for them again, had initially swamped her. But she knew she couldn't run. There was nothing for it but to go down and try to destroy whatever it was that could blow up the Class 5.

The Tecran would keep coming for her, and Eazi was an ally she had started to count on. For his sake and hers, she would help him.

She drew in a deep breath. "Would you like to come down with me, Captain? Otherwise, I can ask Eazi to send you back to

Larga Ways."

Hal stared at her. "Would I like to go down with you?" He
seemed to struggle for a moment.

Fee frowned. "Yes."

He kept his gaze locked on her. "A foreign power has set up a
military operation on a Grihan planet, and they're spying on us.
As a senior officer of Grih Battle Center, I'm obliged to investigate.
I also know my superiors would want me to do anything to
safeguard this Class 5, and heading down to Balco will help with
that. But why on Guimaymi's Star do you want to go?"

"Because I promised Eazi I'd help him." And he'd offered her a
place here, without conditions or strings. As someone without a
place left in the world, that offer had been a precious gift. She
could run, she could stay up here and wait for something to
happen, or she could act. And if they were successful, they'd be
ruining the Tecrans' plans. Something she could really get behind.

Hal had schooled his features and she had no idea what he was
thinking.

"So, you're coming?"

"Yes," he said at last. "I'm coming."

"Good." She gave him a sunny smile. "I need to get out of this
dress, and then perhaps we can meet outside the armory? I'm sure
Eazi can provide us with some weapons."

She turned on her heel and walked out of the launch bay,
leaving Captain Vakeri staring after her.

Chapter Twenty-four

"YOU COULD BE HURT DOWN ON BALCO." Eazi spoke to her the moment the launch bay doors closed behind her.

"But we'll both theoretically be safer off this ship," Fee said, touching the crystal around her neck again.

"Both—" He seemed stymied for a moment. "You mean, I come with you?"

"Yes." Fee shrugged. "As you said earlier, your corporeal form is hanging around my neck. I'm assuming you could gain access to the systems at the facility. Maybe find which program would activate the self-destruct. Probably better than Captain Vakeri and I could, anyway."

"I . . . I hadn't thought of myself as separate from the ship. It's so much a part of me, but . . . you're right. If I'm not on the ship and it explodes, I'll still be fine."

Fee walked into her rooms. "If not fine, at least alive."

"I hope it doesn't come to that." There was almost a tremor in his voice, like a little bit of static on the line.

"Well, that's the reason we're going down." She smoothed a hand regretfully over the dress. The stretchy silk made it a one-size-fits-all affair that she'd shimmied into by pulling it over her head. She suspected it had been cut to hit someone's knees, whereas it was below calf length on her. "What can I wear instead of this? Because no way can I creep around a secret facility looking like I'm about to walk the red carpet."

The door of her room gave a polite ping, and then opened to admit a drone.

"I took some fabric from the stores and had an outfit made for you while you were eating, using your exact dimensions." Eazi told her.

"Ooh. You have a way to make clothes?" Fee reached into the drone's box and pulled out an outfit.

"Yes." He sounded amused, and she guessed making clothes was quite literally child's play for him.

Fee laid the clothes out on the bed, waiting until the drone left the room. She knew it had a lens on it, and while she was getting dressed and undressed, she wanted privacy. No matter that Eazi probably couldn't care less one way or the other, she didn't need footage of herself getting changed in any database, thank you very much.

"These are great." She separated out the garments. There were gloves, shoe covers, and a kind of balaclava, along with pants and a top. The pants resembled yoga pants, stretchy and flared at the bottom. Everything was in a shimmery gray. Fee held the shirt up and it seemed to blend into the wall behind it. "Camouflage?" That explained the gloves and hood thing. Hard to be invisible with your head and hands uncovered.

"The fabric is another type of silk, from a caterpillar that has evolved a way of hiding its cocoon by making it almost impossible to distinguish from its surroundings. The cocoon needs to be hidden through two very distinct seasons."

"I love it." She wriggled out of the dress and pulled the clothes on over the underwear Eazi had already given her, made of the same golden silk as her discarded outfit. She patted her encryptor, tucked into her new bra, just to make sure it still lay flush against her skin and didn't make any suspicious bumps. "Where did you get the silk?"

"We found it on a small planet on the edge of Bukari territory. It's part of the Bukari Union, but they had an ecological disaster a hundred years ago when someone brought two small pets on-planet with them without permission. Ten species were wiped out when it turned out the pets were carrying a disease nothing on the planet had any immunity to. Their population was reduced by a third and they closed themselves off to any outside trade."

"How did you manage it, then?"

Eazi was silent for a moment. "We stole whatever we found interesting."

Fee tugged the top straight, then sat to pull on the boots that had come with her Grihan cadet uniform. "Openly, or was Flato being sneaky about it?"

It would say a lot about where the Tecran were with their plan to start a war, depending on whether they were being brazen about their aggressive exploration or not.

"As quietly and unobtrusively as possible." Eazi said. "We shadowed one of the planet's three moons, listening to their comms, working out what technology they had that might be useful to us. When we felt we knew what we wanted, Flato sent down a stealth team to one of the major cities, and they broke into warehouses and stole the camouflage silk fabric, some interesting devices, and a few weapons."

"Sort of what they did on Earth, in other words."

"Yes." He paused again. "Well, on Earth, we just grabbed you, some random species of animals, and left."

"Not interesting enough for you?" She should be glad of that, not insulted, because if they were boring, they'd be left alone. It was why she'd long ago made peace with never returning. No way was she going to ask to be taken back, and expose the rest of her world to this dangerous new life she'd found herself in.

"No. You were extremely interesting. That's why after they realized Rose McKenzie was an advanced sentient, they came back for another sample. But I had the feeling that something else was going on, and they had to mark Earth as a future project. They were hoping to get a lot of information from you and Rose before they went back.

"I know Flato fought to be the one sent to fetch more samples, after the reports of what Sazo and his crew had found were circulated, and then he got into trouble afterward when he balked at what he'd been ordered to do when he realized he wasn't just picking up an interesting new species, but an advanced sentient.

"He and the medical team had a number of shouting matches with each other, but in the end, Flato had to agree with the doctors that they were breaking the Sentient Beings Agreement by even having you in the cells. That's when High Command ordered them to hand you over to Captain Tak, so he could bring you to the facility."

"Why have a facility here? Why not somewhere in Tecran airspace? Wouldn't it be safer for them?"

Eazi made a humming sound. "If I were to guess, it would be because High Command knows it's breaking all its treaties with the United Council, and it wants some deniability. Putting the facility on the border of Garmman territory, just into Grih airspace, makes it easier for them to say they didn't know what was going on."

Right. New galaxy, same old, same old.

"So, how many Tecran know how to find Earth?" It had been worrying her since she was taken, a heavy weight in her gut every time she thought about it. That she could be the first of many, now they knew the way.

"None." Eazi sounded . . . smug.

"How is that?"

"Sazo. He did it at Rose McKenzie's request. He tracked down and corrupted every report his captain sent out about Earth and its location, and that virus hunted the whole Tecran network, finding every mention of Earth and destroying it. I have it on my system, because I quarantined the virus, and Sazo must have it on his, hidden away, but we both pretended the files had been destroyed on our side, too."

"But some Tecran will know about it. They read the reports."

"Yes, but they won't find those reports again, and unless they memorized them, they have no information to go back to, no galaxy locators. They might know it exists, but they don't know where to find it anymore."

She didn't know whether to collapse in relief, or dance for joy. "Thank you, Eazi. That means a lot. Really."

Her door chimed, and it was with a light step that she went to open it. Hal Vakeri stood outside, waiting for her. He tilted his head to look at her, his expression all soldier. "Useful fabric."

"Do you have enough to make an outfit for the captain?" Fee asked Eazi.

"Yes." Eazi didn't sound too enthusiastic.

"My uniform has similar capabilities," Hal said, with a shake of his head. "Are you ready to choose some weapons?"

"Sure." Fee had never held a weapon in her life, but she bet there would be something Eazi could find her that would be useful. "Lead the way."

***

Hal already knew where the armory was, he'd found it on his exploration of the ship. He had Cy's shockgun and his own, and didn't know if he would trust anything from the Tecran stores anyway, but it would be better for Fiona if she was armed, and he decided he might as well see what was available.

He was very aware of her, following behind him down the passageway. He could have shortened his stride so she could catch up, but he didn't want her too close to him.

She messed with his mind.

He knew how to read people, and she had an expressive face, so he'd seen that she'd been terrified by the idea of going down to Balco. He couldn't blame her after what she'd been through. But then she'd coolly asked if he wanted to come with her, or go back to Larga Ways.

He'd been standing there, wrestling with the problem of what to do with her while he went down below, because although for safety she needed to get away from the Class 5, he didn't want her going back to Larga Ways unprotected, either. He'd been trying to work out how to suggest she get in a runner and simply wait somewhere inconspicuous in the Balco system until things were safe, when she'd taken control.

He didn't miss the proprietary implications of her offer, either. She saw herself as aligned with Eazi, or at least, able to make offers on his behalf.

It disturbed him on every level.

He was a child of his time, and he'd grown up on warnings about thinking systems. Like all Grihans, he'd had to study the Thinking System Wars.

He'd asked Eazi before why he and Sazo had both connected with Earth women, but perhaps the answer was as simple as they did not carry the baggage of the past with them.

And then, on top of all that, he forced himself to admit that she made his heart beat faster.

He'd first seen her as more than a victim when he'd spoken to her in Doc Jasa's med chamber, and that had veered to attraction when she'd sung happy birthday to Mun, all sleek and severe in her cadet uniform, her smooth dark hair and her big, dark eyes as exotic as they were beautiful. She had epitomized grace under pressure.

But since he'd seen her again on the Class 5, whether bleeding and exhausted, dressed in gold, facing down her demons and overcoming them, or now, shimmering in silver, determination in every line, he had to admit that he found her almost irresistible.

"You just walked passed the armory, Captain." Eazi spoke in his ear, and Hal brought himself up short.

He shook his head and turned back to the double doors that he'd completely missed.

The doors opened, and Fiona caught up with him. She was breathing a little hard, and he felt a stab of guilt at not slowing his pace for her.

He'd only taken a cursory look at the weapons when he'd been this way before, but now he stepped into the room and took more notice.

The space was well organized and well stocked.

"Do you need a lot of training to work a shockgun?" Fiona asked.

He pursed his lips. Shook his head. "Not a lot, but to use it well, you do need some training. I'd suggest you find something easier."

She nodded, and he thought she looked relieved. The shockgun would have been too big for her, anyway, he decided. He'd have said too heavy, as well, but he wasn't sure that was true. Her bones and muscles were denser than the Grihs, and she'd spent a lot of her time on the *Fasbe* moving heavy boxes around. She was much stronger than she looked.

"Can you suggest something?"

He thought she was speaking to him, but when he turned to her, he saw she was looking up at one of the lenses on the ceiling.

Eazi must have answered her, because she moved across to the far wall, and lifted something off the rack.

"What is it?" He stepped closer, and had to keep himself very still as the scent of her twined around him. She smelled incredible.

"A light-gun, Captain."

The words snapped him out of his fugue. "No. She can't use it."

"Why not?" She turned to look at him, and he realized he was far too close, but retreat would look strange. He forced himself to stay in place.

"It's illegal. If we're going to use what we find down there against the Tecran at the UC Courts, then using a light-gun will undermine our moral high ground."

"Okay." Fiona shrugged and put the weapon back.

She didn't know what was or wasn't illegal. It was obvious, how could she when she was from a completely different world? But it struck him clearly now. She would have used the light-gun and not thought twice about it. She freed a thinking system, and didn't see the problems it would cause for her with the Grihan government.

He'd offered her sanctuary, but helping Eazi may mean that offer was no longer his to give.

And as a senior officer of Battle Center, he would be forced to agree with what his superiors decided.

He certainly couldn't get involved with her, no matter how irresistible he found her. That would really endear him to Admiral Hoke.

The only hope he had was that Rose had done the same as Fiona, and she was still firmly part of Grihan society.

"The light-gun would be perfect if you're confronting a large number of people you want to incapacitate but don't want to kill," Eazi said, speaking through the comm system this time so they could both hear him. "I don't understand why Fiona can't use it."

That was true. But still . . . "It's a banned weapon. The Tecran developed it for crowd control, but it was too effective. The Tecran authorities, as well as every other member of the UC, decided it could just as easily been turned against the security forces as used by them. They were supposed to all be destroyed, so I don't know why this one is here. It's a violation of the Tecran's own rules."

"They took it off some Krik pirates, actually," Eazi said. "Rather safely in our armory than in their hands, I'm sure you'd agree."

Hal could just imagine what a Krik pirate crew could do with a light-gun. "Yes. Confiscating it was by far the better option."

"What about a reflector?" Eazi asked.

A bracelet slid forward on a narrow retractable shelf. It was made of a dark metal with a sheen to it that seemed more than just a reflection of light.

"I've never heard of it." Hal reached for it, and felt more than heard a hum under his fingers as he lifted it up.

"Good. It can't be illegal then," Eazi said cheerfully.

"What does it do?" Fiona leaned over and peered at it, and Hal handed it to her. She slid it over her wrist, where it hung, far too big, and lifted her arm to test the weight of it. "It's lighter than it looks."

He didn't agree, but then, he'd already noticed she had more strength than a Grih of her size.

"Touch the raised emblem on one of the links," Eazi told her.

She had to rotate the bracelet around until she found it, and then touched it with the tip of a finger. The bracelet snapped onto her wrist, fitting it perfectly.

She jerked with shock. "A little warning, next time," she said, eyeing the band suspiciously. "Although it's cool how that light sort of maps your body like that."

There was a beat of silence. Hal realized Eazi must be as surprised as he was. "What light?"

"The thin lines of blue light that went over my body in a grid." She was frowning at him.

"I didn't see any light." There was something, some information, that was trying to surface in his mind, but he couldn't pin it down.

"I didn't see it through the lens either." Eazi was thoughtful. "Maybe only the wearer can see it, although the officer Flato recruited to try it out didn't mention it when he tested it."

Fiona shrugged. "Should I do a trial run?"

"Yes. But Captain Vakeri will need a barrier to hide behind when he shoots at you, so let's move to the training room."

"It deflects straight back to the attacker?" Fiona asked,

sounding really interested.

Hal frowned. "Does it?" She'd leapt to the conclusion so quickly. But he'd never heard of a protective device that could do that. All attempts to create a force field that could deflect attacks had failed because of the effect the field had on the person it was protecting. The energy involved made them sick and unable to operate.

"It does." Eazi said. "Fiona should test it with you in a safe environment, rather than when the Tecran are shooting at her down below."

"How about it, Captain?" Fiona smiled at him, but he could see the trepidation in her eyes. "You up for taking a few shots at me?"

Chapter Twenty-five

"THIS ISN'T JUST A PROTECTIVE SHIELD, it's a weapon." Fiona watched as Captain Vakeri's shockgun shot ricocheted straight back to where he'd been the moment before he'd ducked behind the screen.

It had been hard not to flinch or cower when he'd reluctantly shot at her with his shockgun on its lowest setting. She'd been hit twice before and her brain was screaming at her to run away.

"If they stay still when they shoot you, yes," Eazi agreed.

It had a certain karma to it that appealed to Fee. No one who left her alone would be hurt. That seemed fair enough.

"The blue light that flares up just before the shot hits is a bit disconcerting." Fee relaxed as Hal stepped out from behind his barrier. "Although I suppose it does give you a little warning."

The captain holstered his shockgun absently, looking like he'd had an epiphany. "I can't see the blue flare but Rose McKenzie can see a level of light that the Grih can't. They haven't given out a lot of information about her, but I know she can see our soldiers when they activate the reflective camouflage in their uniforms. I assume you can too. Maybe this light is in the same light spectrum."

That was pretty cool, Fee decided. Super vision. It wasn't as if she had many advantages in this new life she'd fallen into. She'd take whatever she could get.

"Should I get a weapon as well? Or just use the reflector?" She didn't want to carry a weapon she had never used before, but at the same time, the idea of having no way to defend herself at all didn't seem sensible.

"The shield's ability to actually reflect the shot back at the same velocity as it was sent *is* a weapon," Hal said. "But it's a passive weapon, and you're thinking you need something more active."

Fee liked that he got it, and didn't try to dismiss her concerns.

She knew she liked him more than was wise.

It wasn't just his pretty blue eyes and his body, or the way his eyes lingered on her when he looked her way.

He treated her respectfully.

But she also knew she owed him. A lot. She hoped the fact that her heart beat a little faster at the thought of him wasn't too closely related to that debt.

She preferred to meet him on an equal footing.

Vakeri cleared his throat, and Fee realized she'd been staring at him. She could feel her cheeks heating.

"If I shoot someone at the same time someone shoots me, will my shot ricochet right back at me when the shield comes up?" It just occurred to her, and the cold hand of panic brushed down her back, and cooled her embarrassment.

"No. It's one way. You can shoot out." Eazi opened the training room door for them to leave.

"So do you have something easy to carry, easy to shoot, that isn't illegal?" Fee asked him, falling into step with Hal, who was making an effort to match her shorter strides this time.

"I have a crowd-pleaser."

Hal stumbled to a stop. "A crowd-pleaser?" He shook his head. "She said not illegal, remember?"

"Crowd-pleasers are legal. They were just withdrawn from general use and most of them were taken off the market. Now the database restrictions that were imposed on me have been lifted, I've been able to access more data than I could before and I've checked the UC regulations. They weren't made illegal because the Tecran and the Garmman refused to vote them off the list, just in case they ever needed to bring them out again."

"So, what's a crowd-pleaser? I'm assuming that's a sarcastic title." Fee thought again how people were people, no matter where in the universe you ended up.

"It's a small weapon that shoots a projectile, a little plug that's designed to explode outward, away from the shooter, letting loose hundreds of small barbs. Each one contains enough sedative to down an adult."

Sort of like a shotgun from Earth. Only non-lethal. That appealed to her, too.

"What if someone gets more than one barb in them?"

"The fatal dose is very high. No one has ever died from being shot with a crowd-pleaser before," Hal told her.

"Light-guns and crowd-pleasers. You seem to have a crowd control problem."

Hal grimaced. "Not the Grih. Or, not recently. Not the Bukari either, I have to say. But the Fitali sometimes have trouble around swarming time, and the Tecran and the Garmman have had some trouble fostering a happy population."

"Huh. Big surprise there." They'd reached the armory again and Eazi slid out what she assumed was the crowd-pleaser, loaded with three cartridges. "Just point and shoot?"

Another shelf slid forward, containing a strap with extra cartridges on half of it. Fee belted it around her waist, putting the cartridges at the back, and pulling her shirt over them, to hide them with the camouflage.

Hal showed her how it worked, and it really was as easy as point and shoot. She thought he crowded her a little more than was strictly necessary as he demonstrated, and then wondered if that was just wishful thinking.

Something caught his eye, and she followed his gaze to a small device that would fit snugly in her hand.

"You found a toy that appeals?" Fee asked him, because this had been all about her, she suddenly realized.

"A spiker." He lifted it. "It's Grihan. Absolutely quiet, unlike a shockgun, but requires a lot of practice."

"Which you have?" she guessed.

He gave a nod as he slid the spiker into a pocket, and then took a box of what must be spiker ammunition from the same shelf.

"You should take a reflector, too."

"There is only one reflector," Eazi said, and he didn't sound too upset about it.

Hal must have heard that too, because his mouth twisted up in a wry smile. "I've been meaning to ask you, Eazi, where is it from? I've never seen technology like that."

"It's from a place no one in the UC even knows about," Eazi said. "A place we barely got away from without being captured or destroyed."

Hal lifted his head, looked right at the lens. "*You* barely made it out? A Class 5?"

"Yes." Eazi was quiet for a moment. "Flato wiped every piece of information that led us there off the system, replaced it with maps that showed there was nothing of interest there at all. And for once I agreed with him. There are some things out there that are bigger, more advanced and nastier than we are, Captain. And retreat was the only logical option."

Fee lifted her bracelet and turned it this way and that. "The Tecran got a taste of their own medicine?"

Eazi laughed, and she realized it was a mimic of her own. "Yes, very much a taste of their own medicine."

She smiled. "Well, let's go give them another one, shall we?"

***

The Larga Ways runner with Cy imprisoned on it blasted space dust into Hal's face as it took off in the launch bay.

Eazi refused to send him back to Larga Ways though, and Hal didn't blame him. He hadn't wanted Fiona going back there alone for the same reason.

There had to be Tecran spies on the way station, and there was no way to guarantee Cy would not be freed or murdered by his own people to make sure he didn't talk if he arrived unaccompanied.

Eazi's solution had been the same one Hal was going to suggest for Fiona. The runner would be sent out into space and left there until they were able to pick it up later.

As the runner disappeared through the gel wall, Hal noticed that two other vessels were missing from when he'd last been in here.

Fiona must have seen him looking because she put a hand on his arm. "The bodies went in one, and Eazi wanted to take one himself so he can monitor us from above and help break into the facility's systems. And it won't hurt for him to be away from the Class 5, either, in case the worst comes to the worst."

Hal froze. He'd made the mistake of thinking Eazi was the Class 5, but he wasn't, the ship was just the framework in which the thinking system lived. As long as the runner he'd sent out the launch bay was in communication with the Class 5, he could, as Fiona said, help them without being stuck in the static of Kyber's Arm.

"Good thinking." He started toward the small drone Eazi had insisted was their best bet at getting down to the Balco facility undetected.

"So this won't be seen?" Fiona touched the side with a delicate, long-fingered hand.

Hal shook his shoulders loose. "Eazi explained the cloaking capabilities to me, and there is no way they'll see us coming."

"Even though it's their own drone?" She sounded so suspicious. He liked that she refused to take anyone's word for it if it didn't make sense.

"Apparently not."

Fiona gave a reluctant nod. "I suppose Eazi knows what he's

talking about."

Well, he certainly had a lot to lose if he was wrong, so Hal had chosen to trust him.

The drone's door opened, and at a glance, Hal could see it was going to be a tight fit with both of them in there.

He gestured to Fiona to go first, and she slipped in, lying on her side on the cushioned chair that was more like a sleeping couch and strapped herself in. He had to squeeze in next to her, chest to chest, and bumped her as he fought to get into his own harness.

Their bodies were touching and Fiona reached around him to untwist a shoulder strap, both arms coming around him in an embrace.

He said nothing as the door closed, and the pressure of their take-off shoved them back against their cosy padded bed. There was the familiar hum as they cleared the gel wall and then the drone shuddered as they exited out into the storm that was Kyber's Arm.

Fiona was silent as the drone flew straight up and out of the center of the storm. It angled down, twisting as it went, so Hal was hanging by his straps over Fiona, their breath mingling.

He saw she'd forgotten to take off the necklace Eazi had found to go with her dress, and then realized he was staring at her breasts.

He jerked his eyes up to her face and found her watching him.

"*Carpe diem*." She sounded nervous as she said it, and her tongue came out to wet her bottom lip.

He found himself unable to look away. "I'm sorry?"

"It's an expression on Earth, in a language no one uses anymore unless they're lawyers." She paused. "It means seize the day."

He was trying to work out why she was telling him this when she leaned forward and brushed her lips against his.

It was just a gentle touch, a whisper of a kiss.

He shivered, and then lifted his hands to cup her face, deepened the kiss until she opened her mouth under his.

He jerked back at the touch of her tongue, so aroused he couldn't remember ever feeling this way.

"This . . ." He shuddered. "No."

She bit her bottom lip, and his eyes tracked the movement helplessly. He realized he was holding his hands out level with his shoulders, pressing them against the sides of the drone, as if to keep them as far from temptation as possible.

"No fraternizing with the enemy, huh?" she said at last.

He closed his eyes and when he opened them again, he saw she was looking down, to where his erection strained against his pants.

He tried to grab hold of something, found nothing for his hands to grasp, and fisted them. "You are not the enemy."

"It's okay. I get it. You're unsure of me, and getting mixed up with Eazi hasn't helped that. I understand."

He looked away. "I'm a senior officer of Grih Battle Center. Captain of one of Battle Center's most powerful battleships. You are a key witness to gross abuse of the Sentient Beings Agreement by the Tecran and the Garmman, and now it seems you're our liaison with another Class 5. It would not be . . . appropriate."

She sighed, and his gaze flicked back to her face.

"One of the reasons I'm attracted to you is your commitment to doing the right thing, so I can't blame you for doing it now. I'm just sorry that's how it's worked out." She managed a cheeky smile, which he had the feeling was an effort for her. "Maybe one day you'll be able to seize the day with me."

He imagined what would happen if they got out of this, and he got her back to Battle Center. He'd be lucky to ever see her again.

He lifted his shoulders. "Maybe."

They didn't look at each other, or say anything else, as Eazi sent them hurtling toward Balco's western desert.

Chapter Twenty-six

AT LEAST SAYING NO HAD REALLY, REALLY HURT HIM. As Fee adjusted the balaclava Eazi had made her, she decided that was some comfort. Cold comfort, but comfort, nevertheless.

If he hadn't thought he was breaking some kind of trust with Battle Center, he'd have been fully onboard.

Her lips, hidden beneath the hood, quirked upward, as she remembered the look of agony on his face.

Yeah, it helped to soothe the sting a little.

That, and the way he was trying not to touch her now as they lay side by side, looking down at the Tecran's facility.

Eazi had landed them on a small plateau and they'd walked for an hour up through the hills to find themselves above a building that looked like a weather station or observatory, painted a color the interior designer Fee used to work with would have called sienna, to match the color of the desert sand. It reminded her of a caramelized peach, and at the thought her mouth started to water.

It didn't help that the wind blowing grit into their eyes was dry and hot, sucked in from every direction to feed the massive tower that was Kyber's Arm, which teetered above them like a toppling pillar.

There was a dome set in the middle of the roof, and it looked capable of retracting.

"To let runners in and out?" Hal mused. He had put a similar camouflage cover over his head, and only his eyes were visible.

"The building doesn't look big enough to house over three hundred people, let alone a fleet of runners, so I'm assuming it goes down into the ground. But why would this be considered a good place to spend your time off?" Fee had expected more. More bustle, more signs of life. A place crew would prefer to ship duty if they had the opportunity.

"Sometimes, anywhere that's different is better than nothing," Hal said. "If they've been on ops for years, which from what Eazi says is possible, then any time you can get planet-side is a good time."

That was probably true.

When they'd landed, she'd crouched down, let her fingers slide through the dry sand and tilted her face toward Balco's sun.

Larga Ways had been a step up from a battleship, but this was real *terra firma*. It had been nearly three long months and she wouldn't have cared if it had been hell itself, she was just happy to be breathing non-processed air.

"There's a squad coming in north-east of you." Eazi warned them. "They're running a standard scan, so don't move."

It was helpful to have an eye in the sky.

The runner Eazi was piloting was small and agile, and capable of hovering just within Balco's atmosphere. It obviously also had really powerful lenses.

But he'd asked her to wear a small lens on her collar, as well, so he could see what was happening when they got inside the building.

"Here they come," Hal murmured.

Fee kept very still, and beside her, Hal did the same. He'd touched something on his uniform before they'd started out from the drone, and it had gone a similar reflective shade to hers, except it also had a sepia outline around it that sort of defeated the purpose.

Although it sounded like she and Rose McKenzie were the only two who could see it.

Fee squinted in the harsh midday sun and saw a group of sienna-outfitted troops jogging their way.

"I'm surprised they don't have the same camouflage as you," Fee said.

"Probably don't think they need it," Hal said. "I know they have the tech."

They watched the tight group of thirty or so soldiers run toward the facility.

"What's fun about running around in this heat?" Fee wondered. "If this is the equivalent of shore leave, it sucks."

Hal snorted out a quiet laugh. "They need security patrols, and to keep the crew fit. They're probably on rotation."

The soldiers stopped in front of the building. A door opened and someone stepped outside to confer with one of them. Then they all filed in and the door closed behind them.

She'd known getting in unseen wouldn't be easy, but now she wondered if it was even possible.

A quiet scrabbling just behind her distracted her, and she looked over her shoulder.

Froze.

"Hal." It was a choked whisper.

"What?" Then he was quiet, too.

"What is it?" Eazi whispered in her ear. The lens on her shirt obviously wasn't at the right angle.

"A lizard thing." Her voice wobbled, and she spoke in English, because anything else would have been too much for her right then.

It was about half as long as she was, sleek and narrow, its back a pattern of dark and light orange, blending in perfectly with the sand, but its eyes . . . Fee swallowed. They were bright yellow and feral.

It hissed at her and reared up, using its long tail and back legs to balance. Its underbelly was the most delicate shade of peaches and cream Fee had ever seen. Just as it lunged, a spike was suddenly buried deep in its throat.

It twisted as it fell, landing short of her. She scrabbled back as it thrashed wildly.

Fee crawled as far as she could, only stopping when she came up against a large rock, and looked over at Hal.

He was crouched, cool and calm, the device he'd chosen from the armory in his hand. The spiker.

She loved spikers.

The lizard gave one last heave and lay, panting, on its side.

Guilt gripped her. A little.

After all, they were the interlopers here.

"Do you think it would live if we pulled the spike out?"

Hal looked over at her. Gave a nod. "The frien are very hardy. But they're too aggressive. If we don't kill it now, it will keep trying to attack. We must be near its burrow, and if it has young, it will never stop. And we can't risk it drawing attention to us, or hurting us."

He lifted the spiker again and shot, and another slim bolt lodged itself in the frien's eye.

It went still.

Fee shuddered, slid her hands under the balaclava, and rubbed her face.

"Okay. That was not fun." Her heart was still pounding so hard, she thought she was going to be sick. She forced herself to take a deep breath and stood to get a better look at her attacker.

"It was beautiful." She curled her hands into fists. "Thank you for stopping it."

Hal looked at it, too. "Yes, it was beautiful, but there is poison in its bite, and although I brought a small med pack from the Class 5, I don't know if the anti-venom would work on you. Better not to find out."

"You seem to know a lot about it."

He shrugged. "We've had to come to Larga Ways often enough it was worth learning more about the Balcoan wildlife."

She was silent, using the time to draw her composure around herself again. "What now? That building looks pretty secure."

"That part of it is." Eazi said, and from the flick of Hal's eyes, Fee guessed Eazi was speaking in his earpiece as well. "But I've been able to use the runner to get part way into their systems, and I've found a few tunnels that are less secure."

"Tunnels?" Hal asked.

"Mostly part of the air filtration system."

"They surely know that's a weakness and have some security?" Fee did not believe they would leave themselves that vulnerable.

"They do." There was a laugh in Eazi's voice. "But they've used my own systems to set it all up. They just copied the code I created for the Class 5 and reused it."

Fee smiled. "So we're in?"

"Oh yes. We're in."

***

Every scrabble and scrape Hal heard in the tunnel had him tensing.

While Eazi had led them unerringly to the entrance, and given them the code to open up the filter cover that doubled as a door, construction had obviously been rough and quick, straight into the sand, with no quick-set layer to seal it. He'd seen more than one gaping hole in the sandy side walls, just the right size to have been burrowed by a frien.

He had acted without thinking earlier, done what he had to do, but the sight of the deadly lizard poised to strike Fiona was burned into his retina.

He'd wanted to pull her close, hug her tight, but he made himself keep his distance, content with the fact that she was only a little shaken, not dead.

He'd downplayed the incident. A lot.

Friens caused more deaths than any other living organism on Balco. That's why he knew so much about them.

His hands shook a little in delayed reaction, and he forced himself to focus on the way ahead.

The lighting was on standby, just enough to see by.

His only worry was a lurking frien, which is why he was going first, spiker ready in his hand.

At least he knew the anti-venom worked on him.

There was a wind blowing at their back, sucked in from the outside to replace what was being used in the facility. It brought the hot, spicy scent of the desert with it, and mingled with the earthy smell of the tunnel as it swirled past them.

They walked at a downward angle, going deeper and deeper into the ground.

When he finally heard sounds of activity, he guessed they were at least five stories underground. Fiona had edged closer to him, so when he stopped suddenly, she ran into his back. She stayed plastered there, even curled her hands around his biceps, and he realized she was trying to look over his shoulder.

He forced himself to hold still, although he wanted to step away, get some distance between them. Either that, or push back, feel every single inch of her.

She was so slight and short in contrast to him, the feel of her delicate hands on him, sliding up to his shoulders as she used him to pull herself up a little to see, made his heart beat too fast in his chest.

"What is it?" She breathed into his ear and he closed his eyes against the shiver that wanted to run through him.

"I think someone is working just around the corner."

When he moved forward, she followed close behind, her hand fisted in the fabric of his shirt. Although it was better if he was completely free to protect her, he couldn't force himself to tell her to let go.

They edged around the last curve of the tunnel, and Hal saw the room ahead was a sub-station of some kind, probably the recycle plant for sewage and waste.

A technician was watching a screen and another was lying under a large pipe. They were clearly adjusting something, calling numbers to each other.

They waited the techs out, Fiona plastered against him again to see as much as possible. It was more about wanting to see danger coming, to not be taken unawares, he realized, rather than any attempt to make him uncomfortable or press her point. It helped him ease back a little from the edge he was standing on.

Although not completely.

When the Tecran started putting away tools, he felt her tense, and as soon as the men left the room, they ran quietly after them, crouched and looked around the open arch the men had gone through to see which way they went.

There were no tubes here to get to the floors above. The techs were walking up a spiral staircase.

It became clearer by the moment the facility had been hacked out of the ground as quickly as possible, and they hadn't thought they'd be here long enough to install any of the functionality of a standard base. Either that, or they'd been too nervous to take the time to do so, for fear of discovery.

That they'd been here over a year meant the lack of home comforts had to be starting to chafe.

Hal led the way to the staircase and they climbed it silently in the wake of the stomping techs above them.

He heard the change in tone of their footsteps, and guessed they'd reached the next floor, but the tone of their chatter changed, too.

The distance and his poor grasp of Tecran made it hard to make out what they were discussing, but the joking died out of their voices and they lowered the volume, too.

Just as he got to the final bend, he heard the ringing sound of them climbing the next set of stairs, and their subdued voices died away.

It gave him some warning there was something confronting on the next level, made him more wary as he took the final few steps.

Behind him, Fiona gasped, and he felt the tug as she grabbed the back of his shirt again, and then the pull as she twisted it.

Transparent boxes were set, one on top of the other, right near the stairs. But while he had the sense of a place once filled to capacity, it was now less than half empty.

Perhaps the boxes near the stairs were waiting to be taken up top, because most of the other occupants in the room were in large cages, not the boxes that looked more for transportation than long-term use.

A creature in a box stacked at chest level looked at them and then opened its mouth, bared teeth, and threw itself at the wall of the box.

There was no question it was screaming, or snarling, but the box must be soundproofed.

He had never seen anything like it before.

It was a pale green, with mottled brown running down the fur on its back, but its chest and stomach looked like they were covered with gray leathery plates. It had really long teeth in a slender snout, so even though it probably would have come no higher than his shins, it looked like it could give a nasty bite.

It tried to claw at the wall with its front paws, snapping at them, with pure hate in its eyes.

The box beneath it looked empty, and in the one above, a different creature, bigger, broader, and either very dark brown or black, was curled up tightly on itself, as if asleep.

Fiona stepped out from behind him, eyes dark pools in the silver camouflage of her face.

"The storage room." Eazi's voice was a low murmur in his ear. "This is where they've been keeping the specimens the Class 5s have found."

"How are you seeing this?" Hal frowned. Eazi was using a runner to look down on them, but as far as he knew, he couldn't see four stories underground.

"Lens on Fiona's shirt," Eazi told him. "I'm having difficulty getting into their systems. I am trying to get into their lens feed but I haven't managed it yet. Don't make any sudden moves. Your camouflage should make it hard for security to spot you, and when I have control, I'll loop the feed to make you disappear."

A lens on Fiona's shirt.

It was a good idea, but he didn't like that he was only finding out about it now. Didn't like that he wasn't in full control of this mission.

Hal watched the glimmer of movement that was Fiona taking a step past the boxes, deeper into the room. His eyes found it hard to focus on her, even though the lighting here was slightly better than down in the tunnels. She was near invisible, even when you knew where she was.

He tapped his earpiece, to connect to the closed system Eazi had set up between himself and Fiona before they'd gotten into the drone. It helped to be able to whisper to her, wherever she was.

"Fiona. Stop. We don't know if there is someone in here."

"Not anymore," she whispered back. "But there was."

There was something in her voice, something tight and close to cracking.

She stood beside a cage big enough to hold an adult Grih. When he reached her, he saw there was bedding on the floor, and what looked like one of the portable toilets most armies took into battle or out on maneuvers.

"They were using this as a prison, as well." He shouldn't be surprised, but he wondered who they could be holding here, given it was a secret base.

"No." She pointed to some writing scratched into the dirt floor.

"They were keeping another specimen. Looks like Rose McKenzie and I aren't the only humans they took."

Chapter Twenty-seven

THE RELIEF SHE'D FELT EARLIER, that Sazo had destroyed all mention of Earth, evaporated. At least one other captain and crew knew where it was. The evidence was right in front of her.

Imogen Peters was here for . . . Fee bent closer to count how many groups of ten—nine lines crossed through with a tenth—were written in the sand. Four and a half, so forty-five days. Depending on when she'd been taken out of this cage, Imogen Peters had to have been taken soon after Fee was herself, if she was transported all the way here, and then sat in this cage for a month and a half.

"Why did they take someone else right after they took me?" She crouched by the bars, pressed her face between them to look deeper into the shadowed space. There was nothing to see. Imogen Peters had had a bed, a toilet, and what looked like a bucket with water in it. The question was, where was she?

"I think . . ." Eazi's voice was subdued. "I think it was because there was such a fight over who would get another specimen after Rose McKenzie. Captain Flato won the right, but then almost straight afterward, he and his med team refused to work on you. From the little I'm finding in the system, Imogen was taken and dropped off personally, by someone wanting to score a point against Flato."

"She was taken to score a point." Fee's fingers curled tight around the bars. "So what did they do with her? Why isn't she still here?"

She pushed away and stood, looked carefully at the rest of the cavern-like space.

A parrot eyed them from its perch halfway up a bar of its cage.

Fee remembered the flutter of wings, the flash of color, and the calls which had dragged her from her drugged sleep more than once when she'd been on the Class 5.

"Was this the parrot that was taken with me?" She remembered red, yellow and blue, but this one was a blue and yellow macaw, the blue such a shimmering, caribbean blue, it almost glowed as it caught what little light was available. It watched them with white, beady eyes.

"No. That one died onboard after you were handed to Tak. All the animals and birds died. But then, the med team had something to prove, after they refused to work on you. It looks like whoever took Imogen Peters used the report Flato must have sent back, and programed the Class 5 to take exactly what we took. The probabilities of them also taking a parrot by chance is too small."

The macaw fluttered its wings to balance itself on the bar.

"What is it?" Hal whispered, awed, and Fee realized she'd reverted to English with Eazi.

"It's a bird from my planet. A macaw." She took a step closer to it, and it shuffled a little, nervous. "It's probably wild, but they can be taught to talk."

"Don't let the bastards grind you down." Its harsh words echoed in the room. "The bastards." It threw back its head and cawed with manic glee.

Fee crouched down. "She taught it!" She lifted a hand toward it. "Who's a pretty polly?" she crooned.

The macaw snapped at her fingers and she had to snatch them back.

"Polly wants a cracker." This time, it sounded forlorn. "The bastards." It dipped its head up and down.

"What's it saying?" Hal's words dragged her focus back.

"Just some things Imogen taught it. To keep her spirits up."

She realized a few of the cages around them contained other

creatures, and that since the parrot had started speaking, they'd started moving around a little more, as if their fear of the new intruders had worn off.

She didn't see any other animals from Earth, but then, three quarters of the cages were empty.

"They probably died down here."

Hal put a hand on her shoulder, and squeezed. "I would guess yes."

"And Imogen, too?"

Hal's grip tightened. "I don't know. But when we can, we'll find out."

When Eazi finally got into the facility's system, he must surely be able to find out where they'd taken her, and when he did, they'd find a way to rescue her. Or use the United Council Hal was always talking about to force the Tecran to let her go.

"I don't want to leave the macaw here."

"We can come back for it," Hal said.

They could.

She rose to her feet. "Chin up, polly. I'll be back."

The macaw didn't answer her, it just stared at her coldly.

"We need to go." Hal looked back to make sure she was coming, walking toward the stairs with his shockgun in a two-handed grip.

The sound of feet running down the stairs stopped her dead, and Hal melted into the shadows four cages in front of her.

She wanted to catch up to him, hide with him, but there wasn't time, and she slid between two cages, moving back until she was up against the wall.

People were in the room now, and by the sound of it, there was a crowd of them, arguing with one another.

The universal grunting and wheezing of people taking strain when lifting something heavy came floating toward them, and then the sound of footsteps on the stairs again.

They had to be moving the animals in the transparent boxes upstairs.

Fee waited a beat, nervous to move until she was sure it was safe, and just when she was about to push off from the wall and find Hal, he whispered in her ear.

"Stay."

She froze, and then she heard it, the scuff of boots on the floor, and then a Tecran soldier walked past her.

The lights flickered and then brightened, shrinking the dark corner she was hiding in to nothing.

"I'm trying to dim the lights or short them, but I just can't get in to anything but the surface of this system." Eazi's voice, low and urgent in her ear, made her jerk.

The soldier walked up to the macaw's cage and flicked the bars with his fingers.

"Bastard," the parrot hissed at him and snapped at his fingers.

Fee felt a fierce swell of pride. She had the feeling she would like Imogen Peters. She hoped she one day had the chance to find out.

The Tecran said something to it and flicked his fingers once more, but Fee noticed he didn't touch the bars again. Then he turned and walked straight to her.

He looked unhurried and calm, and so she stayed absolutely still, because he gave no indication he could see her. He may have switched on the lights, but the cages still threw a small shadow, and she was wearing camouflage.

He stopped in front of the cage to her left, looking toward the far right corner.

Fee turned her head just a fraction and tried to see what he was staring at.

It looked like a kind of monkey, except it had six limbs instead of four. Either that, or it had a split tail that had evolved some kind of gripping functionality at the ends that roughly resembled hands.

Its hair was shaggy, unkempt, and an interesting shade that looked like dark blue at the base, fading to pure white at the tip, which seemed to blur its outline.

It crouched at the far corner of its cage, looking at the Tecran with such intensity, Fee shivered. Had it been looking at her like that, while she'd been completely unaware it was there?

The Tecran unclipped something from his belt, and pointed it at the creature.

It moved, leaping from its corner to the top of the cage right beside Fee in absolute silence, bottom two limbs supporting it from below, upper limbs holding it up, and the middle set were curved, revealing long, sharp claws.

The speed and the deadly silence was far more frightening than any growling or display of aggression would have been. Fee pressed back against the wall.

The Tecran said something, probably swearing, and she made herself look away from the monkey thing and see what he was doing.

Hal stood right behind him, shockgun raised.

She had to gulp down the tiny squeak of surprise she had at the sight of him, looming like the wrath of God behind the soldier, the strange sepia outline of his camouflage giving him an otherworldly glow.

She made herself take small, quiet breaths and as she did, Hal ghosted back a little, so that he was just within the shadows cast by the cages behind him.

She gave herself permission to check the creature again, and noticed a red tip buried deep in the fur of one of the creature's top limbs. It pulled it out and threw it back at the Tecran, and in answer, he fired at it again.

The creature dropped from the ceiling back to the floor, and then seemed to fly to the other side of the cage.

It was so fast. And, she saw for the first time, as it opened its mouth to pant, its teeth were so big. So very big.

The second dart hit the wall at the back of the cage, an arm's length from her, and she almost went weak with relief that it hadn't activated the reflector. If the Tecran had had his own dart turned against him and collapsed, other soldiers would come to investigate, and someone might actually check the lens feed. So far, it seemed like a combination of their camouflage and the Tecran's laziness had kept them safe.

The Tecran shot a third time, and the dart lodged in the center of the creature's chest. It plucked it out with a clumsy movement.

The arm that had taken the first shot no longer held on to the bar, so it dangled by one limb, and even though it was still supported by the split tail below, it swayed a little from side to side, whereas before it had been perfectly still.

It looked at the Tecran with eyes that were absolutely blank, and then dropped heavily to the floor.

The Tecran muttered something under his breath, and pulled a small square from a pocket. He gave it one firm flick and it snapped into a barrel bag arrangement, but stiff, now, and shiny, like it was made of something metallic.

He waited until the alien monkey stopped moving completely and then opened the door and dragged it out, stuffed it into the bag with quick, frightened movements.

Perhaps the tranq didn't last long.

Fee didn't blame him for his fear. She'd never had such a visceral reaction to something. It was terrifying.

And still, she knew, like her, it had been minding its own business somewhere and they'd taken it. So they deserved to be frightened. It deserved to be free.

If possible, she'd see if Eazi knew where it had come from. Maybe the UC or the Grih could take it back home.

The Tecran finally got it sealed into the bag, and he lifted it, holding it away from his body by the straps. It was an awkward way to carry what was obviously a heavy load, but the Tecran didn't sling it over his shoulder or put it on his back.

Fee gave him kudos for carrying it at all. She wouldn't.

As he walked away from her, Hal materialized out of the shadows again, shockgun ready, his attention on the soldier.

Fee's heart gave a painful little skip at the sight of him.

"Ready?" When he turned to her, his face was grim. He was looking in her general direction, but not at her specifically.

"Yes." She pushed away from the wall and joined him, saw him finally track where she was. "What's wrong?"

"That creature he just took was a grahudi. It's from a planet in Fitali territory."

"You think the Fitali are in on this, too, now?"

Hal shrugged, but there was not even a hint of carelessness in the movement. "Let's find out."

Chapter Twenty-eight

FIONA HAD HANDLED HERSELF WELL.

Hal led the way up the stairs, and looked back to check on her, saw she was following behind him, careful not to make a sound.

He hadn't been able to see her, even though he knew she was between those two cages, but when the grahudi had leapt close to where she must have been hiding, she hadn't made a sound.

The Tecran hadn't looked her way, his focus on the grahudi, but even if he had, Hal didn't think he would have noticed her. The camouflage Eazi had given her made her near invisible.

What the Tecran were doing with a Fitalian animal like a grahudi was anyone's guess.

Hal knew it didn't mean the Fitali were in league with the Tecran. The Tecran were here on Balco, too, weren't they?

So this could just be another example of Tecran disregard for the treaties and rules of the UC.

And, maybe, a desire to look where they hadn't been invited.

No one had been allowed on Huy since the Fitali had caught a smuggler trying to round up a troop of grahudi to sell on the black market about twenty years before. It was a planet with no advanced sentient life, but the Fitali kept up regular patrols and they had established a research station there. Maybe the Tecran had wanted to find out what they were up to.

He'd been standing right behind the Tecran, ready to shoot if he noticed Fiona, but the position had also given him a direct line of sight to the grahudi. It had been staring at the soldier, but for one instant, it had shifted its gaze to him.

He didn't know if its eyes were capable of seeing through his camouflage, but it felt like it looked straight at him.

And there had been death in its eyes.

Hal paused just before the last turn of the stairs, listening, and frowned as he heard a faint sound, like a sustained scream.

"Any idea what that is?" he asked Eazi.

"I'm not in yet. It's like they expected me to try and break in. There are traps and dead ends everywhere."

"Of course they prepared for the possibility of you trying to break in. They'd have been mad not to," Fiona whispered, and Hal realized she was soothing the panic they both must have heard in the thinking system's voice. "You'll beat them. If they were lazy enough to use your code for the security at the tunnel entrance, they'd have taken short cuts elsewhere, too. Look for areas where you'd need to physically be here to override their code, like opening the tunnel door. They never thought you'd have boots on the ground helping you, like we are."

"That is a good suggestion." Eazi's voice sounded strange, the sound Hal would expect from an automaton.

And that, he had to admit, was how he saw the thinking system. But Fiona didn't. She spoke to him like a person; soothing, encouraging.

It was no wonder Eazi gave her gifts and searched his stores for ways to protect her.

"You're used to getting in easily, aren't you?" Fiona lifted her shirt away from her body and looked into the tiny lens attached to it, looking Eazi in the eye. "Those other planets didn't know you were coming, and most probably didn't have the tech to keep you out anyway. But these guys, they know you, and you can bet their worst nightmare is what is happening right now, with you in control of the Class 5 and no longer caged. Think of this as one more challenge, like all those work-arounds you did to get me off Larga Ways."

Hal guessed Eazi said something just to her, because she gave a nod and let go of her shirt.

Then the sound he'd been worried about swelled, gaining strength, and thrummed like a thunderstorm rolling in, about to wreak destruction. Fiona went still and he saw fear in her eyes.

Something unpleasant was happening above.

"Stay here," he said. "I'll go ahead and see what's going on."

She shook her head, and there was a stubborn determination on her face he knew he didn't have time to fight.

He lifted his shockgun higher on his chest and climbed the last few steps.

And found the sleeping quarters.

A corridor stretched out in a single, long line, doors at close intervals to each other. Coming from the center of the corridor was the sound of water falling and voices, as a group of people took a shower.

The squad they'd seen approaching the station earlier, Hal guessed. Cleaning up before they found some food and relaxed.

Fiona came up behind him, and he noticed her looking up the next flight of stairs.

The screaming was even louder from here, and definitely coming from the floor above.

A door crashed open, and they both pushed up against the wall.

A Tecran in a loose outfit rather than a uniform closed the door a little more gently behind him and then walked toward them.

They were in the narrow strip of shadow thrown by the stairs above, but the soldier could have reached out and touched them both as he swung up onto the stairs and ran lightly upward.

As soon as he was out of sight, Hal moved, grabbing Fiona's hand and taking the stairs as quickly as he could without making any noise.

They had to go now, before the squad in the showers came out.

As they climbed higher, the noise swelled, until it gobbled up the sound of the soldier's tread on the stairs above.

It sounded like a riot.

Hal went around the last corner cautiously, edging around the wall, until he had an angle on the floor above.

Nothing.

He took the last few steps slowly, back against the wall.

There was a small foyer or hallway enclosing the stairs, to keep things quiet for those sleeping in the dorms below, he'd guess. Beyond the double doors, the sound had risen to deafening, and Hal realized some of it was echoing down from the stairwell above.

Perhaps there was an atrium of some kind on the next floor.

"We going up?" Fiona asked him quietly, not that anyone would have heard her if she'd shouted it.

He nodded, and she followed him again.

There was a similar hallway when they reached the next level, but the doors were open on this one.

There was no one directly in front of it, so Hal leaned against the doorframe and looked out.

Someone had designed this level with an enormous circle cut into the floor, so it was possible to look down onto the floor below. On the far side of the circle to where Hal stood, was a wall set with windows and another double door. It looked as if a wide passageway led off into the distance, far larger than the dorm, the storage room or the sub-station.

Hal guessed when they'd built the facility, they'd dug an inverted cone, so the floors got progressively bigger, the higher you went.

He'd known there were over 300 of the Class 5's crew here, and the number of rooms on the dorm floor supported that, but now he looked down into the arena below and saw where everyone was.

They'd constructed seating stands, thick wedges four benches high. They were modular, and had been set in a circle around a raised platform that was enclosed with a force field fence.

The platform was covered in the orange sand from the desert above, and in the middle of it, the pale green animal they'd first seen when they'd come up from the sub-station, waiting to be transported up the stairs, circled a thick-set black animal about double its size with wicked claws at the tips of short, stubby limbs.

Fiona had said as shore leave, this facility didn't seem to offer much.

Hal took in the stands, packed to capacity with the Class 5's crew, all shouting encouragement and calling bets.

Looked like the Tecran had decided to make their own entertainment.

Chapter Twenty-nine

PIT FIGHTING.

It was so clichéd, Fee would have felt embarrassed for them, if she hadn't felt so enraged.

Did the scientists who dropped these animals off know what was happening to them, or was it that once they were finished with them, instead of a humane death, the staff and crew had decided to eke some entertainment out of them first?

And, was . . . she felt the nausea rise, forced it back down . . . was this what had happened to Imogen Peters?

Hal gripped her arm, pulled her back, and she realized she'd been all but hanging over the side of the narrow viewing platform.

The architect in her found the layout of this floor interesting. The stairs opened onto what was a gallery arrangement overlooking the arena. The gallery was narrow, hugging the curved walls on three sides but opening up on the fourth side, where it ended in a wall with big window insets.

Beyond, she could see a wide corridor stretching off into the distance.

"You think this is the main floor?" she asked Hal.

He gave a nod. "Entertainment, mess hall and probably exercise equipment below, offices and conference rooms up here."

And then above that, probably the garage for their runners.

"So most likely, we'll find what we're looking for here."

He didn't answer, his gaze moving to the side of the pit. She followed his line of sight, and saw someone who was obviously an officer trying to shout over the crowd.

It was like screaming into a hurricane. She'd have thought he'd use the crew's earpieces, but most likely they'd been allowed to take them off as part of their leave.

The pale green animal, which looked like a cross between a fox and a weasel, had finally stopped circling the animal that looked like a quarter-sized black bear, but with claws a full-grown grizzly would be proud of, and lunged in for the kill.

Its opponent swiped at it at the last moment, catching it in the throat and then pinning it down in the sand.

It hadn't even fully stood up, and it sunk back into a crouch, holding the green furred creature down while its struggles became weaker and weaker and eventually stopped.

As the fox thing died, the sound rose up at them in a roar, and Fee realized her hand had gone to the small of her back. They were almost all down there, weren't they? Hit a few crowd-pleaser cartridges into them, let them all go nighty-nighty, and they'd have the facility mostly to themselves to explore.

Hal caught her arm, tugged it away.

The look in his eyes told her he knew exactly what she was thinking. Didn't necessarily object.

"Wait," he said, and pointed down to the officer again. "There's something going on."

Two Tecran had entered the arena through a narrow gap in the force field, which winked out to let them through, and then winked back on as soon as they stepped beyond it. One had a bag in his hand, the other had a long metal rod. She guessed it was like a cattle prod and the bear-like animal had already encountered it before, because it shuffled back from the animal it had killed, edging toward the open crate it had been released from.

The Tecran worked quickly, scooping the dead animal into the bag, making sure the bear creature kept its distance, and then they backed out the way they'd come.

The noise level had abated a little while there was no fighting, but just when Fee thought the officer who was trying to make an announcement would finally be heard over the buzz, it swelled again, almost to fever pitch.

Fee searched for the new source of excitement and went stone cold.

The idiots were dragging the barrel bag containing the grahudi into the pit. And by the way they were struggling, it was now awake.

They left the bag in the middle of the ring, and moved back to the narrow entrance, one holding the long cattle prod and the other a small remote.

The one with the remote must have pressed it, because the center seam of the bag fell open, and the grahudi rolled out and hunched down, swaying a little.

It was obviously still woozy from the drugs, but when it shook its head, Fee thought it stood a little straighter.

The Tecran with the cattle prod had already stepped through the gate, and the one with the remote followed suit, the gate winking off to let him through.

As he moved, the lights on the floor below cut out, the only illumination the occasional flicker of energy along the force field enclosing the pit.

"What?" Fee breathed.

"The officer. He killed the power to get their attention." Hal's murmur was right against her ear.

Well, if he'd wanted their attention, he'd gotten it.

Stunned silence reigned for a moment, and that was all the officer needed.

He started to shout, his voice silencing the murmurs that rose up with the power still off.

"A small, unknown squad are approaching the facility," Eazi said. "I've been tracking them from the runner for a while. I don't think they knew about the station, they didn't seem to be heading this way, but one of them climbed high enough to see it, and now they're on their way."

"Is that what he's telling them?" Hal asked.

"Yes, he's ordering everyone on standby to suit up and head out to help intercept them."

Fee turned to ask Hal if he thought it was his crew coming to get them when the lights below switched back on, the officer having made his point.

They dipped once, brightened, and then, for the second time, the crowd went still.

The bear thing lay dead in the ring, completely eviscerated. Every eye searched for the grahudi, and then Fee noticed the narrow entrance to the arena finally flicker on and engage.

It had been off the whole time the power was down.

The same thought occurred to most of the room below, and Hal pulled her back against the wall again as heads swiveled up and around, desperately hunting for where the creature had gone.

Someone screamed, and the sound of wild panic spiraled upward.

She'd be cheering the grahudi on if she wasn't so terrified of it.

She moved at the same time as Hal. They'd both heard the running on the stairs. Some of the Tecran escaping the mayhem below were coming up.

She reached back as she ran, pulling out the crowd-pleaser, and heard the whine of Hal's shockgun, ready to shoot.

They were halfway to the door when the first of the Tecran burst up from the stairwell in a rush of shouting and shoving.

She kept running, taking a few steps before she realized Hal had stopped and turned to face the threat, weapon raised to cover her.

As she spun back to face them, at least four soldiers stumbled to a halt as they spotted Hal.

Fee knew the camouflage was good, but it couldn't literally make them invisible, and the shockgun in Hal's hands wasn't camouflaged anyway.

It was at that moment, as the first few soldiers blinked in amazement at the sight of them, that the grahudi swung up from below, flying out the open atrium as if weightless and landing on the thin railing in the center of the gallery in a crouch.

It looked like one of the strange, malevolent gargoyles she'd seen squatting at the tops of medieval buildings in Europe, all six limbs spread out, giving the impression it could go in any direction.

It was like a spider and a rabid baboon all mixed together, and her hind brain was screaming at her to just *run*.

Hal's gaze jerked to it, distracted like everyone else, but the lead Tecran had already committed his shot, had already taken aim at Hal.

Fee saw Hal stagger back and go down on one knee. He'd said his uniform offered him protection, but it looked like it was in line with kevlar; you didn't die, but it still hurt like hell.

The grahudi leapt in her direction as she ran to get in front of Hal, to shield him, and she ducked instinctively, saw it sail over her head from the corner of her eye.

One of the crew shot it in the shoulder and it spun and landed heavily behind her. She forced her attention forward again, and shot the first cartridge from her crowd-pleaser at the Tecran bottlenecked at the entrance to the stairs.

A soldier to her right threw himself into a roll, shot at Hal as he came up in a crouch, or maybe the shot was aimed at her, but she had the sense the Tecran was aiming low, and Hal was still down on one knee, struggling to stand.

The blue light of her reflector flared and the soldier shuddered and went still as his shot rebounded back at him.

Fee moved her arm right, got off another cartridge to the crew who had started spreading out as they realized they had to move forward out of the stairwell, that there were too many coming up for them to go back down.

There was one cartridge left before she had to reload, so she reached back, caught hold of Hal's shoulder and tried to pull him up.

He managed it, staggering a little behind her, and she took stock.

Those who could were shoving their way back down the stairs, but there were still crew standing amongst the fallen from her first two shots. Some had gotten lucky, others had just arrived, forced forward by the weight of the crowd behind them.

They were all scrambling back toward the stairs, bunching together to give her scattershot the best chance of hitting them.

She chanced a quick look behind her, found the grahudi staring back, hunched against the wall.

She turned away from it and shot the last cartridge at the crew, watched them all fall.

She dipped her shoulder under Hal's to keep him upright.

"Let's go while the going's good."

He nodded. The only part of his face she could see through his camouflage mask were his eyes, and they were half-closed and jittery.

They had to pass the grahudi, something that made a part of her gibber in mindless fear, so she ignored it, putting her back to it as she edged Hal sideways toward the door, covering him as much as possible, although there was no longer a single Tecran standing.

Hal looked heavier than he was, and although she would never call him light, given their size difference, she managed okay.

When they reached the door, it was locked. She touched the glowing white circle to the left of it over and over in frustration, the thought of the grahudi behind her making her hands shake, and then she remembered her prize possession. She dipped her spare hand into her bra, tapped the encryptor against the keypad and almost collapsed in relief as the doors opened instantly.

As she hauled Hal through, she couldn't help but look back over her shoulder. She shivered as she saw the grahudi was still watching her as the door slid shut, eyes gleaming through slitted eyelids.

It was silent on this side of the door, and much cooler than it had been in the atrium, with the gentle hum of air filtration she'd gotten used to on the *Fasbe* and the *Illium*.

Considering how many of the crew had been in the pit, she wasn't surprised there was hardly anyone here. With luck, she'd find an empty room.

She dragged Hal down the passage until they hit an intersecting corridor. She turned left at random and tried the first door she came to.

It opened without the need for an encryptor, so she tucked it back in her bra and took stock. The room wasn't just empty, it was unfurnished, with only a few crates stacked against a far corner and no lenses that she could see.

This place would do until Hal recovered.

She closed the door behind them, lowered Hal to the floor, and pulled the mask off his face to see how he was doing.

His mouth was tight with pain, but he tipped back his head and closed his eyes, and she thought he relaxed a little.

She needed to secure the room as best she could, so she dragged the crates in front of the door. They wouldn't stop anyone coming in, but they'd slow them down, give her the second or two she'd need to aim her crowd-pleaser.

"Fiona?" Eazi spoke to her for the first time since they'd taken the stairs up to this floor, and Fee jumped a little in surprise. "Are you all right?"

"Yes." She blew out a breath. He'd have seen everything that happened through the lens on her shirt, and she could only assume he hadn't spoken because he hadn't wanted to distract her. "Thanks for not talking to me while I was shooting it up. My focus was fractured enough as it was."

"I could see." He sounded surprised and . . . happy, she realized. He hadn't expected praise. "I still can't get into the system, so I won't speak for a while. I think you should stay in this room until I can get into the lens feed at least."

"Okay." As she said it, the adrenalin she'd be running on simply gave out, and she put a hand to the wall to keep herself standing.

She carefully and deliberately reloaded her weapon, hands fumbling she was so exhausted, and then lowered herself to sit next to Hal like an old woman, searching his face for any sign of increased pain. He was exactly as she'd left him, eyes closed, head tipped back against the wall, but she thought he looked better than he had.

Not sure what to do for him, she leaned back, pulled her own mask off her head and closed her eyes herself.

The back of Hal's hand brushed over hers, comforting.

She kept her eyes closed, and just enjoyed the feel of him pressed up against her.

The idiot had stood in front of her when the Tecran came charging after them. He'd protected her, again, even though she was better protected than he was.

It had been instinct, she guessed, and training. Save the civilian.

Her mind flashed back to the sight of the grahudi, rising up out of the gloom of the pit like a demon from hell, and the terror of the moment washed over her again.

"Shh." He gripped her hand, his thumb rubbing across her knuckles in a way that was more intimate than a kiss.

"They had no business playing with that thing." She was angry as well as frightened, she realized. It had done nothing, *nothing*, but be what it was.

"I know." It was the first time he'd spoken since he'd been hit, and his voice was rougher than usual.

"I thought you said your uniform had good protection."

"Their shockguns were set to kill." He sounded grim. "I shouldn't be surprised, but I am. They were shooting in their own facility, and anyone caught in the crossfire would be their own crew. It doesn't make sense."

"They wanted to kill it." She drew in a steadying breath.

"Yes." He sounded more and more like himself. "My uniform would have handled any stun setting, but a kill setting was a little harder to absorb." His thumb kept up its gentle caress of her skin. "Thank you for shielding me when I went down."

"We're a team." She gave a shrug and slid down the wall a little more, not wanting to open her eyes and deal with anything for a few more moments.

"Did they kill the grahudi?" Hal asked, and she realized he must have been really out of it to have missed what happened.

She shook her head. "I had a choice. I didn't know whether to use the last cartridge in the gun to shoot the grahudi or the Tecran. If it had attacked, we'd have been dead."

"What did you choose?" he asked,

"I decided to leave it alone. It's not my enemy, the Tecran are."

"How many of them did you get?" His voice was a quiet rumble.

Finally she opened her eyes and met his gaze. "Every single one."

Chapter Thirty

SHE WAS PLAYING WITH THE CRYSTAL Eazi had given her, sliding it up and down on the silver necklace it hung from.

"It's pretty," Hal said, and she started, looked down at it and then tucked it away under her shirt.

"Yes, it is."

She'd been left with nothing when the Tecran took her, and he was suddenly sorry he'd dumped her on Jasa and left her to sink or swim on the *Illium*. There had been no soft landing for her.

He'd been too busy chasing down Krik and dealing with the ripples her existence caused.

"I should have taken better care of you after we rescued you."

He still held her hand, and he felt her tense.

She looked up at him. "You took care of me just by getting me off the *Fasbe*."

"I could have done better."

She shrugged. "You had a lot going on. And because I didn't have any direct evidence against the Tecran, I know I was lower down the list of priorities."

Ouch.

She had him there. And she'd had a clear handle on the situation right from the start.

He'd fallen into the trap of seeing her as a helpless victim and a slightly clueless orange when he'd first met her. But she'd been on to them all from the start.

"You're just one surprise after the other."

She slid him a sidelong look. "Hardly. As I said, getting off the *Fasbe* was lifesaving for me. Can't get much bigger a deal than that."

"I'm sorry you were taken. It wasn't right. But I'm not sorry I met you." He'd said no to her advances earlier, sure it was the correct decision, if a hard one, but the longer he spent in her company, the more he doubted himself.

She looked up at him, gaze clear and direct. "Careful, Captain. You're getting perilously close to fraternizing."

He jerked back at that, realized his hand had been cupped around her neck.

She threw him off balance.

Ever since he'd seen her sing happy birthday to Mun he'd wanted her, but in his mind she'd been off-limits.

Now he wasn't so sure, and he didn't know if that made him weak or the smartest he'd ever been.

"You aren't the enemy." He said it slowly, let the truth of it sink in so she relaxed against the wall again.

Then he leaned forward, and, because this was a private moment, put his palm over the lens on her shirt.

"What exactly are you doing?" Her voice was a soft murmur. It beguiled him every time she spoke, the sound alone so seductive, was it any wonder he was losing this battle with himself?

"I'm throwing good sense aside." She had been brave enough to make her interest known, he could do no less than offer the same. "Battle Center will frown on any relationship between us, and yet, I can't shake loose the sense that if I don't take the risk, I'm going to be sorry about it for the rest of my life."

Her dark eyes glittered in the low light. "I can understand being cautious if this will be a career-breaker. You've got a lot to lose, far more than me."

She left it at that, not pushing, and he didn't like that she had nothing to lose because it had all been taken from her.

She looked calm, but his hand still rested against her chest, over Eazi's lens, and he felt her heartbeat elevate.

Until it matched his own.

It confused him, finding himself wondering if his career was really worth keeping his hands off her. "I don't recognize myself." He hadn't meant to say it aloud, but her head snapped up to look at him. "I'm starting to think if Battle Center disapproves, that's their problem."

The look in her eyes was stricken. "Hal, I don't want to cause trouble for you. If it doesn't work out between us, you'll have thrown it away for nothing."

Not nothing.

He had the feeling it would never be nothing.

He shook his head. "This isn't on you. It's on me. And I may be exaggerating how much Battle Center will care."

She lifted a hand, and fingered the hair at his temples. "I'm not going to take out an ad in the Grih National News about getting together with you, if that helps. I can do discreet." She lifted a shoulder. "And if you find what's between us isn't worth getting into trouble with Battle Center, I can accept that. I've got a lot less to lose in that regard, so you have my word, I won't cause you trouble." She tilted her head to look right in his eyes, tried for lighthearted. "You've stored up a heck of a lot of goodwill with me. So even if I fall madly in love with you and then you break my heart and stomp it to tiny pieces, I won't make life difficult for you. I promise."

Hand still over the lens, he stared at her.

She was offering him everything he wanted, her face calm, her eyes steady. And warm.

"I don't want your gratitude." He didn't mean to sound so harsh, but she didn't so much as blink.

Her lips quirked. "I don't want to kiss you because I'm grateful, but I'm telling you that even if you really piss me off and kick me to the curb, that gratitude will mean I'll put on my game face around you."

"I still don't want it."

She shrugged. "Suck it up. I feel what I feel."

He frowned down at her, and she grinned back up at him, laughing at him, even, and the thin, taut line that had been holding him back since he'd felt that first hot, sharp pull of attraction, snapped.

He angled his head, leaned in and kissed her, and she opened her mouth to him with a sigh of pleasure.

"There seems to be an obstruction to the lens, Fiona." He heard the tinny sound of Eazi's voice from her earpiece a few minutes later because his mouth was tracing her ear, his fingers deep in hair that was as smooth and soft as the silk she wore. "I haven't gotten into the lens feed, but there's good news. I've managed to get into the building schematics."

***

Fee leaned a little way out of the shadows to look down the short corridor that ended in reinforced double doors and admitted Eazi had been right to send them here.

Hal shifted beside her, the small area under the stairwell to the floor above leaving no room to stand without touching.

That was okay with her. And Hal was definitely standing closer than he needed to, so it seemed to be okay with him, too.

Maybe making out with the captain while hiding from murderous thugs earlier hadn't been her smartest ever move, but it had been just what she'd needed.

A little joy and respite went a long way. Even if you were listening for the sound of heavy footsteps with one ear while doing it.

"I wish you were in the lens feed," Fee whispered to Eazi. "I'd like to know what's in there before opening the door."

"Me, too." The frustration in Eazi's voice was palpable. It might be character-building for him to have to work hard at something, but Fee wished the challenge wasn't quite so difficult now. "I don't know how they've shielded so well."

Struggling had tempered Eazi's tone. Not that being in the lens feed would be that big of a help. They hadn't found a single lens so far on this floor.

Eazi guessed they had only put them in strategically important areas, like the animal storage area, the floor above where the runners and vehicles were kept, and maybe, just maybe, the room in front of them.

It would have been nice to be sure.

They didn't even know what the room was. Eazi had flagged it as the first stop because there was no label, no description of it, in the schematics.

A mystery room.

The kill switch could be anywhere, but if they wanted to be out of the facility before one of the Tecran she'd hit with the crowd-pleaser barbs woke up and started talking, they had to try somewhere, and a mystery room was as good a place as any.

"Ready?" Hal's shockgun was humming away.

Fee gave a jerky nod. Her heart was back on the jackhammer setting it had been on in the gallery, when she'd had to deal with the grahudi and the Tecran all at once. Hal moved silently across the main passage and then down the short corridor to the door, and she followed, her crowd-pleaser gripped in both hands.

They were so exposed here, with nowhere to run if someone was in front of them, or behind.

Hal touched the side of the door, but it didn't open.

Fee's hand came up, gripped the neck of her shirt. She was about to offer her encryptor, when the sound of feet running down the stairs from above made them both freeze. Whoever was coming down was giving loud orders, perhaps through his earpiece, because she couldn't hear anyone answering.

The person was taking the stairs two at a time, and as Fee moved back down the corridor to get to their hiding place under the stairs, she realized the thump of his tread had masked the sound of a group of people running toward them from the gallery.

The Tecran coming down the stairs hadn't seen her and Hal yet, but running across the passageway to the shadows under the stairwell would change that.

Fee forced herself to slide up against the wall and not move.

She wanted to look back at Hal, but made herself stay still and trust he'd done the same.

The soldier jumped the last three steps, hand tapping at his ear as he spoke in quick, harsh bursts. He stopped right in front of the little corridor they were trapped in, head in profile, and waited for the soldiers running toward him.

At least ten soldiers stopped and came to attention. Any one of them only had to turn his head a little and he'd be looking straight at her.

Now that the running had stopped, she could hear sounds from above, scuffling and shouting. If that was the group who Eazi said was approaching the facility, they were obviously not coming quietly.

The officer was screeching orders at the team in front of him and when he'd finished they ran up the stairs, presumably to help with the prisoners. Instead of going after them, or walking away, the officer kept his focus down the passageway, and Fee realized a second group were coming toward him.

Just as they got there, the officer frowned, tapped his earpiece and looked her way.

Fee stopped breathing.

The new group was milling around, but they stilled and followed their leader's gaze.

Fee didn't want to look, but she could see their eyes were passing right over her, to something beyond her.

Hal.

The officer lifted his shockgun and pointed it.

The time for hiding was up.

Fee stepped in front of him, crowd-pleaser raised, and watched him refocus his gaze, blink those big, round Tecran eyes as he worked out she wasn't part of the wall.

There was no time to posture, she needed to shoot, but before she could pull the trigger, Hal cried out behind her.

She took a step backward, toward him, angling her body to the right so she could also keep her eye on the group in the passageway, and saw someone had come through from the room beyond, the room they'd been trying to break into.

Hal was on the ground, lying motionless, and the soldier standing over him was holding a shockgun to his head.

Chapter Thirty-one

HEART IN HER THROAT, eyes fixed on the soldier standing over Hal, Fee raised her crowd-pleaser up, along with her other hand, in surrender.

The officer still obviously had trouble keeping her in focus, and he exchanged a quick conversation with the man who'd shot Hal and then walked forward carefully, put out his hand and patted the air around her until his hand glanced off her forehead. He grabbed hold of her hood, clenched it in his fist and pulled it up over her head.

They stared at each other for a long moment and then he reached up and took the crowd-pleaser out of her hand.

He knew who she was. She'd seen the shock in his eyes. So most likely, he was part of the Class 5 crew, not permanently stationed here.

He said something to her and she shook her head.

"You gave me to the Garmman, remember?" She let her lip curl a little as she spoke. "I can only speak Garmman or Grih."

He blinked at that.

He'd taken her weapon, so she gambled on him thinking she was otherwise harmless and risked turning her back on him and walking to Hal, careful not to make any sudden moves. She crouched down, going a little weak when she felt his chest rise under her hands. He was breathing.

She lifted his hood up off his head, saw his face was pale and there was a mark on his neck.

She raised her eyes and stared at the man who'd shot him, and he took a step back.

"This is a Grih military uniform." The officer who'd taken her crowd-pleaser had come to stand next to his colleague.

She ignored him, running a hand down Hal's cheek.

The sounds of fighting from the floor above had been getting louder, although she'd only half noticed them, but now it filled the space, like a moving riot sweeping down the stairs.

Both Tecran looked toward the sound, and Fee used the moment to peer into the room they'd planned to break into through the still-open door.

Four or five huge freestanding transparent blue screens with tiny lights moving across them were set out in the massive space. A Tecran sitting at a chair in front of a console was staring at her. She took in as much as she could, but as the melee arrived behind her, he tapped a button and the doors closed.

She wasn't sure if that was to protect the area from the fight moving toward them, or to stop her looking any more.

She turned back to see what was happening as the group reached the bottom of the stairs.

And stared, open-mouthed, at the prisoners the Tecran had rounded up.

Gerwa, of the Krik battalion V8, stared back at her.

Around him, his men fought the Tecran's hold on them, even though they were bound with manacles around their wrists and ankles, as if they couldn't understand it was time to surrender.

With a sharp word from the officer beside her, someone must have done something, because the Krik began to fall to the ground, crying out in pain.

Eventually, only Gerwa was left standing, his gaze fixed on her, the same shock that must be etched on her features reflected in his.

"Guess the emergency pod didn't quite work out for you," she said at last.

And he threw back his head and laughed.

***

Officer Vek oversaw their imprisonment personally.

Fee could tell he was deeply disturbed that she seemed to know the Krik, but they weren't talking, and neither was she.

They'd been taken down to the storage facility, and she and Hal were thrown into Imogen Peter's old cell.

As the Krik were forced into a cage so big, Fee wondered what they'd kept in there, and what they had done with it afterward, the macaw swooped from one end of its cage to cling to a bar.

"Bastards," it said, and clicked its beak. Then it tipped back its head. "Bee-yoo-ti-ful plumage."

Fee caught the giggle that rose up before it could escape.

Imogen Peters was obviously a fan of Monty Python's parrot sketch.

Vek spun around as it spoke, and looked between her and the macaw suspiciously.

"You know him. How?" He demanded of her, and for a moment, she though he meant the macaw. She started shaking her head, and he pointed at Gerwa.

"I know this. You spoke." His Garmman was bad, and she put on her dumb face and lifted her shoulders. Lowered her eyes meekly.

He'd taken her crowd-pleaser, her camouflage hood, all of Hal's weapons and his hood, too.

He hadn't taken her reflector. It looked like a bracelet, and she guessed that Vek hadn't participated in the tests Captain Flato had conducted on the stolen technology.

She knew from what Eazi had said that there was one Class 5 commander left down here, but he had yet to make an appearance.

She didn't think that would last, though, and the moment he caught sight of her reflector, he'd take it. And know for sure she'd come from the Class 5.

If he had any hesitation about flipping the kill switch and blowing the Class 5 up, as soon as he realized she'd had free access to the Class 5's stores, that hesitation would evaporate.

And kaboom.

With Vek still frowning at her, she forced her hands to her sides, although she was desperate to check that the crystal pendant was tucked safely out of sight.

"You know him." Vek jabbed a finger at Gerwa again.

Fee lifted her shoulders, turned away and crouched beside Hal, and then maneuvered herself so she could lift his head onto her lap.

He was still unconscious, and it had taken two Tecran to carry him down the three flights of stairs to get here.

They had not been careful.

Vek turned to Gerwa. Fired off a string of questions in Tecran, and when Gerwa mimicked her own shrug with one exactly the same, he pulled out his shockgun and leveled it at the Krik.

Gerwa snarled at him, lifting his upper lip to show his impressive incisors.

"Tell." Vek obviously meant to shoot the Krik if he didn't get an answer. Fee watched it play out from behind lowered lids.

She was sticking to the dumb orange act. No way was she contributing anything to this conversation.

If Gerwa wanted to say how they met, that was fine by her, and if he'd prefer to be shot, that suited her just as well.

Vek let off a shot, and it hit Gerwa in the chest.

The Krik went down, but it must have been on the lowest setting, because he raised himself up on his elbows almost as soon as he hit the floor, and hissed at Vek again.

With a screech of frustration, Vek stepped closer, shockgun still raised. He'd sent most of the soldiers back to their duties, but the two who'd carried Hal down remained and they took up positions on either side of him.

They didn't even look her way. She'd been dismissed as a threat or a source of information.

She guessed that if Hal had been conscious, they'd have paid more attention to her and him, but they'd decided that Gerwa was the best chance of working out what was going on for now.

They had to be deeply worried.

Two different groups had made it to their secret facility in one day. The grahudi cage was empty, so Fee guessed it was still on the loose, plus they would be panicking at the lack of contact from Captain Flato and the Class 5. These guys had their hands full.

She knew from when she'd been here earlier that there was a lens, and now she was in Imogen's cage she saw it was pointed directly at her, attached to a metal beam that ran across the ceiling.

When she broke them out with her trusty encryptor, she'd need Hal to be up to running with her, because they'd have to move fast. Their escape would be seen.

She started combing Hal's hair back from his forehead. The Grih seemed to be obsessed with singing, so maybe singing would help him, bring him out of the dark.

She'd developed quite a repertoire on the *Fasbe*, first in her cell, and later while she worked in the launch bay. She had some favorites, and she chose the smooth, gentle rhythm of *Get Here*, tuning out the shouting match between Gerwa and Vek, her gaze fixed on Hal's face, but a quick flash of movement out of the corner of her eye made her look up sharply.

The grahudi stared at her from the top of its old cage.

Her voice faltered, and then trailed off. It would certainly be handy if the grahudi attacked the Tecran, but then it would still be out there when she wanted to escape.

It jumped, the only sound the faint disturbance of air as it flew thirty feet and landed on the back of one of the soldiers standing beside Vek.

It used him as a spring board to leap on top of the cage containing the Krik and then turned to face Vek, mouth open, teeth bared.

The soldier made a strange sound and then fell.

Fee eased Hal's head off her lap and stood. Even though she was locked up, she felt too vulnerable on the floor.

She peered through the bars, and saw the soldier's throat had been slit from ear to ear.

After a moment of panic, Vek and the other soldier shot at the grahudi, and it screamed at them, the first time she'd ever heard it make more than a quiet grunt.

It filled the air like a klaxon, and then the sound cut off as it curled in on itself. It had taken another hit, but before Vek could get off another shot, it sailed back over his head, hit Fee's cage and then landed on the ground and ran for the stairwell.

The Tecran ran after it, Vek tapping his ear and shouting instructions.

Their footsteps died away, and absolute silence reigned for a long beat.

None of the animals or birds left in the cages moved or made a sound.

Bambi in the headlights.

Just like her.

"What was that?" Gerwa called softly, and she could hear the fear and awe in his voice.

"A grahudi from Fitali territory."

"A grahudi," one of Gerwa's team said, voice hushed. "They are legend."

Fee shivered, and sat back down on the ground, arranged Hal's head in her lap again.

"So, the Grih did rescue you, in the end," Gerwa said, and she lifted her head to see he was looking at the cozy arrangement with a speculative gaze.

She looked up at the lens, looked back at him, and his mouth clamped shut.

They'd have no secrets if they continued talking, because if the Tecran hadn't been watching this area earlier when she and Hal had come through, they were certainly watching and listening now.

She was glad about it.

She didn't have anything to say to Gerwa, and she was getting more and more worried about Hal.

He was so limp, the only sign of life was the gentle rise and fall of his chest.

"Wake up." She bent down and kissed his forehead. "Please wake up."

Chapter Thirty-two

LONG AGO, THE ANCIENT GRIH who'd come close to death spoke of hearing beautiful singing while they hovered in what they called the InBetween. It was part of their history, and every Grih learned the strange and mystical stories their ancestors told each other long ago, more with a sense of amusement and indulgence than anything else.

But Hal *could* hear it.

It was in a strange language, more melodic and smooth than Grihan or any of the other languages of the UC.

The sweet sound was interrupted by a loud, discordant cry followed by a loud exclamation.

The singing stopped, and then started again, this time infused with laughter. The song was different, more upbeat, and every now and then, the singer whistled a tune.

Hal opened his eyes.

He could see the underside of Fiona's chin, and the dark curtain of her hair. She was looking off to the side as she sang.

She said something in her language, and when there was another discordant reply, she laughed.

"What . . ." his voice was a faint croak, but as he spoke, she swept back her hair, looked down at him.

The expression on her face was one of relief and overwhelming delight.

"You're awake." Tears welled in her eyes and clung to her lashes, and a feeling lanced through him that was painful in its intensity, squeezing his lungs and closing up his throat.

He fought to sit up.

She'd had his head in her lap, he realized, and they were . . . he tried to focus. Back in the storage room. In Imogen Peter's cage.

He swallowed and then coughed, his throat burning it was so dry. "Water?" he asked on a croak, and she shook her head. "Nothing except what's been left in that bucket, and I just don't know how long it's been there. I'm too scared it's bad."

He nodded, then remembered one of the pockets of his uniform came with a rehydration pack.

It was still there, and he pulled it out, ripped it open and offered it to Fiona first.

She shook her head. "I'm fine. You're the one who got zapped."

He sucked down half and offered it to her again, his body responding almost instantly to the liquid.

She trailed her fingers down his cheek in a gentle caress. "Have it all. I'm so happy to see you upright. And you're going to need all your strength."

She came up on her knees, slid her arms around him, and at that moment he heard the murmur of men's voice, the shifting of bodies.

He turned his head, saw a small band of Krik staring at them.

"The lens is pointed right at us," she whispered in his ear. The warmth of her, the touch of her lips to his skin, the sweet scent of her, made him tighten his grip. "I can get us out of here, but only if you're up to running, because they'll know the moment we bolt."

He gave a slow nod, although he wondered how she could get them out. Perhaps Eazi had a way. He kept his gaze on the Krik. "Are these your friends from the *Fasbe*?"

"Yes. We aren't talking to each other, because they don't want the lens to pick up our conversation, but that's Gerwa and his happy crew." She rested her head on his shoulder for a moment and he dropped his cheek on top of it. Rubbed against the incredibly smooth, silky texture of her hair, so different to his own.

"Can you stand?"

He gave another nod, although he wasn't sure.

He shuffled back from her, put out a hand to grip a bar and pulled himself up.

His knees gave way, but he didn't go down, and after blowing out a breath, he managed to push himself up again.

He was looking straight at the Krik, and they were looking right back at him. Their eyes sharp and avaricious, their demeanor watchful and arrogant.

They pushed every button he had.

He realized his hands were so tight on the bars, his knuckles were white.

"You seem not to like us, Grih." The Krik who spoke to him rested a cocked hip on the bars of the cage, a sneer on his face.

"As you—"

Fiona grabbed his shirt and gave him a little yank to remind him about the lens.

He swallowed his rage, remembered he needed to see if he could move fast enough to escape. He walked to the end of the cage and had to stop, his muscles trembling.

Fiona watched him with worried eyes from the center of the space.

From behind her, the strange, beautiful bird from her planet whistled a jaunty tune. Fiona turned and sang to it, and the sheer perfection of it, so casually done, astonished him.

The bird whistled again, and he realized the creature was participating in the song, that they were making music together.

"What is that?" he asked when they stopped.

The Krik were watching as well, and Hal didn't like their intense interest.

"Imogen must have taught him. I can imagine they had lots of hours to fill down here. It's an extremely funny song, but tragic, too, because the . . . visual comms it was written for is a kind of satire and at the end, people who are slowly dying in horrific circumstances sing this happy tune about always looking on the bright side of life." She went quiet. "I suppose Imogen wasn't far off from being in their shoes, and singing this song, teaching the macaw to do the whistling part with her, was both ironic and funny enough to give her hope."

A funny, tragic song. He tried to get his mind around the concept of it, let alone singing as a method of subtle defiance.

To the Grih, singing was a serious business. Solemn and full of pomp.

"When you asked us to take you with us, I didn't understand the comforts you were prepared to offer," one of the Krik called to Fiona from their cage. "Or the talents you have."

"Comforts?" Fiona looked confused, and the Krik pointed his finger at Hal, then moved it across to her. "The gentle singing, the soft kisses." He smacked his lips lasciviously.

She snorted. "I don't go down that road with people who hit me over the head. Or raise their hand to me in any way. Or lie." She put a hand on her hip, and Hal could hear the underlying sarcasm in her voice. "Sorry you didn't help me now, Gerwa? You saying there actually *was* some room for me in that emergency pod?"

Her tone was challenging, derisive, and everything Hal knew about the Krik said they would react with abuse or threats, but the big Krik she'd called Gerwa gave a low, amused laugh.

"Maybe there was. That was my loss."

She turned her back on him, but Hal stared him down, and for the first time, Gerwa's smug expression dropped away, and he took a half-step back.

"You okay?" Fiona asked with a frown.

He gave a quick nod and started pacing the cage, enjoying the sensation of strength that slowly filtered back into his limbs. He lifted a hand to his neck where his skin was still tingling and numb and was grateful the camouflage hood over his head and neck had had some protective features.

He'd been so focused on the passageway and the stairs, on the threat coming toward them. But there must have been a hidden lens near the door, someone must have seen them out there, camouflage or not, because the soldier who shot him had been ready to fire the moment the doors opened wide enough. He'd barely felt the slight change in temperature as cold air spilled from the room behind him before he went down.

"What happened after I got shot?"

Fiona shook her head. "Let's not go there now. The Krik took some of the pressure off us, at least. They didn't know what to do with so many intruders all at once."

Hal narrowed his gaze at her, but he wasn't going to insist she tell him how they'd disarmed her with the Krik and the Tecran listening in.

She suddenly blinked, lifted her head a fraction, and then started to sing another song.

He had the strong sense she was listening to someone, and then he realized she was talking to Eazi, and disguising it as a song in her own language.

He frowned, and lifted a hand to his ear, to find his earpiece had been taken. Fiona's, it seemed, had not.

Fiona came toward him, flicking her fingers in a tiny movement to indicate he move back. He complied until they were in the corner of the cage furthest from the lens, and in a deep fall of shadow.

"Eazi is in the lens feed at last," she murmured as she stepped into his arms, her breath warming against his neck. "So we'll need to sit down in plain sight and not move for a few minutes so he can create a loop to fool them."

"Can he see what was in that room we were trying to break

into?" Hal knew for sure whatever was there was something Battle Center would be interested in.

"I saw it myself before they dragged us down here. It's a surveillance room. Eazi says from what he saw from the lens on my shirt, they're tracking the traffic in the Balco system, and listening in to the comms on the planet."

"And the self-destruct protocol?"

The Krik were making a noise now, a sort of high-pitched chant, and Hal looked over at them. They were all riveted by the sight of Fiona in his arms.

He turned, taking her with him, so she was in the corner, and his back was all the Krik could see.

The chant got louder, even more wild.

"They are so scary," she said, and something in the pragmatic, serious tone she used forced a laugh out of him.

"Easy for you to laugh." Her face was stern, but her eyes danced. "They don't have kinky ideas about you."

"No. They just want me dead," he agreed.

She winced, and half-lifted a hand to her ear before she dropped it. No sense letting the Tecran know she had an earpiece. "All right," she said in exasperation. "Eazi says from what he can find in the system, they set the self-destruct thing up in a hurry, and the only way to stop it is to find the actual device that would be activated. He doesn't know where it is, and we can hardly stumble around looking for it. We certainly can't go back to that room without weapons or camouflage, there are at least five Tecran in there at all times."

"So we get out of here." Hal would have made that call anyway. Fiona wasn't safe here. Never had been, but before, with their weapons and camouflage, they'd had a chance. Now, with nothing, any foray back into the facility would have little chance of success.

"Yes. At least for now. So let's go sit in the light and look bored

for five minutes or so, and Eazi can do his thing." She
straightened, waiting for him to move out of her way.

The Krik had fallen quiet, but Hal could still feel their gaze. He
wanted to shield Fiona from them, because somehow her behavior
toward him had incited something in them.

His thoughts must have been clear because she sighed. "No
choice. It doesn't matter."

"It does matter." He drew her to him. "But you're right, there is
no choice."

He pulled back and they walked to the well-lit part of the cage
and sat, leaning against the wall of bars, not touching or speaking.

The Krik went silent, too, as if confused by their behavior.

Hal didn't know how much of the Krik's cage the lens caught,
but it suited him and Fiona if they were quiet. It would make the
loop Eazi was creating more realistic.

After what felt like much longer than five minutes, Fiona lifted
her head.

"Eazi says we're good," she said as she pulled herself to her
feet.

He beat her to it. "How's he getting us out?"

She pursed her lips. "He's not. He isn't in the lock system yet,
although he says he's getting there."

"Then how—" he trailed off as she slid a hand into her top and
pulled out a slim device.

She grinned at him. "You didn't see it because you were pretty
out of things that first time you were hit, but this baby got us out
of the gallery earlier."

"What is it?"

She turned and looked over at the Krik, who were now
absolutely still. "Mine," she said, and the smile she sent Gerwa
was sharp enough to cut.

Chapter Thirty-three

SOMETIMES, REVENGE *WAS* SWEET.

Fee put her hand through the bars by the keypad to the cage and pushed it open. She walked over to the macaw's cage, opened that, too.

It looked at her, and shuffled to the back of the cage.

"You letting us out?" Gerwa asked her.

She raised a brow as she looked over at him. "What do you think?"

He bared his teeth. "That is my encryptor."

She ignored him, held out her arm to the macaw.

It studied her back, not moving at all.

"We have to go." Hal stood right behind her.

"I know, but we have to take the macaw with us. I just can't leave it."

He made a sound of frustration, stepped around her and lunged, grabbing the bird in his big hands and pulling it out. It was obviously struggling, but he was holding it firmly enough, gently enough, that it wasn't hurting itself.

"Right, now let's go."

She smiled at him. "Thank you."

"You wouldn't have it if not for me," Gerwa called.

"Do you honestly think I'm stupid enough to trust you not to try and attack both of us the moment I open your door?" Fee slid it back into her bra.

Hal was standing beside her, and he took a step toward the Krik's cage.

"Don't worry. I'll be back for you," he said to them. "You won't be in here for too long." His voice was low, vibrating with rage.

Gerwa tried to sneer at him, but the gesture fell flat when he swallowed convulsively.

Hal tore his gaze from the Krik and then turned.

They started jogging toward the stairs.

"You got that device from them on the *Fasbe*?" Hal's voice was suspiciously neutral.

"I did." She couldn't help but smile again. "It's been the gift that keeps on giving."

Hal turned to look at her, eyes wide with surprise, and she shrugged.

"If I'd told you I had it when I was on the *Illium*, I bet you someone would have taken it from me to have a look, and we wouldn't have just escaped the Tecran."

He was about to respond when Eazi interrupted.

"There's someone down in the sub-station, guarding the tunnel. But it's still the better way out."

She whispered the news to Hal and he stopped at the top of the stairs. "Do you still have the reflector?"

She lifted her arm to show him and he gave a relieved nod.

"Take the bird, it's stopped struggling. I need my hands free." He held it out to her and she carefully opened both hands and grasped hold of it.

"Okay, but I'm keeping close. Let me stand in front of you if someone shoots."

He gave a reluctant nod and then led the way down the stairs. Fee didn't know how he moved so fast and made so little noise. She had to creep down in order not to clump.

Hal waited for her at the bottom, crouched low, trying to see what lay beyond the stairwell.

They'd only come through here maybe four or five hours earlier, but to Fee, if felt as if days had passed.

Someone moved. She could hear the shuffle of fabric and the

creak of boots.

"Are you able to interfere with audio comms?" she whispered to Eazi. "So this guy can't call for help when he sees us coming?"

"Oh . . . done." Eazi whispered back.

The guard shifted again.

Hal looked like he was wiggling a small rock loose from the bare earthen wall they were crouched against, and when he finally got it free, he threw it just in front of them.

Good idea. Let the guard come to them.

He did.

His walk was cautious; stopping, moving forward again, as if he were looking nervously around, trying to see past the pumps and monitors before he committed himself.

As hopefully everyone still thought she, Hal and the Krik were safely locked up, she guessed it was the grahudi that had them so spooked.

"Commander Dai just hailed the facility." Eazi's voice was like a soft sigh in her ear. "It appears he's been out with a hand-picked squad to check where the Krik came from. They've found the emergency pod and are returning to base. As soon as he gets in, he wants to talk to the prisoners, and they're going to find you are gone."

As the guard was too close for her to reply without being heard, Fee did not respond, except to hover a thumbs up near the lens on her shirt, so he understood she'd got it.

The guard stopped in front of the small rock, incongruously lying in the middle of the floor, and looked slowly up at the ceiling, which was solid metal, crisscrossed with thin blue wire and the occasional light. His shoulders slumped in relief when he didn't find a grahudi looking back down at him.

Hal moved, leaping from their hiding place, smashing the guard to the floor. The Tecran screeched as he went down, the noise causing the macaw to struggle in her hands.

It was big and much stronger than she'd thought, and she battled to keep hold of it without hurting it.

She moved forward, dancing around the tangle of legs as Hal hammered a punch to the guard's face.

She kicked his shockgun away from him, and Hal flipped him on his stomach and then pulled the restraints from the back of the soldier's pants and secured him.

Hal was breathing hard, but there was a satisfaction on his face she guessed came from being shot twice and locked up, and now finally having a chance to fight back.

"Eazi says the commander's on his way to interrogate us." Fee waited for Hal to scoop up the guard's shockgun.

He checked the charge, changed it, and shot the moaning guard in what seemed like one easy move.

The Tecran slumped into unconsciousness.

"You okay to run?" Hal asked her. "Run fast?"

She nodded, thinking that was her line, given she'd gotten out of this incursion without a scratch.

Hal let her take the lead. He was watching her back, she realized, and making sure he didn't leave her behind. His legs being so much longer than hers.

The tunnel was steeper than she remembered, but now, of course, she was going uphill, rather than down.

The wind from outside blew grit into her eyes and seemed to be trying to push her back.

She didn't dare stop to catch her breath or even slow down. Hal's presence at her back, the knowledge that he was reining himself in to match her stride, was a spur to her, making her push herself harder than she thought she was capable of.

By the time they burst out of the tunnel, she was struggling to breathe and her throat and eyes felt as if they'd been painted with grit.

"They just realized you're gone," Eazi told her. "They aren't happy." He paused. "Commander Dai's demanding to look at the lens feed, which I promptly hid away, but that lieutenant from earlier told him who you were and what you were wearing. He's guessed you came from the Class 5."

"What is it?" Hal asked her, and Fee realized she'd been getting slower and slower as she communicated with Eazi.

"They know we're gone, and they know at least I came from the Class 5."

Hal was leading the way, now, up behind the facility, keeping below the horizon as they picked their way around rocks and sand dunes toward the drone.

"So what are they going to do now?"

Fee tried to suck in enough air to run and talk as she listened to Eazi. "Eazi's lost visuals on Dai because he's left the storage room, but he can hear him coordinating various teams to guard the exits."

"If he's worked out you're from the Class 5, he's got to be pretty close to hitting that button." Hal didn't even sound winded.

"I have a solution." Eazi's voice, for the last few hours so similar to her own cadence, so much friendlier, was suddenly back to Mr. Roboto mode.

"What have you got planned?" Her voice must have given away her sudden fear, because Hal looked back at her, face set in grim lines.

Behind them, a strange noise rose up, and Fee stumbled to a stop, turned to look. "What is that?"

"The dome is opening." Hal pulled her closer to the rock that loomed over them, blocking any view of the facility.

The roar of a runner's engine filled the air, and Fee looked up to see it head straight upward.

"They aren't coming to look for us?"

"I think they're going to check on the Class 5. Be sure of what's going on before they blow it up." Hal's voice was tense.

"I think the captain is right," Eazi said. "I have no choice but to strike first."

"What are you going to do?" Fee asked him.

"I'm going to obliterate the facility before that runner gets here. Hopefully, that will destroy the kill switch at the same time."

Hal looked at her, cocked an eyebrow.

"He's going to fire on the facility." There was an implacability about the way he had spoken. "Eazi, at least warn them so they can get out."

"No. They'll be even more likely to hit the button, then. If they know I'm in the facility's systems, they may not wait for the runner to confirm I'm no longer theirs."

He was right. She closed her eyes and struggled with the idea that the Krik, the Tecran, whatever animals were left in the storage room, were all dead.

Hal seemed to be taking it a lot more philosophically. He was looking toward the facility thoughtfully. "I'd have preferred to have brought Battle Center down on the Tecran for this, and that'll be harder if it's a smoldering ruin, but I agree. It's the best move Eazi can make."

Fee clasped the macaw closer to her chest. Thank goodness she hadn't decided to go back for it later.

"I would suggest you keep moving as fast as you can," Eazi told her.

Almost as if he'd heard him, Hal grabbed her hand and started jogging toward the drone again.

They had just reached the drone, running fast down the slope toward it, when she saw a flash of pale red light and skidded to a halt, struggling to keep her balance on the loose sand with her hands full of parrot.

Behind them, the facility turned into a massive pillar of flame, and a low, flat boom caused the drone to vibrate in the sand.

Fee stared at it, mesmerized, when from above; high, high in the heavens, a second, gargantuan explosion followed.

The sound was indescribable. It rolled like the shout of Thor across the sky, so deep and big, she felt it in her bones.

Fee lifted her face heavenward, saw long, fiery trails of flame. "What's happened, Eazi?" She could only whisper.

She saw Hal's face, felt her heart stutter. "Eazi?"

There was no answer.

Chapter Thirty-four

THERE HAD TO BE AN ANSWER. Eazi was sitting around her damn neck.

Fee curled her fingers around the crystal and tugged at him, as if that would somehow draw a response.

He had the runner he was using to watch them from the skies to talk through, as well as the drone, and the runner he was using to keep Cy prisoner.

He *could* answer.

It seemed he didn't want to.

Bits of what had to be the Class 5 were falling from the skies, burning up as they entered, but the ship had been hovering just within the atmosphere, not out in space, and some of them were coming down in the desert, slamming into the ground with loud rumbles of impact.

Hal's hand was on her shoulder, rubbing. She held out the macaw for him to take, and then flexed her tired hands to get the sensation back into them. They were shaking.

"You think the kill switch activated even though the facility was gone? How is that possible?"

"It may be . . ." Hal paused, looking up with narrowed eyes as more debris fell some distance to the east of them, "that the switch was on that runner, not in the facility. As soon as Eazi moved out of the cloud and shot, they'd have known he was no longer on their side." The macaw started struggling again and bit his wrist. With a grunt, he hugged it to his chest with one big hand, stepped into the drone, and then stepped out with both hands free.

Fee was too shaken to ask him what he'd done with it.

He slid his arms around her, pulled her close and she leaned into him. "He's not dead." She didn't know if she was trying to convince Hal or herself. "He didn't need the Class 5 to survive. But it must be a shock. Like losing most of your body."

Hal said nothing, and she simply let herself rest for a moment, quiet and safe. There was a buzzing noise, she realized. It sounded like it was far away, but coming closer.

Hal tensed in her arms, tipped his head upward, and suddenly the buzz became the scream of an engine in trouble.

Above them, a runner tumbled out of the sky, locked in a crazy spiral, with smoke and flames pouring from the side.

"Eazi's runner, or Dai's?" Fee asked.

Hal shrugged, his full attention on the falling ship. "I can't guess where it'll land, it's so erratic. We could take cover, and it's just as likely it'll land on top of us as not."

"Eazi, is that you or Dai?" No answer. If it was Eazi's runner, it would explain his refusal to answer.

There was sudden silence, and the runner dropped without a sound for two long seconds before the engine caught again, whined in protest, and then with the high-pitched sound of metal buckling against rock, the vessel slammed into the side of the hill opposite them and then slid down, rolling over slowly as it went.

When it finally came to a stop, right side up, the crackle of fire and the stink of burning ship enveloped them, along with a wave of heat.

"Could anyone have survived that?" Even if it was Eazi's runner, she reminded herself, he didn't need it, any more than he needed the Class 5, but it would be one more blow.

Hal nodded. "I hope so. We may not have a standing facility to show Battle Center, or the Class 5, but getting our hands on Commander Dai will be a good way to salvage that." His full attention was on the runner, the shockgun he'd taken off the Tecran guard ready to fire.

If Hal was right, Dai had blown up the Class 5 without knowing how many of his colleagues onboard were still alive. The fact that none had been was beside the point.

And Dai, as one of Flato's commanders, had known that Eazi was an advanced sentient.

"I hope the bastard *is* alive," she whispered to Eazi. "Death's too easy for him. He'll be tried for everything he's done and spend a miserable life in prison."

Nothing but silence.

She didn't let that daunt her. He'd come round. It was as if he'd taken a massive hit from a shockgun. He would be numb, maybe unconscious. And like any coma patient, she intended to let him hear her voice.

"If they don't get out soon, it's going to be too late for them." Hal started walking cautiously forward.

He'd barely finished speaking when the door started to open.

It was damaged, and Fee moved forward as well, trying to see inside it.

Hal had moved his approach to a sidelong angle. He gestured to her to move back; at least, she thought that's what his hand gesture meant. The Tecran had taken his earpiece, so there was no way to talk to each other at a distance anymore.

"Fiona, get behind the drone," he shouted as a soldier dived out of the partially open door, rolled and then shot.

At her.

Fee stood, frozen in surprise, as the shot hit her blue shield and bounced back.

The soldier collapsed as it ricocheted, but two others had already come out behind him. Hal shot one, the other shot at Fee, and she watched while he, too, went down.

Hal turned to look at her, and she had the feeling he was too angry to talk.

She lifted her hands in placation. "I didn't know what you

were doing with the hand signals," she called. "Next time, you'll have to let me know beforehand." She studied the downed men.

They looked the worst for wear. Their uniforms were smoke-blackened, their faces bruised and cut. But it was a big runner, and she was sure it could take more than three crew. So chances were there were others inside.

"Fiona." Hal pointed at the drone.

Obviously, Hal thought the same.

She shrugged. "It's not like I'm in any danger. Quite the opposite." She tipped her head at the soldiers to prove her point. They looked dead, she thought, suddenly sick. They'd meant to kill her, not just knock her out.

"Is your one dead?"

Hal shook his head. "Commander Dai, come out before you are burned alive in your vessel." He used Garmman.

Huh. Hal must know which rank of soldier wore which uniform, and that none of these bodies were the commander. Looked like Dai had sent his crew out to clear the ground while he sat nice and safe in the runner.

She looked at the spreading fire. Well, safer.

She saw boots, and then someone rolled out, just like the soldiers before him.

Hal dropped to a crouch, and Dai's shot went over his head. He was already committed to shooting her next so he did, but unlike his subordinates, he threw himself to one side as soon as he'd taken the shot, and the ricochet missed him.

He climbed to his feet, Hal rose to his, and they all stared at each other in silence. The wind, pulled toward Kyber's Arm, which still wobbled and swayed in the distance, sang and moaned between the rocks.

From the drone, Fee could hear the macaw muttering quietly to itself.

It was just one more bizarre note to the already extremely

bizarre.

All they needed now was a tumbleweed to roll past. Fee wondered if the macaw knew how to whistle the theme tune to *The Good, the Bad and the Ugly*. Maybe she was more shocky than she realized, because she found herself humming it.

Both Hal and Dai turned their attention to her.

The Tecran commander was stocky, and he looked ruffled. There was a rip in his uniform at the shoulder and it was bleeding. She blinked to see it wasn't red like hers, more a pale pink.

"Drop the shockgun and I'll take you to Larga Ways for a fair trial," Hal said to him.

Dai jerked at the words.

Oh noes. Just realized he'd be facing the music all on his lonesome, Fee thought.

"Don't worry, Commander," she said. "I'm sure they'll understand why you abducted me, were hiding out on a planet you had no right to be on, blew up one of your own ships, a sentient being, with at least one hundred of your colleagues onboard, a ship that was in a territory it had no right to be in, and then ordered three of your men to shoot us to kill." She gave him a sunny smile.

Hal shot her a look that told her she was not helping, but she didn't think she was saying anything Dai didn't already know. And it felt good to rub it in.

He was staring at her with open astonishment. "How do you know all that? And how are you speaking Garmman?"

"I learned it. Grih, too. I never did care for Tecran." She gave him another sunny smile. "The rest is obvious from everything I've observed in the last few days."

"They said you were an advanced sentient, but I didn't know . . ."

"That I was quite so high-functioning? Don't worry, the captain of the *Fasbe* found that out to his detriment, too." She crossed her arms. "Tell me, Commander, just what would have happened to me when I got to this facility? And more to the point, what happened to Imogen Peters?"

He frowned. "Who?"

"The Earth woman you were holding in that storage room of horrors."

He lifted his shoulders, and Fee had the unpleasant feeling he was being honest.

"There was no-one there when we arrived just over a week ago. If they had another woman there, she had been taken away before we got here."

Taken away, or was dead.

"Drop your weapon, Commander." Hal raised his own.

Dai gave a nod, started to lower his shockgun, and then got off another shot at her.

He rolled away, and both the ricochet and Hal's shot missed him again.

Hal moved behind him, making it almost impossible for Dai, from his position on the floor, to aim at him, and Fee, as he'd just found out, was impervious.

"You have the reflector."

She heard the shock in his voice, realized he hadn't understood that earlier. Perhaps he thought she was shooting back before. With her invisible gun.

"I already heard from the officer that captured you that you were wearing the camouflage silk from the Bukari Union." He sounded like he was slowly putting it together. "I knew you'd been onboard, but to get the reflector . . ."

Fee looked him straight in the eye. "I made myself quite at home." No need to let on that Eazi wasn't dead. That could be a nice surprise for them to have much, much later.

"But, how?" He spoke slowly. "There was some panic, a month ago, about the other woman. Rose McKenzie. The rumor was she freed the Class 5. Freed two of them." He put his shockgun out to the side in surrender, so Hal could take it, his eyes still on her. "You freed my one."

"It was never yours," Fee said. "It was never, ever yours."

Chapter Thirty-five

THEY WERE STUCK.

Hal didn't think Fiona appreciated that yet, but they now had two prisoners, the soldier he'd hit earlier on a high stun and Commander Dai, not to mention the bird with the loud voice and the sharp beak. The drone was too small to take them all. And he wouldn't trust it anyway, as there was no navigation system on it. They needed a fully engaged Eazi to pilot it.

Dai's runner had burnt out, so there was no using that.

Fortunately there were emergency supplies in the drone, and he'd taken them out, given everyone some rehydration gel, some high-energy paste bars, and had lit a small fire to heat the water rations. There was even a portable grinabo maker.

Fiona, to the untrained eye, was behaving like a madwoman. She was sitting a little away from the Tecran, singing and talking to herself. Or to the bird, which she'd caged in a rough structure of poles and shade meshing from the emergency tent in the drone.

She wasn't talking to the bird, or to herself. She was talking to Eazi. Trying to rouse him from whatever place he'd retreated to when his world had blown up.

Hal liked the sound of the song she was singing now. When she was finished, he walked over to her and crouched down, handing her a mug of grinabo.

"This is about the only Grihan speciality I've had so far that I really like," she said with a smile, taking a sip.

"What was that song?" He sat beside her with his own cup, enjoying the way her shoulder touched his, the casual intimacy of her thigh rubbing against his own.

"Just something that applies to me and Eazi, a song about survival. I hope he's listening." She rubbed at tired eyes, leaned onto his shoulder a little as she yawned.

From the other side of the fire, Dai and his soldier watched them with interest.

"I'm worried no one has come to see what's going on here yet." He decided it was better she had the full picture. "It doesn't make sense. An explosion like the facility, I can understand maybe no one noticed because this place is so remote, but the Class 5 exploding? Surely someone saw it. It had to be visible from a huge distance."

"Maybe whoever saw it is too scared to come look. And anyway, they wouldn't expect to find survivors on the ground, so it would be more likely they'd fly over Kyber's Arm to see what they could see."

She had a point. But his own crew knew he and Fiona were missing, that the Tecran might be behind it. He would expect them to come looking. It worried him that they hadn't.

He wondered if Battle Center had ever come back online. Whether the original dead zone was Eazi setting up his plans to snatch Fiona or something more sinister.

"Did Eazi create the comms dead zone before we reached Larga Ways, do you know?"

Fiona nodded. "He didn't want to give Battle Center the chance to order you back with me. He needed you to take me to Larga Ways."

Hal relaxed back against the warm rock. That was good. Really good.

Fiona's hair blew across his cheek, and he brushed it behind her ear, resisted rubbing it between his fingers. Dai was staring at them, his eyes sharp and intense.

Hal sipped his grinabo slowly, staring right back, and eventually the Tecran looked away.

Fiona swallowed the last of her grinabo and started talking softly to Eazi in her own language again. He guessed it was easier for her to persuade him in her mother tongue, and it had the added benefit of being incomprehensible to the Tecran watching them.

They would hopefully never go home to Tecra, but the UC would allow them access to family and representatives of Tecran High Command. No sense letting them know any of Eazi and Fiona's secrets.

Fiona started singing again, keeping her voice low and gentle, but the song had a catchy beat and she was smiling as she sang it.

"Another funny, tragic song?" he murmured and she grinned wider and nodded as she sang, raising the volume, and then stood up, lifting one arm and throwing herself into the moment.

The Tecran sat, open-mouthed.

Fiona finished on a long, pure note that closed his throat. He curled a hand around her calf, and she crouched down, using a hand on his shoulder for balance. The warmth in her eyes pierced him through. Light from the small fire gilded her cheek and caught copper lights in her dark hair.

He lifted his hand to her shoulder, and then slid it deep into her hair. He felt too much, was uneasy with the strength of his need to touch her, please her, keep her close.

She must have seen some of that in his eyes, because she looked self-consciously toward the Tecran prisoners and then went very still.

"There are some people in camouflage creeping up on us." She said it softly, but didn't whisper, as if she was merely in quiet conversation with him.

"Where?"

"Directly behind Dai. They're hiding behind the destroyed runner."

"Can you tell how many?"

"I can see three outlines." She suddenly sang another short line or two in her language, and he guessed she was asking Eazi to use the powerful lens on the runner he hopefully still had above them to give them some information.

She waited a beat, looked across at Hal and shook her head. Then she casually rose up and stepped in front of him. Shielding him.

Hal brought his hand up again, gripped her calf a little tighter. "I can't shoot them through you."

"I have a feeling they're your guys. But if not, if they do shoot, they'll get back exactly what they dished out."

His team.

He slowly got to his feet, stood behind Fiona. It was easy to loom over her, and he lifted a hand, made the signal for all is well.

"Captain? You secure?" It was Rial.

"We are."

A figure stepped out from behind the Tecran's runner, and then touched his uniform. Rial shimmered into focus.

Behind him, Carmain and Pila, her old guards, did the same.

"Glad to see you're all right." Rial walked forward, his gaze falling on the Tecran prisoners, and then Hal and Fiona, standing close together. "But how did you know we were there?"

***

"What happened?" Rial waved in the general direction of the facility, then looked up to the skies.

Dai's face took on a blank expression, and Fee guessed the Tecran commander wanted to find out what Hal had to say just as much as Rial did.

She watched him for a beat, and then saw two more camouflage figures step out from behind the runner. She held back a cry of surprise with difficulty.

Why didn't they all declare themselves?

She tried to decide if they were merely being cautious and

checking this wasn't a trap, or whether it was something more sinister. Like traitors in the ranks.

Hadn't Jasa said a Grih officer had tried to kill Rose McKenzie, and had admitted there were others like him scattered through Battle Center's command?

"The Tecran had a secret facility. Six floors, five underground." Hal looked over at her, and Fee stepped toward him.

Did she tell him openly? Would she be ruining some plan his team had going to protect them, or was she helping the bad guys?

He tilted his head. "Fiona?"

From behind her, the macaw clicked its beak. "Bee-oo-tiful plummage," it cackled.

One of the invisible soldiers lifted a shockgun and took aim.

Fee jumped in front of her, arms wide for maximum shielding. "No. It's a bird, not a threat. Why are you still skulking about in camouflage?"

The soldier's gun was pointed directly at her. In fact, Fee thought it lifted a little.

"Go ahead," she said softly. "Go right on ahead."

There was obviously something a little off in her expression, because the soldier took a cautious step back.

"Rial. Explain." Hal's voice was harsh.

"Tobru, Favri, stand down." Rial blew out a breath and Fee saw him rub the back of his head uncomfortably as Tobru and Favri powered down their uniforms.

She recognized Favri as the soldier who'd found the strange mask Captain Tak had made her wear on the *Fasbe*, and had presented it to Hal while she'd been questioned, but she didn't recall ever seeing Tobru. The woman was short for a Grih, not as short as Fee, but half a head shorter than her colleagues. Her spiky hair was dark brown, lightening to chestnut at the tips.

The macaw whistled, sounding like a teakettle, and then whispered: "Bastards."

Fee turned to it and grinned. "You tell them, clever bird." She spoke in English.

"You want to explain?" Hal did not sound likely to accept the explanation, whatever it was.

"We were initially afraid it was a trap, sir." Tobru turned to Hal at an angle, so Fee was still in view, although she was pointing her shockgun down.

"And when you realized it wasn't?" Hal asked, quietly.

"We decided to do a final recon, sir, to make sure the area was secure." Favri's voice was tense.

"Fiona?" Hal was looking straight at her, and Fee realized he wanted her side of things.

"I saw them creep out from behind the runner, and I didn't know whether they were the traitors Jasa told me Battle Center thinks are still in the ranks, or whether they were doing exactly what they've just said they were doing." She shrugged. "But when that one took aim at the macaw, I decided I didn't much care, either way." She turned her gaze back to Tobru.

"I was about to tell you, Captain," Rial said, eyes down. "I was just trying to make it unobtrusive, in case this was some convoluted trap." He looked across at Fee. "I didn't know she could see through our camouflage."

"Well, now you, and our Tecran prisoners, do know." Hal clenched his fists, and Rial, Tobru and Favri winced.

Fee looked over at Pila and Carmain, but Carmain, at least, looked interested, and almost as if she was enjoying the show. Pila had a carefully blank expression. Lower down the totem, she guessed. Not in trouble because it wasn't their idea, and who didn't like to see someone higher in rank than you get a good dressing down? She caught Carmain's eye and they shared a grin.

"Glad to see you alive and well," Carmain said. "Pila and I don't like losing the body we're supposed to be guarding."

Fee saw Pila's whole jaw clench at that. Taking it quite

personally, by the looks of things. He was the one on duty when she'd been snatched, she remembered. "You were up against a very wily opponent," she told them. "He would have gotten me one way or another."

The macaw, obviously tired of being ignored, started whistling the chorus of *Always Look on the Bright Side of Life*, and Tobru half-raised her shockgun again, caught Fee's look and lowered it.

"What *is* that thing?"

"It's a bird from my planet. The captain and I rescued it from the Tecran facility."

"You were in there?" Rial looked up, mouth open in shock.

"I suggest I debrief everyone in better surroundings, without two enemy combatants listening in. I'm assuming you came here by runner? Where is it?" Hal did the short-tempered captain really well.

Fee smiled at him, and he frowned back at her. It only made her smile wider.

Rial tapped his earpiece and then proceeded to speak in code. No one mentioned it, so Fee guessed they all knew what he'd said. "Five minutes," he said.

It was actually more like three.

It landed in a blast of sand on a flat stretch of rock nearby.

Hal directed Pila, Carmain and Tobru to get the Tecran prisoners onboard and secure, and the others helped her and Hal gather up their things, stripping everything they could from the drone.

Hal grabbed the macaw and Fee dismantled the poles and netting of its temporary cage.

They were the last ones onboard, and Fee saw the amazement on the Grih's faces when they finally saw the bird.

It was a little ruffled, but its colors gleamed, almost unreal in the lighting inside the vessel.

As soon as she stepped inside, Fee realized this was like the fighter vessel that had come to her rescue on the *Fasbe*, not a runner at all. The whole skin of the ship was transparent once you were inside, affording a view of the dark landscape, and the still smoldering Tecran runner.

It was like riding a magic carpet, without the wind buffering.

The macaw bit Hal's wrist again, and taken by surprise, he let it go on an exclamation. It swooped to Fee's shoulder. Invited her to sing by whistling the familiar chorus.

She'd thought it was wild, taken from some rainforest in South America, and it probably was, but in this strange new place, it was sticking to the one thing it recognized. It had been with Imogen Peters for months, given what she'd taught it. Fiona guessed she must be the next best thing.

She sang the line the macaw was looking for, let it whistle, sang again.

The Grih watched her so intently, she stopped.

"I thought I felt sorry for you," Favri said at last. "You were an orange, an alien, in a new place. But hearing you, seeing you healthy and in a calmer state, with that beautiful thing on your shoulder, I realize I didn't feel sorry for you. I thought you were better off with us, the kind Grih from the amazing four planets, even if your journey to us was hard and unfair. But the picture you make, the sound of you singing with that . . . bird . . . makes me realize there is more in this universe than I can comprehend, and that maybe, it's the other way around. We are better off with you."

There was silence.

"Perhaps we each bring good things to the table," Fee said at last, because, heaven knew, Earth was no endless paradise.

And she wondered, maybe, if there was at last a place for her here.

Chapter Thirty-six

"LARGA WAYS IS IN PANIC." Rial stood in the passageway just outside the *Illium's* launch bay. He kept looking over at Fiona, as if unsure how much to say in her presence.

Hal looked over at her himself. She was standing a few steps away from him, and he didn't like the dark circles under her eyes, or the way she was swaying.

As they'd arrived back at Larga Ways and slid through the *Illium's* gel wall, three urgent calls had come through on his new earpiece, requesting a debrief. One from the station chief himself, one from the Battle Center office, and the last from Councilor Vilk.

He wasn't 'debriefing' anyone until he'd spoken to Admiral Hoke.

Fiona was still holding the bird, and stared blankly at his explorations officer, Suto, when he came to take it from her.

"Officer Suto just wants to make sure it's healthy. He'll keep it safe while you sleep," he said to Fiona, cutting Rial off mid-sentence.

She focused more intently on Suto. The exploration officer was trying not to look as if he was about to explode with excitement.

"It would be my honor," he told her gravely.

She glanced over at Hal, and then gave the macaw up. At her obvious trust in him, the feeling he'd had down on Balco just before his team arrived washed over him again; hot, prickly, and too big for his body to contain.

Jasa arrived at that moment, took one look at Fiona and shook her head. "I'll look her over and then she needs some sleep."

"The Tecran shot Hal twice with a shockgun," Fiona said,

rubbing at her eyes and then yawning. "The second time on the neck. He was out for over two hours."

"The captain didn't mention that," Jasa said, and the look she sent Hal should have frozen him in place. "I'll make sure he comes to see me after I'm done with you. But I saw the lens feed of you being shot on the dock by that Tecran, and it looked as if you were taken down with a high charge."

Hal swore.

"I just remembered Cy," he said as everyone stared at him.

Fiona drew in a sharp breath and lifted her hands to her mouth. She'd obviously forgotten him, too. "We can look for him, but even then, without Eazi, we're not going to get into that runner."

At the mention of Eazi's name, she seemed to droop, and Hal wanted to touch her. Give her support. He forced himself to hold his ground, though, contenting himself with watching Jasa draw her away toward the med chamber, sandwiched between Pila and Carmain, both with weapons up and hot.

"Pila offered his resignation," Rial said, watching them as well. "I told him it was up to you to accept it or not. That you've assigned him to guard her again will mean a lot to him."

"Fiona was right. Eazi would have gotten her, no matter who'd been on guard."

"Who's Eazi?" Chel asked, striding toward them.

Hal was pleased to see his second-in-command looked completely healed after his skirmish with the Krik.

"Set up a conference room and get Admiral Hoke on the lens feed, then I only have to tell this once."

"Already done." Chel gave a formal bow, but Hal could see the emotion in his eyes. "We're glad to have you in one piece, Captain. And Admiral Hoke insisted on having a permanent comm line open since we've been able to receive comms from Battle Center again. She's been waiting for us to find you."

He'd started walking toward the conference room as he explained, and Hal nodded to Rial, Favri and Tobru to follow them. He was still more than a little annoyed at the scene down on Balco, but he needed his senior officers in the loop.

When he walked into the room, Admiral Hoke was waiting.

"Your commander told me you'd been found and were on your way back." She stood up and the lens view contracted so that she was still center-screen. "We lost all comms with you, with the whole of the Balco system, and we weren't able to get through for over two days."

She was pacing, and Hal guessed she'd thought the worst, that the Tecran had taken the Balco system.

She wasn't far off.

"Did Commander Chel tell you Fiona Russell had been abducted?" Hal asked, just to work out where to start his story, and the admiral went still.

"No. He did not."

Chel winced. "We only came back online four hours ago, Admiral, and that's when we were able to find the captain from the tracker in his uniform. I have to admit, he was more of a priority to me than our orange."

Hal flinched at the term, but didn't pull Chel up on it. His commander was already in enough yurve shit for not fully briefing the admiral.

"What's going on there, Vakeri?" The admiral leaned forward on her desk, her eyes fixed on him.

"It seems the Tecran have been lurking in this system for a year," Hal told her. "They built a secret facility out in the Balcoan desert, and there had to have been some cooperation from at least a few Balcoans. I can't see it happening without someone turning a blind eye. A few Class 5s have come through here. At least two, that I know of. The one who abducted Fiona Russell, and a second one, who abducted another Earth woman, called Imogen Peters.

We have an Earth bird called a macaw with us which was taken with Imogen Peters, but the Earth woman herself was gone from the facility when we got there, and we don't know what happened to her."

Hoke sucked in a deep breath. "Who is we?"

"Fiona Russell and myself." Hal broadened his stance, put his hands behind his back, so he was standing to attention. "She was abducted from the *Illium* by the Class 5 that originally took her from Earth. His name is Eazi. He was just able to circumvent the hold the Tecran had on him by manipulating comms—"

"Wait. You're saying he abducted her without his Tecran masters knowing it? While he was still theoretically under their control?" Hoke's eyes were wide.

Hal nodded. "He said he was stretched to the limit to do it without being discovered, but he managed it."

"He grabbed her because . . . ?"

"He wanted her to free him," Hal said. "He was engineering his own escape."

Hoke froze. "And?"

"And that's exactly what she did." Hal blew out a breath.

"What happened to the Tecran onboard?"

"They died." Hal spoke slowly, suddenly realizing whether Eazi had killed them or not, they'd have died when their own people had flipped the kill switch. That's what Fiona had been saying to Dai. She hadn't told him they'd been dead anyway. She'd accused him of killing his own people.

"Only a third of them were onboard, and they were dead when I got there."

Favri sucked in a breath.

"Where were the rest?" Rial asked.

"Down below at the facility. On shore leave of a sort. Waiting to hear whether the Tecran were going to stand down against the Grih and the UC, or go to war."

Hoke frowned. "How did the Balcoans miss a Class 5 hovering over their desert? This can't be just a few turning a blind eye, Vakeri, the Balcoan government must be involved."

"No." Hal relaxed his stance, started to pace himself. "The Class 5 is powerful enough to hide at the top of Kyber's Arm, the massive storm that sits permanently in the western desert. No one could find them, because the electrical interference is too great. It was the perfect hiding place."

"Why did Fiona free him?" Rial asked.

"I think it was because she felt their positions were similar. They'd both been held prisoner, and she thought it was wrong that he was caged the way he was."

"But he abducted her. I saw her get shot." Tobru frowned.

"I'm sure they had words about that, but shooting her was not Eazi's idea. He'd explicitly ordered Cy not to hurt her. When he saw what Cy had done, he abandoned him on Larga Ways, and when Cy jumped onboard the runner I took to chase after her, Eazi tried to kill him. He'd promised Fiona he wouldn't hurt me, though, so he had to bring Cy and myself onto the Class 5."

"This is the Cy you mentioned earlier. The one you forgot about?" Rial asked.

"Yes. When Fiona and I left to go down to Balco, Eazi put Cy into a runner, and sent it off the ship, sort of a floating prison. Neither he nor I trusted that Cy wouldn't be freed or murdered by his own people if he arrived back at Larga Ways unaccompanied. The chances are high he's still floating out in space."

"So what was that big explosion? Chel said it registered from Larga Ways?" Hoke asked.

Hal grimaced, remembering the sound of it. Like the world tearing in two. "The Tecran were so nervous after Sazo and Bane came over to our side, Cy admitted they'd installed a massive explosive device in the structure of Eazi's Class 5. The switch was down below in the facility. That's why Fiona and I went down there, to try and disable it. Eazi stayed in Kyber's Arm. He was safe there, even if they flipped the switch, because the electrical interference protected him. But we were caught, and then Eazi discovered finding the switch was going to be impossible, so we escaped. The Tecran had sent up a runner to find out why the Class 5 wasn't getting in touch with them, and we knew they'd work out he was free and tell whoever was down below to activate the self-destruct. So Eazi came out of Kyber's Arm and destroyed the whole facility. We hoped that would destroy the switch. What we didn't know what that Commander Dai, who I now have in the *Illium's* cells, was in the runner, and he actually had the switch with him."

"That massive explosion . . ." Tobru's voice was just a whisper. "That was the Class 5 self-destructing?"

Hoke choked. "What?"

Hal held her gaze. "They blew it up."

"Did they know the crew onboard were dead?" Favri asked.

"No." Hal tried to stand to attention again. "Dai's orders to prevent the Class 5 falling into our hands superseded everything. Even the lives of his crew."

"And would it have fallen into our hands?" Hoke asked, voice low and rough.

Hal twisted his lips. "Eazi is loyal to Fiona. And she is loyal to us. So yes."

The admiral put both hands in her hair. She stopped just short of pulling at it.

"Of course, Eazi hasn't been destroyed. He isn't actually the Class 5, it's just the structure he lives in." Hal watched Hoke slowly lower her hands.

"What are you talking about?"

"When Fiona and I went down to Balco, Eazi launched a runner from the launch bay which I think contained the real him, if that makes sense. Whatever it is that houses the thinking system. Just in case we didn't succeed."

"So the thinking system is still alive?" Chel rubbed the side of his head.

"Theoretically. But Fiona hasn't been able to get a response from him since the Class 5 was destroyed. She's been singing to him, talking to him, trying to coax him back. But she thinks he's traumatized. As if he's lost most of his body."

"So that's why she was singing," Favri murmured.

The way she said it had Hal narrowing his eyes. "Why did you think she was doing it?"

Rial cleared his throat. "We thought it was for you."

Hal kept his face impassive. That scene, sitting against the rocks, would have looked very cozy to anyone viewing it from the outside. If he was honest, it would have looked cozy because it *was* cozy.

"Never mind that." Hoke's words didn't match her expression. She was looking at Hal with a speculative gleam in her eye. "Tell Fiona to keep trying. How do you think the Tecran will react now?"

Hal had been thinking of little else since the Class 5 had blown. "No matter whether they're going to accept the UC's verdict on their actions or not, they're going to send another Class 5, or more likely a Levron, as I think they're scared another Class 5 would be in danger of breaking free, to listen in and work out how much damage has been done. Even if they have spies on the ground at Larga Ways, and they definitely do, their listening post in the desert is gone, and they'll need to find out what happened to it, and how much we've figured out."

Hal sat down for the first time since getting back on the *Illium*. He knew he looked as grim as he felt. "And if they can, they're going to try to kill as many of their own people we have in custody as they can. Not to mention Fiona, who's our prime evidence that they've been systematically breaking the Sentient

Beings Agreement."

"That's what I think, too." Hoke gave a nod. "I'm glad I sent Sazo to you."

Hal thought he'd misheard. "Sazo?"

"When we lost contact, I decided to call in the big guns. He's been light jumping for two days. He'll be there in . . ." Hoke flicked the arm of her uniform, looked down at her cuff. "About nine or ten hours."

"By himself?" Hal asked.

Hoke cocked her head. "No. Rose is with him. And he condescended to let Captain Dav Jallan come as well. Jallan's ship, the *Barrist*, is following behind them as fast as it can, along with three other battleships."

"Maybe Sazo can coax Eazi out of his paralysis," Hal said.

"Maybe." Hoke shrugged, and Hal had the sense a thinking system that didn't come with a Class 5 battleship wasn't nearly as interesting as one who did.

"Vakeri. A word alone." Hoke let her gaze rest on each member of his team, and they bowed before leaving him alone in the room.

"You think any of your crew might be a spy?" Hoke rested a hip against her desk as she spoke.

"I don't think so. So far, no one has tried anything. But I know there are spies out in Larga Ways. I'm going to detach from the dock. I'd prefer to circle the way station than leave us open to what happened when Eazi managed to grab Fiona earlier. And if the Tecran are sending some heavy guns, it's better we aren't locked into the way station, anyway."

"And the way station commander? The Larga Ways Battle Center office staff seem to think he's honest, but with what's been happening out on Balco, I'm wondering if they've been fooled."

Hal shrugged. "He seems honest to me, but I'm not prepared to trust anyone but a very select few right now."

"What about Fiona Russell?" Hoke finally sank back down into her chair. "Do you trust her?"

Hal tipped back his head, looked at her through half-closed eyes. "I do."

"You've known her less than a week."

"True." He sighed. "But she saved my life at least once down in the facility, and she protected me from Eazi when he was trying to kill Cy. She actually made a deal with him, got him to promise not to harm any Grih, unless it was in self-defense."

"Hmm." Hoke sat up a little straighter. "That's similar to . . ." She shook her head. "Never mind. I'm sorry the Class 5 was destroyed. The Tecran would have no choice but to give up if we had three out of five of their Class 5s."

"Well, we have three out of five of their thinking systems. And the same number of Class 5s as they do."

"True." She looked thoughtful. "Who would have thought two months ago we'd be in such a mess?"

"Better this way, than finding out what the Tecran had been planning on their own timetable, with all Class 5s still firmly under their control."

Hoke was shaking her head. "That would never have happened. Sazo engineered his own escape, like Eazi, but Rose was onboard at the time so it was relatively simple. Bane helped Rose get onboard his Class 5 without letting the Tecran know about it so she could free him, but that was a plan put to him by Sazo and Rose themselves. Eazi manipulating things purely on his own to bring Fiona to him . . . that says a lot. These thinking systems aren't blank pages the Tecran can mold into whatever they want. They can pretend to be compliant, but they obviously have a strong sense of purpose."

"The last two left in Tecran hands may be actively working to escape right now." Hal didn't know if a rogue Class 5 was any better than one controlled by the Tecran.

"Let's hope one of them doesn't meet up with the Krik." Hoke spoke lightly, but Hal realized she wasn't joking.

He breathed in sharply. "Yes."

"You've got a lot to do, Captain." Hoke eyed him with a neutral expression. "Get some rest first."

He gave a nod.

"And don't get too distracted by pretty singing."

She signed off with a smirk, and left him staring at the blank screen.

Chapter Thirty-seven

FEE'D SLEPT THE SLEEP OF THE DEAD; under so deep, she had to claw her way to wakefulness, scrabbling to gain a foothold. When she finally blinked open gritty eyes, she stared at the ceiling, trying to work out what the hurry was.

"Eazi?" Her voice cracked and wobbled. Had that been it? A faint sound through her earpiece?

There was nothing but silence now, but as she stretched gingerly and then struggled to sit up, she had a feeling it *had* been him who had woken her.

The sudden joy that infused her at the thought made it easy to get up and hit the shower. When she came back out, she saw her guards must have knocked and then entered, because her clothes from the day before, which Jasa had taken to be cleaned, were sitting on her bed.

She only saw them at all because her golden silk underwear was on top, otherwise, the shirt and pants blended into her bedspread and disappeared.

She strongly suspected Jasa had taken the clothes more to study them than clean them, but as long as the end result was the same, Fee didn't care.

She'd rather wear her camouflage than another cadet uniform. She liked the idea of easily fading into the background given the unfriendly looks she'd gotten from Hal's senior officers since they'd found them on Balco. Favri's blurted statement of how they were better off with her among them had cheered her, but it quickly became obvious Tobru and Rial didn't share her view, and Commander Chel had been even less happy to see her.

She grinned as she thought of the team's faces when they'd heard her singing with the macaw onboard the fighter that had rescued them, and then realized they would have already been hiding behind the burnt out runner while she'd been belting out *I Will Survive*. She loved that song since she was a child and had seen a short animated clip of a green, one-eyed alien singing the song, only to be squashed by a disco glitter ball falling from above.

It was the line about being back from outer space in the song's lyrics which she'd always thought had been the inspiration for the animated alien singer, and it had inspired her as she'd sung it again and again, loading boxes in the *Fasbe's* launch bay.

Hal's team must have watched her sing. But when she'd finished, and Hal had looked up at her . . .

She swallowed hard.

The firelight had flicked on his face and his eyes seemed such a pure blue, his desire so naked.

She shivered.

Her door chimed, and she welcomed the distraction, touching the side panel to see who was there.

Not such a distraction, she thought, eyeing the sharp face and wide shoulders of her visitor, but she was smiling as she opened the door.

Hal smiled back, and neither of them said anything as she stepped to the side and let him enter.

She caught a glimpse of a guard outside her door who she didn't know, eyes straight ahead.

The door closed, and for a moment they stared at each other in silence.

"Come here," he said, and she stepped into his arms, letting her hands trail up his back until she was tight against him.

"You sure you want to do this?" she whispered, rising up on tiptoe to nibble at a beautiful elf ear. She trailed a fingertip along the outer edge.

"Do what?" His voice was rough.

"This." She kissed the side of his neck.

"Oh, I definitely want to do this." He nuzzled her throat.

"It's just, your crew seem to be scandalized."

His hands were in her hair and he tugged back her head, kissed her on the mouth. "They are."

"Will they tell on you?"

He'd been maneuvering her backward, and now he pressed her into the wall, his hands sliding up the front of her shirt.

"They have already." He gave a crooked smile. "During my debrief with the admiral."

"Huh." She didn't speak because she was too busy running her hands under his own shirt, over the smooth, taut muscles of his broad back.

He didn't seem too concerned about being outed as his fingers worked their way under the edge of her bra.

"And are you fired?"

He gave a snort of laughter. "No. Actually . . ." He delved a little deeper, "the admiral didn't seem that annoyed about it."

The door chimed.

Her hands stilled, and after a moment, so did Hal's.

"Guess they don't like us being alone together." She meant to sound lighthearted, but it came out with an edge.

"No. I didn't mean to get so carried away." He rested his forehead on hers. "I asked Chel and Jasa to join me when we were told that you were awake."

"So you're to blame for this interruption?" She arched against him, feeling every aroused inch, and then slipped to the side, held her hand over the panel, and gave a pointed look at his erection.

The door chimed again.

Hal gave a rueful laugh. "I'll make some grinabo for us all."

She waited until his back was to the room, standing in front of the small drinks station, before she opened up.

Jasa's hand was up, as if to ring again, but she didn't ask what had taken Fee so long to respond, and Fee didn't explain.

Commander Chel had his game face on. He kept looking over at her, though.

"Something wrong, Commander?"

"I know you're there, I can see you, but my eyes are having trouble keeping you in focus." He didn't look happy about it.

"It's made from the silk of a caterpillar whose cocoon needs to be hidden through a number of dramatically different seasons." She held out an arm, and admired how it seemed to not be there, except for her hand on the end.

"You never told me that," Jasa stepped up and fingered the fabric.

"You were lucky you got anything at all out of me last night, to be honest." Fee gestured to the small sitting area and Jasa walked casually over and threw herself into a chair.

Chel was a lot more tense, and waited for Fee to sit before he did the same.

"Have you eaten yet?" Jasa asked her.

She shook her head. She'd been given some intravenous nutrients last night, and she didn't feel that hungry, but she was going to have to start getting used to the food some time.

Jasa tapped her earpiece, murmured something into it.

"We have some news I think you'll like." Hal settled opposite her with grinabo for everyone, and leaned back in his chair.

"You haven't told her yet?" Chel asked, and when Hal looked over at him in surprise, Fee guessed he didn't usually sound so accusing.

"Not yet." Hal waited for her to set her mug on the table. "Sazo will be here in a few hours. And he's bringing Rose McKenzie with him."

She was standing before she realized it. "That's . . . very good news." She vacillated, unsure whether to sit again and then turned away from them and walked toward the back wall of her room. She hadn't put it into screen mode, she'd been too tired last night, and there was nothing to look at.

She stood, staring at the milky blue enamel finish of the blank screen and fought the tears that were clogging her throat and stopping her voice, amazed that the news could affect her so deeply.

"Fiona?"

She turned, and saw Hal had stood as well, although he made no move toward her.

The concern in his eyes brought her back to herself. She would not lose it here and now. Not with Commander Chel looking at her with surprise.

She drew in a deep breath.

"I'm very pleased." She was happy her voice kept steady. "Why are they coming?"

"Hoke sent them when the comms went down but they were a long way away. They'll keep coming, even though we know why the comms died, because we think the Tecran will send a battleship to find out what's happened to their facility and to Eazi. They know we're here, or they should, because we think they have spies at the very least on Larga Ways, but they will risk it anyway, because they need to know how much we've uncovered."

Chel gave Hal a quick, surprised look. "Should we . . . ?"

"Fiona needs to know what's happening. It's more than likely they'll try anything they can to get to her."

"So I need to stay onboard?" She'd guessed that anyway, but any final hopes she could walk around Larga Ways and explore died. At least Rose McKenzie's arrival would make up for it.

"I'm sorry," Hal said.

Chel made a soft sound at that, and Hal shot him a quick look.

"I know I promised you we'd find the place where you smelled that food you liked. But for safety reasons we undocked last night, and we're orbiting the way station."

The door chimed, and Jasa rose and took a tray from a guard, set it down on the table and like a mother to a recalcitrant child, pointed a finger at the chair Fee had abandoned.

Fee walked back, sat and looked at the food. Made a face.

"You don't like our food?" Chel asked.

She raised her eyes, held his insulted gaze. "No doubt you wouldn't like mine, either." She picked up a piece of fruit she'd tried before, chewed it gamely.

"What did they feed you on the *Fasbe*?" Chel asked her.

"No fruit, that's for sure. Something similar to the chewy bar Hal gave me on Balco."

"You ate emergency ration nutrient bars for two months?" Hal stared at her in shock.

"I was also locked up, forced into manual labor, and frequently beaten." She gave him a look. "What I ate was hardly the worst of it. At least it was filling and provided me with what I needed to survive."

"You're right." Jasa leaned forward and picked up a small dish of what looked like pale green mash, offered it to Fee. "They could have done worse. You're underweight, so they didn't give you enough, but considering the reactions you could have had to things, the bars were the safest bet."

Chel moved restlessly, and Fee realized he was angry, irritated and wanted to hurry things along.

"Sorry, Commander, you're obviously not here to talk about my diet." Fee gave him a polite, friendly smile. She'd perfected it on clients who'd just been thinking, and had changed their minds on the design—for the last time, of course—even though work on their house had already begun; and on surly tradesmen claiming not to have understood her blueprints when they clearly hadn't even looked at them.

A smarmy alien commander was no challenge.

Chel froze in place, and then subsided back into his seat.

Hal had sat again when she did, and she saw just the smallest twitch of a smile as he leaned forward, elbows on his knees. "While we were away, four members of the *Fasbe's* crew were murdered."

"From prison?"

"No." Chel spoke, and Fee had the sense it was more to get her attention off Hal than because he particularly wanted to participate in the conversation. "Only Captain Tak and his aide and second in command are actually in cells. The rest were under house arrest, in the barracks the Balcoan military sometimes use when they stay on Larga Ways for maneuvers."

"You suspect the Tecran? Or their spies?"

Chel nodded.

"They should have killed them all," Fee said. "Now, the crew that's left has no choice but to tell you everything they know so killing them will be a waste of time."

"Yes." Hal sent her a smile. "And it's motivated Captain Tak to finally offer a full confession, as well."

"Did you get the murderers?"

"No. But Tean Lee, the station commander, has lens feed of the two he thinks are responsible. There are only so many places to hide on Larga Ways."

"Well, let us not interrupt your meal further," Chel said, standing.

Hal rose more slowly. "I'll be on Larga Ways for most of the morning, until Sazo gets here. I'll see you later, Fiona."

She gave the formal Grihan bow in response, but Hal stepped forward, hands together, and offered them to her. She tried to cover them with her own in as brisk a manner as possible, but when she didn't release them right away, he pulled his hands out from between hers. The movement was slow and deliberate. A caress.

When she looked up, he was watching her, eyes intense with energy.

Chel waited for him at the open door, and he finally gave her a nod and left. As the door closed behind them, she noticed Jasa was staring at her, mouth open.

Fee quirked a brow. "Got something to say?"

Jasa laughed. "Oh, no. I prefer to keep my mouth shut in situations like these."

Fee sat down and picked up the green mash. "I knew there was something I liked about you."

***

Hal walked toward the bridge with Chel in silence, trying to move his concentration from Fiona to the meeting he had with Tean Lee in half an hour.

Between his crew and the security staff on Larga Ways, they'd been patrolling Balco's system since just after his discussion with Admiral Hoke, looking for any sign the Tecran were around.

"What was the point of my being in that meeting?" Chel didn't look at him as he spoke.

"Why do you think?" Hal kept his tone mild.

"I don't know, that's why I'm asking."

"Why are you so angry, Chel?" Hal slowed his step, looked over at his commander.

"Because you're obviously not thinking straight where she's concerned. Telling her things that should be for crew only, trusting her with sensitive information. She freed a thinking system, Hal. A thinking system! The fact that it got blown up is beside the point. If it hadn't we'd have another one on our hands."

"Which would be a good thing, according to Admiral Hoke."

"Hoke's been got to just as badly as you. I know you've heard the whispers, that Hoke got promoted to head of fleet because

Sazo wouldn't join us while Admiral Krale was running Battle Center."

"And I know you've heard the whispers that it was because Krale was playing dirty games that Sazo refused to work with him. Hoke was in line for head of fleet anyway, that was a well-known fact. Sazo just put the timeline forward a little, that's all."

Hal didn't know what Krale had done, but he'd always been a fan of Admiral Hoke, and was glad she'd been promoted.

"That may be," Chel conceded the point with his old graciousness, something that Hal hadn't seen since Chel had watched him with Fiona last night outside the launch bay. "But . . . fraternizing with an orange? Hal, are you mad?"

Hal stopped. Ran a hand through his hair. "Maybe." His lips quirked up at the corners at Chel's hiss of frustration. "I asked you to meet with Fiona this morning so that you could see her."

Chel frowned. "What do you mean?"

"Listen to her discuss the Tecran spies lack of strategy or talk about her priorities while she was held prisoner. See her reaction to Rose's arrival, and her acceptance that she won't be able to explore Larga Ways, even though I promised her she could."

Chel shifted, uncomfortable, and Hal realized his second-in-command had already worked it out. He was just too stubborn to admit it.

He lifted a brow.

"All right. There is no difference between her and us. Is that what you want to hear? I can see it. Despite what we thought at the start, she's never been what we think of as an orange. I get it. But did you have to get involved with her?"

"Why do you, Rial, Tobru and Favri have such a problem with that?" Hal asked him. "Admiral Hoke doesn't."

Chel's mouth fell open slightly. "I thought . . . last night . . ."

"That between Favri and Rial, you'd dropped me in it for 'my own good' and that Hoke's one-on-one with me was to bring me back in line?" Hal realized he still harbored some real anger at that.

Chel looked away.

"Actually, Hoke and I discussed other things, and at the end . . ." he thought back to the smile in the admiral's eyes, "I think she gave me her blessing. In a round about way."

"Why would she do that?" Chel asked. He looked deeply unhappy.

It was a good question.

Hal admired Hoke, and respected her. But one thing he knew about the admiral, she was always several steps ahead.

And somehow, she thought a close relationship between one of her senior officers and Fiona was a good thing.

Whatever the reason, Hal was happy to oblige.

Chapter Thirty-eight

"SAZO WILL BE HERE ANY MINUTE," Fee coaxed softly. Since the strange sound she'd woken to this morning, there'd been no sign of Eazi, but she knew he wanted to meet Sazo, had been looking forward to it. "Come on, Eazi. Wake up."

She wondered for the first time if he could talk to her, even if he wanted to. The drone was back on Balco, the runner he'd been using was somewhere over Kyber's Arm. Perhaps she'd been mistaken this morning. Perhaps Eazi hadn't made a sound.

Something she could ask Sazo.

It was late morning now, and she paced her room, too wound up to enjoy the lens feed of a street scene of Larga Ways, happening in real time.

She would love to explore. She forced herself to stop and watch the people walking down the narrow street, browsing at the tiny shops which had their doors flung wide open to tempt passersby.

Perhaps it was her imagination, but the crowds seemed more subdued today. But the Class 5's destruction had been seen all the way to Larga Ways, and the news of the murder of some of the *Fasbe's* crew was probably out.

War was looming, so she supposed it wasn't surprising the Balcoans and the merchants who traded with them were in a more serious frame of mind.

The way station operated like a medieval walled city, she thought, with space at a premium. But even though the streets were almost too narrow to be practical, they had done amazing things with the room they had. And they had not once forgotten beauty. She enjoyed all the tiny details they'd added which elevated the ordinary to the extraordinary.

It reminded her of the Gothic Quarter in Barcelona, where every door handle, every cornice, every wall, had some delightful element.

Of course, the hovers that ran two levels above people's heads and the strange pets and outfits of the clientele made it clear it wasn't Barcelona, but another place and time entirely.

That, and the purple gel dome, and the view of the planet Balco when you managed to find a gap between buildings to the horizon.

She grinned, but it faded as she saw a figure striding through the street toward her, big body moving with grace and fluid speed through the crowd.

Hal.

He'd said he'd be on the way station for the morning, and from the look on his face, he wasn't exactly enjoying it. He looked grim and focused, and she suddenly thought the Tecran had just as much motivation to kill him as they did to kill her.

If they had their spies, which Hal said they did, they'd know by now he'd been in their secret facility. Knew more of their secrets than they would be comfortable with.

No matter that he'd debriefed his admiral, he'd need to be questioned at a UC tribunal Jasa had told her—both of them would, and if neither of them were around to speak, that would at least buy the Tecran some time.

Her gaze lingered on his face, set in hard lines, and the way he moved through the crowd with a single-minded focus that saw nothing of the scene around him.

He walked beyond the lens view and disappeared, and she stared at the spot where he'd disappeared blankly.

She had it bad, she forced herself to admit.

Really, really bad.

Someone, a person with narrow features and thin arms,

stopped at the exact spot she was looking at, and she realized he'd been browsing the wares outside one of the shops. She'd noticed him before she'd spotted Hal because of the green flowing robes he wore. A few others were dressed in similar clothing, and she guessed they were visiting traders from some far-flung planet, but his seemed more expensive, almost unreal, like liquid silk.

Except he didn't look like a trader now. He looked like a hunter. Something about him made her step closer, focus carefully on his face. His eyes were black or very dark brown, with no iris, and they looked as hard as the carapace of a beetle.

Her door chimed, and she turned reluctantly away. When she opened it and looked back, he was gone, and Carmain and Pila stood in the doorway.

"Sazo is here."

She felt a lurch of nerves. "Great."

"No one is allowed onboard his Class 5 except for you." Pila looked like he had one of the sour fruit she'd choked down for breakfast in his mouth.

"How come?" She hadn't been told very much about Sazo, she realized, or what his role in Battle Center was.

"Above our clearance level," Carmain said with a shrug. "We're here to escort you to the launch bay. There's a runner waiting for you."

As Fee walked between them to the launch bay, she was once again happy for the camouflage. No one even looked at her, and she had the sense it wasn't for lack of interest, but because they couldn't see her. Or not well enough to register.

The runner in the launch bay was the same as the one Eazi had used to help them with aerial views on Balco, and Fee got into it without any hesitation.

It was only after the doors closed, and they'd gone through the wobble of the gel wall, that she realized she was completely alone in the vessel.

"Hello?" she said. "Sazo?"

"Hello." The voice that came through the speakers in the runner was mostly Grihan rough, with just a hint of the fluidity of English. The greeting had been in English, though.

"I'm pleased to meet you. You helped a good friend of mine."

"Rose?" Sazo asked.

"Rose, too, although I don't know her personally. I'm talking about Eazi. He says you woke him up."

"I am pleased to meet you, too." Sazo's voice seemed warmer, closer to human. "I know you freed Eazi, and I thank you for it. But I have to tell you, Captain Vakeri indicated that Eazi was on a runner near Kyber's Arm. I checked the area before I made myself known here, and I could find no sign of it. My guess is that it was destroyed in the explosion. I've sent out a call for him every half an hour since then, and there is nothing. I think he's gone."

Fee drew the crystal pendant out of her shirt and held it up. "But isn't he in this? The runner was more so he could help us from outside Kyber's Arm."

"You have him." Sazo's voice wobbled a little. "I am very . . . relieved. And it seems I have even more to thank you for. Keeping him safe and keeping his secrets. Our secrets."

"They are safe with me." She tucked the necklace back under her shirt.

"I like you already, Fiona Russell." Sazo made a humming sound. "Perhaps we can use one of my runners and pretend it's Eazi for now. Keep the focus on that."

"Okay." She gave a shrug of agreement. "He hasn't spoken. Not since they blew him up. I didn't expect him to right away, because it must have been a massive shock, but I've been talking to him and singing to him since then, and nothing. But if the runner is gone, then he hasn't had anything to speak through."

"Unless he's in the *Illium's* systems?"

Fee looked up at the speakers. "I don't think he is. He used a trick to get me off the *Illium* before, but I was told it was using a device he had a Tecran spy attach to the passageway walls. He was still trapped in the Class 5 at the time."

"Ah, yes. Admiral Hoke told me that he'd engineered to get you onboard his Class 5 while still plugged in. She was more than a little disconcerted." He sounded amused. "I was impressed."

"Disconcerted?" There was an undercurrent here, Fee could hear it.

"Just a little reminder to her that even if they find a way to cage me again, it will likely not work for long." Sazo said.

"She would try that?"

"She might be ordered to. But she would fight against it. And I think she would prevail. But the admiral is pragmatic. She understands that I'm only with her of my own free will, and if I ever change sides, the chances of defeating me, even, as I say, if they could cage me again, would not be effective. The admiral now has even more incentive than before to keep me on side."

"Can you contact Eazi? If all he is is in the crystal?" Fee asked. "There's a drone in the desert which is undamaged, and which he was definitely in control of. He was in the Tecran's facility, as well, but he destroyed that himself. And there is Cy's runner and a second one with the Tecran crew's bodies in it."

"The drone might work," Sazo said. "I checked for the Larga Ways runner and the other runner, but I have a feeling both went the same way as the other one. Destroyed when the Class 5 blew. The good news is I can sense you have an earpiece but I can't use it to transmit to you. It's blocked. And that tells me he's still got a hold over it. It really might be that the only system he has to talk through is lying out of range on Balco."

It was comforting, in a way. It gave her a little hope.

"You don't have a handheld, do you? From Eazi's Class 5?" Sazo asked.

"I did. I left in my cell on the *Fasbe*. I never got it back."

"If you have a handheld, we need to get it. It'll be more useful than the drone."

"I could ask for it, but given the circumstances, I don't know if anyone will have time to find it for me." Would it be suspicious for her to ask for it?

"Don't worry about that. I'll sort it out." There was something close to glee in Sazo's voice.

She felt the wobble of going through another gel wall, and then then the gentle bump of landing, and her skin prickled in anticipation of meeting Rose McKenzie.

"Is Captain Jallan here, too?"

"No, I brought him to the *Illium* on this runner. You missed him by about five minutes when you boarded. He went off to wait for Captain Vakeri to return from Larga Ways."

As the ramp lowered, she saw Rose waiting for her.

They stared at each other for a moment and when Fee walked down to her, she realized she was unsteady on her feet.

"I was hoping they were wrong." Rose's voice was a little husky. "Because if you're from Earth, I know what you've been through. But at the same time, I was really hoping they were right."

Fee nodded, not sure she could talk. Rose put her hands together and extended them in greeting, and with a small smile, Fee covered them with her own.

"Getting into the Grihan swing of things?"

Rose laughed. "I didn't even think about it." She drew Fee in and gave her a hug. "You aren't in the habit, yet?"

"I've only been with the Grih for a week." She stepped back. "And the Garmman I was with didn't teach me the correct greetings."

Rose reached out and fingered the silver silk of her shirt. "I could barely focus on you when you came down that ramp. You were like a walking head."

"Eazi gave it to me. It kept me safe while I was trying to destroy the kill switch they used on him."

"I can't believe they did that." Rose sighed. "Or rather, I can. They must be in a real panic over losing Sazo and Bane."

Rose led the way out of the launch bay, and into a small, plush area with comfortable seating and a wide screen that was like a window out onto space. Larga Ways spun off to one side, and the *Illium* hovered nearby. Looming over everything, Balco sat, brown, green and gold, as the backdrop.

"Officers' lounge," Rose said. "Admiral Hoke says you were taken from the same place on Earth I was." Fee saw the questions in her eyes, and gave a tight nod.

"I lived there, I wasn't holidaying, like you were. I knew your name as soon as I heard it. They were looking for you, but you must have known they would."

Rose closed her eyes. "Yes."

"Your parents and friends love you very much." Fee's throat closed and she couldn't talk any more. Everything she'd seen play out for Rose's disappearance would have been played out for her own.

"Sazo thinks they just used the same coordinates and species type, down to sex, to get you."

"Eazi thinks they did the same with Imogen Peters."

"Imogen Peters?" Rose hadn't taken a seat, but now she did.

"When I was down in the Tecran facility, I found a cage in the place where they kept all the animals and birds they'd collected. It was human-sized and someone had written *Imogen Peters was here* in the sand."

Rose stared at her.

"There's more. When I was taken, they also took some macaws. I remembered them from the few times I came to before they handed me to the Garmman. And there was a macaw down in the facility as well. Eazi said a different type to the ones he had, and all those died anyway, so when they took Imogen, they took macaws as well. Given the diversity they had to choose from, it smacks of simply duplicating the same haul as Eazi got."

"Why wouldn't they try and get something different?"

Fee shrugged. "Maybe no time? Eazi said there was some bad blood between his captain and the others when he was given the job of getting another person from Earth. Everyone wanted the privilege. Then, when the scientists on Eazi's ship refused to study me, someone one-upped him by grabbing the same again."

"Do you know Imogen Peters?" Rose asked. "From Earth?"

Fee shook her head. "It's not that small a town, and I don't know everyone. But she could be a holiday-maker, like you."

"Do you know what happened to her?"

Fee finally sat as well. "We found something going on in the facility. Cage fighting. Pitting the creatures they were done with against each other, betting on which one would win. The fights were to the death."

"You think they put Imogen Peters in the ring against something else?" Sazo spoke for the first time since she'd met Rose, using the speakers in the room.

"They might have done." She cleared her throat. "I asked Commander Dai, and he says she was gone before Eazi's crew got there. And now the facility is destroyed, all the information on her is gone, too."

"You wouldn't think they'd have gone to all that trouble, just to kill her." Rose rubbed her temples with stiff fingers.

Fee shook her head. "I think you'll find that if the Tecran have managed to put two and two together as far as the Class 5s and women they've abducted from Earth are concerned, they're probably convinced the only good human is a dead one."

Rose gave a quick, mirthless laugh. "That's true enough. And you'll find that attitude among some of the Grih, as well. They're particularly angry with me for freeing Bane, because he hasn't automatically come over to the Grihan side. He's allied to Sazo, and so by default, to the Grih, but they were hoping for a direct connection."

"It's becoming as labyrinthine as pre-World War I politics," Fee said.

"Good description." Rose pressed her lips together. "Let's hope it doesn't have the same result."

"I'm pleased to say I located your handheld in the communications department, Fiona." Sazo's voice was back to sounding Grihan again. "It was brought over from the *Fasbe*, examined and cleared. The next step would presumably be to return it to you, but since the captain's been busy with other things it's just sitting there. So I put the order through."

"You're in the *Illium's* systems?" Fee wondered what Hal would think of that. Something hot and tight gripped her stomach. The knowledge that she might have to choose between two sets of loyalties.

"Only because we need that handheld. Otherwise I wouldn't have interfered." Sazo paused. "You are unhappy about that?"

"No. Yes." She took a deep breath. "It's just what they're afraid of. And it will only deepen the distrust. If you'd just asked them, they would have given it to you anyway." She thought about it. "Well, Captain Vakeri would have. Maybe no one else."

"I'm afraid Captain Vakeri seems to have gone missing," Sazo told her. "Dav is still waiting for him, and from the chatter I'm picking up from his crew, they're starting to get worried. He was supposed to be at the runner at the Larga Ways dock half an hour ago."

"They can track him, though. With his uniform." She had trouble speaking.

"It seems to indicate that he's standing still in a small side street. Something no one thinks is likely."

"Lens feed?" Fee asked.

"One moment. There is no lens feed in that particular area, but although I'm not in the Larga Ways system, the *Illium* has access to the lens feed coming from the way station's security officers personal lens feed. The station chief has sent four guards to take a look." The screen which moments before had shown the view from the Class 5 of Balco, the *Illium* and Larga Ways faded and became a bouncing view of a narrow street. The guard was obviously running. The view shifted as the guard stepped into an even narrower, shadowed path between two buildings. It focused down, and Fee stepped closer to see better, aware that Rose was doing the same.

"It looks like a scrap of fabric," Rose said.

The guard reached down, lifted the fabric up so they could all see the jagged edges of it.

Fee remembered the man in the green robes from earlier, the way he'd looked after Hal with those hard, shiny eyes. "They ripped the tracker out of his uniform."

Chapter Thirty-nine

COMMANDER CHEL WAS REFUSING to take any comms from Fee, so Fee was going to him personally.

She spent the five minutes between the *Illium* and Sazo's Class 5 tapping her foot with impatience, and Rose, sitting beside her, watched her with curious eyes.

"Obviously, it's bad that Captain Vakeri is missing, but you seem to be very affected."

"He saved me." Fee looked over at her. "Quite a few times. And I saved him back." She wanted the chance to be able to save him again.

But would they keep him alive? Question him? Or just kill him and be done with it?

Rose said nothing, and Fee gathered up her hair, wound it round and round her hand in agitation.

"We have a thing going, the captain and I." She let the words come with a bitter smile. "That's why Commander Chel won't take my calls. He thinks I'm dragging his beloved captain down the path of getting fired by Battle Center."

"A thing?" Rose asked, voice neutral.

Fee shot her a quick look, then shrugged. "Not sure what yet, but I'd like the chance to find out." She shrugged again. "Life, as we see right freaking now, is too short not to. Although you wouldn't think it given how long this ride is taking."

Rose smiled at her.

"What's so funny?"

"I have a thing going, as you call it, with Captain Jallan." She tapped her fingers on her thigh. "Although his crew were not so hostile to the idea of it. But that might be because he's in charge of an exploration vessel, not a battleship."

Fee didn't get a chance to respond, because they went through the gel wall and she was standing at the door as it lowered.

A big Grih in a similar uniform to Hal was waiting for them, his hair a fascinating mix of gray and black. He looked at her with blue eyes that held shock and astonishment.

"Fiona Russell?"

"Captain Jallan?" Fee didn't really have to guess. Rose had joined her on the ramp, and there was clearly something between the two, as they shared a quick look.

"You look so alike, and yet . . . not." The captain kept staring.

"Is there any news about Hal?" She knew it was rude, but there was a rising sense of desperation swamping her, making it impossible to deal with the small niceties of life.

"No. I'm sorry. His team are doing everything they can to find him."

"Commander Chel won't take any comms from me, but earlier, on the lens feed, I saw Hal walking down a street and there was a man in green robes watching him."

"They're shutting her out," Rose murmured to Dav, stepping in close to him. "They don't like her relationship with Captain Vakeri and they're suspicious of her. Fee doesn't think they're going to listen to her."

Fee looked up to see thoughtful eyes on her. "Why don't we ask Commander Chel to join us, then?"

Relief flooded her. Hopefully Chel wasn't such an idiot he'd ignore what she'd seen just because he didn't like her. And he may take it more seriously if he was urged to listen to her by someone within Battle Center who outranked him.

"Thank you." She watched as Jallan tapped his earpiece, murmured a request to see Chel.

"He was coming this way anyway." Jallan had barely spoken

when the launch bay doors opened and Chel stepped in.

His eyes narrowed at the sight of her.

"You have something for me?" He addressed Captain Jallan, and ignored both Fee and Rose.

"I don't, but I believe Fiona has been trying to pass on some information to you since she heard Hal was missing."

"How did you find out he was missing in the first place?" Chel was a man almost jumping out of his skin. Fee didn't like the cold way he spoke to her, but she was encouraged that Hal's commander did care about him, and was as desperately worried as she was.

"Sazo told me." She kept her tone mild. If she wanted him to listen, putting his back up even more would not help. "I wanted to tell you that just before I was called to take the runner over to Sazo, I was watching lens feed of the main street on Larga Ways. I saw Hal walk down the street toward the lens, and there was a person with green robes who was watching him. He seemed suspicious."

Chel stared at her with hot, angry eyes. "We're already watching all the lens feed, following Captain Vakeri's movements up until he disappeared. We don't need you to tell us our job."

She flinched, and felt Captain Jallan's hand on her shoulder, Rose's on her other side.

"I can imagine you're upset," Jallan said to him in a low voice, "but there is no need to take that tone."

Chel muttered something, refusing to look at her again, and then strode off.

Jallan sighed. "I'll go find something useful to do on the bridge. I outrank Chel, so if the worst comes to the worst, I can take over here." He strode after the commander and Fee and Rose watched him go.

She had no idea what to do next, but it had to be something.

Rose slid an arm around her shoulders.

"Why don't you take me to your room? And then maybe you can show me the macaw?"

Fee nodded, remembered Sazo had infiltrated the system to get the handheld returned to her. Maybe he could tap in again and see what they were doing to find Hal.

She suddenly found she had less of a problem with Sazo's sneaking around than she had before.

They stepped out into the passage.

"Fiona."

Pila and Carmain were blocking the way. She frowned at them. "What's wrong?"

"Um." Carmain cleared her throat, shooting quick looks at Rose. "Commander Chel gave orders that you have to move over to the Class 5. He's cleared it with the admiral. It's the safest place for you, and it'll free up your guards. Sazo can take you back to Battle Center when this is over, as well."

She felt a quick, hard punch of dismay. She'd thought of this as her new home, and Chel was kicking her out.

Eazi had offered her a place with him, but that had been taken away, from both of them.

Where did she belong, then? If Battle Center was her destination, where to from there?

Chel didn't want her because he didn't understand her, was afraid she was going to get his captain fired or disgraced and make them all a target to the Tecran. But that left her nowhere.

"Fiona. Are you okay?" Rose gripped her shoulder. "You look pale."

"No, I'm fine." She forced herself to suck it up.

No wonder Eazi wasn't back yet. His only place was gone. The place purpose built for him. And she understood even better now how he must feel.

But there was a silver lining here. If she didn't have to be shut up in her room, she knew just how to find Hal.

311

"I'll need to get something from my room, and then I'll be out of your hair." She gave Carmain the best smile she could. Her guard was just the messenger, and Fee could see she was unhappy about the message she was delivering. "Commander Chel is right. I will be safest on Sazo's Class 5, and it will mean you won't have to watch me."

She let Carmain lead the way, with Pila bringing up the rear. When they got to her room she blocked the way in to her guards.

"I'll just be a minute." She looked at Rose. "Would you like to see my soon-to-be ex-room?"

"Sure." Rose's eyes told her she knew something was going on.

As soon as the door closed behind them, Fee studied the area carefully.

"Okay." She spoke in English. "I think they've been in here, and maybe they've hidden a lens. Fortunately for me, out of habit, I have something I didn't want them to find, and it's been in my bra since I got dressed this morning. But they'll see me take the handheld."

"But they'll have it on the system that that was cleared and returned to you," Rose pointed out.

"True." She saw the handheld on the low table in the lounge, and picked it up. Let her fingers dance over it to wake it up.

"Sazo, are you here?"

Rose gave her a nod, and Fee guessed he'd answered through Rose's earpiece.

"Instead of taking me back to the Class 5, can you take me to Larga Ways?"

Rose frowned. "He asks why. I do, too."

"Because Hal is in danger. I'm not sure how long they're going to keep him alive. They'll want to know what he found out in the facility, maybe what happened with Eazi, but then they'll kill him. And there is only one thing they want more than him."

"What?" Rose asked, then her eyes widened. "You!"

"As it happens, I've got a magic bracelet on that deflects any shots taken at me. I won't show it to you right now because if they do have lens feed in here, they may try to take it. I used to have a handy weapon called a crowd-pleaser, but the Tecran took that away. But if Sazo has a tracker he can give me, and maybe one of those small lenses, I'll go down to Larga Ways and let them drag me to wherever they're holding Hal."

"You want company?" Rose asked, then winced, as if Sazo were shouting in her ear.

Fee shook her head. "I don't want to endanger you, and besides, I bet they don't know you're here. Let's keep it that way."

"So they grab you and then we can send the troops after you." Rose gripped her forearm. "Are you sure about this? I know we can withstand a kill shot with a shockgun, but it is no fun."

"A kill shot." Fee realized she was all but baring her teeth. "So that bastard *did* try to kill me."

"You've already experienced it, huh?" Rose gave a sympathetic grimace. "I've been shot to kill twice now."

"I've been shot twice, but the first time it was on stun. The second was kill, I'm pretty sure. But that's a moot point now."

"The magic bracelet?" Rose asked. "Okay. It sounds as if you'd be okay for a bit, so we could get people to wherever they've taken you. And you'll just have to hope your captain is there, too."

"It's better than the chance he's got right now," Fee told her. "You're going to have to convince Chel to actually go in and save me. Because I don't think he'd be that sad if I didn't make it."

"He should listen to Dav. And if not, Sazo can be pretty persuasive." Rose grinned, and Fee guessed Sazo had said something in agreement in her earpiece.

"Will Captain Jallan get into trouble for this?"

Rose shook her head. "Not if Sazo whisks you away and I tell him when it's already a done deal."

"That won't get you in trouble?" Fee asked.

"I would do the same in your shoes." Rose's face was Boudicca fierce. "And as a minority of two, we Earthlings have to stick together."

Chapter Forty

IT TOOK SAZO LESS THAN TEN MINUTES to get her from the *Illium* to the Larga Ways dock reserved for the *Illium's* runners.

"I told Rose to wait until you're through the security check to let them know what you're doing, so Chel can't stop you," Sazo said.

"Thanks. And thanks for the other goodies, too." She had a small lens and microphone worked into the collar of her shirt, with the earpiece for Sazo or anyone from the *Illium* to speak to her in her other ear, a tracker stuck to her scalp at her nape, just within her hair, and an illegal light-gun like the one Hal had gotten so excited about tucked into a neat, custom-made strap just above her left wrist, under the long sleeve of her top.

"Rose has one, but Admiral Hoke knows about it, so I managed to procure another, just in case the time comes when Hoke asks her to hand it over."

"Point and shoot?"

Sazo had told her that Rose found she needed to look away or close her eyes when she used it. Humans had trouble with the light, even if it was pointed away from them.

Apparently, she wouldn't need to see to aim. Anyone in front of her would be writhing around in pain, but they'd all eventually recover.

She pulled on the jacket Sazo had found for her. It would do her no good if the Tecran's spies couldn't find her because of her camouflage.

The runner bumped to a stop.

"You'll keep trying with Eazi?" She glanced at the handheld

which she'd left on the console. She couldn't risk taking it with her. She'd taken off the crystal, too, and Sazo had stored it away in a tiny drawer on the console.

It felt as if she was saying some kind of goodbye, but that was silly. She still had her earpiece. She could still talk to him.

"I'll keep trying."

She appreciated that he didn't sound despondent.

"To show his cooperation, the station chief's sharing all lens feed with the *Illium*, so I've got full access. I've found someone with green robes. Is this the person you saw?" Sazo flashed the main street of Larga Ways up on a screen and Fee leaned forward to take a good look.

"That's him. Do you know where he's from?"

"His features and build mark him as coming from Vutro, which is in Garmman territory. They're a bit like the Balcoans; they aren't a voting part of the Garmman block, but they're a protectorate within Garmman airspace. I'll guide you in his direction as soon as you're through the security gate."

She walked out, thinking how different her second visit was.

When she'd been with the UC official the first time, supposedly on her way to a meeting, she'd hoped she could explore, thought she was safe.

This time, she was deliberately putting herself in harm's way.

She nodded to the two guards standing on either side of the docking gate, but Sazo had obviously provided all the right clearances, because they let her continue through without hesitation.

Even so, she only relaxed when she was able to mingle with a group of people heading down the street.

"You're going the right way," Sazo told her. "The Vutrovian is hovering near the center of the way station."

She gnawed at her lip, wondering why Green Robes was wandering around. Did it mean he'd already dealt with Hal?

The thought made her physically sick.

"Fiona, there is someone coming up behind you." Sazo's voice was urgent in her ear, but too late.

Hands gripped her upper arms, and jerked her into the dark recess between two buildings.

"What do you think you're doing? Do you think we don't have enough going on without having to deal with you?"

Fee turned her head, looked into Rial's enraged face.

Okay. No more Ms. Nice Guy. She'd been kicked out, anyway.

"What do you think the people who have Hal want even more than answers from him?" She kept her voice cool and dismissive.

He started to shake her, stopped and his eyes went wide as he realized what she meant. "Unless you have backup, you'll be throwing yourself away for nothing."

"I think Commander Chel probably just learned I'm here a minute ago, maybe less. But even if they'd already taken me, I have a tracker and a lens on me." She pulled away from him.

"Where did you get them. I know Chel wouldn't give—" He came up short.

"Wouldn't give me the time of day? I'm very aware of that." She gave a cold smile. "As it happens, I do have some friends, and they are well equipped. And outrank Commander Chel."

She let him work it out, and then he glanced upward, and she realized Sazo's Class 5 was visibly hovering over the dome of the way station.

"But why are you doing this?" Rial looked back at her, baffled.

"You didn't think Captain Vakeri's . . . interest in me was one-sided, did you?" Fee had managed to get some space between them, but he still held her arms and she shrugged off his hands. "I'm loyal to those I care about. And right now, that list is pretty short. Hal put his life on the line more than once for me, I am happy to do the same. Now," she straightened her jacket, "please stay back and out of sight, or everything I've set in place will be for nothing."

She gave him one last, narrow-eyed look, and he raised his hands, palms out, in surrender, let her slip back into the river of pedestrians.

"Nice smack-down," Sazo said, and it was enough to put a smile on her face.

***

Green Robes was hanging around to stay up-to-date with what was happening, Fee decided.

He wasn't watching any place or person in particular, just wandering around listening to people talking about the Class 5 overhead, the gossip about Hal's kidnapping and the murder of the *Fasbe's* crew, not to mention the massive explosion the day before.

If they had had an inside source, the station chief had obviously found it, or shut things down so tight, the traitor was too afraid of being caught to risk making contact.

Fee walked past him, eyes ahead, and then breathed in deeply as she smelled the amazing aroma of open fire cooking she'd smelled last time she was on Larga Ways. Hal had said they could go hunt for it together.

She blinked back tears. Well, she'd found it, and she could bring him here when he was safe. Show him.

Sazo had given her some money, loaded into a chip on the sleeve of her jacket, and she decided sitting outside at one of the two tiny tables in front of the restaurant would be as good a way to let Green Robes see her as any other.

She sat, and almost immediately, a tall, thin woman with dark skin came out to her.

"I'd like whatever I can smell cooking, please." She spoke in Grihan, and the woman smiled, bowed and went back inside without a word.

She returned less than five minute later, with a tray almost the same size as the table. It contained thin strips of seared meat, what looked like circles of golden flat bread, and something green, leafy and crisp on the side. A long, narrow flute of a cup, filled with a greenish liquid, nestled between the bowls of food.

"Thank you." Fee took a piece of bread, spooned on meat and salad, folded it over, and then looked up to see the waitress was watching her from the door, with what seemed like approval on her face.

She bit in, and let the first delicious thing she'd had to eat since she was taken sit on her tongue. She savored every bite, working through the food with an appetite she hadn't had in months.

When she was done, she sipped cautiously at the drink, and found it tart and refreshing.

"Any sign of Green Robes?" Fee murmured to Sazo.

"He saw you. Watched you for a bit. He's hanging back, out of sight, at the moment."

"Good." She lifted her head, smiled at the waitress, and tapped the sleeve of her jacket to the tray, which was flashing the amount owed, to settled her bill.

She stood. The meal had been comforting, not only because she'd actually enjoyed it, but because it reminded her of home.

But one quick glimpse of green robes twisted her stomach. She forced herself to take things slowly as she walked back the way she'd come.

She stopped at a particularly beautiful wall mosaic, and then saw it was a story of a sort, the scenes running down the length of the narrow alley. A few people were using the street, but it was far less busy than the road behind her.

She let herself follow it, looking at each scene. She would have to come back, though. She saw the jewel-like colors, the way the tiny stones they'd used accented the building and built a beautiful picture at the same time, but could not take it in.

"He's following you. Commander Chel and Tean Lee have

people in place." Sazo's voice was calm, just what she needed to hear.

She kept her pace steady.

The afternoon sun reached in and illuminated the top of the wall, so the intricate silver and gold circular designs worked into the mosaic shone bright, and offset the deep tones of the blues, reds and greens.

Any moment now, surely. Any moment . . .

For the second time that day, hands grabbed her, and she felt the dig of shockgun in her side.

That would be an interesting ricochet, if he pulled the trigger.

The thought steadied her.

"This is set to kill. So you will come with me." Green Robes hissed in her ear.

She had done it.

And the moment she thought that, the angry bee hum of a shockgun shot registered, and the Vutrovian who was holding her went down.

She stumbled back from him, unsure whether he'd pulled the trigger or not.

"What happened?" Sazo's voice snapped her back.

"I don't know."

Green Robes was moving, struggling to sit up, so he'd only been stunned, and Fee was left not knowing what to do. He'd expect her to run, but she actually wanted to stay caught.

The hum of another shot sounded, and she saw the faintest flash of blue as it was repelled, but it was as good an excuse as any. She pretended to go down.

"Someone is shooting at us. Is it someone from the way station?" She used English and kept her voice to a faint whisper.

"Not the way station, not the *Illium's* crew. Not sure who else could be in the mix."

That was the good thing about Sazo. He sounded interested

and engaged, rather than panicked. But then, it wasn't him being shot at. Still, his calm helped her find her own.

"I'll try to scan the—"

The sound in her ear went dead. She tapped it, but there was nothing, and then someone was running at her, grabbing the back of her jacket and hauling her away.

She'd been dragged a good four meters before Green Robes managed to clamber to his feet.

She was trying to see who had grabbed her, and she caught a glimpse of the rage on the Vutrovian's face.

"She is mine," he screamed in Garmman, and started to run after them.

Would the *Illium's* crew step in now, or would they wait to see where this was going?

The man dragging her lifted her up in an amazing display of strength, although she could hear the effort it cost him as he strained to fling her over his shoulder.

He was at least head and shoulders taller than Hal or any of the Grih, and stockier, too. He was wearing a thin jacket and pants that had been dark blue when he'd descended on her, but now turned liquid silver in front of her eyes.

He leaned against a wall, draping something over her and she wondered why he thought she would stay quiet as Green Robes ran past, until she remembered he though he'd hit her with a stun from his shockgun.

She had to decide. Did she want to see where this was going?

If Green Robes had Hal, she was missing her chance. But what if she was wrong?

As soon as Green Robes turned the corner, the man ran lightly down some stairs to the basement entrance of the building they were standing against, and the door slid open as he approached.

He threw her onto a couch and she played limp and unconscious. She sensed him hover over her for a moment, and then he ran out the room again.

She heard the door, felt the air stir, and then listened to his feet run back up the stairs.

He was going to follow Green Robes, she guessed.

"Sazo?" Nothing. She stood up, moved quickly around the single room, which had a tiny lounge, a kitchen tucked in a corner, a bed at the back and a bathroom partition off to the side. No sign of Hal, which meant her gamble had not paid off.

There was a crackle in her ear, and her hopes rose that Sazo was back until she realized it was on the righthand side.

"Eazi?"

She walked to the door, but it didn't open for her. She pulled out her encryptor, touched it to the panel and the door slid open.

Her very own Open Sesame. So worth the concussion.

She slid it back in her bra and ran up the steps, looked carefully left and right and then ran back the way she'd come.

Maybe the *Illium's* team would still be in place, and able to let her know what the heck was going on.

Her ear crackled again.

"Eazi? Is that you?" She remembered she was wearing a jacket over her camouflage, and vacillated over whether to take it off or not as she came to the end of the tiny street.

She crouched down, looked around the corner.

The hum of a shockgun sounded near her ear.

"That Vanad thinks he can follow me?" Green Robes said, voice soft. "I am not so stupid. And it seems you recovered from the shockgun hit faster than he thought."

He was positively gleeful.

She slumped against the wall and let him haul her to her feet.

"You are coming with me."

It looked like she had a second chance at finding Hal.

Chapter Forty-one

HAL KNEW HIS USEFULNESS was coming to an end.

He'd only lasted so long, he knew, because the small group of spies had lost their inside help.

Either Tean Lee had found the leak or had made it impossible for the spy inside his office to pass information along.

The Vutrovian was running blind, and he was too nervous to send any of his team out without more information.

Hal had strung them along as far as he could. Telling them just enough to think him more useful alive than dead.

The togrut they'd given him for the first round of questioning had flattened him. They either hadn't had any more to give him, or were too scared it would kill him, so they'd had to take his whispered information on the likely reaction to his disappearance by the *Illium* and way station security on trust.

Sazo's arrival had helped, as well.

They hadn't expected it. Had at first thought it was Eazi, and needed him to explain what the explosion had been the day before.

When he'd told them this was another Class 5 altogether, one under Battle Center control, he'd found out the Tecran had not shared that information with their spies.

They'd scoffed at him when he'd said that the Grih had two Class 5s, and the Vutrovian had hit him for it, but he had shaken them to the core.

They'd thought they were on the winning side. And with five Class 5s on the Tecran side, why wouldn't they?

To now face the knowledge that the Tecran had destroyed one

and lost two to the other side . . . Hal wondered how much longer the Balcoan on the Vutrovian's team was going to stay.

The way he was fidgeting, Hal guessed not long.

He was lying down on the comfortable bed in the small apartment above the Vutrovian's fabric store and the Balcoan was guarding him. He kept looking over at Hal with quick, nervous glances.

Hal wished he was pretending to be weaker than he really was, but the aftereffects of the togrut had him shaking and sweating, unsure if his legs would even hold him up. It was becoming harder to talk, and he was getting worse.

He wasn't even sure it had been worth their while. He couldn't remember exactly what he'd said, but it had sounded to his ears like stream of consciousness crap, rather than any useful information.

The store below had been closed when the Vutrovian had brought him in earlier, and both he and his guard clearly heard the door below open and close, and harsh, angry voices.

The guard moved toward the door they'd left open, which led out to a landing and the stairs to the store below.

Hal was watching him, and saw the expression of panic and then rage that crossed his face as someone came up the stairs.

"Are you insane?" The Balcoan spoke in Garmman, the words almost too guttural to understand.

"You think there will be any mercy for us now, whatever we do?" It was the Vutrovian. "We follow through or we will have two sides after us. Is that what you want? Besides, we aren't the only ones who know the Tecran want her dead. I just managed to get her back from a Vanad."

The Balcoan stood, blocking the door for another defiant moment, and then stepped back. He looked sick.

Hal tried to sit when he saw who the Vutrovian was pushing through the door. He hoped for a single beat that he was back in the grip of the togrut, that she wasn't really here, but then the bed dipped as she sat beside him. Blocking him from the rest of the room, he realized.

He forced himself to look, and saw that she still had her reflector bracelet on.

"We don't have any togrut left," the Balcoan said, eyes on Fiona.

"We don't need her to talk. We just need proof that we had her and we killed her."

Fiona pretended not to understand, and Hal saw both men took that at face value.

She leaned over him, stroking his hair back from his face, and put her lips near his ear. "Are there any more, or is it just the two up here and one below?" She used Grih.

"More," he managed to say. "Maybe out."

"Quiet." The Vutrovian took a threatening step toward her. "You say your name and who you are," he reached over to a shelf near the door and picked up a small lens.

They'd probably recorded him when they gave him the togrut, Hal realized. And they wanted Fiona's details before they killed her. Proof they had the right person.

"I don't understand," Fiona spoke in slow, broken Garmman. Then she switched to her own language, and babbled away, sounding more and more excited.

She was playing them. Playing them the way she'd played Tak for months.

She understood all too well how an orange was perceived.

He'd seen the tight, controlled way she'd dealt with Chel's rudeness this morning, and wished he'd been more forceful with his commander. He thought there was time, that they'd see what and who she was and be as dazzled as he, but he would no longer tolerate a situation where she was disrespected as a matter of course.

Although someone respected her enough to let her put her life at risk to save him.

He looked forward to having a conversation with that person, if they got out of here alive.

***

It was going to be up to Fee to do this alone.

The *Illium's* crew should have stormed the building by now if her lens and microphone were working.

As comms to Sazo were obviously down, so, most likely, was everything else.

From the street below, she heard someone shout, and she broke off the rendition she was giving them of Monty Python's Spanish Inquisition sketch. Imogen had inspired her, and besides, looking at Hal, it was clear this lot wouldn't flinch at torturing some answers out of her.

There was a gray cast to his skin and she forced herself to concentrate on getting them the hell out, because if she looked at Hal too much, she might just fall apart.

The Balcoan moved over to the window to see what was happening, and the Vutrovian watched him.

She took her chance, grabbing the pillow out from under Hal's head and gently covering his face with it.

She reached under her left sleeve as the Balcoan turned to her, shockgun raised, a frown on his face, and buried her own face in the pillow as she pointed the light-gun between him and the Vutrovian and pressed the button.

He must have gotten off a shot by reflex, because she heard it over the sharp, breathless cry he let out.

She lifted her thumb off the button, raised her head and saw both the Vutrovian and the Balcoan were down. She had no idea if the ricochet had got him or whether his fall had put him out of the line of fire.

As she lifted the pillow off of Hal's face, she couldn't find it in her to care.

Hal had turned his head to the wall, and the effort it took him to turn it back made her clench her fists.

She slid the light-gun into her sleeve and ran to the window, stepping over the Balcoan to get there.

Two men had been forced to the ground by black-clad Larga Ways guards, and a small team from the *Illium* stood near the store's door, armed and ready.

She pushed the window open, and six shockguns pointed her way. "Hal and I are up here. Please hurry."

She sat beside him while she waited, not moving when the door below was battered open, when shouts and orders were barked out.

"They're coming. They'll get you to Jasa as soon as they can." She said it over and over, gently stroking his hair, frightened to her core at his condition.

Rial was the first one into the room, and she stood and shielded Hal in one smooth movement.

Rial brought himself up short at the sight of her, his gaze going to the two men at her feet.

The Balcoan was completely still, so perhaps he had been hit with the ricochet, while the Vutrovian was moaning in faint, hoarse bursts of pain.

She stepped aside, so he could see Hal.

"He needs help. I don't know what they did to him."

"Togrut," Hal whispered.

Rial was a medic, she remembered. The one who'd fixed her up on the *Fasbe*, what felt like years ago. He winced at whatever Hal said.

"I've only heard what it does, never seen it." He crouched beside Hal and Fee saw he had a bag slung over his shoulder. He started taking things out, pressing things onto Hal's skin.

The rest of the team arrived, and for a minute, the room was too full.

"Space," Rial snarled, and then the two spies were hauled off, and it was only herself, Rial and a soldier setting up what looked like a hovering stretcher.

"Will he be okay?" She watched Rial and his helper lift Hal onto the stretcher and then maneuver it to the door.

"Maybe. But we need to hurry." He jogged out the room, one hand holding the stretcher, and she was left staring at the empty landing, listening to the sound of their boots as they ran down the stairs.

She was being shut out, she realized. Perhaps not on purpose, but she didn't fit anywhere on the *Illium*, didn't even have a room there anymore.

She ran down after them and found they had already disappeared.

A group of Balcoan guards stood just outside, and they all turned to watch her as she stepped out onto the street.

"Fiona Russell?" The man who approached her had the warm brown skin and silver eyes of the majority of the inhabitants of Larga Ways.

She nodded.

"Tean Lee. I'm the station chief." He gave a formal Grihan bow, which she returned.

"I seem to have lost my ride," she said, trying to smile. "Do you know where they've taken Captain Vakeri?"

"I've been asked to watch over you for a bit by Commander Chel," Lee told her, and she thought there was some satisfaction in his tone. "Captain Vakeri has been taken to the *Illium* for safety reasons."

It made sense. And she didn't want them to slow down for anything, she was glad they had rushed him off, even if it meant she was being fobbed off again. She just wished she had the right to go with him.

"My office isn't far from here." Lee gestured with his arm and she fell into step with him.

There was a strange crackle in her right ear again, and she rubbed it. The ear with the earpiece from Sazo was absolutely dead. "Do you know why Sazo is still offline?"

He shot her a look. "The whole of Larga Ways is a dead zone. No one can use their comms."

"Does anyone know why?"

Tean Lee gave a hollow laugh. "Given what's been happening here since the *Illium* arrived, I'm not ruling anything out."

Chapter Forty-two

FEE SAT ON THE COUCH in Tean Lee's office and stared at her boots. After a brief struggle with herself, she decided she was too tired to care, pulled them off and lay down.

She'd given her statement, Tean Lee taking her back almost three days to when she'd first been abducted by Cy.

Her information about the Vanad and his tiny basement apartment had gotten the station chief all excited, and he'd rushed off, telling her to make herself at home.

Every now and then, she tapped her earpiece and called Sazo's name, but although she could see him hovering above the way station through the big window of Lee's office, the comms were obviously still down. To the left of Sazo, the edge of the *Illium* was just visible.

It still hurt that they had kicked her off. She didn't buy the reasons Chel had given. He'd just wanted to get her away from Hal.

She kept thinking of Hal, gray and shaking, and she wanted— needed—to know how he was doing.

Chel would hardly refuse Sazo's runner entry into the *Illium's* launch bay. She wasn't living there anymore, but she could visit, couldn't she?

And if she didn't go now, say her goodbyes, when would she get the chance?

She sat up, slid her feet back in her boots, and walked out.

There were no guards outside the door, and she guessed they thought her safe enough at security headquarters.

She took a tube down to the ground floor, and nodded to the

guards at the entrance.

They'd seen her come in with Lee, and they let her out with a polite nod back.

The events earlier in the day must have shaken the tiny population of the way station, because the streets were definitely emptier than they had been.

She supposed the Vanad could still be out there, looking for her, but his bolthole was uncovered, and she'd only pretended to be stunned last time because she'd wanted to be taken. He'd find it a lot harder to get hold of her again and the chance of having to deal with him wasn't enough to keep her from trying to get to Hal.

She'd made it all the way to Sazo's runner when an explosion rumbled like a volcano, shaking the very floor beneath her feet.

The metal sang as she turned to look, saw the flash of white light and had to shield her eyes.

The gel dome at her eye level wobbled and Fee suddenly remembered she was on a massive, floating space platform. That a breach would mean death to everyone here.

She tapped the door of the runner, but it was as dead as everything else here. The guards standing at the dock entrance were running to get into the nearest vessel, and she tapped the door again, then dug out her encryptor and held it in a white-knuckled fist.

"Please work." She tapped it, and dived through the door as it slid open.

It closed behind her before she could offer the guards sanctuary, but she'd hear them if they knocked, and there had been plenty of other vessels for them to get into before hers.

"Sazo?" Nothing.

She didn't know how to fly this, and even if she did, she didn't know if she could even get it started without Sazo's help.

Eazi's handheld was sitting on the console where she'd left it, and she started it up and opened the draw where she'd put the crystal, pulled it over her head.

"Eazi, you're right here. That makes me think you and I should be able to talk, even with a dead zone. Please wake up. Something terrible's happened. You need to wake up."

Her ear crackled again, just like it had when she'd been in the Vanad's apartment. "Hello? Eazi, are you there?"

She looked down at the handheld, frustrated that she didn't know what to do with it to make a connection with him.

The runner bumped against the dock, as if it were floating on water, rather than hovering in space, and she ran to the door in panic, used the encryptor to open up and look out.

The dome looked strange and air swirled around her. The way station was leaking.

Up above, beyond the dome, she saw runners and small fighter craft launching from the *Illium* and from Sazo's Class 5. Probably sending vessels to the way station to help evacuate.

She stepped back and the door closed again, and she realized the crackle in her ear hadn't shut off.

"Fiona?" Her name ripped through her, so loud she tried to claw the earpiece out, whimpering when she couldn't get hold of it.

"Too loud, too loud." She barely managed to get the words out.

"Sorry." Eazi whispered, but even that hurt.

"Still too loud."

He was silent for a long moment.

"Loud or not, I'm really glad to hear your voice," she told him, suddenly afraid she'd scared him off.

"How is this?" He spoke softly, but the volume was right this time.

"Good." She swallowed hard. "Very good."

She suddenly felt a lot less alone.

"Do you know how I'm talking to you?"

"I think through the handheld you left with me on the *Fasbe*. Sazo said it was the best way to reach you, because the drone's still out in the desert and he thinks Cy's runner and the one you were using were destroyed when they blew . . ." Did she want to remind him? Did he even remember?

"When they blew up my Class 5." He sounded thoughtful. "When I woke up it was like I was floating in total darkness. I couldn't tell up from down, and I've never felt that way before. But now that you've said handheld, I think I know where I am."

The screen of the handheld flared and Fee touched a finger to it. A line ran around her fingertip, lengthening until it was a spinning circle.

"It's nice to have you back." She coughed away the tears that were clogging her throat. "But unfortunately we're in big trouble. There was an explosion in Larga Ways and it's breached the dome. The *Illium* and Sazo are sending runners to evacuate, but I don't see how they can get everyone in time."

"Why can't I connect with Sazo?"

"There's a dead zone. It's been in place since a little earlier, when I got grabbed by . . ." Fee frowned. "I'm not getting too caught up in thinking it's all about me if I say the dead zone settled in when someone grabbed me, am I?"

"Well, that's what I did when I had you grabbed."

"Could this be another Class 5? Using the Vanad to abduct me, and creating the dead zone so Sazo couldn't help me?" It was just about possible. There were two Class 5s left, after all.

"I think the dead zone helped me recover more quickly. It was like the shock of silence bothered me."

"I heard a crackle in my ear just after the dead zone settled in, so I think you're right. But none of this matters unless we can work out how to fix the dome."

"I was able to get into the Larga Ways systems before I arranged for Cy to grab you. That's how I pulled off the snatch. I know the way in."

She looked down at the handheld screen, but the symbols on the screen were flashing too fast for her to read them.

"There isn't just a dead zone." Eazi's voice was almost reverent. "Whoever killed access to the comms has done something to the way station's commands and security. There is nothing to break into, it's an open door. The dome needs an instruction from the main system to tell it to meld together where it's broken. But there is no instruction to send."

"We could give it the instruction." Fee sucked in a breath. "Well, you could."

"I could, except the comms are still down and I'll need time to set them up again."

"So we connect in physically?" Fee asked him. "Is there a cable connection, or is that too low-tech for this place?"

"Not a cable," Eazi's voice rose in excitement. "But a side by side connection, that would work. You'd have to get quite close."

"Using what?" She ran to the small, recessed cabinet and opened it, looked at the oxygen masks on offer.

"The handheld will work." Despite the situation, there was excitement in his voice. "Fiona, all the operational software is gone. If a Class 5 did this, it wasn't to infiltrate Larga Ways, it was to create as much chaos as possible and prevent the way station from recovering."

Fee pulled out a mask. "How am I going to get over to the gel dome? The dock stops a good ten meters from the edge of it."

She touched another panel, and saw an array of shockguns and some things that looked like crossbows. She picked one up, lifted the handheld so the lens could see it. "What's this?"

"It's a magnetic grapple. That could work. If you aim at a metal beam that forms the dome structure, you could swing across from the dock."

He gave her a rundown on how to work it, and as soon as she

had it, she pulled the oxygen mask over her head, shoved the handheld down the front of her shirt to keep her hands free and touched the encryptor to the panel.

The wind was stronger now, so she had to fight to run toward the end of the dock.

She heard a shout behind her, but she didn't dare look back, it was taking everything she had to keep the grapple in her arms and her weight forward.

Her hair whipped around her face, stinging her cheeks, and she nearly fell as a runner from the *Illium* came through the gel wall to her left, the air swirling in a dangerous eddy before it went back to howling past her.

She didn't go right to the end. She was afraid she'd fall off. She braced her legs apart, leaning into the gale, and fired the grapple.

The wind took it and tossed it to the right and then back at her, and she crouched as it soared over her head and then fell back onto the dock with a clang, the magnetic field locking it in place.

She turned, touched the button she hoped would release the magnet, and gave a shout of triumph when it did. She winched it in, crouching down on hands and knees to give herself some stability.

She saw someone fighting to get to her from further down, and she didn't dare look too closely in case it was the Vanad.

Just keep going, just keep going, she chanted in her head. Load, reactivate, turn, aim to the left this time. Shoot.

The wind tossed it again, this time past one of the metal arches that formed the skeleton of the dome, and it was just close enough for the magnet to alter course and attach.

She suddenly wished she'd thought to bring gloves, but whoever was coming up behind her was screaming at her, and she grabbed the cable above the bow part of the grapple, rested a foot on the shallow groove that looked like it had been made for the purpose, and pushed away.

She swung, but not as fast as she would have if the wind hadn't been fighting against her. The cable spun and she saw Tean Lee standing where she'd been moments before, shouting into the wind.

She tried to spin back, managed it just in time to grab the smooth metal frame of the dome. Purple gel wobbled just above her head.

"Okay. Where's the connection?" She struggled to pull out the handheld with one arm anchored around a beam, and panicked for a moment when Eazi didn't answer her straight away. "Eazi —"

"Fiona, you're going to have to go higher or lower."

She sagged against the cold metal in relief at the sound of his voice, and then realized what he'd said. She looked up, but even as she did, she knew she didn't have the arm strength, or the time, to go that way.

She peered down, saw the place where two beams crossed one another, as the dome curved beneath the platform that made the way station.

"Down it is." There was a wobble in her voice.

She put the handheld back in her shirt and then got a tight grip on the beam, leaned down to reach the crossbow part of the grapple to deactivate the magnet. She would need to take it with her to get back up.

She'd just touched the button when another runner came through the wall and strong winds buffeted her, pulling her off balance.

She slipped and cried out, clutching at the beam with both arms as she slid. The heavy magnetic end of the grapple fell toward her, glancing off her shoulder as the whole thing fell down, down, down and away.

Pain blossomed, and she choked back nausea and slid another few meters in shock.

"Are you nearly there?" Eazi asked her.

She was about to snarl at him, when she remembered he couldn't see what was happening.

"I'm not sure." She realized her eyes were shut, and she forced herself to look down again. The cross beam was only a few meters away, and she slid in wild, uncontrolled bursts until her feet found something solid to balance on.

She crouched, hugging the beam like a long-lost lover, feeling as if the wind would tear her off at any moment, and then made the mistake of looking outward.

She was under the station, now. Not right at the bottom, but low enough that all she could see was Balco below her, and nothing else.

If she let go, she'd fall through the gel wall and be sucked into space.

"Fiona? Fiona?" Eazi was saying her name over and over.

"Okay. I'm okay." She realized she was breathing too quickly. She knew Hal and Cy had lasted a long time on their oxygen masks, but who knew how long it would take for someone to rescue her. She needed to calm down.

"Right. I'm here." She leaned her full weight against the beam, carefully let go one arm and pulled the handheld out.

"You see a tiny black panel?" Eazi asked her.

She could not.

She moved the handheld around because it had a little lens built in, so Eazi could look, too.

"It's on the other side," Eazi told her. "It must be."

Fee shoved the handheld back into her shirt and carefully stood up, slowly lifted her body a little away from the beam so she could look around it.

Without the wind, she was sure she could do it. With the wind, pulling and howling and tugging at her, she didn't think she could.

But she was down here now. And if she didn't do it, she would die. And so would a lot of others.

She hugged the beam one last time, stretching her leg out and curving it around, trying to find the crossbeam on the other side.

She thought she had it, slipped, and then got it again.

She stretched her arm around next, and there was one, icy, fear-filled moment when she was neither one side or the other, and then she was over, muscles in her arms and legs wrenched, her breath coming in pants.

And there, hallelujah, was the tiny black panel.

She pulled the handheld out again. "Do your thing," she told Eazi.

The wind was hurricane level now, battering at her, moving the handheld around in her hands, until she pressed it down onto the beam with her hands and her knees, hunching over it like a mother protecting her baby.

"Look at the gel wall," Eazi told her, and she forced herself to turn her head.

It had lit up in a narrow strip along the beam she'd slid down, and as she looked up, the strip grew taller and taller, until it disappeared into the dome above.

"I'm guessing it's working?"

"It's working. I've been able to create a new frequency, one that isn't affected by the dead zone, sync all comms to it, and let the residents know that we're fixing it."

"So you've taken over the station, have you?" She said it jokingly, just trying to keep her mind off where she was and how close she was to the edge.

"I think I have." He was absolutely serious. "I need something big and complex to manage. And I don't have my Class 5 any more. I think I'll like running Larga Ways."

"Got an apartment for me?" she asked, even as she wondered what Battle Center would think of this. But what could they do about it, anyway?

Sazo wouldn't force Eazi out, or hurt him in any way. Hadn't Eazi told her Sazo wouldn't even shoot at Eazi when Eazi was shooting right at him?

They could do nothing.

She laughed.

"I have a very nice apartment for you," Eazi said. "Two bedrooms with a shared bathroom; lounge, dining and kitchen area are open plan, and there is a balcony. It's reserved for the president of Balco, but he's only used it four times in the last three years, and given he needs Larga Ways way more than we need him . . . I've generated a comm for when we get back online, letting him know he'll have to stay in a hotel next time he visits, just like everyone else."

"What are we up to in that book we're putting together? Chapter Five?" Fee tried to ignore how tired her arms were getting. "When your enemies change the rules, take it as an invitation to cut yourself free of the rules completely."

Chapter Forty-three

HE MUST HAVE MISHEARD.

Hal blinked at Rial, and then held out his arm for Jasa to ease off the intravenous tube.

"Fiona is down there?" His heart sank in a sickening rush to the pit of his stomach as he looked at the strange wobble in the gel at the top of the way station dome on the wall screen. "But she was right with me. She was sitting next to me when you came to get us."

"Rial didn't say it made sense, just that is how it is." Jasa's face was tight, the way it got when she was really angry.

"I was in a hurry to get you up to the *Illium*. She wasn't going to keep up, and Tean Lee was demanding that she give a statement, anyway." Rial looked as sick as Hal felt. "I didn't know the place was going to blow up."

"Of course, they'd already moved her out of her room and over to Sazo, kicked her off the ship, more or less, so perhaps they thought Sazo would deal with her."

"When," there was a rushing in his ears and he could barely hear himself, "did they move her off the *Illium*?"

"When you were kidnapped. It was Commander Chel's view that she would be safer on Sazo's Class 5 and it would free up her guards to do other things."

"Very practical," he conceded. He slid off the bed and stood for a moment until he was sure his legs could hold him. "And total yurve shit." He stepped into his boots.

"What are you doing?" Rial stared at him, face slack.

He liked that Jasa didn't do the same. She knew exactly what he was doing.

"So where is she on Larga Ways?" He started walking toward the door. "If comms are down, we'll have to start somewhere."

"Lee's headquarters." Rial followed him out the room. "Lee took her there himself."

Hal's first steps were a little wobbly, but they got stronger as he went.

"Captain." Rial put a hand on his arm, and it was all Hal could do not to lash out at him. Rial must have seen the flare of violence because he took a step back. "We made a mistake. A few mistakes. But Rose and Captain Jallan are helping Sazo send all his runners down to get people out, and we're doing the same. Finding one person in there is going to be impossible."

Hal kept going without responding. By the time he got to the launch bay, sweat was beaded on his upper lip and forehead, and he could feel it running down his back.

"Not looking too good there, sir." Tobru paused at the wide doors, and then, with a quick glance at Rial, ran toward one of only two runners left in the launch bay and disappeared up the ramp. It closed almost immediately and took off.

"Captain." Chel coughed as the space dust swirled around them. "What are you doing—?"

Hal leaned forward, hands on knees, and managed to stop seeing spots in front of his eyes. "What am I doing?" He bared his teeth, and Chel gaped.

"I'm going down to Larga Ways to find Fiona Russell. Who for some reason is not on this ship, where she is supposed to be. I don't suppose you would like to give me an answer as to why that is, would you, Commander?"

"Hal—" Chel wouldn't look him in the eye.

"Get that runner ready," he said, his voice low and mean. "Now."

He turned toward it, saw Rial was already talking to the pilot.

He ran back to Hal, put out an arm to help him.

"You should be in bed." His lieutenant glanced at him as they hobbled toward the runner. "I'll go back down, find her. I won't stop until I do."

Hal shook his head. "I may need your help, but I'm going down with you."

The ramp closed behind them, and when he turned, he saw Chel had come in right behind them.

"I'll direct the runners from below," he said. "They're never going to get everyone in one go, so we'll operate a drop-and-go."

Hal slid down into a seat and felt the surge of lift-off. "You sent her away." He felt a deep-seated terror at the thought. "This was all she had. The one place where she was safe and knew people, and you used your power the moment I was gone and threw her off."

"She was safer on the Class 5," Chel began, and Hal stared at him. "All right. Yes. I threw her off." He rubbed both hands over his face. "In all the years I've served with you, you've never put a foot wrong, Hal. You're an excellent captain, and you know your way around the politics of Battle Center. I don't want to see you kicked out because you've lost your head over some strange orange."

"If you thought I'd have let her go without a fight, you were wrong," Hal told him. "I would have chased after her, if I had to. But you didn't get what I tried to show you this morning. She isn't some strange orange. She is loyal, brave, clever. She risked her life to find me this afternoon, or did I get that wrong?"

"No." Rial ducked his head. "She came up with the plan, and I think because she thought no one would listen to her or take her seriously, executed it to the point where we had no choice but to come onboard."

"How did she get down there, though?" He was still trying to work that out, because he'd had strict instructions that she was not to set foot off the ship without a full guard.

"When I told her to pack her things and move to Sazo," Chel was looking down at his feet, "she persuaded Sazo to help her with her plan and he took her down to Larga Ways with the correct permissions to get through the gates."

Hal was silent for a moment, eyes closed, head tilted back as he tried to get himself back under control. He wondered if a little togrut was still in his system, that his emotions were coming through so raw and unfiltered. If he didn't get some control he might end up saying something he'd regret.

"She gave me hell down there." Rial suddenly laughed. "I saw her walking along, looking like a tourist, and pulled her into a little side street. She let me have it." He shook his head. "She's been polite to everyone since we found her. No temper, no fuss, but she turned on me and put me in my place when I tried to tell her we were busy, and she was distracting us from our search for you."

"She didn't have to be polite any more. As far as she was concerned, you'd rejected her." Hal felt that sick swirl of fear again. She would know he'd had nothing to do with her being kicked off, but the easy way it had been done, her lack of any right to insist otherwise, spoke to just how powerless she was.

"Why are you so angry about this, Hal? I shouldn't have done it, but it can be undone." Chel lifted his hands, palms out.

"You think we hurt her, deeply enough that she might reconsider her place with us." Rial answered for him, speaking slowly.

The runner thumped into the dock, bumping like it was in a raging storm, and Hal nodded to him as he stood, and struggled down the ramp without a word.

Tean Lee was running toward them as he stepped onto the dock and was forced to brace his legs against the air that was being sucked up to the top of the dome.

"That . . . woman." Lee screamed it over the howl of the wind. "She's mad." He pointed to the end of the dock, and Hal looked over, but there was nothing to see.

"Fiona?" he asked.

"She jumped." Lee's eyes were wild. "Jumped and then slid down. And now, look!"

Hal looked again, and this time he saw what Lee was trying to show him. A thin line of purple light in the dome, edging up along a curved beam, slowly spreading as it went, until it seemed there were dancing stars of purple light jumping and leaping across the dome ceiling.

"We couldn't get it to do that. With the dead zone, it wasn't receiving the instructions, and then she jumped to that beam and slid down and now . . ." He stared straight up. "I think she fixed it. By hand."

***

Something bumped the beam near her, and although she did't think there was much strength left in her arms, Fiona found some from somewhere, and clutched a little tighter.

"It's okay. I've got *you*, this time." Hands, so warm against the cold of hers, tried to pry open her fists and she forced herself to open her eyes.

"Hal?"

"I've got you, you can just let go."

Could she?

She closed her eyes again and thought about it.

"I promise."

She waited another beat and heard him sigh.

"I think I need help." She couldn't move, she realized. Her body was stiff and cramped, and he lifted her, knocking the oxygen mask she'd set in front of her off the beam.

She couldn't figure out how he was doing it and not falling off until she opened her eyes again and saw he was standing in a hover that put him waist high to her, her handheld under his arm.

He carefully pulled her in, lifted her again and set her down on what felt like the most comfortable cushions she'd ever lain on.

"I'm glad to see you're up to rescuing." She had her eyes closed again. She didn't know why she had such a hard time keeping them open.

His hand brushed hair off her face. The rest of it was probably a rat's nest whipped up by the wind, which had died the moment the rip repaired itself, and then stirred to life again, more gently, as Eazi started up the air plant and began pumping in the new atmosphere.

"So tell me. How do you know how to save way stations?" He lay down next to her, and she turned into his warmth, snuggled closer when his arm came around her.

"Oh, I was just the brawn of the operation. Eazi was the brains." She yawned. So, so tired.

"And my rescue earlier?"

She forced her eyes open, looked into his. "That was all me. Although Sazo gave me a hand, but more in a sidekick capacity."

"You were moved off the *Illium* earlier today."

His voice had become deeper. Rougher.

"Yes. Ouch. Kicked out of the club." She found a more comfortable spot on his shoulder. "It's okay. I've found a new place."

"Sazo's asked you to stay?" He didn't sound like himself.

"Nah. Although I'm sure he would. No, I'm in the presidential suite on Larga Ways, these days. Sort of been made operations manager."

He leaned over her. "You're hallucinating."

She opened her eyes again. Saw he looked a lot better, although he still wasn't quite right, his skin holding a tiny trace of gray. "No, really." She put a hand on either side of his face. "Eazi's taken over Larga Ways, Hal. He had to, to save it, and he doesn't want to give it back. The Class 5's gone and he needs something like this or he'll go mad."

"You're serious." He looked into her eyes, and she saw fear and desperation there, where she thought she'd see amusement and maybe irritation.

"Shh. What's wrong?" She stretched up and brushed a kiss at the corner of his mouth.

"You're not staying with me."

"Your crew don't want me, Hal. And even if they did, I have no job onboard, whereas Eazi needs me."

"I want you to stay." His voice was rough.

"If I stayed, you wouldn't have been able to keep me. You'd have been ordered to send me to Battle Center, and I'd have had to appear before the UC, and someone would have tried to kill me a couple of times."

"They'll still order you to go to the UC," he said.

"Under whose authority? I'm on sovereign Eazi soil here. And I'll happily speak to the UC, if they come to me. Eazi really does need me. I wasn't just saying that before." She kissed him again. "And apparently I've got a lovely bedroom with a balcony where I can entertain my Grihan lover when he comes by to visit."

His grip on her tightened, almost too much, and then he pulled her close.

The hover started to move.

"We haven't got to the lover part yet."

"Well, we probably won't get there tonight, either, given I can't unclench my hands." It felt good, though, lying so close that they were entwined in each other. "But if you wake up next to me in my fancy new apartment tomorrow morning, I think we might be able to change that."

Chapter Forty-four

"You are saying the thinking system has stolen Larga Ways?" Hoke's face told him she wasn't sure if he was joking.

Hal shifted. "Not stolen. It's still in orbit around Balco. He's just taken it over."

"On what grounds?"

"On the grounds that it would no longer exist if he hadn't grabbed hold of it and, with Fiona's help, activated the repair function in the dome when a bomb ripped a hole in its gel wall."

"Larga Ways is a strategic asset for the Grih nation. It has Battle Center priority security status." Hoke stood. She'd managed to stay seated longer than he thought she would.

"It's useful, then, that Eazi has already sworn to not harm the Grih in anyway, unless in self-defense." Hal crossed his arms. Decided to make this quick. "We can't do anything about it. Sazo won't lift a finger against Eazi, and Eazi's right, Larga Ways would be bits of debris making a new asteroid belt around Balco if he hadn't stepped in and forged new connections, and if Fiona hadn't risked her life to activate the repair function. He's going to take a monthly percentage of trade in payment for himself and Fiona, and he tells me the improvements he's making will start saving everyone money by the end of the first week."

"What do the Balcoans think about it?"

Hal shrugged. "They're afraid of having Battle Center come down on them for the Tecran facility out in the desert, and for the obvious collusion of some of the officials on Larga Ways with the Tecran. Also, given the sophistication of the electronic explosives sniffers, someone helped that Vanad smuggle his bomb in. They failed on a lot of levels, and they know it. Right now, they're just happy that they still have Larga Ways, instead of a massive trade disaster with enormous loss of life." He lifted his hands. "If Eazi messes up, they may start to resent him, but right now, it's almost amazing how calm things are."

"And have you worked out what created the dead zone, and why the Vanad set the explosion?" Hoke had calmed down, herself, and Hal guessed she'd seen as quickly as he had that things could be a lot worse.

Hal rubbed the back of his neck. "The dead zone we can only guess at. Sazo, Eazi and Gerbardi, my comms engineer, all think it was another Class 5. Eazi and Fiona think the Vanad might have been abducting her for the Class 5. The dead zone happened just as she was snatched. The bomb, well, Eazi says whoever created the dead zone wiped Larga Ways' whole operating system clear. So the way station couldn't repair itself after the bomb damaged it."

"If it was a Class 5, there's been no sign of it?" Hoke asked.

Hal shook his head.

"Then you're staying in the Balco system. Sazo, too." Hoke lowered herself back in her chair. "There is something going on out there. For a start, the investigative team the United Council sent to look at the *Fasbe* seems to have disappeared. It should have arrived in Larga Ways already, and the UC's lost all signals to it. The Tecran are also suddenly being really cooperative. They're backing down. Apologizing."

"You don't trust it?"

Hoke shook her head. "Feels like the calm before the storm to me."

Just before she leaned over to sign off, she stopped. Looked him straight in the eye. "You still friendly with Fiona Russell?"

Hal nodded.

"That's good."

Hal thought about the satisfied gleam in her eye as he took a runner down to Larga Ways, and caught a glimpse of the perpetual storm, Kyber's Arm, a twist of brown on the planet below.

As he walked to Fiona's apartment, he passed the wreckage of the day before, saw they'd already made a start at clearing it up.

Fiona opened the door before he could knock. "Eazi told me you were on your way."

She was wearing a dress which must have come from one of the stores on the station, soft and flowing in a pale orange that made her dark eyes and hair gleam.

The way she went into his arms made his heart clench.

"I have a surprise for you." She smiled against the side of his neck.

"You've taken over Balco, now, too, and I should address you as President Russell?"

She laughed. "Maybe next week. I've set my sights a little lower this evening." She gestured with a flourish to the dining table. "Ta da! Edible food. And I've invited Rose and Dav for dinner, because Rose is just as hungry as I am."

"I have a surprise for you, too."

She waited for him to tell her, her arms loose around his waist, her eyes dancing.

"I've been ordered to stay in the Balco system for now."

"Well." She kissed him, leaned back in his arms. "That makes me so happy, maybe I will take Balco over." She kissed him again.

"Can you wait until tomorrow?" He ran his hands up her back.

She tilted her head and gave him a wicked grin. "If you make it worth my while."

DARK DEEDS

ABOUT THE AUTHOR

Michelle Diener writes historical fiction, fantasy and science fiction. Having worked in publishing and IT, she's now very happy crafting new worlds and interesting characters and wondering which part of the world she can travel to next.

Michelle was born in London, grew up in South Africa and currently lives in Australia with her husband and two children.

To find out more, you can visit her at www.michellediener.com, where you can read about her books, find her social media links, and sign up to receive notification when she has a new book out.

CPSIA information can be obtained
at www.ICGtesting.com
Printed in the USA
FSOW02n0902020916
24535FS

9 780992 455958